W9-AHD-634

Dearest Rogue

"[This] superbly executed historical romance is proof positive that this RITA Award–nominated author continues to write with undiminished force and flair. When it comes to incorporating a generous measure of dangerous intrigue and lush sensuality into a truly swoonworthy love story, Hoyt is unrivaled."

—*Booklist* (**starred review**)

"4½ stars! Hoyt takes an unlikely pair of characters and, through the magic of her storytelling, turns them into the perfect couple...A read to remember."

—*RT Book Reviews*

"Sexy, sweet, and emotionally satisfying...*Dearest Rogue* is everything the reader of a Regency historical wants; it's funny, fast-paced and has plenty of historical flavor and a romance that develops as naturally as a flower opening in the sun. Fans of the Maiden Lane series will cheer for this couple."

—*BookPage*

"Hoyt's exquisitely nuanced characters, vividly detailed setting, and seemingly effortless and elegant writing provide the splendid material from which she fashions yet another ravishingly romantic love story."

—*Booklist* (**starred review**)

Darling Beast

"4½ stars! Top Pick! *Darling Beast* is wondrous, magical, and joyous—a read to remember."
—RT Book Reviews

"A lovely book that I very much enjoyed reading. I love the Maiden Lane series and can't wait until the next book comes out!"
—BookBinge.com

Duke of Midnight

"Top Pick! A sensual tale of forbidden love...Plenty of action and intriguing mystery make this a page-turner."
—BookPage

"Richly drawn characters fill the pages of this emotionally charged mix of mystery and romance."
—Publishers Weekly

"4½ stars! Top Pick! There is enchantment in the Maiden Lane series, not just the fairy tales Hoyt infuses into the memorable romances, but the wonder of love combined with passion, unique plotlines, and unforgettable characters."
—RT Book Reviews

"Hoyt's writing is almost too good to be true."
   —Lisa Kleypas, *New York Times* bestselling author

"There's an enchantment to Hoyt's stories that makes you believe in the magic of love."
                    —*RT Book Reviews*

PRAISE FOR
ELIZABETH HOYT'S
MAIDEN LANE SERIES

Duke of Pleasure

"4½ stars! Top Pick! Hoyt…[is] a powerful storyteller whose novels have a depth of emotion and originality that lifts the genre to new heights. Always unique, wonderfully romantic and highly sensual, Hoyt's stories take readers' breath away."
                    —*RT Book Reviews*

"Hoyt once again successfully deploys her irresistible literary triumvirate of marvelously engaging characters, boldly sensual love scenes, and elegant writing brightened with just the right dash of dry wit."
                    —*Booklist*

"So many ingredients make this story phenomenal. First and foremost, the chemistry between our hero and heroine. It drives the narrative and we can't get enough of their interactions."
             —HeroesandHeartbreakers.com

Duke of Sin

"4½ stars! Top Pick! Hoyt delivers a unique read on many levels: a love story, a tale of redemption, and a plot teeming with emotional depth that takes readers' breaths away. Kudos to a master storyteller!"
—*RT Book Reviews*

"A darkly humorous and lushly sensual historical romance...Hoyt truly outdoes herself in *Duke of Sin*."
—**HeroesandHeartbreakers.com**

"Hoyt has created two dynamic characters...[The book] includes a delicious collection of hot and steamy scenes. A wonderful balance of comedy and pathos, Hoyt's latest is a deeply satisfying read."
—*BookPage*

Sweetest Scoundrel

"While I've long been a fan of the Maiden Lane series, I think this is my favorite."
—**FictionVixen.com**

"4½ stars! Maiden Lane and its inhabitants have long captivated readers, and the latest series installment is just as enchanting as fans could desire...It is a story that takes your breath away and leaves you uplifted. Hoyt does it again!"
—*RT Book Reviews*

"I *loved* it. I loved Artemis. I loved Max, and I loved their story. I have enjoyed every Elizabeth Hoyt book I have read (and I have read most of them)."

—All About Romance (LikesBooks.com)

Lord of Darkness

"*Lord of Darkness* illuminates Hoyt's boundless imagination...Readers will adore this story."

—RT Book Reviews

"Hoyt's writing is imbued with great depth of emotion... Heartbreaking...An edgy tension-filled plot."

—Publishers Weekly

"*Lord of Darkness* is classic Elizabeth Hoyt, meaning it's unique, engaging, and leaves readers on the edge of their seats...An incredible addition to the fantastic Maiden Lane series. I Joyfully Recommend Godric and Megs's tale, for it's an amazing, well-crafted story with an intriguing plot and a lovely, touching romance...Simply enchanting!"

—JoyfullyReviewed.com

"I adore the Maiden Lane series, and this fifth book is a very welcome addition to the series...[It's] sexy and sweet all at the same time...This can be read as a standalone, but I adore each book in this series and encourage you to start from the beginning."

—USA Today's Happy Ever After blog

"Beautifully written...A truly fine piece of storytelling and a novel that deserves to be read and enjoyed."
—TheBookBinge.com

Thief of Shadows

"An expert blend of scintillating romance and mystery... The romance between the beautiful and quick-witted Isabel and the masked champion of the downtrodden propels this novel to the top of its genre."
—*Publishers Weekly* (starred review)

"Amazing sex scenes...A very intriguing hero...This one did not disappoint."
—*USA Today*

"Innovative, emotional, sensual...Hoyt's beautiful blending of the essential elements of a fairy tale into a stunning love story enhances this delicious 'keeper.'"
—*RT Book Reviews*

"All of Hoyt's signature literary ingredients—wickedly clever dialogue, superbly nuanced characters, danger, and scorching sexual chemistry—click neatly into place to create a breathtakingly romantic love story."
—*Booklist*

"When [they] finally come together, desire and long-denied sensuality explode upon the page."
—*Library Journal*

"With heart and heat rolled into one, *Thief of Shadows* is a definite must-read for historical romance fans! Hoyt really has outdone herself...yet again."

—UndertheCoversBookblog.blogspot.com

"A balanced mixture of action, adventure, and mystery and a beautifully crafted romance...The perfect historical romance."

—HeroesandHeartbreakers.com

Scandalous Desires

"Historical romance at its best...Series fans will be enthralled, while new readers will find this emotionally charged installment stands very well alone."

—*Publishers Weekly* (starred review)

"4½ stars! This is the Maiden Lane story readers have been waiting for. Hoyt delivers her hallmark fairy tale within a romance and takes readers into the depths of the heart and soul of her characters. Pure magic flows from her pen, lifting readers' spirits with joy."

—*RT Book Reviews*

"With its lush sensuality, lusciously wrought prose, and luxuriously dark plot, *Scandalous Desires*, the latest exquisitely crafted addition to Hoyt's Georgian-set Maiden Lane series, is a romance to treasure."

—*Booklist* (starred review)

"Ms. Hoyt writes some of the best love scenes out there. They are passionate, sexy, and blazing hot...I simply adore Ms. Hoyt's books for her sensuous prose, multifaceted characters, and intense, well-developed story lines. And she delivers every single time. It's no wonder all of her books are on my keeper shelves. Do yourself a favor and pick up *Scandalous Desires*."

—TheRomanceDish.com

"*Scandalous Desires* is the best book Elizabeth Hoyt has written so far, with endearing characters and an all-encompassing romance you'll want to hold close and never let go. If there's one must-read book, especially for historical romance fans, it's *Scandalous Desires*."

—FallenAngelReviews.com

Notorious Pleasures

"Emotionally stunning...The sinfully sensual chemistry Hoyt creates between her shrewd, acid-tongued heroine and her scandalous, sexy hero is pure romance."

—*Booklist*

Wicked Intentions

"4½ stars! Top Pick! A magnificently rendered story that not only enchants but enthralls."

—*RT Book Reviews*

Notorious Pleasures

ELIZABETH HOYT

Notorious Pleasures

FOREVER

NEW YORK   BOSTON

This book is a work of fiction. Names, characters, places, and incidents are the product of the author's imagination or are used fictitiously. Any resemblance to actual events, locales, or persons, living or dead, is coincidental.

Copyright © 2011 by Nancy M. Finney
Excerpt from *Duke of Desire* copyright © 2017 by Nancy M. Finney

Hachette Book Group supports the right to free expression and the value of copyright. The purpose of copyright is to encourage writers and artists to produce the creative works that enrich our culture.

The scanning, uploading, and distribution of this book without permission is a theft of the author's intellectual property. If you would like permission to use material from the book (other than for review purposes), please contact permissions@hbgusa.com. Thank you for your support of the author's rights.

Forever
Hachette Book Group
1290 Avenue of the Americas, New York, NY 10104
forever-romance.com
twitter.com/foreverromance

Originally published by Vision in 2011
Mass market reissued: October 2014, December 2017

Forever is an imprint of Grand Central Publishing.
The Forever name and logo are trademarks of Hachette Book Group, Inc.

The publisher is not responsible for websites (or their content) that are not owned by the publisher.

The Hachette Speakers Bureau provides a wide range of authors for speaking events. To find out more, go to www.hachettespeakersbureau.com or call (866) 376-6591.

Printed in the United States of America

OPM

10 9 8 7 6 5 4 3 2 1

ATTENTION CORPORATIONS AND ORGANIZATIONS:
Most HACHETTE BOOK GROUP books are available
at quantity discounts with bulk purchase for educational,
business, or sales promotional use. For information,
please call or write:

**Special Markets Department, Hachette Book Group
1290 Avenue of the Americas, New York, NY 10104
Telephone: 1-800-222-6747 Fax: 1-800-477-5925**

*For my agent, Susannah Taylor, who understands
the importance of crab legs.*

Acknowledgments

Thank you to my marvelous editor, Amy Pierpont, and to my perceptive copy editor, Carrie Andrews!

Notorious
Pleasures

Chapter One

*Once upon a time, in a land quite on the other side of the
world, there lived a queen both beautiful and wise.
She was called Ravenhair....*
—from *Queen Ravenhair*

The daughter of a duke learns early in life the proper etiquette for nearly everything. What dish to serve roasted larks in. When to acknowledge a rather risqué dowager countess and when to give her the cut direct. What to wear while boating down the Thames, and how to fend off the tipsy advances of an earl with very little income at the picnic afterward.

Everything, in fact, Lady Hero Batten reflected wryly, but how to address a gentleman coupling vigorously with a married lady not his own.

"Ahem," she tried while gazing fixedly at the molded plaster pears on the ceiling overhead.

The two people on the settee appeared not to hear her. Indeed, the lady gave a series of loud animal squeals from under the skirts of her atrocious puce-and-brown-striped gown, which had been flipped up to cover her face.

Hero sighed. They were in a dim little sitting room off the library of Mandeville House, and she was regretting choosing this particular room in which to fix her stocking. Had she picked the blue Oriental room, her stocking would be straight by now and she'd already be back in the ballroom—far away from this embarrassing predicament.

She lowered her eyes cautiously. The gentleman, wearing an anonymous white wig, had discarded his embroidered satin coat and was laboring atop the lady in his shirt-sleeves and a brilliant emerald waistcoat. His breeches and smallclothes were loosened to facilitate his endeavors, and every now and again a flash of muscled buttock was visible.

Sadly, she found the sight mesmerizing. Whomever the gentleman was, his physical attributes were quite... astonishing.

Hero tore her gaze away to look longingly at the door. Really, few would find fault with her should she turn and tiptoe from the room. That was exactly what she would've done when she'd first entered had she not passed Lord Pimbroke not two minutes before in the hallway. For, as it happened, Hero had noted the atrocious puce-and-brown-striped gown earlier in the evening—on *Lady* Pimbroke. Much as Hero was loath to embarrass herself, her own feelings were not, in the end, as important as the possibility of a duel and subsequent injury or death to two gentlemen.

Having come to this conclusion, Hero nodded once, took off one diamond earbob, and lobbed it at the gentleman's backside. She'd always quietly prided herself on her aim—not that she used it much in everyday life—and she was rather gratified to hear a yelp from the male.

He swore and turned, looking at her over his shoulder with the most glorious pale green eyes she'd ever seen. He wasn't a handsome man—his face was too broad across the cheekbones, his nose too crooked, and his mouth too thin and cynical for true masculine beauty—but his eyes would draw any female, young or old, from across a room. And once drawn, their gaze would linger on the look of arrogant male virility he wore as naturally as he breathed.

Or perhaps it was merely the, er, *circumstances* that gave him the look.

"D'you mind, love?" he drawled, the anger in his expression having changed to faint amusement when he'd caught sight of her. His voice was gravelly and completely unhurried. "I'm busy here."

She could feel heat suffusing her cheeks—really, this was an impossible situation—but she met his gaze, making quite sure hers did not wander lower. "Indeed. I *had* noticed, but I thought you should know—"

"Unless you're the type who likes to watch?"

Now her face was aflame, but she wasn't about to let this...this *wretch* get the better of her verbally. She allowed her gaze to drop swiftly and scornfully down over his rumpled waistcoat and shirt—fortunately the tail hid his open breeches—and back up. She smiled sweetly. "I prefer entertainments in which I'm not in danger of falling asleep."

She expected her insult to anger him, but instead the rogue tutted.

"Happens a lot to you, does it, sweetheart?" His voice

was solicitous, but a sly dimple appeared beside his wide lips. "Falling asleep just as the fun's about to begin? Well, don't blame yourself. Like as not, it's the gentleman's fault, not yours."

Good God, no one ever spoke to her like this!

Slowly, awfully, Hero arched her left brow. She knew it was slow and awful because she'd practiced the movement in front of a mirror for hours on end at the age of twelve. The result made seasoned matrons tremble in their heeled slippers.

The devilish man didn't turn a hair.

"Now, as it happens," he drawled obnoxiously, "my ladies don't have that problem. Stay and watch—it'll prove instructive, I guarantee. And if I have any strength left over after, maybe I'll demonstrate—"

"Lord Pimbroke is in the hallway!" she blurted before he could finish his dastardly thought.

The mound of puce-and-brown-striped skirts quaked. "Eustace is here?"

"Quite. And heading this way," Hero informed Lady Pimbroke with only a touch of satisfaction.

The gentleman exploded into action. He was up and off the lady and throwing down her skirts to hide her pale, soft thighs before Hero could even blink. He caught up his coat, made one swift, appraising glance about the room, and turned to Hero, his voice still unhurried. "Lady Pimbroke has torn a ribbon or lace or some such thing, and you've kindly consented to help her."

"But—"

He placed his forefinger against her lips—warm, large, and quite shockingly inappropriate. At the same time, a male voice called from the hallway.

"Bella!"

Lady Pimbroke—or Bella—squeaked in fear.

"There's a good girl," the rogue whispered to Hero. He turned to Lady Pimbroke, bussed her on the cheek, and murmured, "Steady on, darling," before disappearing under the settee.

Hero had only a moment to watch Lady Pimbroke's pretty, insipid face go ashen as she realized fully the peril she was in, and then the door to the sitting room crashed open.

"Bella!" Lord Pimbroke was big, reddened, and quite obviously intoxicated. He glanced belligerently around the room, his hand on his sword, but froze in consternation when he saw Hero. "My lady, what—?"

"Lord Pimbroke." Hero casually stepped in front of the settee, obscuring a large masculine heel with her wide skirts.

She employed her left eyebrow.

Lord Pimbroke actually backed up a step—quite gratifying after the reception her eyebrow had received from the rogue—and stammered. "I...I..."

Hero turned to Lady Pimbroke, touching lightly the horrid yellow braiding on the elbow of her gown. "That's fixed, I think, don't you?"

Lady Pimbroke started. "Oh! Oh, yes, thank you, my lady."

"Not at all," Hero murmured.

"If you're done here, m'dear," Lord Pimbroke said, "then perhaps you're ready to return to the ball?"

His words may have been a question, but his tone of voice most certainly was not.

Lady Pimbroke took his arm rather sulkily. "Yes, Eustace."

And with a perfunctory good-bye, the two left the room.

Almost immediately, Hero felt a tug upon her skirts. "Hist! I can hardly breathe under here."

"They may return," she said serenely.

"I think I can see up your skirt."

She moved back hastily.

The rogue rolled out from under the settee and stood, towering over her.

Nonetheless, she glared down her nose at him. "You weren't—"

"Now, now. If I was, do you really think I'd tell you?"

She sniffed, sounding rather like Cousin Bathilda at her most priggish. "No doubt you'd boast of it."

He leaned over her, grinning. "Does the thought have you all hot and bothered?"

"Is your wig growing tight?" she asked politely.

"What?"

"Because I would think your swelled head would make it quite uncomfortable."

His smile became a trifle grim. "My head isn't the only thing out of proportion, I assure you. Maybe that's why you came in here? To sneak a peek?"

She rolled her eyes. "You have no trace of shame, do you? Most men at least pretend to be abashed when caught in wrongdoing, but you—you strut about like a feckless cockerel."

He paused in the act of donning his coat, one arm thrust out, the sleeve half on, and widened his beautiful green eyes at her. "Oh, of course. Moralizing. Naturally you must hold yourself superior to me when—"

"I saw you engaging in adultery!"

"You saw me engaging in a pleasant *fuck*," he said with slow emphasis.

She flinched at the crudity but stood her ground. She was the daughter of a duke, and she would not flee from a man such as he. "Lady Pimbroke is married."

"Lady Pimbroke has had numerous lovers before me and will have numerous lovers after me."

"That does not forgive *your* sin."

He looked at her and laughed—actually *laughed*—slow and deep. "And you are a woman without sin, is that it?"

She didn't even have to consider the matter. "Naturally."

His mouth twisted cruelly. "Such certainty."

She stared, affronted. "Do you doubt me?"

"Oh, no, far from it. I believe absolutely that the thought of sin has never once crossed your perfect little mind."

She tilted her chin, feeling a thrill of excitement—she'd never before argued with a gentleman, let alone a strange one. "And I begin to wonder if any thought of righteousness has ever crossed your *shameless* little mind."

He watched her a moment, a muscle twitching in his jaw. Then he bowed abruptly. "I thank you for going against your own inclinations and saving me from having to kill Lord Pimbroke."

She nodded stiffly.

"And I hope most fervently that our paths never cross again, my Lady Perfect."

Unaccountably, Hero felt a pang of hurt at his dismissive words, but she made sure not to let the weak emotion show. "I will certainly pray that I never have to suffer *your* presence again, my Lord Shameless."

"Then we are in agreement."

"Quite."

"Good."

For a moment she stared at him, her breasts pressing against her stays with each too-fast breath, her cheeks hot with emotion. They'd drawn closer in the heat of their argument, and his chest nearly brushed the lace of her bodice. He stared back, his eyes very green in his loathsome face.

His gaze dropped to her mouth.

Her lips parted and for an endless second, she forgot to breathe.

He turned and strode to the door, disappearing into the dim hallway beyond.

Hero blinked and inhaled with a shudder as she looked dazedly around the room. There was a mirror hanging on the wall, and she crossed to it to peer at her reflection in the glass. Her red hair was still elegantly coiffed, her lovely silvery-green dress properly in place. Her cheeks were a little pinkened, but the color was becoming. Strangely, she didn't appear all that changed.

Well. That was good.

She threw back her shoulders and swept from the room, her step graceful but quick. Tonight of all nights, it was important she present a serene, lovely, and *perfect* aspect, for tonight her engagement to the Marquess of Mandeville was to be announced.

Hero tilted her chin at the remembered sneer of the stranger as he'd mouthed the word *perfect*. What could he possibly have against perfection anyway?

GODDAMN ALL SELF-SATISFIED, *perfect women—and that red-haired wench in the sitting room in particular!*

Lord Griffin Reading, strode toward his brother's ballroom in a foul mood. Damnable chit! She'd stood there disapproving and priggish and dared to look down her narrow nose at *him*. She'd probably never felt an honest human urge in her entire, too-sheltered life. The only sign of her embarrassment had been the pink blotches climbing her delicately pale throat as she stared at him. Griffin grunted. That censorious face should have caused any man's pride to wilt.

Except, as it happened, he'd had just the opposite reaction—and it wasn't because he'd not reached completion with Bella, either. No, the prospect of being discovered by an irate husband, followed speedily by a bloody duel at dawn had cooled his ardor quite thoroughly, thank you. By the time he'd rolled out from under the settee, he'd been calm in both body and mind. Until, that is, he'd exchanged heated words with that holier-than-thou madam. His cock had seemed to look upon the argument as some kind of bizarre preamble to bedsport, despite the lady's obvious respectability, her hostility to him, *and* his own instant dislike of her.

Griffin paused in a shadowed corner, trying to calm himself as he fingered the diamond earring in his pocket. He'd found the thing under the settee and had meant to give it back to Lady Perfect before her tart tongue had made him forget the trinket altogether. Well, served her right to lose her pretty earring if that was how she talked to gentlemen.

He rolled a shoulder. When he'd entered the ballroom half an hour ago, he'd not even had time to greet his mother and sisters before Bella had waylaid him with her naughty suggestion. Had he known her husband was attending the ball as well, he'd never have let himself be drawn into such a dangerous tryst.

Griffin sighed. But it was too late now for self-recriminations. Better to simply file the embarrassing episode under *Things Best Forgotten as Soon as Possible* and move on. Megs and Caroline probably didn't care one way or the other that he'd disappeared, but Mater would no doubt be keeping an eagle eye out for him. No use in putting it off. With a last tug at his neckcloth to make sure it was straight, Griffin entered the ballroom.

Lights blazed from crystal chandeliers high overhead, illuminating a veritable crush. This would be the event of the season, and no member of London society wanted to miss it. Griffin began to weave his way through the mass of colorfully dressed bodies, his progress made slower by the frequent need to greet old friends and curious acquaintances.

"How kind of you to attend, darling," a dry voice said at his elbow.

Griffin turned from a duet of simpering young matrons blocking his way and leaned down to kiss his mother on the cheek. "Ma'am. It's good to see you."

The words were rote, but not the sudden emotion behind them. He hadn't been to London in almost a year, and it had been over eight months since his mother had visited him at the family estate in Lancashire. He tilted his head, studying her. Her fine hair, knotted elegantly under a lace cap, might have a few more gray threads, but otherwise her dear face was unchanged. Her brown eyes, bracketed with crinkled laugh lines, were far too intelligent, the soft-bowed mouth pursed to hide a fond smile, and the straight eyebrows were faintly arched in a perpetual amusement that matched his own.

"You're as brown as a nut," she murmured, reaching up

to touch one finger to his cheek. "I suppose you've been out riding the lands."

"Perceptive as always, my dear mater," he said, offering his arm.

She linked her elbow with his. "And how is the harvest?"

A point of pain throbbed in his temple, but Griffin answered cheerfully, "Well enough."

He felt her worried look. "Truly?"

"It was a dry summer, so the harvest was smaller than anticipated." A pretty gloss on what in fact had been an abysmal harvest. Their land was not particularly fertile to begin with—something his mother already knew—but there was no point in making her fret. "We'll do well with the grain, never fear."

He was deliberately vague about what exactly he'd be doing with the grain. That was his burden to bear for his mother and the rest of the family.

His answer seemed to reassure her. "Good. Lord Bollinger is showing interest in Margaret, and she'll need new gowns this season. I don't want to overstretch our funds."

"That's not a problem," he replied, even as he swiftly calculated in his head. It would be a near thing as always, but he should be able to get the monies—providing he suffered no further losses. The pain in his temple intensified. "Buy Megs all the fripperies she wants. The family purse can stand it."

The line of worry between her brows eased. "And, of course, there's Thomas."

He was braced for the subject of his brother, but somehow he wasn't able to prevent the slight stiffening of his muscles.

Naturally Mater sensed it. "I'm so glad you came, Griffin. Now is the time to put that little contretemps behind you two."

Griffin snorted. He hardly thought his brother considered the matter a "little contretemps." Thomas acted with propriety in all things, and he'd not have argued with Griffin over anything trivial. To have done so would be to let emotion rule him, which for someone as proper as Thomas was anathema. For a moment, Lady Perfect's wide gray eyes came to mind. *She*, no doubt, would've gotten on famously with his priggishly correct brother.

Griffin made an attempt to appear pleased at the prospect of seeing Thomas again. "Of course. It'll be wonderful to talk to Thomas."

Mater frowned. Obviously he needed to work on his pleased expression. "He misses you, you know."

He shot her an incredulous look.

"Truly, he does," she insisted, though he noticed two spots of color had flown into her cheeks—even Mater had doubts about Thomas's reception of him. "This estrangement must end. It's not good for the family, it's not good for you both, and it's not good for *me*. Why it ever dragged on this long, I'll never know."

Griffin caught a flash of moss green out of the corner of his eye, and he turned, his pulse picking up. But the lady wearing the dress had already disappeared into the crowd.

"Griffin, pay attention," his mother hissed.

He smiled down at her. "Sorry, thought I saw someone I wanted to avoid."

She huffed. "I'm sure there are any number of disreputable ladies you wish to avoid."

"Actually, this one is rather too reputable," he said

easily. His hand had drifted to his coat pocket, and he fingered the little diamond earring. He ought to return it to her, he supposed.

"Really?" For a moment, he thought his mother might be diverted from her harangue. Then she shook her head. "Don't try to change the subject. It's been three years since you and Thomas began this wretched argument, and my nerves are terribly frayed. I don't think I can take one more freezing letter between the two of you or dinner watching my every word for fear I'll raise the wrong topic of conversation."

"Pax, Mater." Griffin chuckled and bent to kiss her outraged cheek. "Thomas and I shall shake hands and make up like good little boys, and you shall dine with the both of us while I'm in London."

"Promise?"

"On my honor." He held his palm to his chest. "I'm going to be so pleasant and thoroughly nice that Thomas won't be able to stop himself from falling on me with pro-testations of fraternal love."

"Humph," she said. "Well, I certainly hope so."

"Nothing in the world," he assured her blithely, "can possibly stop me."

"Happy?"

Hero turned at the deep male voice and saw her dear elder brother, Maximus Batten, the Duke of Wakefield. For a moment, her mind blanked at the question. In the two months it had taken to arrange her engagement to the Marquess of Mandeville, Maximus had asked her several times if she was content with the match, but he had never asked her if she was *happy*.

"Hero?" Maximus's straight dark brows drew together over his rather arrogant nose.

She'd often thought that Maximus's looks suited his rank perfectly. If one closed one's eyes and tried to paint the perfect duke in one's mind, Maximus would appear. He was tall, his shoulders broad but not heavy, his face long and lean and just a tad too coldly commanding to be truly handsome. His hair was dark brown—though he cropped it close, as he habitually wore immaculate white wigs—and his eyes were brown as well. Brown eyes were often thought warm, but one impatient glance from Maximus was enough to disabuse anyone of *that* notion. Warmth was the last thing one would associate with the Duke of Wakefield. But despite all that, he was still her brother.

Hero smiled up at him. "Yes, I'm quite happy."

Was that relief she saw in those stern eyes? For a moment, she felt a traitorous flash of irritation. Maximus had shown no sign before this moment that her happiness might be a factor in the match. The consolidation of lands and interests, the strengthening of his parliamentary alliance with Mandeville, those were the important considerations. Her feelings, as she well knew, played no part at all in the negotiations. And that was fine with her. She was the daughter of a duke, and she'd known from the cradle what her purpose and place in life was.

Maximus compressed his lips, surveying the crowded ballroom. "I wanted you to know that there is yet time for you to change your mind."

"Is there?" She glanced about the ballroom. Mandeville House was exquisitely decorated. Blue and silver swags— the Batten family colors—intertwined with Reading scarlet and black. Vases of flowers stood on every table, and the marquess had hired and outfitted a veritable platoon of footmen. Hero looked back at her brother. "The contracts are settled and signed already."

Maximus frowned in ducal displeasure. "If you truly wished to escape this engagement, I could break it."

"That's very generous of you." Hero was touched by Maximus's gruff words. "But I am quite pleased with my engagement."

He nodded. "Then I think it time we joined your intended."

"Of course." Her voice was steady, but her fingers trembled just a bit as she laid them on her brother's deep blue sleeve.

Fortunately, Maximus didn't seem to notice. He led her toward one side of the ballroom, moving unhurriedly but with his usual determination. Sometimes Hero wondered if her brother even realized that his way was made smoother because people were quick to step out of his path.

A man stood by the dance floor, his back to them. He wore somber black, his wig a snowy white. He turned as they approached, and for a moment Hero's heart stuttered in disbelief. Something in the set of his shoulders and the jut of his chin in profile reminded her of the rogue she'd argued with just minutes before. Then he faced her, and she curtsied gravely to the Marquess of Mandeville, chiding herself for her silly imagination. It was hard to think of anyone *less* like Lord Shameless than her betrothed.

Mandeville was tall and appropriately handsome. If Mandeville smiled more often, his looks would come perilously close to beautiful. But one felt somehow that beauty in a marquess would be gauche, and *gauche* was the last thing one could call the Marquess of Mandeville.

"Your Grace. Lady Hero." Mandeville executed an elegant bow. "You are even more lovely tonight than usual, my lady."

"Thank you, my lord." Hero smiled up at him and was pleased to see a faint softening of his usually somber lips.

Then his gaze moved to the side of her head. "My dear, you're wearing only one earring."

"Am I?" Hero automatically felt both earlobes, her face heating as she remembered what had happened to the missing earring. "Goodness, I must have lost one."

Hastily she removed the lone diamond earring and gave it to her brother to place in his pocket.

"That's better," Mandeville said, nodding approvingly. "Shall we?" he asked the question of her but glanced at Maximus.

Maximus nodded.

Mandeville signaled to his butler, but already the room was growing quiet as the guests turned toward them. Hero pasted a serene smile on her face, standing straight and still as she'd been taught from the nursery. A lady of her rank never fidgeted. She disliked being the center of attention, but it rather went with being the daughter of a duke. She glanced at Mandeville. And a marchioness would draw even more stares.

Naturally.

Hero suppressed a small sigh and inhaled and exhaled slowly, softly, and imagined she was a statue. It was an old trick to get through events such as these. She was a hollow, perfect facade of a duke's daughter. Really she—the woman within—didn't have to be here at all.

"My friends," Mandeville boomed. He was well known for his oratory in parliament, his voice rich and deep. Hero rather thought there was a touch of the theatrical about it as well, but of course she'd never say so to his face. "I welcome you all here tonight for a very important celebration: the engagement of myself to Lady Hero Batten."

He turned and took her hand, bending and kissing her knuckles very prettily. Hero smiled and curtsied to him as their guests applauded. They straightened and were immediately surrounded as the guests surged forward to offer their congratulations.

Hero was thanking a rather deaf elderly countess when Mandeville called behind her. "Ah, Wakefield, Lady Hero, I'd like to introduce you to someone."

She turned and met wickedly amused light green eyes. Hero could only stare, speechless, as Lord Shameless bowed and took her hand, brushing smooth, warm lips over her skin.

Distantly she heard Mandeville say beside her, "My dear, this is my bother, Lord Griffin Reading."

Chapter Two

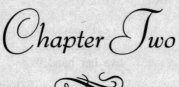

*Queen Ravenhair had ruled her kingdom fairly and
peacefully ever since the death of her husband, the late
king. But it is not an easy thing for a woman to wield
power in a world of men. For though she had advisors
and ministers and men of letters, she could not fully
trust any of them. Which was why every night Queen
Ravenhair stood upon her balcony and held a
little brown bird between her cupped palms.
She would whisper her secrets and worries to
the bird and then, opening her hands, let him fly free,
high into the night, carrying her cares with him....*
—from *Queen Ravenhair*

Hero took a deep, steadying breath and fixed a social
smile—neither too wide nor too small—upon her face. It
was a very middling expression that in no way revealed
the shock of finding out that Lord Shameless would soon
be her brother-in-law. "I'm very pleased to meet you, Lord
Griffin."

"Are you?" He was still half bent over her hand so only
she could hear his murmur.

"Naturally."

"Liar."

Her middling smile became a bit rigid as she hissed under her breath, "Don't you dare cause a scene!"

"A scene? Me?" His eyes narrowed, and she realized that she might have made a tactical error.

Hero tried to retrieve her hand, but the awful man tightened his hold as he straightened unhurriedly. "How delightful to finally meet my new sister. You don't mind if I call you 'sister,' do you, my lady? I feel as if we already know each other. Soon we'll be rubbing shoulders at every family gathering—dinners, breakfasts, tea, and the odd snack here and there. The prospect simply takes my breath away, dear little *sister*. What a jolly family we'll be."

He grinned wickedly at her.

Hero's soul revolted at this rogue using such a familiar term. He was in no way *fraternal* to her. "I don't think—"

"I'm so sorry to hear that," he murmured.

She grit her teeth and surreptitiously yanked on her hand. His grip held firm.

"Lord Griffin, I—"

"But pray will you dance with me, my lovely new sister-to-be?" he asked with jaw-dropping innocence.

"I don't—"

He raised his eyebrows at her words, his green eyes sparkling with sly mirth.

"—*believe*," she gritted, "that would be a good—"

"Of course." He bowed his head, his eyes downcast. "Why would such a proper lady wish to dance with a wastrel such as I? I'm so sorry to have importuned you."

His lips actually trembled. Hero felt her face heating. Somehow he had made *her* the villain of this piece.

"Well . . ." She bit her lip.

"It's a pretty offer, Hero. What do you say?" Maximus rumbled beside her.

She started, just a little bit, but Reading squeezed her fingers in warning. Good Lord! She'd almost forgotten they were in the midst of a crowded ballroom. Such a thing had never happened to her before. No matter where she was, Hero was always completely conscious of being a duke's daughter, completely conscious of how she should act.

She looked at Reading in consternation and saw that he had lost his mocking smile. In fact, there was no expression at all on his face as he turned to his brother. "With your permission, of course, Thomas."

Standing together, she could see now the similarities between the brothers. They were of the same height, but beyond that they both tilted their square chins in a certain way, as if challenging any other man in the room. Studying the brothers, Hero thought that Reading's countenance looked the older of the two, though she knew he was the younger by several years. Lord Reading's eyes were deeper set, more lined, and much more cynical. He looked as if he'd experienced lifetimes more than Mandeville.

Mandeville had not answered his brother, and the pause was growing awkward. The dowager marchioness stood between the men and was looking anxiously at her elder son. Perhaps she communicated something silently to him.

Mandeville nodded abruptly at his brother and smiled, though only his lips moved.

Reading immediately turned and started leading her toward the dance floor. His pace seemed unhurried, but

Hero found herself halfway across the room before she knew it.

"What are you about?" she hissed.

"A minuet, I believe."

She gave him a speaking glance at the childish witticism.

"Now, now, dear sister, mine—"

"Stop calling me that!"

"What, *sister*?"

They were on the dance floor now, and he pivoted to face her as other couples took their places around them.

Hero narrowed her eyes. "Yes!"

"But you will soon be my sister," he said slowly and patiently, as if talking to a not-very-bright toddler. "The wife of my elder brother, above me in rank if not in age, always to be deferred to. What else should I call you but sister?" He widened his eyes so guilelessly she nearly laughed.

Fortunately she was able to restrain herself. Lord knew what Mandeville—let alone her brother—would think if she giggled like a schoolgirl at her engagement ball. "Whyever did you ask me to dance?"

He feigned hurt. "Why, I thought to celebrate your wondrous engagement to my brother, of course."

She raised her left eyebrow, sadly ineffective though it was.

He leaned toward her and whispered hoarsely, "Or perhaps you'd like to discuss the particulars of our meeting in front of both our families?"

The music began and Hero sank into a curtsy. "Why would I mind? It seems to me that you have more to lose than I should the circumstances of our meeting be made public."

"One would think so," he replied as they circled each other. "But that supposition does not take into account my brother's incredibly stodgy personality."

Hero frowned. "What are you trying to insinuate?"

"I'm *stating*," Reading murmured, "that my brother is a narrow-minded ass who, if he had discovered you in that sitting room with Belle and me, would have immediately leaped to several unfortunate and wrong conclusions."

The movements of the dance parted them for a moment, and Hero tried to grapple with the notion of a man with a mind so blackened he would think the absolute worst of his own brother.

When they again met, she said softly, "Why are you saying these things to me?"

He shrugged. "I merely speak the truth."

She shook her head. "I think not. I think you strive to alienate my affections from your brother, which is a very wicked thing to attempt indeed."

He smiled, though a muscle jerked under his right eye. "Lady Perfect, we meet again."

"Stop calling me that," she hissed. "I do not think Mandeville is as ill-willed as you seem to believe."

"I hesitate to contradict a lady, of course, but you have no idea what you're talking about."

She glared. "You are insulting, sir, both to your brother and to me. I cannot think what your brother has ever done to you to deserve such infamous treatment."

He leaned over her, so close she caught the scent of lemons and sandalwood. "Can't you?"

She couldn't repress a shiver at the implied threat of his proximity. She wasn't a small woman—in fact, she stood taller than many of her female acquaintances—but

Reading was male and loomed at least a foot over her. He was using that physical fact to intimidate her.

Well, she wasn't so easily intimidated. She snorted softly and turned to look him in the eye. "No. No, I can't conceive of a wrong so terrible that you would vilify your brother's character to me."

"Perhaps, then, your imagination is defective," he said, his eyes hooded.

"Or perhaps it is *you* who is defective."

"In your eyes I probably am. After all, I do not possess the perfections of my brother. I am not a leading member of parliament, and I do not have his beauty or his grace. And"—he leaned close again—"I do not have his lofty title."

For a moment, she stared at him in disbelief; then she laughed softly under her breath. "Are you so jealous of him that you think I'm marrying your brother only for his title?"

She was gratified to see him jerk his head back, a scowl on his face. "I am not *jealous*—"

"No?" she interrupted him sweetly. "Then perhaps you're merely a fool. Mandeville is an honorable man. A good man. And, yes, a man respected by his peers and by everyone he deals with, as well as my brother's friend and ally. I am proud to be his fiancée."

The dance broke them apart, and when they rejoined, he nodded stiffly. "Perhaps you are right. Perhaps I'm merely a fool."

She blinked, caught off guard. The rogue she'd thought him would not admit so readily to a human failing.

He glanced at her, a corner of his mouth quirking up as if he knew her thoughts. "Will you tell Thomas about our meeting?"

"No." She didn't even have to think about it.

"That's wise. As I've said, my brother would not think the better of you for your involvement."

Uncertainty whispered in her mind. As much as Hero didn't want to believe it of Mandeville, her fiancé might just jump to the wrong conclusion.

She shook off the thought and looked Reading in the eye. "It's *your* reputation that I seek to preserve with your brother."

He threw back his head and laughed, the sound rich and masculine, drawing stares from the other dancers. "Didn't you know? I don't have a reputation to preserve, my Lady Perfect. Put away your shield and sword; lay down your shining armor. There is no dragon to slay for me. Nothing to protect at all."

"No?" she asked, sudden curiosity making her speak without forethought. She'd heard a few whispered rumors about her fiancé's mysterious brother, but they'd been maddeningly vague. "Are you so irredeemable?"

"I am a veritable blackguard." He circled her, pacing slowly to the music, whispering so only she could hear. "A seducer, a rake, the worst sort of profligate. I am notorious for my pleasures—I drink too much, wench with abandon, and belch in mixed company. I have no discretion, no morals, and no desire for either. I am, in short, the devil himself, and you, my dearest Lady Perfect, would do well to avoid my company at all costs."

A BURST OF male laughter made Thomas Reading, the Marquess of Mandeville, glance at the dance floor. Griffin had thrown his head back as he laughed with unbecoming abandon at something Lady Hero had said. Fortunately, the lady appeared less amused. Still, Thomas couldn't help the instinctive tightening of his shoulders.

Damn Griffin to hell.

"Your brother seems to be enjoying his dance with my sister," Wakefield murmured.

Thomas looked at the duke and met cool brown eyes. It was always deucedly hard to puzzle out what Wakefield was thinking, but at the moment the man could've modeled for a male sphinx.

Thomas grunted and turned his gaze back to where Griffin paced about his intended bride. "He does indeed."

Wakefield folded his arms across his chest. "Hero has been sheltered all her life—as is proper for her station—but her personal morals are of the highest. I know she will not fall even if presented with temptation."

Thomas nodded, feeling a flush of mortification creep up his neck. He had an urge to tug at his neckcloth at the duke's veiled admonition. "I believe you, Your Grace. Lady Hero has my complete faith, and I shall never treat her in any way other than with respect."

"Good." Wakefield clasped his hands behind his back and was silent a moment as they both watched the dancers. Then he said quietly, "The clause is ineffective."

Thomas glanced at him sharply. In an effort to act against the scourge of gin drinking among the poor of London, they'd attached a gin clause to parliament's Sweets Act last June. The clause gave a bounty to informers who brought in illegal gin sellers.

"Every day more gin sellers are hauled before the magistrates," Thomas said slowly. "How is this ineffective?"

Wakefield shrugged. His voice was low and controlled,

but his ire was plain. "They drag in the poor women who sell that devil's drink in wheelbarrows. Wretches who make only pennies a day. What we need is to catch the men distilling the gin. The powerful ones who hide in the shadows growing rich off the backs of those poor women."

Thomas pursed his lips. On the dance floor, Lady Hero was frowning at Griffin and the sight relieved him. "Catch enough of the gin sellers and it will impact the makers as well—I assure you. The clause is only months old. We must give it time, my friend."

"I haven't time," Wakefield replied. "London is wasting under this plague. More citizens die than are born in our great city. Bodies litter the streets and garrets of the East End. Wives are deserted by their drink-destroyed husbands, babes killed by their drunken mothers, children abandoned to die or prostitute themselves. How can England prosper if the workers deteriorate in mind and body? We will wither and fail as a nation if gin is not eradicated from our city."

Thomas knew that Wakefield was concerned about the gin problem, but to care so deeply about this one cause? Such passion didn't fit the man he knew.

A movement from the other side of the dance floor caught his eye and scattered his thoughts. A woman stepped to the edge of the crowd. Her skirts were a flaming orange over primrose petticoats. Her hair was a deep, impossible wine-red, her lips and cheeks artificially rouged. Every man on that side of the dance floor watched her as she flirtatiously rapped her male companion's arm with her folded fan. He said something, and she arched her white throat and laughed, making her breasts jiggle.

"...only if a man of substance is brought to account for gin making," Wakefield said.

Thomas blinked, realizing that he'd missed most of what his companion had said. He turned his head to the duke, but out of the corner of his eye he could still see the woman playfully drawing her fingers across the slopes of her breasts. "Wanton baggage."

"Who?"

Damn, he'd spoken aloud and now Wakefield waited for an answer.

Thomas grimaced. "Mrs. Tate." He jerked his chin to indicate the woman across the room. "Every time I see her, she has a different beau, all younger than herself. The woman should be hauled up on indecency charges. Anyone can see that she's five and thirty if she's a day."

"Eight and thirty," Wakefield murmured.

Thomas turned to look incredulously at him. "You know her?"

Wakefield's eyebrows rose. "I believe most of London society knows her."

Thomas glanced back at Mrs. Tate. Was Wakefield speaking of biblical knowledge? Had the duke bedded the woman?

"She has a quick wit and an easy manner," Wakefield was saying lightly. "Besides, she married a man three times her age. I don't begrudge her a little merriment now that she's widowed."

"She flaunts herself," Thomas gritted. He could feel Wakefield's look.

"Perhaps, but only with unmarried gentlemen. She is careful not to dally with a man otherwise engaged."

As if she'd heard the word *engaged*, Lavinia Tate

suddenly looked up, her eyes meeting his across the distance that separated them. He knew, even though he could not see them now, that her eyes were a plain brown. That, he thought with satisfaction, was something she couldn't change. Her eyes were and always would be ordinary brown, no matter how much paint she employed.

She held his eyes and lifted her chin in a challenge that would bring any red-blooded man to attention. It was a look as old as Eden, as old as Eve daring Adam with a bit of over-ripened fruit.

Thomas deliberately looked away from her proud gaze. He'd tasted that fruit once, and though it had been difficult, he'd weaned himself from its heady sweetness. The woman was a jade, plain and simple. And if there was one thing he'd had enough of in this lifetime, it was jades.

LADY HERO'S FACE was calm and grave and almost beautiful—and she looked not at all impressed by Griffin's dramatic recitation of his sins.

"I had already decided you were a rake," she said as he halted before her. She sank into a graceful curtsy. "But as you are to be my brother-in-law, Lord Reading, I think avoiding your company entirely may be somewhat difficult."

The woman certainly knew how to prick a man's illusions about himself. Once again he was hit with the awful irony that *this* woman out of all the women at the ball should be the one Thomas had chosen as his bride. A woman who made no bones about her displeasure with Griffin. A woman who had seen him at his very worst—and showed no signs of forgetting the sight. A woman who was proud of her snowy-white soul.

Lady Perfect—a perfect lady for his perfect brother.

He eyed her with disfavor, watching as she arched her damned left eyebrow in pointed query. She wasn't quite a beauty, his brother's fiancée. Instead she had that sort of elegance that was found sometimes among the upper crust of English society—creamy pale skin, a slightly overlong face, properly neat features, and hair that was red without going so far as to be gauchely ginger.

He'd seen her type a hundred times before, and yet... something about Lady Hero was decidedly different. For one thing, most of the ladies of her rank would've simply left him to his fate in the sitting room. Yet she had gone against her own rigid morals to save both him and Bella. Had she acted out of compassion for two strangers? Or merely a stolid code of ethics that superseded even her own distaste for what she'd found in the sitting room?

Griffin looked about. The music had halted, the dance was at an end, and he was supposed to escort her back to stodgy Thomas. Which he would do, of course—just not yet.

He bowed, proffering his elbow in feigned docility. "Sad, isn't it?"

She looked at his arm with sudden suspicion, but was forced by her own rigid propriety to take it. Griffin tamped down a surge of triumph.

"What is?" she asked, her voice wary.

"Oh, that a woman as pious as you should have to put up with the company of a rake like me merely because of polite convention."

"Humph." She lifted her chin as he led her slowly through the crowd. "I hope I know my duty."

He rolled his eyes. "Buck up. Enduring my presence in your life will surely give you points toward sainthood."

If he hadn't turned to look at her at that very moment, he would've missed the twitch of her soft, pink lips. Egad. Lady Perfect had a sense of humor! He'd seen her smile, but the expression had been fixed and immobile. What would a genuine smile look like on her face? What would happen if she actually laughed?

Intrigued, he bowed his head toward hers, inhaling the scent of flowers. "If you aren't marrying my brother for his title, then why?"

Wide gray eyes looked up, startled, into his. She was so near he only had to lean an inch or so closer and his lips would touch hers. He could find out what she tasted like, if she would break under his tongue and run soft and sweet like honey.

Good God! Griffin jerked his head back.

Fortunately, she seemed to have missed his confusion. "What do you mean?"

He inhaled and glanced away. They were nearly across the room now and moving in the opposite direction from Thomas, though she didn't seem to notice. He was playing with fire, but he'd always found danger terribly tempting.

"Why marry Thomas?"

"My brother and he are friends. Maximus urged me to make the match."

"That's all?"

"No, of course not. My brother would not have considered Mandeville for me if the marquess weren't well regarded, kind, and a man of substance." She rattled off his brother's attributes as if listing the points of a breeding ram.

"You don't love him?" he asked with honest curiosity.

She knit her brows as if he'd burst into Swedish. "I

have no doubt that I will someday have affection for him, naturally."

"Naturally," he murmured, feeling again that idiotic triumph. "Rather like a favorite spaniel, perhaps?"

She stopped dead, and if she hadn't been restrained by her propriety, he had the feeling she would've set her hands on her hips like an irate fishwife. "Mandeville isn't a spaniel!"

"A Great Dane, then?"

"Lord Griffin..."

He tugged her forward, leading her toward the outside edge of the ballroom. "It's just that I've always thought it would be nice."

"What?"

"To be in love with one's wife—or in your case, one's husband."

Her face softened for a moment, her gray eyes going a little foggy, her sweet lips parting. Griffin found himself drawn to her fleeting emotion. Was this a glimpse of the true Lady Hero?

Then she was back to being Lady Perfect, her spine erect, her lips firm, and her eyes giving nothing away. The change was rather fascinating. What had made her into such a chameleon?

"How romantic," she drawled in a bored, social voice that set his teeth on edge, "to think that love has anything to do with marriage."

"Why?"

"Because marriage at our rank is a contract between families—as you well know."

"But can't it be more?"

"You're deliberately being obtuse," she said impatiently. "You don't need me to explain society's rules to you."

"And you're being deliberately thickheaded. My parents had it."

"What?"

"Love," he said, trying to keep the irritation from his voice. "They loved each other. I know it's rare, but it is possible, even if you've never seen it—"

"My parents, too."

It was his turn to look confused. "What?"

Her head was bent so that he saw only her mouth, curved down in sadness. "My parents. I have memories of...of a deep affection between them."

He remembered suddenly—awfully—that her parents had been killed. It had been a cause célèbre over fifteen years before—the Duke and Duchess of Wakefield murdered outside a theater by common footpads. "I'm sorry."

She inhaled and glanced up, her face unbearably vulnerable for a moment. "Don't be. Hardly anyone mentions them to me. It's as if they'd never existed. I was in the schoolroom when they died, but I have a few fond memories of them, before...before it happened."

He nodded, feeling a protective tenderness for this proud, prickly woman. They strolled in silence for a moment, the crowd surging around them, but making no contact. It was as if they were strangely apart. Griffin inclined his head to one or two people as they met, but he kept walking, forestalling conversation.

"Perhaps you're right," she said after a bit. "Marriage with love between the partners is surely the ideal."

"Then why settle for less?"

"Love may grow between a husband and a wife after marriage."

"It also may *not* grow."

She shrugged, looking pensive. "All marriages are gambles of a sort. One tries to even the odds by choosing wisely—a man who is well liked, comes from a good family, and is kind."

"And the Readings do have a lack of madness in the family that is somewhat refreshing in aristocratic lineages," he murmured.

She wrinkled her nose up at him. "Would you rather I marry into a family with a history of madness?"

"No, of course not." He frowned, trying to articulate why her rather cold-blooded decision to marry his brother bothered him. Lord knew he wasn't worried about *Thomas's* heart. "You said yourself that a love match is ideal. Why not wait to make one?"

"I *have* waited. I've been out for over six years."

"You've been looking for true love all this time?"

"Maybe." She shrugged, obviously irritated. "Or something like true love. Besides, how long would you have me wait? Months? Years? I'm four and twenty. I have an obligation to marry and marry well. I cannot wait forever."

"An obligation." The words were sour on his tongue, though the thought wasn't new. Didn't all ladies of her rank have an "obligation" to make a good match?

She shook her head. "What if I met my true love at sixty? What if I never meet him? There is no guarantee that I will. Would you have me remain a spinster on some faint hope?"

He glanced at her curiously. "You believe that you do have one true love?"

"Perhaps not *one* true love, but someone, surely. I think...yes, I think that we are each certainly capable of falling in love—perhaps deeply in love—and that somewhere out there is a person who will reciprocate that love." She wrinkled her nose, suddenly looking self-conscious. "You no doubt find talk of true love foolish."

"Not at all. I do know romantic love is real. I've seen it, after all."

"And do you think a rake such as you could fall madly, deeply in love with one woman?" Her words were meant to mock, but her tone was serious.

He shrugged. "Perhaps, though it sounds a deucedly uncomfortable state to find oneself in."

"Then you've never been in love?"

"Never."

She nodded. "Nor have I."

"A pity," he said, pursing his lips. "I wonder how it would feel? To be swept away by a grand passion? To give everything for only one person in the world?"

Her lips curved wryly. "So idealistic for a rake. Really, you do spoil my prior understanding of what the word entailed."

"This is my social face," he said lightly. "Don't confuse it with the animal beneath."

She looked at him searchingly for a moment before nodding as if coming to a conclusion. "I'm hardly likely to do that considering how I first found you."

He smiled to cover a twinge of disappointment.

"But if you're so idealistic, my lord," she said, "about the connubial state, then why aren't you happily married with a score or more of offspring?"

"I'm idealistic about *love*, my lady, not marriage. To be tied to one lady for the rest of my life, surrounded by small, grubby urchins?" He shuddered in mock horror.

"No, I shall gladly cede the matrimonial state and all its attendant duties to my brother."

"And if you do one day find yourself in love?" she asked softly. "What then, my lord?"

"Why, then, all shall be lost, my lady. A rake's life crumbled to ruins, a splendid specimen of the bachelor state brought low by the bonds of matrimony and a delicate hand. But"—he lifted an admonishing finger—"that is, as you yourself have pointed out, very, very unlikely. My one true love may be a lady living in farthest China. She might be a crone of ninety or a babe of two. I may never meet her in this lifetime, and I thank God in advance for that fact."

He'd teased a slight smile onto those soft lips, and his heart beat faster at the sight. A smile—a genuine smile—from this woman was like total nudity from another. And what a very odd thought that was.

"Why, my lord?"

"Because"—he bent so close that his breath moved a wayward red curl by her ear—"while *I* may be far from perfect in your eyes, I do assure you that my *life* is perfect as it is. I enjoy my rakish ways, my freedom, and my ability to, er, *dally* with as many ladies as I might want. For me, true love would be a complete and utter catastrophe."

HERO STARED UP into Reading's roguish light green eyes. He'd used a euphemism instead of the crudity he'd employed in the sitting room, but his words were no less shocking because of that.

She swallowed, imagining a legion of ladies sprawled across his bed, his well-muscled buttocks thrusting in that mesmerizingly rhythmic movement. Dear Lord, she should be offended at the vision, but instead she wanted to press her palms to her cheeks to cool the heat rising there. She watched as Reading's eyelids drooped and his wide mouth opened to say something that would no doubt scandalize her even more.

Fortunately, they were interrupted.

"Might I have my fiancée back?" Mandeville said in a voice that was a little too hard-edged to be jovial.

The teasing gleam left Reading's eyes, taking with it any softness in his face. What remained was an expressionless and rather daunting mask. Without his habitual humor, Reading might have been the type of man others followed into near-hopeless battle: a leader of men, a statesman, a visionary.

What a very odd thought to have about an admitted rake!

Hero blinked and realized that Mandeville was offering his arm. "My dear?"

She smiled, dropping a curtsy for Reading before taking her fiancé's arm.

Reading swept into a bow so extravagant it verged on mocking. "My congratulations to you, Thomas, on your engagement. Lady Hero."

He nodded rather more curtly to her and then turned to disappear into the crowd.

Hero let out a breath she did not know she was holding.

"I hope he wasn't too trying," Mandeville murmured as he led her toward the dance floor.

"Not at all," she said, nodding to a passing matron.

She felt more than saw his sharp look. "Some ladies

find him very enticing." His tone was so neutral it might as well have been a warning shout.

"I'm sure they do," she said gently. "The hint of danger and that wicked grin no doubt have many a feminine breast aflutter. But I've always found a man who knows his responsibilities and keeps them far more attractive than one who spends his life playing."

The arm beneath her hand relaxed fractionally. "Thank you, my dear."

"For what?"

"For seeing so clearly what others do not," he said. "Now, would you care to dance with your betrothed?"

She smiled up at him, liking how the lines about his brown eyes crinkled when he looked at her. "I'd be delighted."

They danced a minuet and a country dance, and then Hero professed herself in need of refreshment. Mandeville led her to several chairs arranged by the side of the room and found her a seat before going in search of punch.

Hero watched him thread his way through the crowd, admiring his wide shoulders and firm stride. As always, he was stopped every few feet by well-wishers and those who merely wanted to be seen talking to the Marquess of Mandeville. She sighed, content. Really, Maximus had made the perfect choice of husband for her.

"There you are!"

Bathilda Picklewood—or, as she was better known in the Batten household, Cousin Bathilda—settled her substantial frame into a chair next to Hero. A distant relation on her mother's side, Cousin Bathilda had raised Hero and her younger sister, Phoebe, ever since the death of their parents. Cousin Bathilda's white hair was crimped into tiny curls about her forehead and was topped by a lacy triangular cap. She wore her favorite plum color, and her magnificent bosom was framed by white lace and black ribbons. From the crook of her arm peered a small black, brown, and white face. Mignon, Cousin Bathilda's tiny, elderly spaniel, accompanied her wherever she went.

"My dear, I must talk to you!"

Since Cousin Bathilda nearly always spoke in exclamations, Hero merely raised her eyebrows. "Yes?"

"You mustn't dance with Lord Griffin Reading ever again!" Cousin Bathilda said with as much urgency as if she were importing state secrets. Mignon barked once as if to emphasize her mistress's words.

"Why not?"

"Because he and Lord Mandeville loathe each other."

"Hmm," Hero murmured, absently scratching Mignon behind her silky ears. "I had noticed a certain strain between them, but I don't know if I would go so far as to call it *loathing*. Perhaps a general dislike..."

"It's much, much worse than dislike, my dear! Don't you understand?" Cousin Bathilda lowered her voice to a whisper. "Lord Griffin seduced Mandeville's first wife!"

Chapter Three

*Far below the queen's balcony lay the royal stables.
There, the little brown bird would come to roost at
night after it had tired of flying. Early every morning,
the stable master personally groomed the queen's favorite
mare. As he curried the horse's chestnut coat, the little
bird would sing above him in the stable rafters. And
sometimes if the stable master listened hard enough,
the bird seemed to be singing these words:*
"High, high on the castle walls
A sweet lady weeps alone at night.
Oh, will no one comfort her?..."
—from *Queen Ravenhair*

It was times like this that being an unmarried lady was particularly galling, Hero thought later that night as she and Cousin Bathilda rode home in the carriage.

"Why couldn't anyone have told me about the scandal involving Mandeville's first wife?" she demanded.

"It wasn't a proper topic of conversation for a maiden." Cousin Bathilda waved a vague arm, nearly clipping Mignon's nose where it peeked out from her lap. "Seduction and affairs and all that. Besides, how was I to know that you'd go off and dance with the man as soon as you met him?"

"He asked me in front of Maximus," Hero said for the third or possibly the fourth time. "Mandeville gave his permission!"

"Couldn't very well have done otherwise, could he?" Cousin Bathilda replied with irritating logic. "Well, what's done is done. You'll just have to be more careful in the future."

"But why?" Hero asked rebelliously. "You don't seriously think I'd let myself be seduced by a rake, do you?"

"Of course not!" Cousin Bathilda sounded scandalized at the mere notion. "But everyone will be watching you closely when the man is anywhere near you."

"It's not fair. *I* haven't done anything wrong." Hero crossed her arms on her chest. "How do we know Lord Griffin seduced Mandeville's wife anyway? Perhaps it's just a nasty rumor."

"Well, if it's a rumor, Mandeville certainly believes it," Cousin Bathilda said. "Do you remember the first Lady Mandeville?"

Hero wrinkled her nose. "Vaguely. She died four years ago, didn't she?"

"A little over three years ago. You wouldn't have moved in her circles anyway. She was quite fast for a young matron, but then she was a Trentlock," Cousin Bathilda said darkly. "Always a feckless lot, the Trentlock family, though quite comely, of course. That must've been what turned Mandeville's head. Anne Trentlock was a beauty, no doubt about it, and the family is old and very nicely situated. Everyone thought the match a good one when it was announced."

Hero couldn't suppress a shiver. Everyone thought *her* match was a good one. "What happened?"

"Lord Griffin Reading is what happened." Cousin Bathilda shook her head. "The man is wild, has been ever since his father's death. The old marquess died when Reading was at Cambridge. Reading immediately left and began living the life of a young roué in London. He associated with the worst sort of lowlifes, seduced married ladies, and was nearly involved in two duels. And through all these scandals, Mandeville was a rock of loyalty. He wouldn't hear anything against his brother even when Reading began to be refused invitations."

"And then?"

"And then Mandeville married Anne Trentlock. It was the match of the season, and naturally Reading was invited." Cousin Bathilda sighed. "It was a year before you came out, dear, but I was there. Anne couldn't take her eyes off Reading—everyone remarked upon it. There was speculation that she would've set her cap on winning Reading instead of Mandeville, had it not been for Mandeville's title."

Hero frowned. "What did Reading do?"

"He acted no differently than usual, but of course he must've taken note of Anne's infatuation."

"And Mandeville?"

"What could he do?" Cousin Bathilda shrugged. "I suppose he tried to keep them apart, but Reading is his brother. It was inevitable that eventually Reading should find an opportunity to seduce his brother's wife."

"Inevitable only if he was a complete cad," Hero muttered. This story was depressing her terribly. She'd known Reading was a rake, but to do such a thing to his own brother was simply appalling.

"Well, yes, but by then we all knew what he was."

Mignon whined and batted a paw. Cousin Bathilda absently scratched her under her chin. "When Anne died in childbirth, the brothers weren't even talking to each other. And there were rumors about the babe. A mercy it did not live, really."

"What a horrible thing to say," Hero whispered.

"Perhaps so—your compassion does you credit." Cousin Bathilda pursed plump lips. "But we must be practical, I'm afraid. Had the child lived with his father uncertain, it would have been a terrible burden, both for Mandeville and for the child himself."

"I suppose you're right," Hero murmured. She wrinkled her nose. She hated this kind of practicality, though—the kind that would bless the death of an innocent baby.

Cousin Bathilda leaned forward in the swaying carriage and patted Hero's knee. "That's all history now. Just remember to keep well clear of Reading and the past will be forgotten."

Hero nodded. She parted the carriage curtains to look out, but the night was black and all she saw was her reflection in the glass. Dying in childbirth was awful enough, but how much more terrible to die having betrayed one's husband? She let the curtain fall. That was a fate she had no intention of following.

The ride home took another twenty minutes, and by that time, Cousin Bathilda was nodding and little Mignon was snoring in her arms.

"Goodness!" Cousin Bathilda yawned as they descended the carriage steps. "What a lovely ball, but I'm for bed now, I fear. I'm not like you young things that can stay up until all hours!"

They mounted the white marble steps of the neat town

house Maximus had bought for Hero, her younger sister, Phoebe; and Cousin Bathilda three years ago. Until then, they'd all lived with him at Wakefield House in one of London's most fashionable squares, but Maximus had said that it wasn't right for three ladies to be rattling about a bachelor's mansion. Hero suspected that this was Maximus's way of ensuring his own privacy, but she didn't object. While their town house wasn't as palatial as Wakefield House, it was quite elegant and comfortable.

Panders, the butler, opened the front door, bowing over a round little belly. "Good evening, my lady, ma'am."

"More like good morning, Panders," Cousin Bathilda said as she handed him her wrap and gloves. "Have one of the footmen take Mignon for her before-bed constitutional and then bring her to my rooms."

"Yes, ma'am." Panders took the little spaniel in his arms, succeeding in remaining grave even as Mignon bathed his chin with her tongue.

"Thank you, Panders." Hero smiled at the butler and relinquished her wrap before following the older lady to the upper floor.

"I am so very proud of you for making this match," Cousin Bathilda said outside her room. She yawned again, delicately patting her mouth with one hand. "Oh, dear, I'm quite done in. Good night."

"Good night," Hero whispered, and turned down the hall to her own room. It was well past midnight, but oddly she didn't feel at all sleepy.

She opened her door and wasn't too surprised when Phoebe's mobcapped head popped up from the covers of her bed. "Hist! Hero!"

Phoebe was the youngest of the Batten children and

looked nothing like either Hero or Maximus. Where both Hero and Maximus were tall, Phoebe was short—barely an inch over five feet—and rather on the plump side, much to Cousin Bathilda's consternation. A fine cloud of curly light brown hair, already falling from her night braid, framed her face, and her eyes were hazel behind small, round spectacles. In her white lawn night rail, she looked all of twelve, though she'd been seventeen for half a year now.

"What are you doing still up?" Hero closed the door behind her, then kicked off her slippers. Four candelabras lit the room, making it bright and warm. "And what have you done with Wesley?"

Phoebe hopped from the bed. "I sent her away. I'll play maid and you can tell me all about the ball." Phoebe wasn't yet out and hadn't been allowed to attend the engagement ball—much to her vocal disgust.

"Hmm. Well, I don't know that there's much to tell," Hero began.

"Oh, don't tease!" Phoebe was already working at the hooks to Hero's bodice. "Was Mrs. Tate there?"

"Yes, and you wouldn't believe her gown," Hero said, relenting.

"What? What?"

"Scarlet. Almost the same shade as her hair. And her bodice was so low it was nearly indecent. I swear I saw Mr. Grimshaw stumble over thin air he was so busy craning his neck around to ogle her bosom."

Phoebe giggled. "Who else was there?"

"Oh, everyone." Hero helped take off her bodice, and then they both began on the tapes fastening her skirts. She kept her eyes on her fingers and made her voice casual. "I met Mandeville's brother."

"I thought he lived in the north of England?"

"He came down for the ball."

"Is he like the marquess?"

"Only a little. They're both tall and dark, but other than that, they're completely different. Lord Griffin Reading has such pale green eyes, startling really. His face is more lined than Mandeville's and thinner. He seems merrier, laughing and joking, but I think he's less happy than Mandeville. And the way he moves..."

Hero looked up and realized that despite her carefully neutral tone, she must've given something away. Phoebe was watching her quizzically. "Yes? How does he move?"

Hero could feel heat stealing into her cheeks. She made a production of stepping from her skirts and shaking them out before draping them over a chair for Wesley to clean and put away tomorrow. "It's rather odd. He seems to be doing everything slowly, and yet when he wants, he's faster than other men."

"Like a cat," Phoebe said.

Hero straightened and looked at her, eyebrows raised.

"You remember that big marmalade tom that hung around the stables at Wakefield House?" Phoebe began to work on Hero's stays. "It was always sleeping or lounging about, but when it saw a rat—bang!—it would be off like a lightning bolt and have that rat in its jaws in seconds. Is Lord Griffin like that?"

"I suppose so," Hero said, remembering how fast Reading had moved just before Lord Pimbroke had entered the sitting room. "Like a great cat."

"He sounds lovely."

"No!" Her voice was overloud, and Phoebe looked

startled. "I'm sorry, dearest. It's just that Cousin Bathilda spent the whole carriage ride home warning me about Reading's reputation. You must stay away from him."

Phoebe pouted. "I never get to meet the really interesting people."

Unfortunately, Hero had a little too much sympathy with Phoebe's complaint. She might be out, but she was allowed to mix with only the very best of society—no one with even a hint of scandal.

"There are plenty of perfectly respectable people who are interesting as well," she said to Phoebe with more confidence than she actually felt.

Phoebe looked at her doubtfully.

Hero wrinkled her nose and capitulated. "At least one can *look* at the scandalous people while conversing with more respectable gentlefolk."

"It doesn't sound as interesting as meeting them."

"No, but I assure you watching Mrs. Tate's progress across a ballroom full of silly gentlemen is quite fascinating."

"Oh, I wish I could've been there." Phoebe sighed.

"Next season you'll be eighteen, and we'll have a grand coming-out ball for you," Hero said as she sat at her dressing table.

Phoebe picked the pins from her hair. "But you'll be already married by then and off doing married-lady things. I'll have only Cousin Bathilda to accompany me, and you know I love her, I truly do, but she's so very *old* and—oh!" Hero glanced in the mirror in time to see Phoebe's head ducking behind her. "Dash it, I've dropped a pin."

"Don't worry about it, dear."

"But it's one of your emerald ones." Phoebe's voice was muffled.

Hero turned on the stool and saw her sister on her hands and knees, patting the carpet. Hero's heart squeezed. The emerald pin was right in front of Phoebe, not more than a foot from her nose.

Hero cleared her throat, feeling a sudden constriction. "Here it is." She bent and picked up the pin.

"Oh!" Phoebe stood and pushed her spectacles up her nose. A frown marred her sweet face. "Silly me. I don't know why I didn't see it."

"Never mind." Hero gently placed the pin in the glass dish on her dresser. "It's dark in here with only the candlelight."

"Oh, of course," Phoebe said, but her frown deepened.

"Shall I tell you how the ballroom was decorated?" Hero asked.

"Do!"

So Hero went into great detail about the decorations at Mandeville House, the refreshments, and each dance she took part in as Phoebe brushed her hair. Gradually her sister's expression lightened, but Hero's heart remained heavy as she watched the reflected light of the four candelabras in her mirror.

They made the room as bright as day.

ST. GILES WAS a veritable hellhole, especially after the bucolic beauty of the Lancashire countryside, Griffin mused early—very early—that morning. He guided Rambler, his bay gelding, through the darkness and across the stinking channel running down the middle of the lane. He couldn't take the shortest route to his destination, because some of the alleys that way were too narrow to accommodate a man riding a horse. And he'd be damned if he left Rambler anywhere here. The horse would be stolen before his master was out of sight.

Griffin ducked his head as he rode under a swinging sign advertising a chandler's shop. No lantern hung by the door of the shop as it would in the better parts of London. In fact, the only light he traveled by was the moon's pale face. Thank God it was a clear night at least.

Up ahead, a low door burst open and two toughs staggered out. Griffin laid his right hand on the loaded pistol stuck in his saddle, but the men paid him no mind. Pausing only for one of them to cast up his accounts into the channel, they wandered off away from him.

Griffin let out his breath and moved his hand from the pistol's grip to Rambler's neck, patting the horse. "Not much farther now, boy."

He rode down the lane and then turned into a slightly larger street, lined with brick and plaster buildings, some with overhanging upper stories. A nondescript door stood in a tall brick wall, hiding a courtyard beyond. Griffin pulled Rambler to a halt by the door. Taking the pistol from the saddle holster, he used the butt to knock upon the wooden door.

Almost immediately a gruff male voice called, "'Oo's without?"

"Reading. Let me in."

"'Ow'm I sure 'tis you, m'lord?"

Griffin raised his eyebrows at the door. "Because I'm the only one who knows about that night at the Lame Black Cockerel when you drank a dozen pints of ale and—"

The door flew open, revealing shifty black eyes in the ugliest face Griffin had ever known, in London or without. The nose was mashed nearly flat, causing the lipless mouth to always be parted so the man could breathe. Stubble perpetually dotted the lined cheeks and chin, like some spreading mildew, broken by old pox marks and scars far less benign. The man was of average height, but his arms and shoulders were disproportionately large, ending with hands that hung like great slabs of ham by his side. Most who saw him assumed he was either a professional boxer or a murderer for hire.

They'd be right on both counts.

"I'm that glad to see you, m'lord," Nick Barnes said. "Me and the boys 'ave been staking out the place, but we could sure use your 'elp."

"Have there been any more attacks?" Griffin swung down from Rambler but kept the gun in his hand and his eyes sharp as he led the horse through the door. Inside, the small courtyard was paved with cobblestones. Buildings rose up on three sides. Griffin had purchased the buildings to either side just last year as a precaution. Now he was grateful for the forethought.

"Some lads tried to come in night afore last, but we beat 'em back right smart," Nick said, heaving a solid oak bar across the courtyard door.

Griffin led Rambler to an ancient stone water trough to let him drink. "Do you think he's given up?"

"The Vicar won't give up until 'e's dead, and that's a fact, m'lord," Nick said soberly.

Griffin grunted. He'd not held high hopes that Charlie Grady, otherwise known rather blasphemously as the Vicar of Whitechapel, would give up so easily. The Vicar had a dirty finger in most of the illegal trades east of Bishopsgate, but recently he'd begun expanding his empire west into the Seven Dials area of St. Giles.

And that had impinged on Griffin's interests.

Griffin gave a last pat to the gelding and turned to Nick. "You'd better show me, then."

The other man nodded and led the way into the building directly across from the courtyard wall.

He opened a stout wooden door reinforced with iron and shouted, "Oy, Willis! You and Tim come 'ere and guard the courtyard."

Two men lumbered out of the building, touching their hats as they passed Griffin. One held a cudgel, the other a long knife that looked suspiciously like a saber.

Nick watched as they took up positions by the courtyard door and then nodded at Griffin. "This way, m'lord."

The lower floor of the building was one large, cavernous room, broken here and there by massive brick pillars, holding up the upper floors. Four large hearths smoldered under great covered copper kettles nearly as large as a man. Various copper pipes sprouted from the kettles, leading to slightly smaller copper pots, which were in turn connected to oaken barrels. The smells of smoke, fermentation, juniper berries, and turpentine were heavy in the humid air. A dozen more men were in the warehouse, a few tending the fires or the contents of the kettles, but most stood about, hired merely for their muscle.

"I've brought in all the other operations," Nick said, gesturing to the copper kettles. "All but the one that the Vicar's boys blew up on Abbott Street."

Griffin nodded. "You've done well, Nick. One position is more easily guarded than many."

Nick spat at the stone floor. "Aye, that it is, but we'll 'ave another problem when the 'arvest grain comes in."

"What's that?"

Nick tilted his head in the direction of the courtyard. "The outer door. It's too small to bring in a wagon full of grain. We'll have to toss the bags over the wall, and while we do, the cart, the boys, and the blasted grain'll be sitting like pullets awaitin' pluckin' for Sunday supper."

Griffin grimaced, not bothering to reply to Nick's succinct analysis of their position. He watched the men stoking the fires beneath the huge copper kettles. Most of his—*their*—capital was sunk into this operation, and the bloody Vicar was set to destroy it all. For the Vicar had declared that he would smash all other gin distillers and make himself king of gin in London.

And as it happened, Griffin was the biggest gin distiller in St. Giles.

SILENCE HOLLINGBROOK WOKE to little baby fingers poking at her eyelids. She groaned and opened her eyes. Big brown eyes framed by an extravagance of lashes met her own. Mary Darling—the owner of the eyes and the baby in question—sat up and clapped pudgy hands, crowing her delight in having woken Silence.

"Mamoo!"

Silence grinned back at her tiny bedmate—it was quite impossible not to, really. "How many times have I told you not to poke at Mamoo's eyes, you little imp?"

Mary Darling giggled. At little over a year old, she had but three words to her vocabulary: "Mamoo," an emphatic "no!" and "Soo" for Soot the cat—who was not nearly as fond of Mary Darling as she was of him.

Silence glanced at the tiny window to their attic bedroom and sat up in horror. The sun was shining brightly. "Oh, no. You should've poked me in the eye earlier. I've overslept again."

Hurriedly she did her morning ablutions, feeling a vague sense that she was forgetting something important. She changed Mary Darling's diaper and dressed them both—and only just in time. A firm knock came at the door. Silence pulled it open breathlessly and looked into the worn face of her elder brother, Winter.

"Good morning, sister," Winter said gravely. He rarely smiled, but there was a twinkle in his eyes as he looked at the baby in Silence's arms. "And to you, too, Miss Mary Darling."

The baby chortled and made a grab for Winter's plain black hat.

"I'm so sorry," Silence said breathlessly as she gently plucked Mary Darling's fingers from Winter's flat hat brim. "I did mean to be down earlier, but, well, I overslept."

"Ah," Winter said, and somehow his very lack of condemnation only made Silence feel worse.

She'd started working at the Home for Unfortunate Infants and Foundling Children over six months ago, but she still felt like she was learning. Running a foundling home that housed nine and twenty children and infants was no small task, even with the aid of Winter and three servants.

Her self-doubts were not helped by the fact that her predecessor had been her elder sister, Temperance. Silence loved Temperance dearly, but sometimes she wondered darkly if Temperance had to be *such* a paragon. In all the years that Silence had visited the home when Temperance had been in charge, she'd found her sister busy, flurried, and sometimes tired beyond bearing, but Temperance had always been in *control*.

Lately Silence had begun to wonder if she'd ever feel in control—of the home, of her life, or of anything else.

"Nell has taken the children down for breakfast," Winter said now.

"Oh! Oh, yes," Silence muttered, shifting Mary Darling to her other hip and trying to extricate a ribbon from the baby's mouth. "No, dearest, it really isn't for eating. I'll go help, shall I?" she said to her brother.

"That might be a good idea," Winter murmured. "I'll see you at luncheon."

Silence bit her lip, remembering how poor Winter had had to dine on cold bread and cheese yesterday because she'd forgotten to put the soup on in time. "I'll be sure and have it ready today, really I will."

A corner of Winter's stern mouth kicked up. "Don't worry so—I wasn't chastising you. And besides, I like cheese." He brushed a finger across her cheek. "Now I'm away to work. If I'm not at the school before the boys, Lord only knows what mischief they'd get up to in my absence."

Winter turned and clattered down the stairs. She didn't know how he found such energy when he not only helped run the home, but also taught in a day school for boys.

Silence sighed and followed more slowly, careful of her footing on the rickety stairs. The Home for Unfortunate Infants and Foundling Children had once been housed in an aging but sturdy building, but that had been before it had burned at the beginning of the year. Now, thanks to the generosity of the home's patronesses, the elder Lady Caire and Lady Hero, a beautiful new home was being built. It would have plenty of rooms, a big kitchen, and a garden for the children to take fresh air in. Unfortunately, the new home wasn't yet built.

In the interim, Winter, Silence, the home's three servants, Soot the cat, and all the home's children—save for two infants boarded out with wet nurses—lived in one too-small, dilapidated building in St. Giles. Silence could have lived in the rooms she shared with her husband, William, but William was the captain of the merchant ship *Finch* and was away most of the time at sea. It had seemed silly to live by herself in the rooms in Wapping and then travel every day all the way to the home in St. Giles.

And there had been Mary Darling.

Silence kissed the little girl's soft cheek as she descended the stairs. Mary Darling had been left on her doorstep nearly seven months ago. It had been a hard time for Silence—William had been at sea, and their parting had been chilly. Mary Darling had been like the first rays of a bright new day. She'd warmed Silence's life, and Silence had hated to part with her, even for as short a time as a night at the home. Silence heard the voices of the children even before she and Mary Darling reached the main floor. A dark, crooked passage led back to the home's kitchen—a big room with blackened beams in the ceiling. Two long trestle tables took up the middle of the room, one for the boys, one for the girls. Mary Darling began bouncing at the sight of the other children.

"All right, sweetheart." Silence picked up a bowl of porridge and a spoon and slid into a space at the girls' table with Mary Darling on her lap. "Good morning, everyone."

"Good morning, Mrs. Hollingbrook!" the girls—and some of the boys—chorused. Even Soot glanced up, chin dripping, from his morning saucer of milk by the fire.

Mary Evening, the girl sitting next to them, leaned close. "Good morning, Mary Darling."

Mary Darling, mouth full of porridge, waved her spoon in greeting, nearly hitting Mary Evening's nose.

"Be careful, Mary Evening," Nell Jones said as she draped a big cloth across Silence's lap and front.

Nell was a merry-faced blond woman, the most senior of the servants and a former actress in a traveling theater. She might be only a bit over thirty years of age, but she knew how to wield an iron hand, and Silence had come to rely on her good sense since taking over the home's management.

"Thank you, Nell," Silence said. Eating breakfast with a baby in one's lap could be a very messy task—as she'd found out in the last months.

"You're welcome, ma'am. And you"—Nell bent and mock-scowled into the baby's eyes—"careful with that great big spoon."

Mary Darling laughed up into Nell's face, splattering porridge down the front of her chemise. Silence sighed and wiped at the spill, taking a spoonful of porridge herself. Breakfast was almost over, and if she didn't eat now, she'd not have another chance until luncheon.

Hurriedly, she ate the thick porridge, taking sips of the hot tea that Nell thrust in front of her. In between her own bites, she fed spoonfuls to Mary Darling, keeping both the hot teacup and the tempting bowl of porridge out of the baby's reach. Mary Darling was old enough to feed herself with her spoon, but the result tended to be incredibly messy.

Around them the children ate cheerfully, aided by Nell and the other maidservant, Alice. The home also employed a manservant, Tommy, who helped with the heavier tasks and ran errands.

Nell suddenly clapped her hands. "Time to clean up, children. We have a busy day ahead of us, for we have a very important visitor coming today."

Silence nearly choked on her last spoonful of porridge. Oh, dear Lord! She'd completely forgotten. Lady Hero was to tour the home today—and not only was Lady Hero their patroness, but she was also the daughter of a *duke*. Silence pushed her bowl away, feeling slightly queasy. Would she ever be comfortable in her position as manageress of the home?

HERO STEPPED GINGERLY from her carriage that afternoon—gingerly because she'd learned very quickly to watch where she placed her feet in the St. Giles streets. To the side, a man lay in the gutter. Hero made a wide circle around him, her nose wrinkling as she caught the stink of gin. Here was yet another victim of that terrible drink, sadly not that uncommon a sight. What misery would be relieved in London if only gin could be eradicated!

Once past the drunkard, Hero made her way down a little lane to where the Home for Unfortunate Infants and Foundling Children was housed temporarily in a rather ramshackle building. Hero sighed silently. As the patroness of the home, she felt guilty whenever she saw the wretched condition of the house the children lived in.

Mrs. Hollingbrook, the home's manageress, bobbed a nervous curtsy as she neared. "Good afternoon, Lady Hero."

Hero nodded, smiling—she hoped—graciously. The fact was that she'd originally become a patroness of the home when Temperance Dews, now the younger Lady Caire, was in charge. Hero had felt an instant friendship with the then Mrs. Dews and had rather enjoyed her interactions with the woman. She'd not found the same rapport with Mrs. Hollingbrook—at least not yet.

Mrs. Hollingbrook was younger and less poised than her elder sister. Her face reminded Hero of a medieval saint—all pale oval solemnity—and like one of those painted martyrs, she seemed to hold a resigned melancholy close to her heart.

"Won't you come in and have a dish of tea?" Mrs. Hollingbrook asked formally as she always did.

She stood aside, letting Hero precede her into the home. Hero stepped over the threshold, trying not to wince at the cracked plaster on the entryway walls. A cramped room lay at the back of the house, and Hero entered it, familiar now with the rhythm of her visits to the foundling home. Inside, four chairs, a low table, and a desk had been crammed into the small space. Hero took one of the chairs, drawing off her hat as Mrs. Hollingbrook fluttered about, supervising the tea.

Finally the other woman settled to pour the tea. "No sugar, is that correct, my lady?"

Hero smiled. "Yes."

"Now where have I put the spoons?" Mrs. Hollingbrook held the full teacup in one hand, the hot liquid sloshing perilously near the rim as she searched the crowded tea tray. "But if you don't take sugar, perhaps you won't need a spoon anyway?"

"I don't think so." Hero took the cup before Mrs. Hollingbrook burned herself. "Thank you."

Mrs. Hollingbrook smiled uneasily and sipped at her own tea. Hero looked down at her teacup. People were often awkward or shy about her, she knew. Her rank awed them. It was a perpetual problem—how to put others at ease.

She inhaled and looked up. "I understand the home has new residents?"

"Oh! Oh, yes." Mrs. Hollingbrook straightened and placed her teacup down carefully on the low table. She clasped her hands in her lap as if about to recite a memorized poem. "Since we saw you last month, my lady, we've taken on two infants—a boy and a girl—and a little boy of four years. The boy, Henry Putman, is—"

Mrs. Hollingbrook stopped here because Hero had coughed. "I beg your pardon, but I thought all the boys were named Joseph at the home?"

"Well, yes, they usually are, but since Henry Putman already had a name—which, as it happens, he was quite adamant about—we thought it best to let him keep it."

"Ah." Hero nodded. "Please continue."

Mrs. Hollingbrook leaned forward. "I've never understood why Winter and Temperance chose to name all the boys Joseph and all the girls Mary. It's incredibly confusing at times."

"I should think so," Hero replied gravely.

Mrs. Hollingbrook smiled quickly and suddenly, the expression lightening her pale face and making her rather beautiful. "Ahem. We also placed two of our girls in apprenticeships this last month. And, with the monies you and the senior Lady Caire gave us, we were able to outfit both girls with new clothes, shoes, stays, a prayer book, a comb, and a thick winter cloak."

"Very good." Hero nodded approvingly. Some of her help was working at least. "Perhaps you'd like to show me the home now?"

"Of course, my lady." Mrs. Hollingbrook jumped up. "If you'll step this way, the children have been practicing all week for you."

Mrs. Hollingbrook led the way into the dark little hallway and up a rickety set of stairs. They passed a first floor, given over, as Hero knew from previous visits, to dormitory rooms for the orphans. On the second floor there was a room for the toddlers and infants and a little room used as a classroom. Mrs. Hollingbrook led her here and opened the door with a flourish. Within, a dozen of the older children stood in two rows, faces scrubbed, and hair still slick from water.

As she entered, they spoke in unison. "Good afternoon, Lady Hero!"

She permitted herself a small smile. "Good afternoon, children."

Her reply elicited a smothered giggle from one of the boys. A sharp glance from Nell Jones silenced the giggle. Mrs. Hollingbrook gave a discreet nod, and the children burst into ragged song—a hymn, no doubt, though Hero couldn't quite place either the tune or the words. She kept her smile firmly in place even as the most enthusiastic girl went flat on a low note and one of the boys elbowed another in the ribs, making the second squeak.

The song ended on a rather screeching high note, and

Hero fought not to wince. She clapped enthusiastically, and the little boy who had assaulted his neighbor grinned at her, revealing two missing upper-front teeth.

"Splendid, children," Hero said. "Thank you for your song. And thank you to your teachers as well."

Mrs. Hollingbrook blushed prettily even as she escorted Hero back down the stairs.

"Thank you for coming, my lady," she said as they made the front door. "The children look forward so to your visits."

Hero knew that Mrs. Hollingbrook was bound to flatter her because she was the home's patroness, but as she took the other lady's hand, it seemed that the manageress truly meant her words.

"I enjoy my visits as well," Hero said.

She wished she could say more. Could promise that the children would be out of this wretched temporary home soon. Could tell Mrs. Hollingbrook that the children would have new beds, a new schoolroom, and a huge garden to run in come spring. Instead she smiled one last time and made her good-byes.

She picked her way back up the street with a heavy heart. She had a feeling her next visit of the day wasn't going to be nearly as pleasant.

"Please take me to Maiden Lane," she instructed the coachman before climbing in the carriage.

She sat and glanced idly out the window as the coach rolled forward. The home depended on her. Now that—

"Oy!" a male voice—a *familiar* male voice—shouted very near.

The carriage shuddered to a halt.

Hero leaned forward. Surely it couldn't be—

The carriage door opened and a tall masculine form climbed in the carriage and settled himself against the red squabs across from her as if he owned the vehicle.

The carriage started as Hero gaped at him.

"We meet again, Lady Perfect," Lord Griffin drawled.

Chapter Four

*Inevitably there came a time when Queen Ravenhair
decided she should remarry. A queen must have a
king and a kingdom an heir, after all. So the queen
consulted with her advisors and ministers and men
of letters to decide who would be the perfect highborn
man to marry. But here she found a dilemma. Her
advisors thought Prince Westmoon the perfect match
for the queen, while the ministers scorned Westmoon
and instead preferred Prince Eastsun. What was worse,
the men of letters hated both Westmoon and Eastsun
and considered only Prince Northwind the perfect
consort for the queen....*
—from *Queen Ravenhair*

Griffin hadn't believed his eyes when he'd seen Lady
Hero step into a carriage in the worst part of St. Giles.
He'd hailed the carriage, told the coachman who he was,
and hastily tied Rambler to the back before jumping in.

Now Griffin watched as Lady Hero narrowed her
lovely gray eyes at him. "Lord Reading. What a delight
to see you again."

He cocked his head as he smiled at her. "Do I detect a
wee bit of sarcasm in your words, my lady?"

Her gaze dropped demurely. "A lady never engages in sarcasm with a gentleman."

"Never?" He leaned forward as the carriage tilted around a corner. "Even when she's been sorely provoked by a gentleman who isn't very, er, gentlemanly?"

"Especially then." She pursed her lips. "A lady always maintains her composure, always chooses her words carefully, and always takes care to use them with circumspection. She'd never mock a gentleman no matter how provoked."

She recited her rules as if by rote, her manner so grave that he nearly missed the gentle wryness in her tone. But it was there. Oh, yes, it was there. He had no doubt that she observed these rules with Thomas, but not with him. That was interesting.

And vaguely worrisome.

"Perhaps I should try harder to provoke," he murmured without thought.

For a moment her eyelashes lifted, and her gaze met his directly, her eyes wide and intrigued, the very frankness of her look, whether consciously or unconsciously, a feminine lure to a man.

He caught his breath.

Then her gaze dropped to her lap again. "What are you doing in St. Giles, my lord?"

"Riding in your carriage." He stretched his legs in the narrow space between the seats. "This *is* your carriage, isn't it?"

Her lips thinned. "Of course."

"Oh, good," he said easily. "I'd hate to have to take Thomas to task because he'd loaned you his carriage to gallivant about the sewers of St. Giles. Unless"—he widened his eyes in pretend sudden thought—"*Wakefield* gave you permission to come here?"

She tilted her chin haughtily. "I'm not a child, Lord Griffin. I hardly need permission from my brother to travel where and when I choose."

"Then Wakefield won't be surprised when I inform him where I met you," he replied silkily.

Her gaze darted away, confirming his suspicions.

His voice deepened to something approaching a growl. "I thought not."

Anger rose in him, swift and hot. He was caught off guard by the intensity of the primitive emotion. What did it matter to him if Thomas's primly perfect fiancée put herself in danger by haring about St. Giles? Common sense said it was hardly his business.

Unfortunately, common sense held no sway with his emotions. Lady Hero in this place was so terribly wrong that he had to restrain himself from grabbing her and bearing her bodily away, ranting all the while about headstrong chits, recklessly oblivious brothers, and the myriad of ghastly fates that could overtake a gently bred lady in London's slums.

Griffin took a deep breath and rubbed his eyes. God, he needed sleep. "St. Giles is not known for its hospitality, my lady," he said as gently as possible. "Whatever brought you here cannot possibly be as—"

"Please don't patronize me."

"Very well." He felt his jaw tighten. Damnation, but he wasn't used to being dismissed so cavalierly by anyone, let alone a woman. "Tell me why you are here."

She bit her lip and looked away.

He smiled tightly. "It's me or Wakefield. Take your pick."

"Since you insist." She smoothed her skirt with her palms. "I'm going to inspect the building site of a home for foundling children."

Whatever he'd been expecting, it wasn't that. "Why?"

She made a quick impatient grimace, so fast he almost missed it. "Because I'm one of the patronesses of the home."

His eyebrows winged up. "Quite commendable. Why keep it a secret from your brother?"

"It's not a secret." She caught his skeptical look and amended, "The part about me being a patroness isn't a secret anyway. Maximus is well aware that I've pledged to help the home. The problem is its location. He doesn't want me visiting St. Giles."

"I applaud his intelligence," Griffin said drily. "Then why sneak out?"

"Because I'm the patroness!" Lady Hero frowned at him like an offended queen, the look only slightly dampened by the freckles scattered across her nose. "It's my duty to make sure the new home is built properly."

"All by yourself?"

"There is another patroness—Lady Caire. But she is out of the country at the moment." She bit her lip. "I would go to Lord Caire, her son, or his bride, the younger Lady Caire—she is the sister to the manageress of the home and used to run it herself—but they have recently married and have retired to Lord Caire's country estate for the next several months."

He stared at her incredulously. "So you're overseeing the building of the home all by yourself at the moment?"

"Yes." Her chin tilted proudly, but her pretty mouth trembled.

He raised his eyebrow at her and waited.

"It's not going very well," she said after a second's hesitation. Her voice was a breathless rush, her hands twisted in her lap. "Actually, it's going terribly. The architect we hired appears to be untrustworthy. That's why I'm going to visit the site today—to see what he's accomplished in the last week."

"Or what he *hasn't* accomplished?" How odd that her small show of trust should make his chest expand with warmth.

She inclined her head. "That, too."

Griffin shook his head. "You must tell Wakefield about your problem. He or his agent can deal with this for you."

She lifted that damned proud chin again. "*I* am the patroness, not Maximus. The duty is mine. Besides," she added a bit less autocratically, "Maximus would probably forbid me from the position of patroness if I told him of my troubles. He was quite unreasonable when he learned of my decision to help the home."

"Perhaps he doesn't like his money being spent for him."

She wrinkled her nose at him. "It's *my* money, I do assure you, Lord Griffin. An inheritance from my great-aunt quite apart from my dowry. I own it free from any interference from Maximus—or anyone else for that matter. I may do with it as I like, and I like helping the children who live at this home."

"I beg your pardon for my misassumption." Griffin held up his hands in surrender. "Why does your brother hate the thought of you helping orphans so much?"

She winced. "It's not the orphans he hates—it's where

they live. Our parents were killed on the streets of St. Giles. His loathing for this place is quite deep."

"Ah." Griffin laid his aching head back against the squabs.

"I was eight when it happened," she said softly, though he hadn't inquired. "They'd been to see a play and had taken Maximus—he was just fourteen. Phoebe and I were much too small to go to such adult entertainments, so we stayed at home."

He frowned, interested despite himself. "What were they doing in St. Giles? There's no theater here."

"I don't know." She slowly shook her head. "Maximus never told me—if he even knows. I remember waking the next morning to the sound of weeping. Our nanny was quite fond of Mama. All of the servants were terribly distressed."

"As were you, no doubt," he said softly.

She shrugged one shoulder, the awkward movement unlike her usual graceful gestures. "Maximus was in his rooms—he wouldn't talk for days—and there was no one to take charge. I remember that I ate cold porridge in the nursery that morning while the adults tramped about and talked on the floors below. No one paid me any mind at all. After a bit, the family lawyers arrived, but they were strange and cold. It wasn't until Cousin Bathilda came a fortnight later that I felt safe again. As if someone was there to take care of me. She wore a terribly strong, sweet perfume, and her black skirts were stiff and scratchy, but it was all I could do not to cling to her as Phoebe did."

She smiled almost apologetically.

The thought of her as a little girl, pale, solemn, and freckled, worrying that there was no one in the world to look after her—to *care* about her—was almost too much to bear.

He looked out the window and noticed absently that the neighborhood had gotten worse, if that was possible. "Will you come here again?"

"Yes." She said the word without hesitation.

"Naturally," he muttered, and scrubbed his hands across his face. The stubble on his jaw scraped his palms. He probably looked like a beast. Christ, just last week a woman had been attacked and left for dead in St. Giles. "Look here, I can't in good conscience let you wander about the streets of St. Giles alone."

She stiffened across from him, her lips parting, no doubt in argument.

He leaned forward, his elbows on his knees, and met her eyes. "I can't and that's final—no matter your reasons or your arguments."

She closed her mouth and tilted her chin away from him, staring out the window.

He couldn't help a small grin—she was so regally offended by him. "But I'm willing to make you a bargain."

Her brows knit suspiciously. "What kind of a bargain?"

"I won't tell either Wakefield or Thomas about your jaunts to St. Giles, if you allow me to accompany you."

For a moment she simply stared at him. Then she shook her head firmly. "I cannot accept."

"Why not?"

"Because, Lord Griffin, I daren't be seen in your company," she said as ice formed along his spine. "You see, I know you seduced your brother's first wife."

*   *   *

READING THREW HIS head back against the squabs and roared with laughter, his strong brown throat working. The sound was merry, but there was an almost imperceptible edge of danger to his laughter that made Hero instinctively tense. She was suddenly aware that they rode in a small, closed space and that she didn't know Reading all that well.

And what she did know of him wasn't good.

She watched him warily as his laughter died. He wiped at his eyes with a sleeve, inhaling deeply.

When he looked up again, the rage that lurked in his eyes made her tense further. "Listening to gossip, Lady Perfect?"

She met his savage look with a steady gaze. "Do you deny the accusation?"

"Why bother?" His mouth made an ugly twist. "You and all the other stupid, quacking, tittle-tattling gossip-mongers have decided the truth. Protestations of wronged innocence would merely make me look foolish."

Hero bit her lip at his hurtful words, staring blindly down at her hands. They were laid one on top of the other, and she was vaguely pleased to see that they didn't mirror her inner turmoil. What did it matter to her if this man thought her "stupid" or "quacking"?

The carriage bumped to a halt. They were at the entrance to Maiden Lane. She looked across the carriage to find Reading watching her broodingly, his pale green eyes hooded.

"It doesn't matter anyway," he said.

"What doesn't?"

"That I have the reputation as a rake and a seducer of

innocents—my *brother's* innocent." He waved one hand wearily, as if the matter was negligible. "I still won't let you risk your pretty neck in St. Giles. Either you let me accompany you and protect you or I'll go to Wakefield and Thomas. Your choice."

He tilted his tricorne over his eyes and folded his arms across his chest, as if settling in for a nap.

She watched him incredulously for a moment, but he didn't move. Obviously, he'd said all he was going to say.

The carriage door opened, and George, one of the two brawny footmen she'd chosen to accompany her, looked curiously in. "My lady?"

"Yes," she said distractedly. She turned back to Reading and cleared her throat. "I'm going to inspect the building site now."

Reading didn't move.

Well! If he was determined to be rude, she wasn't about to stay and try to get the man to respond. Hero got up and descended the carriage with George's help.

Lifting her skirts, she picked her way down Maiden Lane to the spot where the Home for Unfortunate Infants and Foundling Children was being rebuilt. But as she neared, her worst fears were confirmed. The building site looked deserted.

Hero dropped her skirts and frowned.

George shifted his weight from one foot to the other. "Shall I see if anyone's about, my lady?"

"Yes, do," Hero said gratefully, and watched as George disappeared into the facade of the construction.

She sighed. It was going to be a wonderful building— if it was ever finished. They'd bought the houses around the burned wreckage of the previous home and had them pulled down. Now the foundation and facade of what would be a lovely brick building took up most of this side of the street. Hero pivoted and glanced at the other side of the narrow lane. The buildings there were built so close it looked as if they propped each other up. Wooden structures against crumbling brick, tilting upper floors precariously hanging over the lane. It was a wonder the whole mess didn't fall down.

"My lady."

George hailed her as he came back, trailed by a disreputable-looking character.

"This's the only one I could find about," George said, indicating the fellow. "Says he's the guard."

Hero looked in astonishment at the man. He held a half-eaten heel of bread and wore a bedraggled blue coat several sizes too big for his frame.

At her glance, he swept a tattered flat hat from his head and bowed precariously low, his graying shoulder-length hair nearly touching the ground. "M'lady."

"What is your name?"

"Pratt." He clutched his hat and piece of bread to his chest, his expression angelic. "If'n it please you, m'lady."

Hero sighed. "Where are the workmen, Mr. Pratt?"

The guard screwed up his eyes as if in deep thought and looked upward. "Don't rightly know, m'lady. I'm sure they'll return in a bit."

"And Mr. Thompson?"

"'Aven't seen 'im in a while." Pratt shrugged and took a bite of his bread.

Hero compressed her lips, glancing away from the man. Mr. Thompson was the architect of the new home and was in charge of building it. He'd been perfect in the planning stages, producing a lovely drawing of a new home with exact specifications. Both she and Lady Caire had been quite pleased with him. But when the actual construction began, Mr. Thompson became less reliable. Materials that were supposedly already ordered had been absent, and then their delivery delayed, causing the crew of workers that had been hired to find other work.

Lady Caire had pushed back her tour of the continent until the foundation had been laid. At that point it had seemed that the worst of the construction problems were over. They had their material, a new crew was hired, and Mr. Thompson's apologies and assurances were profuse. But a mere month after Lady Caire's departure, things began to go wrong again. Construction was slow; the expense reports Mr. Thompson submitted didn't make sense to Hero; and when she made polite inquiries, he either gave vague answers or ignored her questions entirely.

And now in the middle of the day no one was at the building site!

"Thank you, Mr. Pratt," Hero said, and turned to walk back to the carriage. "Is he sufficient to guard such a large site?" she asked George quietly.

George looked a little startled at having his opinion asked. He scratched his chin. "No, my lady, I don't think so."

Hero nodded. George was only confirming her own fears. She'd have to hire more guards immediately if nothing else.

She had half expected Reading to have deserted her, but as she entered her carriage, she saw that he slouched against the squabs in the same pose as when she'd left him almost an hour before. She sat and watched him as the carriage lurched forward.

He wore a rather shabby brown coat with a bottle-green waistcoat and dark brown breeches and boots. His long legs took up most of the space between the seats, his scuffed boots nearly under her seat. His black hat was still tipped over his eyes, and she noticed for the first time that his jaw bore a heavy stubble. Had he been out all night since the ball? He hadn't moved when she entered or when the carriage started, and she could hear a faint snore coming from his parted lips. Her gaze dropped to those lips. The bottom was fuller in sleep, lax and sensuous, contrasting with the deeply masculine shadow of the stubble about his mouth.

Hero looked quickly away.

"Have you decided?" he asked, making her start.

She inhaled. Had he been feigning sleep all this time?

He sat up and stretched lazily, then glanced out the window. "Headed home, are we?"

"Yes."

"How was it?"

"Worse than I thought." She pursed her lips. "The architect appears to have decamped."

He nodded, unsurprised. "And my bargain?"

"You mean your blackmail."

He shrugged. "Call it what you like, but I'm not changing my mind. You go with me or not at all."

She stared at her hands in her lap. Her fingers had curled into fists. She had no doubt that he would indeed tell both her brother and her fiancé if she did not take his "bargain." Mandeville would disapprove, but it was Maximus who would put a halt to her seeing the home—and possibly to her being the patroness. She listened and obeyed her brother in all other matters, but not this one. She saw again the sweet faces of the children as they struggled with the hymn they'd practiced for her.

Hero glanced up. Reading was watching her as if he knew the thoughts going through her head. She lifted her chin. "Why?"

"Why what?"

"Why this sudden worry for my person? Why do you wish this bargain?"

She expected more anger, but instead a corner of his mouth kicked up, and if possible, he slouched more in his seat. "You're a suspicious woman, Lady Perfect. Perhaps my soft heart compels me to come to the rescue of reckless maidens."

"Humph." She narrowed her eyes at him. "I don't trust you."

"That's quite wise," he said, widening his eyes mockingly.

She looked out the window. What choice did she really have if she wanted to continue to visit the home?

"Very well," she said, facing him again. "You may accompany me next time I visit St. Giles."

"Good." He yawned and then stood to rap on the ceiling of the carriage. "You can send a note to my house whenever you wish to go. Thirty-four Golden Square."

For a moment she was diverted by this news. "You're not staying at Mandeville House?"

His lips twisted. "No."

The carriage jolted to a stop and he was out the door, pausing to turn and say, "I'll be by your house at nine tomorrow morning."

She leaned forward. "But I hadn't planned on going to the home again so soon!"

"Yes, but I think I can help you with your problems with the architect," he said slowly and patiently. "Nine sharp. Agreed?"

His green eyes pinned her, and she could only nod her head mutely.

"Good," he said again.

He leaped from the carriage and slammed the door shut. In a minute the carriage jerked forward.

Hero released a breath as she let her body relax, and for the first time she wondered, *What had Reading been doing in St. Giles?*

HERO NERVOUSLY DESCENDED her front stairs the next morning. Nine of the clock was very early for Cousin Bathilda—or any other fashionable lady—to be abroad, but it would be just her luck to be caught in the company of her notorious future brother-in-law. But when she looked up and down the street, she saw no one.

No one at all.

For a moment her shoulders slumped in something perilously close to disappointment. She'd have to send back the carriage, already waiting in front. Well, he was a rake, after all. What did she expect? Morning jaunts with respectable ladies were probably not his thing at all. In fact—

"Miss me?"

The masculine murmur came so close to her back that she jumped and gave a little shriek. Hero turned to glare at Reading, who looked thoroughly disreputable and rumpled.

"Have you been out all night again?" she asked without

thinking, and then had time to realize her mistake as heat crept up her neck.

He laughed as he handed her into her waiting carriage. "Of course. We rakes never sleep at night. We have far more, ah, *interesting* things to do in the dark hours."

"Humph." She lowered herself onto the cushions.

The strange thing was, even though his words irritated her immensely, she felt a flutter of excitement that he had indeed showed up for their appointment.

"You, on the other hand," Reading continued as he sat across from her, "look fresh and well rested. A lovely morning lily, in fact."

She eyed him suspiciously. What should've been a compliment sounded oddly like an insult coming from his mouth.

He smiled innocently, the curve of his wide mouth cutting deep lines into his cheeks. His jaw was stubbled darkly in contrast to the white of his wig.

"You look like you could pose for a cautionary engraving entitled 'Dissolute,'" she said sweetly.

He barked with surprised laughter. "My lily has thorns, it seems."

"Lilies don't have thorns, and, anyway, I'm not your lily."

"No, merely my dear future sister."

She debated telling him—again—not to call her his sister, realized any protest on her part would probably only urge him on to more irritating behavior, and sighed, giving up the matter. "Where are we going?"

He stretched his legs between them, his boots brushing the silk of her primrose morning gown. "I have an old friend I'd like to introduce to you."

"Why?"

"He's an architect."

"Really?" Hero looked at him curiously. "Where did you meet him?"

He gave her a sardonic look. "I do spend some time among respectable people now and again."

"I didn't—"

He waved aside her flustered apology. "I met Jonathan Templeton at Cambridge."

"I heard you left after only a year," she said slowly.

"You did call me feckless," he reminded her. "But not everyone I met at university was as irresponsible as I. Jonathan's father was a vicar with very little income. The only reason he was at Cambridge was because a friend of his family had kindly taken it upon himself to pay for Jonathan's tuition. He repaid his friend's kindness by studying day and night."

She cocked her head, watching him. "And what did you study at Cambridge?"

He snorted. "Besides wenching and drink, you mean?"

This time she didn't rise to the bait.

After a moment, he looked down at his hands, a half smile on his face. "Classical history, if you can believe it."

"Did you enjoy it?"

He shrugged restlessly. "Not enough to stay, obviously."

"I read Herodotus in the Greek," she blurted.

He looked up at her. "Did you indeed? I wasn't aware Greek was on the curriculum for fashionable debutantes these days."

"It isn't, of course." Why had she told him that? "Never mind."

She stared at her hands in her lap, wishing she could better control her words around him.

"What did you think of his description of Egypt?" he asked.

She peeked up at him to see if he was mocking her, but he seemed serious. She hesitated, then leaned forward. "I thought their burial practices perfectly hideous."

His face relaxed and fine lines appeared at the corners of his eyes as he smiled. "But fascinating, yes? All that mucking about with myrrh and frankincense."

She shuddered delightfully. "Do you think his report true? So many of the other things he writes about seem quite fanciful."

"Such as Arion the harper who rode about on a dolphin's back?"

"Or the winged serpents that guard the frankincense trees in Arabia."

"Or the giant camel-chasing ants?"

"Camel-chasing ants?" She wrinkled her brow. "I don't remember that part."

"Hard to see how you could miss it." He grinned at her. "In India?"

"Oh, of course—the ants that dig up gold!" she cried.

"Those are the ones." He shook his head. "Old Herodotus certainly liked a good story, but you know there are some very odd things in the world. Who's to say that the Egyptians didn't really stuff myrrh into their dead grandfathers? Or that there aren't really giant furry ants in India terrifying the camels?"

"But you must admit it seems a little unlikely."

"I admit no such thing, my lady." The smile still played about his lips. "Have you read Thucydides?"

"No, I'm afraid not." She looked down at her hands again. "The tutor who had taught me Greek had to leave due to his poor health. The ones who replaced him didn't altogether approve of my studying Greek. French is much more important for a lady. Besides, I soon was busy with dancing lessons, and singing lessons, and painting lessons. There's so much one must learn before one makes a debut into society."

"Ah," he murmured. "Do you like painting?"

She inhaled and looked up frankly. "I loathe it."

He nodded. "I have a copy of Thucydides somewhere about. Would you like to borrow it?"

"I don't..." She paused and looked at him. She should decline his offer. Becoming any more involved with Reading than she already was was a sure way to disaster. And he'd sensed her thoughts—his face was already closing in preparation for her dismissal.

"Yes. Please," she said before she could think any more.

A wide smile lit his face. "Very well."

The carriage halted and Reading glanced out the window. "Here we are."

He helped her out, and Hero saw they were in front of a neat, but by no means wealthy, town house. Reading knocked on the door.

"It's awfully early to be calling," Hero hissed.

"Don't worry. He's expecting us."

And indeed the door opened to reveal a young man in a somber brown wig and round spectacles.

"My lord!" he cried with an infectious grin. "It's so good to see you."

"And you, Jonathan." Lord Griffin squeezed the other

man's hand. "Lady Hero, this is my friend Mr. Templeton. Jonathan, Lady Hero."

"Good God!" Mr. Templeton exclaimed, losing his smile. "I had no idea Lord Griffin meant to bring a lady of your rank, my lady. I mean, that is, it's a pleasure to meet you, my lady."

Hero nodded to Mr. Templeton, conscious that her position in society had once again put a damper on things. She sighed silently.

Mr. Templeton glanced about dazedly and then gestured inside. "Won't you come in?"

She smiled at him, trying to put him at ease. "Thank you."

They were shown into a small sitting room, sparsely furnished but meticulously clean.

"I've called for some tea," Mr. Templeton said. "I hope that meets with your approval, my lady."

"That sounds lovely." She chose a straight-backed chair while Reading wandered over to a single bookcase to peruse the shelves.

Mr. Templeton glanced uneasily at his friend. "Lord Griffin said that you wished to consult with me about a project?"

"Yes." Hero folded her hands on her lap and explained about the Home for Unfortunate Infants and Foundling Children, the plans to build a new orphanage, and the problems they were having. By the time she'd finished her recitation, the tea had arrived and Reading had wandered back from the bookcase.

"What do you think, Jonathan?" he asked as he accepted a cup of tea from Hero. "This architect they've hired sounds like a bad 'un."

Mr. Templeton shoved his spectacles up his forehead and rubbed the bridge of his nose. "Much as I hate to malign a fellow architect, the fact is I've heard of this person." He looked apologetically at Hero. "It's rumored he's fled the country because of his debts."

Hero drew in her breath. If their architect truly had absconded, then they'd lost the monies that she and Lady Caire had already paid for the new home. She had more of her inheritance, but it came in the form of an annual income, of which she'd already withdrawn this year's amount. Where was she to find more money?

"Can you do anything for Lady Hero, Jonathan?" Reading asked.

"Yes, yes, of course I can." Mr. Templeton put down his teacup. "I can look over the plans your architect had drawn up and see what work needs to be done on the building. I can, in fact, with your approval, take over the project."

"That would be wonderful, Mr. Templeton," Hero said. "But I must be frank. With my copatroness out of the country, my funds are limited. I can pay you an amount right now, but the rest of your wages will have to wait until I can find more funds."

Mr. Templeton nodded. "Thank you for your frankness, my lady. I do appreciate it. Shall we say that I'll begin the work and when I need further funds, I shall inform you?"

"Yes, that sounds like a good plan." It would certainly give her some time in which to come up with the "further funds." Hero stood. "I shall have the plans we have sent around to your house here, along with the directions to the home. Thank you, Mr. Templeton."

He rose hastily to his feet, bowing. "It's my pleasure, my lady."

He showed them both to the door, where Lord Griffin bid farewell to Mr. Templeton before helping Hero into the carriage.

"Where will you find more money for your home?" Reading asked.

"I don't know at the moment."

"Would you consider a small loan?"

She looked at him, startled. "You know I can't accept money from you."

"Why not?" he asked softly. "I wouldn't tell anyone. It would be a small transaction just between you and me. You could pay me back when you are able."

Her mouth opened silently. He would have her in his power if he made a loan to her . . . but that wasn't what made her curious. "Why are you making this offer to me?"

He blinked. "Do you have an objection to my money?"

"You don't know me well. I don't even think you like me." She opened her hands in her lap. "For what purpose are you making this offer? I don't understand."

He tilted his head back, staring at her. "I think it perfectly obvious. I have the money and you need it."

"Do you make such offers to every lady who needs money?" She began to blush the moment the words left her mouth as she realized the possible double meaning, but she held his gaze defiantly. Would he take the easy way? Turn this into a joke?

But he didn't. He looked irritated now, but he answered her nonetheless. "No, of course not."

She simply looked at him.

He leaned forward suddenly, his elbows on his knees. "Money is the one thing I'm good at. You can trust me completely in this matter. I don't cheat. I don't steal. When it comes to financial dealings, you can rely on me."

He said it almost like a confession, and she was strangely touched, as if he'd shared something deeply personal with her.

Yet she'd only known this man for less than forty-eight hours. Years of practicality held her back. "I do appreciate your kind offer," she said carefully, "but I think I must decline it for now."

He nodded as if he'd expected her answer and sat back. "My offer is still open should you change your mind."

She suddenly felt lighter, even though she'd refused his money. He was on her side. She wasn't working alone anymore. "I haven't thanked you, have I?"

He shook his head, a smile playing about his mouth.

She inhaled, fighting down her own silly smile. "Well, I do thank you. Mr. Templeton seems like a competent architect and, perhaps more importantly, an honest one. I would never have found him without your introduction."

He shrugged. "I'm glad to be of service."

"There is one question I have for you, though."

"Only one?"

"Why were you in St. Giles yesterday morning?"

If she expected confusion or denials of wrong-doing, that wasn't what she got. Reading grinned and knocked on the ceiling of the carriage to signal the driver to stop.

"I was in St. Giles on business," he said as the carriage halted. He opened the door and looked back at her over his shoulder. "Wicked, wicked business."

He jumped down and tipped his hat to her. "Good morning to you, my Lady Perfect."

He slammed the door and the carriage started forward.

Hero sat back against the squabs, whispering, "And good day to you, my Lord Shameless."

Chapter Five

*Well, this was quite the problem as you can imagine!
For Queen Ravenhair trusted—and distrusted—her
advisors, ministers, and men of letters all equally.
How to choose which of the three princes would make
the perfect husband? After puzzling on the problem for
several days, the queen mounted her mare and announced
to a gathered throng of her subjects that she had come
to a decision. She would invite all three gentlemen to
her castle and there hold a series of trials to discover
her perfect consort and the man she would wed.
All the court cheered.
But the stable master, standing by the head of
the mare, was silent....*
—from *Queen Ravenhair*

The first thing Griffin noticed as he entered Mandeville
House that night was the multitude of candles. That and
the two footmen and the butler who rushed to take his hat
signaled that Mater had decided to turn a simple family
dinner into an Event.

Griffin sighed.

Dinner with his family was wearisome enough without
the extra frills.

"My lady has already sat down," the butler said, his tone

managing to sound both obsequious and disapproving at the same time.

"Of course she has," Griffin muttered. It wasn't enough that he'd have to endure a formal dinner with Thomas and his perfect fiancée—he must be late as well.

He stifled a yawn as he followed the butler up the stairs to the dining room. The few hours of sleep he'd been able to catch between leaving Lady Hero in her carriage and waking belatedly to dress for dinner didn't seem nearly enough.

"Lord Griffin Reading," the butler announced as if everyone in the room didn't know him already.

"You're late," Caroline, the elder of his two sisters, said. Caro had always enjoyed stating the obvious. She was considered a beauty by most, but Griffin privately thought that ill humor overrode any amount of glossy dark locks and large brown eyes. "Where have you been?"

"In bed," Griffin said succinctly as he made his way down the room to his mother. He stopped to touch the cheek of Margaret, his younger sister. "Been well, Megs?"

"Oh, Griffin!" she said. "I *have* missed you."

She smiled up at him, her round cheeks rosy. Megs was the youngest of the family at two and twenty and Griffin's personal favorite.

He grinned and continued to the foot of the table. There were seven at the long table: Thomas at one end with Lady Hero to his right and Caro on his left; Mater was at the other end with Wakefield on one side and Lord Huff, Caro's husband, on the other. Megs was between Caro and Wakefield. Which left the last empty chair standing between Huff and Lady Hero. She was wearing a sort of misty green tonight that made her red hair blaze like flame in the candlelight.

Griffin bent and kissed his mother's cheek. "Good evening, Mater."

"You needn't boast of your debauchery," Caro sniffed.

Griffin raised his eyebrows. "It's only boasting if I tell who was abed with me."

"Please refrain for all our sakes," Caro said.

Griffin met Mater's gaze, which was part amused, part exasperated.

"You shouldn't tease your sister," she murmured.

"But it's so easy," he whispered back before straightening and moving to take his seat.

"You've missed the fish," Huff said.

His brother-in-law was a short, burly man. Caro had inherited the Mandeville height and stood several inches taller than her husband—a fact that mortified her to no end but that Huff didn't seem to notice at all. Actually, Huff didn't seem to notice much of what his wife did. Nevertheless, he was fond of Caro in an absentminded sort of way, and Caro was quite happy with her match since Huff was one of the richest men in England.

"Was it any good?" Griffin murmured back.

"Cod," Huff said somewhat obscurely.

"Ah." Griffin took a sip of the red wine that had just been placed before him. The social niceties out of the way with his brother-in-law, he really had no choice but to turn to Lady Hero. "I hope you are well, my lady?"

He'd seen her only hours before, but the clarity of her gray eyes was something of a shock nevertheless. He remembered her stubborn insistence that *she* help her home for orphan children, even if her brother disapproved of her endeavor. Then there was that moment after they'd visited Jonathan when they'd seemed to find a strange accord. His offer of a loan had been on pure impulse; he'd never done such a thing before in his life.

And it had felt right. He'd wanted to help her, share her burden with her. He didn't care one whit about the foundling home, but *her*...

What was it about her? He found himself staring into those diamond-clear eyes, watching as the dark pupils at their center grew larger as she looked at him. He leaned closer as if to catch the exhalation of her breath in his own nostrils.

Oh, this was not good.

Beyond her, Thomas cleared his throat.

Lady Hero blinked. "I'm quite well, thank you, my lord."

Griffin nodded and let his gaze slide past her. "And you, Thomas?"

"Fine," Thomas clipped. "I'm quite fine."

"Oh, good." Griffin smiled briefly and took another sip of the wine. Maybe if he drank enough, this dinner would be bearable.

"I heard a terrible story yesterday," Caro said as she took a prim little sip of wine. "An entire family found starved in one of those wretched hovels in the East End."

"How horrible," Meg said softly, "to starve for want of a bit of bread."

Caro snorted. "Bread would've done them no good. It seems the entire family, including a suckling babe, supped upon gin and nothing else until they quite withered away."

Griffin noticed that Lady Hero had set down her fork.

The Duke of Wakefield stirred. "I'm not surprised—I only wish I were. We hear these types of tragedies almost daily, and I fear we will continue to do so until gin is eradicated once and for all from London."

"Here, here." Thomas raised his glass at the head of the table.

Griffin's mouth twisted. "How do you propose to do this, Your Grace, if I might be so bold as to ask? If the people want to drink gin, surely trying to make them stop is a bit like attempting to empty the ocean with a soup spoon."

Wakefield's eyes narrowed. "If we can shut down the distillers of this foul beverage, we will have won half the war. Without a supply, the poor will soon find some other healthier thing to drink."

"If you say so," Griffin murmured as he sipped from his wineglass. Had the duke ever worried about his family's money? He thought not.

A plate of boiled beef was set before Griffin just as Megs said from across the table, "Huff was telling us earlier about a ghost that is said to haunt the coffeehouse he attends."

"Nonsense!" Caro muttered.

Griffin raised his eyebrow at his normally staid brother-in-law. "A ghost, Huff?"

Huff shrugged his shoulders, sawing vigorously at the beef on the plate before him. "Ghost or spirit. Said to bang a drum incessantly at night. At Crackering's Coffeehouse. Have it on good authority."

"*Inside* the coffeehouse?" Lady Hero murmured. "But is anyone there after dark?"

"Must be," Huff said. "Otherwise who would have heard him?"

Griffin caught Lady Hero's eye and could've sworn the

lady was suppressing a smile. He hastily looked to his own plate.

"I've heard there is a ghost or phantom in St. Giles," Caro said somewhat surprisingly.

"Does he bang drums?" Griffin asked gravely.

Caro wrinkled her nose. "No, of course not, silly. He kills people."

Griffin widened his eyes at his sister.

"With a sword," Caro said, as if that settled things.

"Where did you hear this?" Mater asked.

"Oh, I don't know." Caro stared into space for a moment, a faint frown marring the creamy skin of her brow, then shook her head impatiently. "Everyone has heard of him."

"I haven't," Megs said.

"Nor have I," Griffin said. "I wonder if Caro is making it up?"

Caro inhaled, her face turning a rather dangerous pink.

Before she could speak, Lady Hero cleared her throat. "Actually, I've seen him."

All heads swung toward her.

"Really?" Megs said with interest. "What does he look like?"

"He wears a harlequin's motley—all black and red triangles and diamonds—and he has a great floppy hat on his head with a red plume. Oh, and there's a pantomime half-mask covering his face." Lady Hero looked around the table and nodded. "He's called the Ghost of St. Giles, but I don't think he's a ghost at all. He seemed corporal enough to me."

There was a small silence as everyone contemplated her words.

Then Mater asked, "But what were you doing in St. Giles, my dear?"

Griffin set his wineglass down, trying to think of an excuse for Lady Hero to have been wandering about St. Giles.

But the lady did not share his anxiety. "I went to view the Home for Unfortunate Infants and Foundling Children along with many other members of society. You remember, Maximus, early last spring. The home burned to the ground—that was when I saw the Ghost of St. Giles. We had to put up the children in your town house. You were away for the month."

Wakefield's mouth twisted wryly. "Ah, yes. I came home to find a game of shuttlecock going on in the ballroom."

Lady Hero pinkened. "Yes, well, we moved them out soon enough."

"You must have been quite frightened," Megs said softly. "A fire *and* a ghost."

"It was very exciting," Lady Hero said slowly, "but I don't think I had enough time to become frightened. People were rushing about, trying to put out the fire and rescue all the children from the flames. The ghost merely disappeared into the crowd. He didn't seem like a murderer—he actually helped."

"Perhaps he only murders at night," Griffin said lightly.

"Or when not in a crowd," Megs added.

"Mondays," Huff said.

Griffin looked at him. "What about Mondays?"

"Maybe he only murders on Mondays," Huff said in a burst of verbosity. "Takes the rest of the week on holiday as it were."

"Huff, you are a genius." Griffin stared at his

brother-in-law with admiration. "A murderer who only kills on Mondays! Why, one would be completely safe from Tuesday to Sunday."

Huff shrugged modestly. "Except for the other murderers."

But this was too much for Caro. She snorted like an enraged cow. "Nonsense! What would a ghost be doing running about St. Giles in a harlequin's motley if he *isn't* killing people?"

Griffin raised his wineglass solemnly. "Once again you've debated us into the ground, Caro. I bow from the field of elocution, bloody and defeated."

Hero made a small squeaking sound beside him as if stifling a laugh.

"Griffin," Mater warned.

"In any case, I hope the ghost confines himself to St. Giles," Megs remarked. "I shouldn't like to run into him tomorrow night."

"What's tomorrow night?" Griffin asked absently. A new dish had been placed before him that seemed to contain jelly with unidentified bits floating in it.

"We're off to Harte's Folly," Megs said. "Caro and Huff, Lady Hero and Thomas, Lord Bollinger and me, and Lady Phoebe and His Grace."

Wakefield stirred at the other end of the table. "I do apologize, but I've found I have a prior appointment tomorrow night. I shan't be able to attend."

"Oh, truly, Maximus?" Lady Hero's voice was softly disappointed. "Who shall escort Phoebe, then? You know she's been looking forward to this outing."

The duke frowned, looking nonplussed. No doubt he was rarely chastised.

"Does she need an escort?" Griffin asked. "I mean, with all of you there?"

A look passed between Lady Hero and Wakefield, so fast that Griffin almost thought he'd imagined it.

"Well, perhaps she needn't come," Lady Hero murmured.

"Oh, but Griffin can escort her," Megs piped up. "Can't you, Griffin?"

Griffin blinked. "I—"

"Naturally we wouldn't want to put you out." Lady Hero was staring fixedly at the plate before her. Her expression was serene, but somehow he knew there was distress in her gaze.

Thomas was watching him, his face remote.

"Griffin," Mater said, and for the life of him he didn't know if she said his name in encouragement or in warning.

And in any case it hardly mattered. Once again he gave into temptation. "I'd be delighted to accompany you all to Harte's Folly."

HIS FACE ITCHED.

Charlie Grady propped one elbow on the plank table he sat at and scratched absently, feeling the bumps and ridges under his fingertips. Freddy, one of his best men, fidgeted in front of him. Freddy was a big bear of a man, all but bald, with a nasty scar running through his lower lip. He'd killed four men in the last month alone, yet he couldn't quite bring himself to look Charlie in the face. Instead, his gaze dropped to the floor, drifted to the ceiling, and just grazed Charlie's left ear. If Freddy had been a fly, Charlie would've swatted him.

He might still.

"Two old women were taken last week by the Duke of Wakefield's informers," Freddy was saying. "Makes the others fearful-like."

"Have any given up their carts?" Charlie asked gently.

Freddy shrugged, his eyes fixed over Charlie's shoulder. "Not yet. They'll sell gin as long as it makes 'em money, but with the informers about, they 'ave to watch their step, move more often."

"It's costing us money."

Freddy shrugged again.

Charlie picked up a pair of carved bone dice from the tabletop, idly rolling them between his fingers. "Then we'll have to see to the informers, won't we?"

Freddy nodded, his gaze glancing away.

"What about our plans for St. Giles?"

"MacKay has left London." Freddy straightened a bit as if glad to be the bearer of good news. "And I 'ad word this morning that Smith was inside 'is still when we blew it. 'E's alive, but the burns are bad. They say 'e won't live more 'n another day or so."

"Good." Charlie opened his hand to stare at the dice in his palm. "And my lord Reading?"

"'E's put all 'is business into one building." Freddy scowled. "It's got an outer wall, and 'e 'as armed guards inside. It's going to be 'ard as 'ell to attack."

"Yet attack it we will." Charlie let the dice fall from his fingers. An ace and a *sice*—a six. Seven was always a lucky number. He grunted, pleased. "Tonight, I think."

"WHERE IS LORD Griffin?" Phoebe asked as Mandeville helped her from the carriage.

Hero turned a little to look out on the Thames as she waited for Phoebe. *Where is Lord Griffin, indeed?*

She, Mandeville, and Phoebe had traveled together to one of the stairs leading down to the Thames. Harte's Folly lay south of the river, and they'd need to take boats to arrive there. Lady Margaret, Lord Bollinger, Lady Caroline, and Lord Huff, arriving in a separate carriage, had already descended the stairs and were no doubt entering a boat right now.

The carriage lanterns cast pools of light that were reflected on the wet cobblestones. It had rained earlier in the day, but the sky was clear now, a few stars already lighting the night. It was unseasonably warm for October—perfect for visiting a pleasure garden.

Hero tilted her face to look up at the moon flirting with a wispy cloud. "He said he'd meet us by the steps. I should think he'll be here soon."

"My brother often has business of his own," Mandeville said neutrally. "Please don't be disappointed, Lady Phoebe, if he does not join us."

"Oh," Phoebe said, looking downcast despite Mandeville's admonition.

Hero felt a spurt of anger. How dare Reading disappoint Phoebe? No doubt he was in some woman's bed even as they stood here waiting for him.

"Come, darling," Hero said briskly. "Let's walk down to the river. It'll take a few minutes to ready the boat, and Reading may yet arrive."

"A sensible plan." Mandeville smiled in approval. "The stairs are slippery. Will you take my arm, Lady Hero?"

He proffered his arm, but she backed up a step, frowning. "Please take Phoebe. I'll follow behind."

He looked at her quizzically. "As you wish."

He offered his elbow to Phoebe, and she took it, shooting Hero a smile. Hero breathed a sigh of relief. Mandeville gestured to a footman with a lantern to precede them, and they started down.

Hero lifted her skirts to peer at the steps underneath as she began her own descent. The stairs were medieval, narrow, and built against the river wall, completely open on the other side. The wind shifted, blowing the smell of the river at her: rotting fish and wet mud, and beneath that the scent of ancient water flowing endlessly to the sea.

Both she and Phoebe wore feathered half-masks and colorful gowns. Phoebe was in a delicious orchid and cream while Hero felt rather daring in bright red with ruby underskirts and decorative bows. Mandeville in contrast was in a black domino and half-mask.

Hoofs clattered on the cobblestones above them. Hero turned to peer over her shoulder, her hand braced against the slimy wall. She wobbled as her heel caught on the edge of the step, her foot twisting and her weight dipping as she lost her balance. Her heart swooped into her belly.

"Careful!" Large, masculine hands grasped her arms, pulling her back against a hard chest. "That's a long way down."

"Thank you." Hero's pulse still fluttered in her throat. "I'm fine now."

"You're sure?" Reading's voice was deep and somehow intimate in the still night air. He hadn't loosened his hold on her.

Below them, Mandeville and Phoebe had halted on the small platform where the stairs turned.

Mandeville looked up. "Coming?"

His face was shadowed in the dark, but Hero caught an edge to his voice.

She pulled and Reading let her arms slide from his grasp. "Yes, we'll be there soon."

Mandeville nodded, turning and continuing down the stairs.

"You're late," Hero murmured as she carefully stepped down.

"Why must everyone tell me that?"

"Because you seem to be continually late?"

"Don't you think I'm aware of the time and my tardiness?"

"No," she said clearly and distinctly as if speaking to a slow child, "because if you *knew* the time, you wouldn't be continually *late*."

Behind her Reading exhaled a laugh. "Touché, my Lady Perfect."

"Don't call me that."

"Why not?" His breath seemed to stir the small hairs at the nape of her neck. "Are you not perfection itself?"

She repressed a shiver. "Whether I am or not, I'm certainly not *yours*."

"Pity," he whispered.

They were at the turning in the stairs and she stopped suddenly. "*What* did you say?"

"Pretty." He raised innocent eyebrows at her. "You and your sister are very pretty tonight."

She stared at him and for the life of her didn't know what to think. His pale green eyes were shadowed behind a black half-mask and domino, and what she could see of his expression was relaxed—but his hand was fisted by his side. Suddenly she was out of breath, the sensation of falling making her sway.

"Careful," he whispered tenderly.

Her eyes dropped to his lips, wide and sensuous, framed by the black of the mask covering his upper face, and she wondered wildly what he tasted like.

"Do hurry, Griffin!" Lady Caro called from the bottom of the stairs.

Hero turned jerkily, glad the dark hid her face from those below. She descended the remainder of the stairs, very conscious all the while of the large male shadowing her.

"Glad you could join us, Griffin," Mandeville drawled when they reached the bottom.

The rest of the party was gathered by the stone dock where two low boats were drawn up. Lady Caroline wore a sapphire dress and half-mask that complemented Lord Huff's deep blue domino. Lady Margaret wore yellow with pink embroidery and bows. Her escort, Lord Bollinger, a slight young man, was in a black domino.

"Phoebe, this is Lord Griffin Reading," Hero said rather breathlessly. "Lord Griffin, my sister, Lady Phoebe."

"I'm so sorry to keep you waiting," Reading said as he bowed gallantly over Phoebe's hand. "Please forgive me."

"Not at all." Phoebe darted a nervous glance at Hero. "There's nothing to forgive. You've arrived just in time."

"Then let us proceed," Mandeville said. "Huff, would you like to take my sisters and Lord Bollinger in that boat and we'll take this one?"

Lord Huff nodded once. "Good plan."

"My dear?" Mandeville held out his hand to Hero.

She took his hand and stepped gingerly into the barge. Lanterns were affixed to tall posts at either end of the boat, and the long benches were covered in soft cushions.

"Comfortable?" Mandeville asked her.

"Yes, thank you." Hero smiled at him. He really was quite solicitous of her welfare.

"Watch your step," Reading said as he helped Phoebe inside. "Wouldn't want you to have to swim the river."

Phoebe giggled as she sat next to Hero. "Oh, this is wonderful! The river is like a fairy kingdom at night."

Hero looked over the water. Lights lit it here and there, coming from boats like theirs, the lanterns reflected in the water. The oars squeaked and splashed as the two wherrymen labored at the stern, and the sound of distant laughter, high and light, floated over the water. Despite the strong river stink, it was rather magical.

"Will there be fireworks, do you think?" Phoebe asked.

"Guaranteed," Reading said.

He and Mandeville sat across from them. Their black dominos made them nearly look alike in the dim light. But where Mandeville sat upright, his hands braced on his knees, Reading sprawled, legs spread wide apart, arms crossed on his chest.

Hero hastily looked away from him, though there was no way to ignore him in such a small space. She thought of that breathless moment on the stairs when her eyes had locked with his. Of the fact that only yesterday he'd helped her with the home and discussed Herodotus with her, and the day before that she'd agreed to let him accompany her every time she went into St. Giles. She felt a dangerous unsteadiness as if she were still on the stairs about to fall. A trembling giddiness made up equally of expectation and guilt.

"Your mother and I took tea this afternoon," she said to Mandeville. "She showed me the menu she has devised for our wedding breakfast."

"Indeed?" He smiled indulgently as Reading glanced away at the water. "I hope it met with your approval?"

"I..." For some reason, she looked at Reading. As if he felt her gaze, he turned back to watch her. He widened his eyes mockingly at her. Hero inhaled, hoping the night hid her blush. "Yes. Yes, she's planned a lovely celebration of our nuptials."

Reading rolled his eyes.

"Good," Mandeville said. "I'm so glad that you and Mother have become friends."

"It would be hard not to." Hero smiled with genuine warmth. "Your mother is lovely."

Reading's lips curled in amusement at that and he looked away.

"We're nearly there," Phoebe said. All this time she'd been peering out over the water. "That's the dock, isn't it?"

She glanced at Hero for confirmation.

Hero was aware that Reading's attention was caught. He was staring at them curiously.

"Yes, dear," she said, catching Phoebe's hand. "That looks like the dock."

But "dock" hardly did the landing area justice. A platform over the river was ablaze with lights, strung on poles. As they neared, Hero could see footmen in fantastic livery helping the rest of their party from their boat. Each footman wore a purple and yellow costume, but each was different: One man was in a striped coat with checkered stockings. Another wore a saffron-colored wig and a purple coat with yellow ribbons. And yet another had a bright yellow coat over a purple spotted waistcoat. They were all whimsical variations on a theme.

Their boat pulled into the dock, and a fellow in a lavender-powdered wig bent to help her from the boat. "Welcome to Harte's Folly, my lady."

"Thank you," Hero said as the rest of her party disembarked.

Phoebe came to stand beside her. "Did you see the primrose in his wig?"

Hero turned and saw that indeed the footman wore a bright flower over his ear.

"I do hope that's not a catching fashion," Reading murmured. He caught Phoebe's eyes. "I'd look rather foolish with tulips about my ears."

Phoebe smothered a giggle with one hand.

"You'd look a right ass," was Huff's pronouncement.

"Thank you, Huff, for your opinion," Reading said gravely.

Huff snorted.

Mandeville cleared his throat. "Shall we?"

He offered his arm to Hero, and she took it as they entered a wooded path. The trees about them were hung with fantastical fairy lights. Hero peered closer and saw that each was a blown glass globe, no bigger than her palm, encasing a light. Music drifted through the decoratively trimmed trees and hedges, growing louder as they advanced. The path suddenly opened, and they emerged from the trees into a wondrous theater.

A paved area spread out before them as if sprung from

the forest floor. Behind that were artfully decaying ruins.
If one looked closely, one could just see the orchestra playing between crumbling pillars. On either side, luxurious
boxes rose, four levels high, some open, some curtained
to give the occupants privacy.

A pretty maidservant, her hair intertwined with laven-
der and primrose ribbons, led them behind the boxes and
up a carpeted stairs to a high box right on the stage.

"I say, this is cracking," Lord Bollinger exclaimed. He
was a quiet young man who seemed slightly overawed by
Mandeville's rank.

Lady Margaret squeezed her escort's arm. "It's simply
wonderful, Thomas."

Mandeville grinned, suddenly looking boyish. "Glad
you're pleased, Meg."

Hero smiled up at him as he held a chair for her. "Thank
you for arranging this evening."

"It's my pleasure." He bowed, but as he rose, his eyes
went over Hero's shoulder and he seemed to stiffen.

The curtains parted at the back of their box, and a
troop of servants entered with supper. Mandeville settled
into the chair next to Hero as thinly sliced ham, wine,
cheese, and prettily iced cakes were laid before them.

"A toast," Huff mumbled, raising his glass. "To the
beautiful ladies present tonight."

"Oh, Huff," Lady Caroline said, but she was blushing
as she drank.

Hero smiled and sipped her own wine, but she couldn't
help glancing over her shoulder as the others bantered. In
the box opposite sat a lady with striking deep-wine-red
hair. Three young and handsome gentlemen surrounded
her, but the woman's eyes were fixed on their box.

Hero followed her gaze. Mrs. Tate was watching Mandeville.

GRIFFIN'S EYES NARROWED as he saw Lady Hero note the redheaded woman across the way. What the hell was Thomas up to? Had he arranged an assignation with a mistress with his *fiancée* present?

Lady Hero casually turned back to the table, her gaze sliding by his. She made no sign, but somehow he could tell: She was upset.

Damn Thomas!

Thankfully the entertainment began at that moment with a troop of brightly clad girls dancing onto the stage.

Griffin watched broodingly, fondling the diamond earring in his waistcoat pocket. What matter to him if Thomas wasn't quite as perfect as Lady Hero thought him? Their arrangement was surely no business of his. Why, then, did he feel an urgent need to drag his brother into a private corner and with a few choice words—and perhaps a fist or two—show him the error of his ways?

"They're so graceful," Lady Phoebe said. She sat beside him, across the dinner table from Thomas and Lady Hero.

"They are indeed." Griffin smiled at her.

Lady Phoebe was so different from her sister she might have been a changeling. Where Lady Hero was tall for a woman and elegantly slender, Lady Phoebe was of only average height with a buxom figure, softly rounded shoulders, and plump arms. Lady Hero carefully guarded her expression and movements like a miser with a handful of gold coins. Lady Phoebe, in contrast, let every emotion play across her face, her expressive lips parting in wonder or curving wide in surprised amusement at the antics of a clown on the stage.

"But where did he go?" she murmured to herself. "The little monkey?"

Griffin glanced at the stage. The clown had been playing with a monkey, but the animal sat now at his ankles, waiting with trained stillness.

He looked back to Lady Phoebe. She was leaning forward, squinting. Suddenly she laughed. "He's back."

Griffin looked at the stage. The clown was making the monkey perform backflips through a hoop. Griffin lifted his wine to his lips, frowning thoughtfully.

The dancers and the clown were followed by a play, *Love for Love,* which was admirably acted, though Griffin hardly noticed. He was too busy watching Lady Hero from out of the corner of his eye.

As the actors were bowing, Thomas stood. "Shall we stroll the gardens?"

The suggestion was obvious, and Thomas never glanced at the box opposite. Still, Griffin was unsurprised when the red-haired lady stood as well. Grimly, he offered his arm to Lady Phoebe.

The pleasure gardens were cunningly laid out. Tall hedges trimmed into fantastic beasts lined the walkways, obscuring narrower paths leading off it, as well as nooks and grottos tailor-made for sophisticated amusements. As he guided Lady Phoebe, Griffin wondered cynically how many of the other ladies they passed were there professionally.

"Oh, look!" Lady Phoebe tugged at his arm as one of the many set pieces came into sight. "How is it done?"

Before them was a pretty outcropping of rock, decorated with a falls. But the falls in this case was of multi-colored lights.

"How clever," Megs murmured. "I can't tell how it's devised. Perhaps one of the gentlemen can educate us?"

"Haven't a clue," Bollinger admitted immediately with honest good humor.

Megs laughed. "Huff?"

"Must be mechanical," Huff said.

"Well, of course it's mechanical," Caro said. "But how does it *work*?"

Thomas frowned. "A pulley system of some sort, I'd wager."

For a moment they all gazed, transfixed, at the moving lights as they seemed to flow over the barren rock.

Griffin stirred. "I think we're overlooking the most obvious explanation."

"Which is, my lord?" Lady Hero raised her left eyebrow.

"Fairies," he replied gravely.

"Oh, for goodness' sake!" grumped Caro, and immediately dragged her husband off, despite Huff's protests.

"Fairies," Lady Hero repeated. Her lips definitely twitched.

"Fairies." Griffin stuck his free hand between the buttons of his waistcoat and struck a learned pose, head tilted back, brow furrowed solemnly, foot thrust forward. "In my opinion—which, by the way, is considered an authority on rainbow light falls—each individual light in this falls is in actuality a fairy running quickly over the rocks."

Megs was grinning, Lady Phoebe was giggling, but Lady Hero nodded as if his nonsense was perfectly possible. "But if they are fairies as you say, why exactly should they run *down* instead of *up*?"

"My dearest lady," Griffin replied with sad pity. "Do you not know that falls only run *down* and not *up*?"

Her mouth had widened, her delicate, pale pink lips trembling with laughter, and his heart suddenly sang. Just like that. With no preliminaries or warning, without reason or goal, he was happy. And looking into her clear gray eyes, he had an idea she was happy as well. How odd that such a thing, such a moment, should compound and redouble until the very fact that *she* was glad made *him* the most joyful man in the world.

For just a moment in time.

Then Thomas, who if anything should've been suspicious of their banter, said rather absentmindedly, "Shall we try this path, my dear?"

And he pulled her away.

"Come on," Lady Phoebe urged, and they and Megs and Bollinger chose another path.

Griffin strolled along, listening with only one ear to their banter and exclamations. He must've interjected enough comments to maintain a normal front, for no one stared at him oddly or pulled him aside to ask just what the devil he thought he was doing flirting with his soon-to-be sister-in-law.

But he knew. Oh, yes, he *knew*—he was in over his head and sinking fast. He might be irritated by Lady Hero's calm acceptance of her own perfection, of her condemnation of him without even a trial, even of her fondness for Thomas, but that didn't change his own body's inclinations. He was attracted to the lady—and what was worse, the lady was attracted to him. This was exactly what he had vowed to never let happen. He couldn't let it go further. He must make a firm pledge to stay *away* from the lady.

Yet, here, tonight, he couldn't stop himself from peering down alleys and grottos, searching for a glimpse of scarlet and ruby skirts, a gingery head, the elegant turn of a neck. *Where* had Thomas taken her?

Damnation! Were they embracing even now?

They'd almost made a complete circumference of the gardens when the first *pop!* exploded overhead.

"The fireworks!" Lady Phoebe pointed.

A glowing red star shot into the night and burst above them, sending green and blue sparks showering down. Their group had stopped in a small clearing, and a crowd of the other guests began gathering about them. Caro and Huff soon joined them. Griffin glanced around but could see neither Lady Hero nor Thomas.

"I say, is that a turtle?" Huff asked beside him.

"No," came Caro's exasperated tones. "It's a spider."

"Looks like a turtle to me," Huff said, unperturbed by his mate's correction.

A flash of scarlet caught Griffin's eye. He turned and saw Lady Hero disappear down a path. Good God, was she alone? Surely she knew better than to wander a dark path at night by herself?

He excused himself from the small group, making sure Lady Phoebe was with Megs and Caro and their escorts, then strode rapidly to where he'd seen Lady Hero. The popping and cracking continued overhead, and suddenly the path ahead of him was lit in bright orange. There at the far end stood Lady Hero looking around.

She turned as he advanced on her. "Thomas?"

He took her arm, too ridiculously angry to correct her. Where the hell was his brother? He pulled, but she dug in her heels, just as blue and yellow lights burst overhead.

"Why the hurry, my lord?" She tilted her face up to his, her eyes mocking behind the feathered half-mask she wore. "Don't you think this romantic?"

Suddenly the explosions were in his head. Griffin stared into those innocently seductive eyes and realized very simply that he couldn't stand it any longer.

He kissed her.

Chapter Six

*What a spectacle there was when the three dignitaries
arrived in the kingdom! Prince Westmoon came in a
carriage made of gold and diamonds and drawn
by twelve snow-white horses. Prince Eastsun rode in a
palanquin encrusted with rubies and emeralds and hung
draperies made of silk. And Prince Northwind arrived
in a great gilded ship with sails of crimson and gold.
All three men were haughty, commanding, and handsome
beyond belief. But only the little brown bird and the
stable master knew that the queen retired to her
bed that night with a heavy heart....*
—from *Queen Ravenhair*

It was stupid and irrational, but Thomas found he couldn't
stop himself from searching out Lavinia Tate. Not even
the difficulty of finding her in the near dark in a maze of
paths and side-paths deterred him. *Three* men? Had she
become a sybarite? A woman controlled entirely by her
physical desires? Thoughts such as these did not improve
his mood, so when he did eventually run Lavinia—and
her three beaus—to ground, his temper was perilously on
edge.

"Dismiss them," he barked at her. He eyed the men.

Two were barely old enough to shave, but the third was a big fellow with broad shoulders.

Thomas flexed his hands. In his current mood, he was of a mind to take on all three.

"My lord," Lavinia drawled. She was wearing another flame-colored dress that should've clashed horribly with her outlandishly red hair, but somehow didn't. In fact, the amount of creamy bosom the décolletage displayed was enough to make a man drool.

Thomas scowled. "Tell them to leave, Lavinia."

She arched an eyebrow at the use of her given name, and for a moment Thomas thought he really would have to choose between retreat and fisticuffs. Then she whispered something to the big fellow, and with a last nasty look, all three turned heel and left.

"Now, then." She folded her arms across her chest as if bracing herself for an unpleasant confrontation with a bill collector. "What is it, Thomas?"

"Three, Lavinia?" His hands clenched by his sides. "And all merely boys."

She threw back her head and laughed. "As it happens, my lord, two of those *boys* are my nephews. And I doubt Samuel would like you calling him a boy."

So the big man *was* her lover. Thomas wanted to drive his fist into something. "He's younger than you."

"As are you," she replied softly. "Yet it didn't keep you from my bed."

For a moment he merely stared at her hungrily, remembering her bed and what they'd done there.

Then she looked away. "What do you want?"

"What do I want?" He advanced toward her, confused by his own need to be near her. "You're the one following me."

"Following you?"

He didn't know what reaction he'd expected from his accusation—perhaps protestations or even tears—but it wasn't this. *This* looked perilously close to pity, her eyebrows drawing together, her lush mouth turning down.

"Thomas, I am not following you."

"Explain, then, how you happened to be here on the very night I attend with my fiancée?"

She shrugged—actually shrugged!—at his angry words. "Coincidence, I suppose."

"And your Samuel?" He was close enough to touch her now, but he daren't. "Deny, if you will, that you brought him here in a pathetic effort to make me jealous."

He sneered his words, but she looked at him wonderingly. "*Are* you jealous, Thomas? I can't think why, since you're the one who broke it off when you decided to marry Lady Hero."

He looked away from her too-perceptive face. "I never said we had to quit, only that we wait a decent amount of time after the wedding. A year at most. I could've bought you a bigger house if you wanted it. A carriage and team."

"The money never had anything to do with it."

"Then what did?"

She sighed. "However provincial it might seem to you, I don't wish to carry on a liaison with a married man. It's rather sordid, don't you think? Besides, I've seen your Lady Hero and she seems a nice girl. I shouldn't like to hurt her."

He grit his teeth, feeling the beginnings of a headache. "Are you saying you care more for my fiancée than me?"

She stared back, that wretched look of pity in her eyes again. "Are you saying you *don't*?"

"What do you want of me?" he demanded. "I cannot marry you—you know that, Lavinia. Even if we were a suitable match, even if you weren't past the age of child-bearing, I simply cannot marry one such as you."

"How chivalrous of you to point out my advanced age to me—yet again," she drawled. "But as it happens, there is no need for such drama. I know we cannot marry, and I refuse to conduct a liaison with you when you are other-wise promised. There really isn't anything more to say."

He felt something very close to desperation. "I thought you cared for me."

Overhead the fireworks began exploding.

"I did. I do." She sighed and let her head fall back, watching the fiery trails. "But my feelings for you really have nothing to do with this discussion. Anne broke your trust long before I came along. I'm not sure you'd trust *any* woman again, let alone one with a past like mine. You've made that abundantly plain. Really, it's a wonder you were able to propose to even a virgin like Lady Hero."

An awful, oily blackness invaded his chest at her words, because she was right, damn her. He'd never bring himself to truly trust her.

"As you've already stated, the thing is impossible." She glanced over her shoulder. "They'll be waiting for me—we'd decided on ices while the fireworks played."

He looked at her mutely, unable to find the words that would make this right. The words that would make her stay.

She smiled rather wearily. "Good-bye, Thomas. I hope you have a happy marriage."

And he could do nothing but watch her walk away from him.

*   *   *

HERO HAD WANTED to know how Reading tasted and now she knew: He was wine and man and need.

Pure, hot need, coursing through her blood like quicksilver, lighting her bones on fire, making her muscles quake until she literally trembled in his arms. He didn't kiss her like she was the daughter of a duke, reverent and slow. No, he kissed her like a *woman*. His lips were hard, demanding things from her, not waiting to see if she had the experience to keep up. His tongue pushed against her lips, insisting on entrance. She opened her mouth eagerly. He swarmed in without hesitation, taking as if she was his by right.

"Griffin," she murmured, her hands clutching at his black domino, unsure of what to do. He pulled her close—so close she felt the muscles of his legs through her skirts. His fingers were in her hair, skimming over her throat, brushing lightly at the tops of her breasts.

She should push him away. What she wanted instead was to take his hand and press those long fingers into her bodice. To guide him until he stroked the puckered tips of her naked breasts. She thought she might very well expire from sheer ecstasy if he touched her there.

A loud *bang!* made her start and break the kiss. The night sky lit for a moment, as bright as day, illuminating his masked face and his mouth, wet and tempting. He pulled back from her, still holding her shoulders and stared at her as if transfixed. Lord knew what her own expression looked like.

Behind them the cheers of the spectators rose.

Hero tried to speak and found she had to swallow before her mouth could form the words. "We need to get back."

He didn't reply, merely caught her hand and turned, striding back up the path. She stumbled behind him, her limbs uncoordinated, her thoughts dazed. Another starburst exploded overhead, green, purple, and red flakes floating to earth. The path was widening; they were nearly to the clearing where the spectators stood.

Reading pulled her suddenly into a dark nook off the side of the path. He turned to face her and yanked her into his arms. Her entire being thrilled as he breathed a foul curse and then captured her mouth again. He devoured her as if she were a sweetmeat and he a man who had gone without bread for far too long. He licked across her lips, biting at the corner of her mouth, groaning somewhere deep in his chest. She opened her mouth eagerly this time, having learned what he—what *she*—wanted.

Another cheer went up.

He tore his head away from hers, muttering, "You taste like ambrosia, and I am a madman."

For a moment they simply stared at each other, and she had the strange feeling he was as confused as she.

He blinked, cursed, and, taking her hand again, led her into the clearing.

The gathered crowd all had their faces tilted upward, watching the display overhead. Hero followed Reading without thought, feeling quite shattered as they wound in and out of the bodies until they found their own party.

"There you are," Phoebe exclaimed as Hero made her side. She clapped and squealed as spinning wheels appeared over their heads. She leaned closer to Hero and shouted, "But what has happened to Lord Mandeville?"

Hero shook her head, her brain stuttering to life. She shouted back, "He went for refreshments and I lost him."

She heard Reading grunt. His lips were grim and she hastily looked away.

"Oh, look!" Phoebe cried.

Bombs burst and turned, sparkling, into a green-and-gold-winged serpent. The fiery creature twisted and then melted into a glowing white shower of sparks.

"It's fantastic," Lady Margaret breathed.

It was. It was the most fantastic fireworks display she'd ever seen—and yet she felt curiously unaffected. Hero was conscious only of Reading's bulk, on the far side of Phoebe. There seemed to be an invisible line between them now, an awareness drawn taut by sensuality and basic sin.

Dear Lord, what had she done?

She touched her mouth with shaking fingers. She'd committed an act of horrible betrayal. She knew that. She was aware of the ramifications and of regret. The possibility of far greater sin and guilt. Of the fact that her very soul was in peril.

And she did not care.

She was in a fever, wanting only to taste his mouth again, to feel his hard body against hers. To find out if his bare skin was as hot without any clothes. To discover his naked chest. To lie with him entirely nude.

She gasped, winded, unable to catch her breath. She'd never thought herself a creature of physical want. Had never experienced this longing before with any other man. It was as if she were the dormant black powder and he a flame that set her alight. Suddenly everything was vivid, clear, and burning. The very night sky rejoiced as if to celebrate her awakening.

Her facade had cracked. She realized with shock that

she was as mortal as anyone else, as fallible as the most fallen woman.

And it did not matter. If he but crooked a finger, she would turn and follow him back into those dim paths. Would twine herself about him and lift her face for his kiss again.

Hero shivered and wrapped her arms about herself.

"Are you cold?" His voice was deep and much too near.

She shook her head, a bit too violently, and backed a step away from him, putting prudent space between them. He frowned and opened his mouth.

"Ah, here you are," came Mandeville's voice from her other side.

She turned and smiled up at him, in near-panicked relief. Mandeville was normalcy. Mandeville was sanity.

Some of what she was feeling must have shone in her eyes.

Mandeville bent closer so she could hear over the cracks and pops. "I'm sorry to have lost you. I hope it caused you no worry?"

She shook her head, still smiling like a fool, unable to speak.

"What were you thinking?" Reading growled close, and at first she thought he accused her. Then she looked up and saw the murderous expression he shot at Mandeville. "It's not safe for a lady alone here."

Mandeville's head reared back. "How dare you?"

Reading made a grimace of disgust, turned on his heel, and strode to the edge of the clearing.

Mandeville looked uncertainly at Hero. "I'm sorry..."

Dear God, she could not take an apology from him

now. Hero laid a hand on his sleeve. "Please, don't worry yourself."

"But I should," Mandeville said slowly. "My brother is right: I should never have lost you in the maze of paths. It was not well done of me. Please forgive me, Hero."

He hardly ever used her given name without her title. Hero felt sudden tears spring to her eyes. This man was so good, so right, and she was a fool to let bright, sparkling physical lust endanger her happiness with him.

She squeezed the arm under her hand. "It's done now and no true harm came of it. Please. Let's talk of it no more."

He seemed to search her face for a moment, even as purple and red lights showered above.

"Very well," he said at last. "It seems I am to marry a very wise lady indeed."

Her lips trembled as she gazed up at him, knowing she did not deserve his praise. This was the man she'd chosen to marry. The decision was made, the contracts drawn up and signed. This would be a good marriage, one of respect and common goals attained between the two of them.

And yet she could not help but turn her head slightly and glance at Reading. He stood apart, his face upturned to the sky as sparkling flames reflected in his eyes.

"GET UP, M'LORD, she's doin' a runner."

Griffin groaned, rolling from his stomach to his back and flinging a shielding arm over his eyes. "Go 'way."

"Can't do that, m'lord," the cheerful voice of Deedle, his valet-cum-secretary-cum-jack-of-all-trades, replied. "You told me to wake you if she went out, an' keep at it no matter 'ow you might complain until you stood up by yerself, and 'ere I am awaking you."

Griffin sighed and cracked an eyelid. The sight that met his gaze was not a pretty one. Deedle was only a bit past five and twenty by his own reckoning, but he'd lost both upper front teeth in that time. It didn't seem to bother him, though, judging by the wide smile that split his face. He wore a wig—one that Griffin had cast off—badly in need of curling and powdering. His muddy brown eyes were tiny and spaced too near, peering down a great angular nose that took up so much of his face that his small mouth and smaller chin seemed to have given up completely and retreated down his neck in defeat.

Deedle grinned at Griffin's open eye and stuck his tongue through the gap in his teeth—a rather unfortunate habit of his. "Like some coffee, m'lord?"

"God, yes." Griffin squinted at the window. True the sun seemed to be high in the sky, but they'd been out until well past midnight last night. He remembered that sweet kiss he'd shared with Lady Hero—and how she wouldn't look him in the eye afterward. He winced. "Are you sure she's moving?"

"The lad I got on watch came running to tell me not ten minutes ago," Deedle replied. "The lady must like the mornings, eh?"

"But not keeping her promises." He sat up, the sheets falling away from his nude chest, and scratched his chin as he contemplated the fair Lady Hero. She was attempting to avoid him. Had his kiss frightened her that much? "You're certain she's headed to St. Giles?"

"She's got that big footman and she's taking the carriage. Bit early for morning social calls." Deedle squinted and shrugged. "Stands to reason that's where she's headed, don't it?"

Griffin sighed. Yes, it did stand to reason.

He climbed wearily from the bed and began splashing in the basin of water. "Have we heard from Nick Barnes?"

Deedle laid out the razor, strop, and towels. "No."

"Damn." Griffin frowned. Nick usually sent word first thing in the morning. Griffin would have to see if Nick was sleeping in—or if something more ominous had happened. But first he must deal with the lovely Lady Hero—and the consequences of last night's impulse.

Fifteen minutes later, Griffin ran down the steps of his rented town house. It wasn't in the most fashionable part of the West End of London, but he'd long ago decided that lodgings separate from Thomas were essential for familial accord.

Rambler was waiting at the bottom of the steps, his head held by a young groom. Griffin patted the gelding's glossy neck before swinging into the saddle and throwing the boy a shilling.

The day was sunny, and Rambler made good time, weaving through the London traffic. Griffin found Lady Hero's carriage not twenty minutes later, stalled behind a herd of pigs.

Lady Hero's coachman merely nodded as Griffin waved at him and entered the carriage.

"Good morning," he said as he sat.

"Go away," she replied.

He clapped a hand over his heart. "Such cruelty from such a fair lady."

She wouldn't even look at him. She stared fixedly out the window, her profile remote and reserved. Only the faint spots of pink on her cheekbones gave lie to her serenity. "You shouldn't be here."

"Well, yes." He stretched his legs and crossed them at the ankle, grappling with a wholly foreign surge of guilt. Outside, a chorus of squealing rose alarmingly. "I *should* be abed, still dreaming, but it's not my fault you decided to rise early and sneak off to St. Giles without me."

She pursed her lips irritably. "This isn't wise."

He noted that she didn't deny her destination. "Have you told your brother or Thomas about your jaunts to St. Giles?"

"No, but—"

"Then I'm coming with you."

She closed her eyes as if pained. "You know we can't do this."

Had he hurt her so much? He cleared his throat, feeling uncharacteristically diffident. "About last night..."

She held up her palm, her face averted. "Don't."

He opened his mouth, but she was as still as a graven image. She seemed to have retreated somewhere deep inside herself.

Damnation! His mouth snapped shut. He turned to look out the window as the carriage began rolling forward. He'd well and truly mucked this up. If he had it to do over, he'd...what? He sure as hell wouldn't take back that kiss.

Griffin sighed and laid his head against the squabs. That kiss had been quite spectacular. He remembered her mouth soft and yielding, her breasts pressed against his chest, and the hard beat of his own heart. He'd been aroused, naturally, but oddly the part that stuck in his mind wasn't the eroticism of their embrace, but the sweetness. It had felt...right—as wrong as that was.

And as truly foolish as it was to have kissed his

brother's fiancée, he'd do it all over again if Lady Hero gave even the slightest sign of acquiescence.

Griffin cracked an eyelid and snorted under his breath. The lady was showing no such signs this morning. She sat ramrod straight in her seat—surely an uncomfortable pose as the carriage swayed—and her face was still averted. She gave every indication of loathing him.

Well, that was for the best, wasn't it?

Griffin sighed. "Why have you decided to go back to St. Giles so soon?"

"Mr. Templeton has agreed to meet me at the site of the new home," she said.

He raised his brows, waiting for more explanation, but it wasn't forthcoming. Fine, two could play at that game. He tilted his hat over his eyes and settled back to regain some of the sleep he'd lost this morning.

The carriage shuddering to a stop woke Griffin some time later. He watched lazily as Lady Hero got up and left the carriage without a word to him. His lips twitched. That certainly put him in his place. He could stay in the carriage and await her return, but curiosity got the better of him. Griffin followed her out of the carriage, looking around.

They were in St. Giles, not far from his still, actually. The carriage was stopped at the end of a narrow lane, too wide to pass through. Griffin saw Lady Hero walking determinedly down the lane with her footman, George. Griffin jogged to catch up. By the time he made her side, she was already in conversation with Jonathan. The architect was all in black, a huge roll of papers under one arm. He turned to greet Griffin, but Lady Hero continued talking.

"...as you can see. Now we're worried that the children will have to stay in their wretched temporary home for the winter. Can you give us any hope, Mr. Templeton?"

She drew breath and Griffin took advantage of the pause by sticking his hand out to his friend. "Good morning, Jonathan. How are you today?"

"Quite well, my lord, quite well indeed," the architect replied, beaming. He glanced at Lady Hero and blinked at her gimlet stare. "Er...now, then, as to the progress of the foundling home, my lady. As you can see, the former architect barely laid the foundations. I've had a chance to inspect the site, and I'm afraid I've discovered several distressing points."

Lady Hero frowned. "Yes?"

Jonathan nodded, pushing his spectacles up onto his forehead. "Most of the foundation is sound, but in places it has already settled and will need to be dug up, shored, and rebuilt. Further, the papers you sent me indicated that special stone, wood, et cetera were bought and stored here. I'm afraid I cannot find them."

"Stolen?" Griffin asked.

"Yes, my lord, or perhaps never truly bought in the first place." Jonathan looked troubled. "In any case, the materials will have to be purchased before further construction is done."

Griffin glanced at Lady Hero and saw that she was biting her lip. "I...I will have to see about obtaining the monies necessary to purchase material. Last time it took weeks for the stone to be shipped."

"Ah." Mr. Templeton rocked back on his heels. "Here I think I have good news, then. I know of a supplier of fine granite who has some already sitting in his warehouse here in London. I have no doubt that he has enough to meet our needs. It isn't the Italian marble that the original plans called for, but the granite stone is pretty enough. Cheaper, too. I believe I can persuade him to extend you the credit on the stone."

Lady Hero seemed to relax. "Wonderful, Mr. Templeton! I shall rely upon you to arrange for the granite to be bought and moved here. Now, perhaps you can show me the problems you spoke of."

Griffin sat on the stone foundation of Lady Hero's home and waited for her to complete her tour with Jonathan. He tilted his head back, feeling the sun on his face. He'd have to take her home after this and then return again to St. Giles to consult with Nick about what to do with the Vicar. Griffin rubbed the back of his neck wearily. He couldn't remain indefinitely in London guarding the still. Perhaps the Vicar could be bought off somehow. Except that Griffin balked at giving the man money. The only other means of eliminating the crime lord was assassination.

Griffin chuckled in disgust. He hadn't sunk quite that low yet.

"My lord!"

He glanced up to see a footman trotting toward him.

Griffin straightened. "What is it?"

"There's a lad at the carriage asking after you. Said to tell you that Nick sent him."

Lady Hero had returned with Jonathan by this time. She looked at Griffin for the first time that day. "What is it?"

"A matter of business." He glanced at Jonathan. "Are you done here?"

"Yes, but—"

"Then let's go." He took her arm and walked rapidly

toward the carriage. He hated to take her along, but he couldn't very well let her wander alone in St. Giles. "Damnation."

She arched her eyebrow at him but kept pace with his stride. The youth waiting beside the carriage was one of Nick's crew. He doffed his hat at the sight of Lady Hero, his eyes widening. He'd probably never seen an aristocratic lady in his life.

"What is it?" Griffin demanded.

The lad jumped, tearing his gaze from Lady Hero. "Nick wants to talk to you, m'lord. Quick like, if'n you can."

Griffin nodded. "Hop on the back of the carriage."

He gave the coachman directions and then helped Lady Hero in before pounding on the roof.

She watched him as he threw himself on the squabs. "How did your messenger find you?"

"I sent word where I'd be," he said absently.

Thankfully she didn't ask any more questions. The carriage was already pulling up in front of the distillery's wall.

"Stay here," he ordered her before leaping from the carriage.

Griffin strode through the gate. Nick was in the courtyard.

"In here." Nick jerked his head toward the distillery, leading the way.

Inside, the fires illuminated the cavernous building like something out of Hades. A small knot of his men was gathered over something that lay on the warehouse floor. As Griffin drew nearer, he saw it was a man.

Or what was left of a man.

The body was tangled, the limbs at angles the joints

weren't meant to bear naturally. Griffin took one look at the face and glanced away.

"Tommy Reese," Nick said, and spat into the straw. "Went out for a tankard of beer yesterday afternoon and was thrown over the wall just 'alf an hour ago, lookin' like that."

Griffin fisted his hands. He remembered Tommy; he couldn't have been more than twenty. "Did he say anything?"

Nick shook his head. "Already dead." He glanced sharply at the silent men and gestured Griffin to the side. "Tortured, I'm thinkin', m'lord."

"No doubt." Griffin grimaced. "Was Reese party to any particular secret of our business?"

"Nah, just started."

"Then the Vicar did this as a warning."

"And to scare the men." Nick lowered his voice. "Already two 'ave run off. Couldn't stop them, though I told the buggers right enough they'd be safer in here."

"Fuck." Griffin rolled his head on his shoulders to stretch his neck, then swiveled to the men. "Well, this is first shot. From now on, no one goes out at night, and during the day you go in pairs. Is that clear?"

The men nodded, though none would meet his eyes.

Griffin smiled widely, though he felt more like howling. "And your pay has just doubled, right? Any man still here by tomorrow gets a fistful of coins. You go out tonight and you'll get that instead." He jerked his chin at the corpse.

One by one, he stared at each man until they all met his eyes and nodded.

Finally, Griffin jerked his chin. "Get on with it."

The men went back to work. No one smiled or looked particularly cheerful, but at least they weren't whispering mutiny among themselves anymore. Nick pulled two of the men aside and gave them instructions in low tones. A moment more and the two men had lifted Reese's poor body between them and taken it out to the courtyard. Griffin turned back to watch broodingly as the stills were stoked.

"My God," came a feminine voice behind Griffin.

He turned and met Lady Hero's accusing eyes. "You're running a gin still!"

Chapter Seven

*Early the next morning, the queen greeted her suitors in
her throne room. She wore a gown of silver and gold, her
midnight-black hair was coiled and twisted beneath a
golden crown, and every man in that room was
amazed by her beauty and bearing.*
*The queen looked at her suitors and asked them
this question: "What is the foundation of my
kingdom? You have until midnight tonight to
bring me your answer."*
*Well, Prince Eastsun looked at Prince Westmoon, and
Prince Westmoon looked at Prince Northwind, and then
all three princes hurried from the room.*
*But when the stable master heard the question,
he merely smiled to himself....*
—from *Queen Ravenhair*

Hero couldn't believe it, but the evidence was right before
her eyes—and nose. The great warehouse held huge copper barrels set over smoldering fires, and the air smelled
of alcohol and juniper berries. This was a gin distillery—
most probably an illegal one.

And Reading wasn't at all perturbed to be found
out.

"What is going on? Was that a *dead man* I saw in the

courtyard?" She looked at him, waiting for an explanation, but he turned his back on her.

Actually, it was the large, burly man by his side who seemed the most embarrassed. "M'lord, the lady—"

"The lady can wait," Reading said quite clearly.

Hero felt her face heat. Never had she been so cavalierly dismissed. And to think she'd let this *cad* kiss her just last night!

She swiveled to leave the awful building, but suddenly he was there beside her, his hard hands holding her arms.

"Let me go," she hissed through gritted teeth.

His face held absolutely no compassion. "I have business here. When I am done, I'll escort you home—"

She wrenched her arms free and turned.

"Hero," he said quietly, then louder to someone else, "See that her carriage doesn't leave without me."

"M'lord." Two men darted past her and out the door, no doubt to help keep her prisoner while Reading did his disreputable "business." She continued sedately to her carriage—she'd not let him see her in a hysterical flurry. Once outside the wall and at her carriage, she ignored Reading's guards and climbed in.

Her wait was short, but even so, she was not in the best of spirits when the carriage rocked and Reading climbed inside. He knocked on the roof and then sat down, gazing out the window. They rolled along for a few minutes until Hero couldn't stand it anymore.

"Aren't you going to tell me what that was about?"

"I wasn't planning to," he drawled—expressly, she was sure, to enrage her.

"That was a distillery."

"Yes, it was."

"For gin."

"Indeed."

She narrowed her eyes at him, feeling anger pounding in her breast. She was perilously close to losing her facade—again. Hero fought to control her voice, but even so the words seemed to scrape against her throat. "Do you have any idea the amount and depth of misery that gin brings to the people who live here in St. Giles?"

He was silent.

She leaned forward and slapped him on the knee. "*Do* you? Is this some kind of lark for you?"

He sighed and turned toward her finally, and she was shocked to see the exhaustion lining his face. "No, not a lark."

Tears bit at the corner of her eyes, and she found to her horror that her voice trembled. "Haven't you seen the babies starving while their mothers drink gin? Haven't you stumbled over the bodies of broken men, mere skeletons from drink? My God, haven't you wept at the corruption that drink brings?"

He closed his eyes.

"I have." She bit her lip, struggled to control her emotions, to control herself. Reading wasn't stupid. There must be some reason for his madness. "Explain it to me. Why? Why would you dabble in such a filthy trade?"

"That 'filthy trade' saved the Mandeville fortunes, my Lady Perfect."

She shook her head sharply. "I don't understand. I've never heard that the Mandeville fortune needed saving."

His mouth twisted wryly. "Thank you. That means I did my job well."

"Explain."

"You know my father died some ten years ago?"

"Yes." She remembered the conversation she'd had with Cousin Bathilda on her engagement night. "You immediately left Cambridge to go carouse about the town."

His smile was genuine this time. "Yes, well, that tale was more palatable than the truth."

"Which was?"

"Our pockets were to let. Yes"—he nodded at her incredulous expression—"my father had managed to lose the family fortune with a series of investments that were ill advised at best. I had no idea of the family's finances. As I was the second son, Father and Thomas considered it none of my business. So when Mater told me at the funeral the straits we were in, you could've knocked me down with a feather."

"And you left school to manage the family's finances?" Hero asked skeptically.

He spread his hands and inclined his head.

"But why you? Wasn't it Thomas's job to find a financial manager?"

"One"—he ticked off his point on a long finger—"we couldn't afford a financial manager, and two, Thomas's head for money is about the same as our dear, late father's. He spent the last of what we had in the week after Father died."

"And money is the one thing you're good at," Hero said slowly. "That's what you told me when you offered me a loan. When it comes to financial dealings, you can be relied on." Did he think that was the *only* thing he could be relied upon to do correctly?

Griffin nodded. "Thank God my mother caught wind of what Thomas was doing. She had a small inheritance of her own that she'd kept hidden from Father. We lived for the first year or so on that bit of pin money until my distillery started bringing in money."

That reminder snapped her attention back to her original concern. "But…gin distilling? Why that of all things?"

He leaned forward, resting his elbows on his knees. "You have to understand. I came home from university to my mother near prostrate with grief and worry, half the family furnishings sold to pay my father's debts, bill collectors calling at all hours, and Thomas nattering on about how fine a new carriage with gilt trim would be. It was autumn and all I had was a rotten harvest of grain, mostly spoiled with damp. I could've sold it to a broker who would've then sold it again to a gin distiller, but I thought, wait a minute, why lose most of the profit? I bought a secondhand still and paid the old rascal I'd bought it from extra to show me how to use it."

He sat back on the carriage seat and shrugged. "Two years later, we were able to afford Caro's season."

"And Mandeville?" she asked quietly. "Does he know what you do to support your family?"

"Never fear," he said with deep and devastating cynicism. "Your fiancé's hands are clean of all this. Thomas worries about far nobler things than where the money comes from to clothe him. His interests lie with parliament and such, not bill collectors."

"But"—her brows knit as she tried to figure it out—"he must have *some* idea of where the money comes from. Hasn't he ever asked?"

"No." Reading shrugged. "Perhaps he does wonder, but if so, he's never said a word about it to me."

"And you've never tried to discuss it with him?"

"No."

Troubled, she stared at her hands. What Reading did to make money was reprehensible, but what of a man who enjoyed wealth without once asking how it was made? Wasn't Mandeville in some ways just as much to be condemned as Reading? Perhaps more so—he had all the benefits without suffering any of the soul-shredding consequences of dealing in gin. There was a name for such a man, she knew.

Coward, a tiny voice whispered deep in her heart.

She pushed the thought aside and looked at Reading. "If my brother finds out what you do, he'll not hesitate to have you brought before a magistrate. Maximus cannot be reasoned with when it comes to the subject of gin."

"Even at the risk of embroiling his dear younger sister in scandal?" He arched an eyebrow. "I think not."

She shook her head, turning to gaze out the window. They'd left St. Giles behind and were rolling through a much nicer area. "You don't know him. He's obsessed with gin and the effects it has on the poor of London— he has been ever since our parents' murders. He believes that gin is to blame for their deaths. I don't know that he would stay his hand, even if you're soon to be my brother-in-law."

He shrugged. "That's a chance I have to take."

She pursed her lips. "What were you discussing with that man at the distillery?"

He sighed. "I have a competitor—though that word is a bit refined for what he is—who is bent on driving me out of business."

She glanced at him, alarmed. "What kind of competitor?"

"The kind who likes to smash stills and throw the mangled body of one of my men over the courtyard wall," he said. "It's the reason I came to London—well, that and your engagement to Thomas."

"Dear God." She shook her head. How could he joke about becoming mixed up with such criminals? "Then that man was—"

"His name was Reese, and his only sin appears to have been going out for a drink yesterday."

She shuddered. "That poor man."

"You needn't worry," he said. "As I've said, Thomas isn't involved."

She looked at him incredulously. Did he really think her so shallow?

"I can understand that you were desperate to right your family's finances," Hero said slowly. "But they are no longer in peril, are they? My brother would have found out if there were financial concerns when he had my marriage contract drawn up."

"Your brother is a shrewd man," Reading said. "I've no doubt but that you are correct. The Mandeville fortune is safe now. He didn't find anything amiss."

"If that is the case, then why continue to distill gin?"

"You don't understand—" he began.

"You're patronizing me again," she snapped.

He looked at her, his pale green eyes suddenly hard. "I have my family to consider, my Lady Perfect. Caro has made a fine match, but Megs is still unwed. If she is to find a suitable match, she needs to dress the part—as I'm sure you understand. I cannot give up the still until she is safely wed—until I am financially stable. We need the money from the still to finance her season."

She closed her eyes and spoke from her heart. "We have had our differences, my Lord Shameless. There have been times in the last several days when I have thought I disliked you quite intensely." He snorted, but she continued. She needed to make her point before she lost her courage. "But I think we have also learned something about each other. I would like to think that we are friends of a sort."

The silence was so complete that she thought for a moment that he was holding his breath. She opened her eyes to find him watching her, his elbows propped on his knees, his green eyes still but with an expression in their depths that made her catch her breath. She clasped her hands, bolstering her bravery.

"Yes, friends," she said quietly, as much to herself as to him. "And as a friend, I beg of you: please quit this way of making money."

"Megs—"

She shook her head violently, cutting him off. "Yes, Lady Margaret needs gowns to catch a husband, but there must be other ways of making money. I've seen how gin destroys lives in the poorer parts of London. You may not care right now, you may only see your family and the money you need, but someday you'll raise your head and look around. When that day comes, you'll realize the misery you and your gin have caused. And when that happens, gin will destroy you, too."

"Friends." He sat back in his seat, ignoring her warning. "Is that what I really am to you? A friend?"

She blinked. She hadn't expected the question. "Yes, why not?"

He shrugged, eyeing her moodily. "Why not indeed.

Friend is such a very…benign…word. Do you kiss all your friends the way you kissed me last night?".

Her eyes had narrowed—she had been waiting for the shot. But still she couldn't quite control a small shudder. *His mouth had been hot.* "I've told you I do not wish to discuss last night. It's in the past."

"And forgotten?"

"Yes."

"Funny." He stroked his chin. "I find it rather hard to forget it myself. Your lips were so very soft, so very sweet when they parted beneath mine."

Her body heated at his words. She couldn't help it, and she felt that same spark of desire. He could light it within her so damned easily.

"Stop it," she said low. "What do you think you're doing?"

It was his turn to look away. "I don't honestly know."

"I'm marrying Thomas," she said. "In only five weeks now. If we are to have any sort of brother-sister relationship, you must forget it."

His mouth twisted as if her words were obscene. "Can you?"

She lifted her chin, saying nothing.

"I thought not," he murmured. "That's ducky. Just ducky."

He reached into the pocket of his coat and drew out a book. He tossed it wordlessly onto her lap and went back to staring moodily out the window.

Hero looked down. It was a volume of Thucydides's *History of the Peloponnesian War.* She traced the embossing on the leather cover, her eyes suddenly welling with tears.

*   *   *

"OH, MRS. HOLLINGBROOK, you have a letter, ma'am!" Nell Jones came into the home's kitchen, waving a bit of paper in the air.

Silence looked up from the sad little lump of biscuit dough she was attempting to roll out. Really, it hadn't been one of her better culinary efforts.

Nell caught sight of the dough and wrinkled her nose. "Here, let me finish that while you have a seat and read your letter."

Silence gladly relinquished the rolling pin. She brushed off her hands and washed them in a basin before drawing up a chair to the kitchen table. Mary Darling had been playing with a pot and a big spoon on the floor, but when she saw Silence sit down, she crawled over and demanded to be held.

Silence picked her up and kissed the top of her head. In the last seven months, Mary Darling's hair had grown in thick and inky black, a mass of corkscrew curls.

She set the baby on her lap and showed her the letter. "Now who do you suppose it's from?" she asked as she carefully lifted the seal.

"Is it Captain Hollingbrook?" Nell asked. Overhead came a thump and then what sounded like a stampede of oxen across the floor. The children were supposed to be doing their afternoon reading under the supervision of the maids, but somehow the daily event often turned into a melee.

Silence sighed and turned her gaze to the letter. "Yes, it's from William."

"You'll be glad of that, I'm sure, ma'am."

"Oh, yes," Silence murmured absently.

She deftly kept the paper from Mary Darling's interested fingers as she read. William wrote about the *Finch* and its cargo, a storm they'd weathered, and a fight among the ensigns.

"Have a bit of patty-cake," Nell said to Mary Darling, and handed her some of the biscuit dough.

A seabird the men had shot and the sighting of a French ship...Silence skimmed down the page, following the neat handwriting of her husband, coming finally to his signature—William H. Hollingbrook. She stared blankly at the page, before she began over again, reading more slowly, searching. But she knew already—there were no jokes they shared between just the two of them, no endearments, no expressions of wanting to come home or missing her. In fact, the letter could've been written to anyone.

"Is he well?" Nell asked.

"Well enough." Silence glanced up and noticed that Mary Darling was carefully breaking off bits of the biscuit dough and placing them in her mouth to chew with a thoughtful expression. "No, sweetheart. 'Tisn't good not cooked."

Nell smiled at the baby. "She thinks it is."

"Won't it make her sick?" Silence asked worriedly.

Nell shrugged. "It's mostly flour and water."

"Still..."

Silence began to unwrap the baby's fingers from the sticky dough. Mary Darling naturally didn't think this a good idea and voiced her protests loudly.

Someone knocked on the front door.

"Shall I see who it is?" Nell asked over the baby's cries.

"I'll get it," Silence said. She scooped up the baby and

swung her around. "Who do you suppose it is? The king or queen? Or perhaps just the baker's boy?"

Mary Darling giggled, distracted from the loss of her dough. Silence set the baby on her hip and went to the door. She pulled it open and looked out. On the step was a handkerchief knotted neatly. Silence glanced at it and then quickly searched the street. A woman was washing her step across the way, two men walked side by side trundling wheelbarrows, and several lads argued over a small terrier dog. No one seemed to be paying her any mind.

Silence bent and picked up the handkerchief. The knot was loose and came easily undone, even using only one hand. Inside the handkerchief was a handful of raspberries, perfectly ripe, perfectly unblemished.

"Gah!" Mary Darling cried, and grabbed two, stuffing them into her mouth.

A small scrap of paper was revealed now, and Silence plucked it out from under the berries. One word was written on it.

Darling.

Silence glanced back at the street as Mary Darling snagged three more berries. It was the oddest thing—no one looked in her direction, yet she felt as if watching eyes were upon her. She shivered and reached for the door, beginning to shut it.

A shout came from up the street, and four men trotted around the corner. Between them they held a ragged elderly woman who struggled in their grasp.

"Let me go, yer buggers!" she shrieked. "I 'aven't done it, I tells ye."

"Dear God," Nell said quietly from behind Silence.

Silence looked at the maidservant and back to the

street. People were peering out of windows and doors, coming to see what the commotion was about.

"Stand back!" one of the men cried. He waved a thick cudgel over his head.

A stream of filthy wastewater poured from one of the houses, narrowly missing the group. The four men trotted faster.

"Informers," Nell spat. "Poor woman. They'll have her up before the magistrates for selling gin and collect a nice reward in return."

"What will happen to her?" Silence abhorred what drinking gin did to the people in St. Giles, but at the same time she knew that most who sold it were simply trying to make enough money to feed and house themselves.

"Prison. Maybe worse. Depends if she can pay for witnesses or not." Nell shook her head. "Come inside, ma'am."

With a last glance at the retreating informers, Silence closed the door and barred it.

"What have you there?" Nell asked.

"Raspberries," Silence said, showing her the kerchief.

"In October? That's dear." Nell turned and started back toward the kitchen.

Dear indeed. Silence picked up a berry and popped it into Mary Darling's mouth. A month before, she'd found a baby's girdle on the step, and the month before that there'd been a packet of sugarplums. In fact, every month since Silence had found Mary on her doorstep, there had been a small anonymous gift left for the little girl.

And each had a note with but a single word written upon it: *Darling.*

The same note that had been left with Mary herself.

The reason Silence had given the baby the name Mary Darling.

"Have you an admirer?" she whispered in the toddler's ear.

But Mary Darling merely smiled with red-stained lips.

"Do you think a man can change?" Hero asked that night at dinner.

She poked at the cold beef upon her plate. It was just her, Cousin Bathilda, and Phoebe, and Cousin Bathilda had pointed out that it was hardly thrifty to have Cook put on a grand meal for a quiet supper at home.

Still. Hero did dislike cold beef.

"No," Cousin Bathilda said promptly. Rarely did she ever *not* have a decided opinion.

"What kind of change do you mean?" Phoebe asked.

The candlelight sparkled on her spectacles as she tilted her head in interest. She wore a bright yellow gown tonight, and it made her seem to shine in the little family dining room. The table was a nice, intimate size, and the fireplace, ornamented with white and blue tile, was just big enough to make the room warm and cozy.

"Oh, I don't know," Hero said vaguely, though of course she *did* know. "Say, for instance, a gentleman has a decided fondness for gambling at cards. Do you think he could ever be persuaded to quit?"

"No," Cousin Bathilda reiterated. She slipped her right hand beneath the table while staring fixedly straight ahead. There was a small scuffle under the table.

Neither Hero nor Phoebe made any sign that they had noticed the transaction.

"I think it might depend upon the gentleman," Phoebe

said thoughtfully. "And perhaps on the nature of the persuasion." She picked up a tiny piece of her beef and slipped her hand beneath the table.

"Nonsense," Cousin Bathilda said. "Mark my words: No lady has ever been able to change a gentleman, by persuasion or otherwise."

"Pass the beetroot," Phoebe murmured to Hero. "How do you know, Cousin Bathilda?"

"It's common feminine wisdom," that lady said. "Take Lady Pepperman."

"Who?" Hero asked. She helped herself to the beetroot, even though *that* was cold as well, before passing it to her sister.

"Before your time," Cousin Bathilda said. "Now listen. Lord Pepperman was a well-known gambler and a very unlucky one at that. Once gambled away his clothes, if you can credit it, and had to walk home in nothing but his smallclothes and wig."

Phoebe snorted and hastily covered her mouth with her napkin.

But Cousin Bathilda was in full sail and didn't notice. "Lady Pepperman was at her wit's end, so she decided she would teach her husband not to gamble."

"Indeed?" Hero asked with interest. She chose a bit of beef and held it under the table. A small, warm, soft nose nuzzled her hand and then the beef was gone. "How did she manage that?"

Panders, the butler, and both footmen were too well trained to show anything but boredom on their faces, but all three men were leaning closer to Cousin Bathilda.

"She told him he could gamble as much as he wanted, but only in his smallclothes!" Cousin Bathilda said.

Everyone in the room—including the servants—gaped at Cousin Bathilda.

Then Phoebe closed her mouth and asked diffidently, "Did that work?"

"Of course not!" Cousin Bathilda said. "Haven't you been listening to a word I've said? Lord Pepperman continued to gamble, except now he was clad only in his smallclothes. Went on for a year or more before he lost nearly everything and tried to blow his brains out."

Hero choked. "Tried?"

"Succeeded only in clipping off the top of his ear," Cousin Bathilda pronounced. "Man was a horrible shot. Can't think why Lady Pepperman married him in the first place."

"Hmm," Hero murmured as she digested this cautionary tale. Truly she couldn't think how she could apply it to Lord Reading.

There was a small silence broken only by the discreet scrape of silverware on plates.

"I saw Lady Beckinhall today," Cousin Bathilda said at last, "at a quite dreadful tea given by Mrs. Headington. All that was provided for refreshments were some very dry little cakes. I am positive that they were stale—at the very least two days' old!—and Lady Beckinhall quite agreed with me."

Lady Beckinhall could hardly do otherwise, Hero thought wryly.

"She informed me that Lady Caire is thinking of extending her stay on the continent through the winter," Bathilda went on.

Hero looked up. "Oh, no. Really?"

"Is that a problem?"

"Well, it rather might be," Hero said.

"Why?" Phoebe asked.

"It's the work on the new home." Hero sighed. "I've had to hire another architect, because the first one embezzled the funds we'd given him."

"My dear!" Cousin Bathilda looked horrified.

"Yes. We'll need more money—quite a bit more money, I'm afraid," Hero said. "And Lady Caire staying away even longer won't help matters."

"What about her son?" Phoebe asked. "Won't Lord Caire and his new wife be returning to town soon?"

Bathilda snorted. "I wouldn't be surprised if he stayed away until spring. He married a brewer's daughter, after all. He'll need his mother's help in getting invitations."

"I don't think Temperance or Lord Caire are particularly interested in society events," Hero began.

Bathilda drew in her breath sharply.

"But you are right," Hero added hastily. "They may stay away from town for even longer now."

"What shall you do?" Phoebe asked.

Hero shook her head and was silent a moment as the footmen cleared the supper plates and brought in a pudding for dessert.

She waited until they were each served, then said solemnly, "I shall have to raise the funds myself somehow."

"You can have some of mine," Phoebe said promptly. "Mother and Father left me a fair amount, or so Maximus says."

"But you can't touch it until you're of a majority," Hero said gently. "Thank you anyway, dear."

Phoebe scrunched her face for a moment. "I'd wager there are other ladies who would like to help the home."

"Do you?" Hero dabbed at her pudding without really tasting it.

"Yes." Phoebe was beginning to look excited. "You could form a...a *syndicate*."

"Like a gentlemen's business syndicate?" Cousin Bathilda frowned.

"Quite," Phoebe said. "Except it would be only ladies—because if you let a gentleman in, he'll want to run things—and it's to give money, not make it. You could call it the Ladies' Syndicate for the Benefit of the Home for Unfortunate Infants and Foundling Children."

"That's a wonderful idea, darling," Hero said, smiling. Phoebe's enthusiasm was hard to resist. "But what ladies would I approach to give away their money?"

"You might try Lady Beckinhall for one," Cousin Bathilda said unexpectedly. "I know for a fact that her late husband left her extremely well-off."

"Yes, but will she want to simply give away her wealth?" Hero shook her head. She didn't know Lady Beckinhall all that well, but the lady had always struck her as more interested in fashion and the latest gossip than charity.

"I'll help you make a list," Phoebe said, "entitled 'Potentially Charitable Ladies of Means.' "

"That will certainly help." Hero laughed.

"Mmm." Phoebe ate some of her pudding with evident appreciation. "I say, why did you ask earlier about changing gentlemen?"

"Oh, I don't know," Hero replied.

"Lord Mandeville seems perfect the way he is," her younger sister commented. "Does he gamble?"

"Not to my knowledge," Hero said.

"Well, if he did, I can't think he'd allow you to confine

him to his smallclothes like Lord Pepperman," Phoebe said.

The younger footman choked, earning himself a severe glance from Panders.

Suddenly an image of Lord Griffin in his smallclothes popped into Hero's head, making her go hot all over. She took a guilty sip of wine.

"No, indeed," Cousin Bathilda said, apparently oblivious to the currents around her. "I'm afraid you'll have to accept Lord Mandeville the way he is, my dear. Fortunately for you, he's quite perfect as he is."

Hero nodded, her mind on Lord Reading, which was why she nearly jumped at Cousin Bathilda's next words.

"Now, Lord Griffin," the older lady said, "is an entirely different kettle of fish. I wouldn't be at all surprised if *he* gambled excessively."

"Why?" Phoebe asked.

"Why, what?"

"Why do you suspect Lord Griffin of such awful things? He was quite lovely to me last night."

Cousin Bathilda smiled and shook her head in a manner that Hero had found quite maddening at Phoebe's age. "Those tales aren't for ears as innocent as yours, my dear."

Phoebe rolled her eyes. "Well, whatever his unspeakable deeds, I like him. He makes me laugh, and *he* doesn't treat me like a child."

Naturally this bit of rebellion set Cousin Bathilda off on a lecture about decorum and the dangers of judging gentlemen solely upon their ability to make one laugh.

Hero looked down at her cold pudding. She could sympathize with Phoebe—she, too, liked Reading. He was at base, no matter what Cousin Bathilda said, a good man. And because he was a good man, she needed to show him why what he was doing was wrong. Not just for the people who were damaged by drinking gin, but for Reading himself. If he continued distilling gin, at some point he would cease to be a good man.

And that was something Hero was quite sure she couldn't bear.

Chapter Eight

That night, the suitors assembled in the throne room and presented their answers to the queen. The first was Prince Westmoon. He bowed and set a single, flawless diamond before her. "Wealth is the foundation of your kingdom, Your Majesty."
Next, Prince Eastsun strode forward. He nodded to the queen and laid a pretty little golden dagger at her feet, all encrusted with gems. "Arms are the foundation of your kingdom, Your Majesty."
Finally, Prince Northwind presented a velvet bag with five and twenty perfect pearls and said, "Trade, Your Majesty, is the foundation of your kingdom…."
—from *Queen Ravenhair*

Griffin cursed the Vicar of Whitechapel as he rode home the next morning. After a sleepless night at the distillery, spent constantly tense, listening for the least sign of intruders, Griffin had nothing to show for it but an aching head. There'd been no sign of the Vicar or his men. All Griffin wanted now was a bite to eat and the comfort of his own bed.

In fact, he was so focused on those two things that he almost didn't notice the carriage lurking discreetly on the cross street down from his town house. Only the glimpse out of the corner of his eye of a familiar coach-man alerted him.

Griffin pulled Rambler to a halt with a muttered curse. What the hell was Lady Hero doing on his street at the unfashionable hour of ten of the clock? His house was only feet away, but Griffin sighed and walked Rambler over to the carriage. He rapped on the window.

Slim fingers promptly pulled the curtains back, and Lady Hero motioned him impatiently inside.

Wonderful. Griffin instructed one of the footmen to take Rambler to the mews. Then he climbed in the carriage. She wore a dark green coat over a lighter green skirt, and her red hair seemed to glow in the dimness of the carriage.

"Good morning, Lady Hero."

"Good morning," she said briskly. "I've an appoint-ment in St. Giles, and since you insist on accompanying me, I thought I'd save you the trouble of tracking down my carriage."

"How thoughtful." He slumped onto the carriage seat.

She frowned at him. "Have you had any sleep at all?"

"No, nor breakfast either."

"Hmm." She looked adorably disapproving. "Sleep, then."

And he was so weary that he didn't even ask what her mission was in St. Giles before laying his head on the squabs and losing consciousness so quickly he might as well have been knocked on the head.

He opened his eyes sometime later to see Lady Hero watching him. Her clear gray gaze was somehow intimate.

"Better?" she asked softly.

He didn't move, enjoying simply looking back at her. "Much, thank you."

She looked at him curiously. "For a self-proclaimed rake, you work harder than any gentleman I know."

He cocked his head. Had anyone else said that, he'd think it a complaint—for an aristocrat to work was no compliment—but Lady Hero's voice was musing. Did she actually approve of something about him?

He lifted a corner of his mouth. "Don't tell the guild of rakes, will you?"

She laughed softly, and then opened a cloth on her lap. "I bought you a meat pie while you were sleeping."

"You are an angel," Griffin said gratefully. He took the pie—still warm—and bit into it, savoring the gravy on his tongue.

"Making money isn't the only thing you're good at," she said quietly.

He arched his eyebrows, still chewing.

A faint flush crept up her elegant neck. "You make people laugh."

He swallowed. "So do fools."

She shook her head, gently admonishing. "You jest, but the ability to laugh is a wonderful thing. Phoebe had a lovely time the other night, largely because of you."

"I didn't do anything extraordinary." He shook his head and took another bite.

"But you did." She looked at him intently. "Phoebe is…is special and very dear to my heart. I can't tell you how grateful I am that you made her laugh that night. Thank you."

His eyes narrowed as he remembered how Phoebe had lost sight of the little monkey on stage. "What did—" The carriage shuddered to a halt, distracting him before he could finish the thought. "Have you decided to inspect the construction again?"

"No." She looked down at her hands. "We've stopped at the temporary foundling home. I wanted to show you something."

"Indeed?" She wasn't meeting his eyes, so he probably wasn't going to like whatever she had in store for him. Still, he ate the last of the pastry and brushed off his hands. "After you."

Perhaps his smile had a bit too much teeth. She glanced at him rather nervously before descending the carriage. Outside, the day was gray and a chill wind blew.

Griffin offered his arm. "Shall we?"

She laid her hand on his sleeve, and he was aware of her touch, light though it was. It was pleasant to be able to guide her down the lane leading to the temporary home. To act the proper gentleman to her lady.

They stopped at the door to the home, and he stepped forward and knocked.

There was no sound from within.

He cocked an eyebrow at her. "Do they expect you today?"

She cleared her throat, a fine pale pink blush climbing her throat. "I didn't tell them I was coming."

He didn't have time to reply to this news before the door was pulled open. A young girl stood before them, an enormous apron pinned to her bodice.

"Good morning, Mary Whitsun," Lady Hero said. "Is Mrs. Hollingbrook about?"

The girl curtsied. "Yes, my lady. Please come in."

Griffin stepped over the sill and noticed immediately the bare boards of the hallway—they were warped. The girl led them into a small sitting room.

"I'll fetch Mrs. Hollingbrook from the kitchen," Mary Whitsun said, and hurried away.

Lady Hero didn't sit and neither did Griffin. He circled the tiny room before halting in front of the fireplace. He tapped his fingers against the mantel and watched as crumbs of plaster fell to the hearth.

Footsteps sounded in the hall, and then the door was pushed open. The young woman who stood there was very pretty, but flustered. Pale brown hair with streaks of light red and blond was bundled untidily under a cap, tendrils stuck to her flushed cheeks. A smudge of flour dotted her chin.

"Lady Hero, we weren't expecting you," she said in a breathless rush as she curtsied.

"No matter, Mrs. Hollingbrook." Hero smiled calmly, which seemed to set the other woman's nerves slightly at ease. "I've brought a friend, Lord Griffin Reading. He's heard me speak of the home and became quite interested. I was wondering if you could show him some of the children?"

Mrs. Hollingbrook's face brightened. "How do you do, my lord?" She bobbed a wobbly curtsy, rising eagerly. "I'll be very happy to introduce you to some of our charges."

Griffin smiled and bowed. "Thank you."

He waited until the lady had turned her back to lead them from the room before shooting Lady Hero a skeptical look.

"What are you up to, Lady Perfect?" he murmured in her ear as he placed a hand against the small of her back.

She glanced at him nervously as he ushered her from the room. They followed Mrs. Hollingbrook back through the house.

The kitchen they entered was cavelike. Griffin had to duck his head so as not to knock himself out on the lintel. Six little girls were crowded around a long wooden table, in the process of rolling out pastry of some kind. As one, they looked up and saw him, then froze like young fawns surprised in a woodland glade.

"Children," Mrs. Hollingbrook said, "we have a special visitor. This is Lord Griffin Reading, a friend of Lady Hero. Please show his lordship your best manners."

"Best manners" must've been a code word. The girls each curtsied with varying degrees of grace.

Griffin nodded gravely and murmured, "How d'you do?"

A small, ginger-headed child smothered a giggle.

Mrs. Hollingbrook chose to disregard this breach of decorum. She laid her hand on the eldest girl. "This is Mary Whitsun, who I believe you already met at the door."

Mary Whitsun bobbed a curtsy.

Lady Hero cleared her throat. "How long has Mary Whitsun lived at the home, Mrs. Hollingbrook?"

"Nearly ten years, my lady," Mary Whitsun answered for herself.

"And how did you come to the home?"

Mary looked quickly at Mrs. Hollingbrook. There was a slight line between that lady's eyes. "Mary was brought to us by a"—she darted a look at the girls—"er, person of ill repute. She was just three at the time."

"And her mother?" Lady Hero asked softly.

"We don't know anything about her parents," Mrs. Hollingbrook said slowly, "but judging by the person who brought her here, it was thought that her mother was a poor unfortunate who walked the streets."

Her mother had been a prostitute. Griffin looked at the girl, wondering how she felt to have such intimate matters of her history discussed in front of her.

The girl met his gaze, her expression stony.

Griffin nodded at her and said gently, "Thank you, Mary Whitsun."

Mrs. Hollingbrook moved to the next small girl in line. "This is Mary Little. She has been with us since she was an infant left on our doorstep."

Mary Little bobbed a curtsy. "Are you the one that's to marry Lady Hero?"

Lady Hero gasped softly beside him. Griffin didn't dare glance at her. "No, it's my brother who is to wed Lady Hero."

"Oh," said the child.

Mrs. Hollingbrook cleared her throat. "And this"—she laid a hand on the third girl in line—"is Mary Compassion. She came to us at the age of two along with her brother, Joseph Compassion. Their parents died within a sennight of each other from cold and ill nutrition."

"And drink," Lady Hero murmured.

Griffin stared at her impassively. She lifted her chin, stubbornly staring back.

"Well, yes." Mrs. Hollingbrook looked between him and Lady Hero, a puzzled frown on her face. "Most of the deaths in St. Giles—the ones that are not from old age, that is—are helped along in one way or another by drink."

"How many die from old age in St. Giles?" Lady Hero asked.

"Few," Mrs. Hollingbrook replied softly. "Very, very few."

Griffin fisted his hands, trying to keep his voice level. "And these other young ladies?"

"Oh." Mrs. Hollingbrook glanced distractedly at her charges. "This is Mary Evening. She has been with us since infancy. She was found on a nearby church step. Next to her is Mary Redribbon, who was brought to us by a local tavern owner." Mrs. Hollingbrook glanced quickly at Lady Hero. "I'm afraid Mary Redribbon was left at the tavern by her mother, who did not return."

Griffin forced a smile to his lips as the little girls dipped in curtsy. Damn it. He wanted to shout that it wasn't his fault if people chose to drink gin. He'd made no woman prostitute herself or abandon her babe in a tavern. If he didn't distill the gin they drank, someone else would.

"And finally, this is Mary Sweet." Mrs. Hollingbrook stroked the curls of the smallest child, who couldn't have been more than three. "Her mother has five other children and attempted to sell Mary when she was but an infant. We persuaded the mother to give her to us instead."

Griffin inhaled. "How very fortunate for Mary Sweet." He glanced at the toddler, who promptly hid her face in Mrs. Hollingbrook's skirts.

"We are fortunate as well," Mrs. Hollingbrook said affectionately. "Now, if you'll come with me, I can introduce you to some of our boys."

"Ah, as to that." Griffin made a grimace of apology. "I'm afraid Lady Hero overestimated the time available to us. We shall have to save the rest of your tour for another day."

"Oh, of course," Mrs. Hollingbrook said. "You're most welcome at any time, my lord."

He smiled and took Lady Hero's arm in a firm grip, propelling her to the door even as she breathlessly said her good-byes. He kept his smile pasted to his face until they were outside.

She tried to take her arm from his grasp. "My lord—"

"Not here," he murmured, trotting her up the lane. He gave instructions to the coachman, helped her into the waiting carriage, and sat.

Then he looked across at her and growled, "What do you think you're doing?"

READING'S PALE GREEN eyes were hard, his lips pressed together, forming white brackets on either side, and his nostrils flared.

He looked so intimidating, in fact, that Hero had to swallow before she could reply. "I'm trying to get you to understand what your gin distilling is doing to St. Giles and the poor people who live here. As a friend—"

He laughed sharply, drowning out her words. "Yes? As a *friend*, what did you think would happen when you took me there? I'd gaze at those tiny girls and have a sudden revelation? Perhaps give all my worldly goods to the poor and become a monk?"

He sat forward. "Listen, and listen well, my lady—I *like* who I am and what I do. I'm an unrepentant rake who makes illegal gin. Don't think you or anyone else can change me—even if I wanted to be changed."

She pursed her lips and cocked her head, staring at him silently. Anger was rising in her as well.

He returned her stare until the silence seemed to irritate him. "What?"

"You, my lord, are not nearly as reckless—or as bad—as you would have me believe."

"What in God's name are you babbling about?"

"Your reputation." She waved a hand. "Your rakishness. You've let all of London think that you left Cambridge on some feckless whim when in fact you left to help your family. You lead others to believe that you live the life of a libertine, without care or worry, when in fact you *work* for your family's sake."

He laughed incredulously. "In case it has escaped your memory, I was in the act of bedding a married woman when we met."

She looked away, that vision making her even angrier somehow. "I never said you were *perfect*. Just not as damnable as you let others believe."

"Is that so?"

She tilted her chin and stared him in the eye. "Yes."

He smirked nastily. "What about my dear brother's late wife?"

Her heart began to beat faster. The carriage was so confining, and his temper was a nearly visible haze of red between them. "What about her?"

"The whole world knows I seduced her under my poor brother's nose, and had she not died in childbirth, along with the babe, no doubt I would've fathered his future heir."

"Did you?" she asked softly.

"Did I what?"

"Did you do all those things the world and your own brother think you did?"

For a moment he stared at her, wild and grief-stricken, and she held her breath, waiting for his answer.

Then he slowly shook his head. "No. God, no."

She leaned forward. "Then why let everyone believe such an atrocious lie? Why pretend to be worse than you are?"

"I'm not—" he began, but she wasn't done questioning him yet.

"Why?" she demanded fiercely. "Why continue in this dreadful gin business? You are better than this, Reading."

"What god gave you the right to sit in judgment over me?" he asked low and awful. "Oh, but I forget: You consider yourself more virtuous than the rest of us mere mortals. You are Lady Perfect, arbitrator of other people's sins, an incorruptible maiden colder than graveyard granite in January."

She gasped, unable to speak for a moment. Did he really see her thus? As a chilly, self-righteous virgin?

"How dare you?" she whispered, and couldn't help the tears that flooded her eyes.

"Damn you."

Her vision was blurred, so she didn't see his movement, but she was suddenly across the carriage, half sprawled on his lap.

"I dare," he muttered, "because I'm selfish and black-hearted and vain. I dare because you are what you are and I am what I am. I dare because I cannot otherwise. I've lived too long without bread or wine, crawling desperate in a lonely, barren desert, and you, my darling Lady Perfect, are manna sent directly from heaven above."

His lips were on hers, urgent and hot. Oh, Lord, she had not known how much she missed his kisses! His mouth tasted of need too long suppressed, but where he might've been rough with her, he was instead gentle.

Very gentle.

His lips pressed against hers, his tongue licking at the corners of her mouth.

"Let me," he pleaded even as she opened her lips.

ʾHe canted his face, pulling her closer, his tongue sliding into her mouth. His beard scratched against the soft skin of her chin, but she didn't care. She suckled his tongue, drawing on it as if it were the sweetest thing she'd ever tasted.

"Let me," he murmured again, and she felt his broad hand on the bare skin just below her neck.

He stroked her as if gentling a kitten, softly, expertly, his hand drifting lower. All her awareness was centered on that hand, on his fingers drawing nearer to the tip of her breast. Her breasts felt tight and heavy in anticipation, and she waited with bated breath for him to touch her. He bit suddenly at her lower lip, distracting her, and then— oh, heavens!—his fingers slid beneath her bodice.

She gasped, feeling his hot skin as he stroked over her hardened nipple. He spread his hand, trapping the tip between his first and second fingers. When he squeezed, she felt the sudden jolt between her thighs.

"Shhh," he murmured, quieting the moan she'd made. "Let me."

She looked and saw that he'd pulled her bodice down, exposing one nipple above her stays. He muttered something, working at the laces of her bodice, and then both breasts were exposed.

For a moment he merely stared down at her, her soft skin framed by his big, tanned hands, his long fingers playing with her nipples possessively.

"Sweet, so sweet," he murmured. "Let me taste them."

He looked at her, and his gaze was feverish, his green eyes gleaming like a demon. That was why she agreed— it must be why—because she could only nod at him.

And then his mouth was where no man had ever

touched her. His tongue stroked across one naked nipple, wet and faintly rough at the same time. She had no idea she was so sensitive there. He took her flesh into his mouth—tenderly, reverently—and she jumped. He pulled strongly, the sensation so exquisitely sweet it verged on painful.

She looked down dazedly, watching his white wig against her breast. This was too intimate an act to be done in a carriage fully clothed. She wanted a private part of him, too, if only a little bit. She pushed aside his wig, pulling it off his head and throwing it to the seat. He never stopped his ministrations, only moved to the other nipple.

Under the wig, his hair was dark and thick, shorn short, almost like fur. She ran her hands over his scalp, flexing her fingers, feeling his hair, warm and surprisingly soft. She closed her eyes in bliss. He was pinching her first nipple between his thumb and finger as he suckled on her other breast. A fire was building at her center, hot and uncontrollable.

"Touch me," he whispered against her breast.

"I...I am," she answered.

She opened her eyes and saw him rub his cheek against her cherry-red nipple. She swallowed at the erotic sight, at the sweetly rough sensation of his unshaven cheek on her sensitive flesh. His eyes were bright and green, watching her, demanding something.

"Not there," he said, and caught her hand, drawing it down between them. Her skirts concealed his lap, and he pulled her fingers underneath, fumbling with his other hand, until suddenly—startlingly—she touched naked flesh.

Her gaze flew to his.

His smile was rueful, yet strained. He looked upon her bare breasts, but what she held, naked, in her hand was hundreds of times more intimate.

"Do you feel me?" he rasped.

She licked her lips, staring into his face. "Yes."

"Stroke me." His eyes half closed. "Please."

She flexed her fingers, exploring this foreign, hot flesh. It was so hard it didn't seem humanly possible. Yet the skin was tenderly soft. She wrapped her hand about him, and his palm closed over hers, strong and unbearably familiar. He showed her how to slowly stroke up until she touched the wide, slick head. She caressed it, feeling the spongy flesh, the tiny indent at the very tip. He made a sound, almost of pain, and then he seized her hand and brought it down the thick stalk again. It was so much longer—so much *bigger*—than she'd ever dreamed.

"Please," he moaned. "Please."

He turned his head and licked across her nipple before gently closing his teeth over the tip. She gasped, her head falling back against his shoulder. He worried her nipple, then let it go to kiss it softly.

"Stroke me," he gasped, and let her hand go.

She did, pulling up over that hard flesh, hidden beneath her skirts. That part of him that made him a man.

"Like this?" she whispered, low and intimate in the rocking carriage. Outside, London passed by. Inside she held a man's penis in her palm.

"Yesss," he hissed before tonguing her other nipple. "Exactly like that."

She looked down and saw herself, displayed before him, a wanton feast, her nipples red and swollen, so sensitive his every touch made her moan. Her hand moved beneath her skirts, and she wondered at her own daring. Perhaps this was a dream, a wicked fantasy come to life in the middle of the day in her own carriage. She stroked a man's bare cock—*Reading's* bare cock—to bring him carnal pleasure. She watched his face, shining with sweat, the intent look he bent upon her nipples, and the breaths that made his great chest expand and contract. It occurred to her that she might never share a moment as intimate as this again with another human being.

His big hands were on her breasts, and he pinched both her nipples at once. She bit her lip at the pleasure-pain, a tear slipping down one cheek. This was real. This was something outside of everyday bland interactions and rote conversation. His mouth was on hers, open and wild, and his hips were thrusting, moving his cock in her hand in an animal rhythm. He squeezed her poor engorged nipples again, pulling at them at the same time. And she *felt*.

She felt alive.

She arched, pushing her breasts into his hands, sucking on his tongue, and feeling an unstoppable rush of pure, white pleasure through her body. And at the same time, as if in sympathy, the male flesh in her palm jerked and gushed hot liquid between her fingers. She pulsed as he pulsed, shuddered as he shuddered, and she didn't want it to end.

When she finally opened her eyes, she was appalled and amazed at the same time.

Green eyes watched her face, lazy and satisfied, and very, very male. For a moment all was peaceful with the world.

And then she remembered. "Dear God. Thomas is to meet me at my house for luncheon."

*   *   *

GRIFFIN'S BODY WAS filled with a warm lethargy, but Lady Hero's words were a douse of icy water. He straightened and glanced out the window. Her house was in sight. He turned to her and for a moment was stunned anew. She lay across his lap, her breasts bared just past the tips of her delicious nipples, her pale cheeks flushed, her diamond eyes dazed by what they had just shared.

Dear God, indeed.

Hastily, he searched his coat pockets and found a handkerchief. He took her hand from beneath her skirts and began wiping his spill off of her fingers.

She snatched her hand away. "I . . . I can do that."

He raised his eyebrows but let her take the handkerchief. He put himself to rights and watched as she finished scrubbing her fingers and then wrinkled her nose at the handkerchief.

"I'll take that," he said.

She nodded and fumbled with her bodice. "Please turn away."

A sardonic reply was on his lips, but he thought better of it. He turned to view the closed curtains over the window. She'd moved off his lap, but he felt the small movements beside him as she adjusted herself. She was ashamed, he could see that clearly, and for the life of him he didn't know how to make this right.

He felt her rise and take her seat on the opposite side of the carriage. He looked up.

She was patting at her hair, refusing to meet his gaze. "I . . . I hope you will not speak of this to anyone?"

He cursed, low and foully.

Her head jerked up and she stared at him with eyes that made him want to weep and bellow at the same time.

Griffin passed a hand across his forehead. "Of course I'll not talk."

She bit her lip, then nodded jerkily. "You need to put on your wig."

"Do I?" He looked about the carriage seat, finally finding it smashed into a corner. The carriage rolled to a stop as he tugged the wig on. "Better?"

"Yes."

They sat there in silence as they waited for the footman to set the step and open the door. Griffin tried to think of something to say. He'd stolen her innocence—in intent if not in fact. There was no going back from that.

Finally, after eons of waiting, the door was opened and she stepped down, her face averted from his. No doubt she loathed the very sight of him now, he thought grimly as he followed her.

"Hero, darling, there you are!" Lady Phoebe called from the top of the town house steps. "Cousin Bathilda is pacing holes in the sitting room carpet, and Cook has burned the soup." Her bright eyes swiveled to him, and she squinted a bit behind her glasses. "And you've brought Lord Griffin for luncheon as well. How clever of you."

Griffin felt Lady Hero go stiff beside him. "I do not wish to intrude on your luncheon, Lady Phoebe. Your sister kindly offered me a ride in her carriage, no more."

"Oh, no, you *must* stay," Lady Phoebe protested. "Cook will fix the soup, she always does, and it's so much nicer with two gentlemen instead of a lonely one, badgered by females all about. Hero, do make him stay."

Lady Hero turned to him and smiled with trembling lips, her eyes tragic. "Please."

He ought to go, he knew that. Knew, too, that she didn't

really want him here. But her very fragility at that moment made it impossible for him to turn away.

Griffin bowed and held out his arm for her. "As you wish, my lady."

She laid her hand on his sleeve, and he remembered with something of a jolt that those same fingers had wrapped around his cock not five minutes ago. Dear God, his brother's fiancée. What a mess he'd made.

They mounted the steps and went inside, her sister all the while chattering and thankfully oblivious to their silence. Lady Hero was so wooden beside him she might have been a walking statue. He had an urge to cover the fingers on his sleeve, to see if they were warm with life.

Did she hate him now? Wish that they'd never done what they'd done in the carriage? He knew he should be regretting those moments, but he simply couldn't. Her delicate breasts had been too sweet, the sound she had made when he'd taken her ripe nipple between his lips too beautiful. Her gray eyes had narrowed in bliss as he'd made love to her. And by God, he'd take that memory to his grave and be thankful of it, no matter the cost.

A footman took her wrap, and Lady Hero glanced at Griffin, then away again swiftly. "I...I just need to freshen up. Phoebe will show you to the luncheon room."

Griffin bowed, watching moodily as she retreated up the stairs.

He turned to Lady Phoebe, offering his elbow. "I'm at your mercy."

She grinned, taking his arm. "It's just us for luncheon—myself, Hero, your brother, and Cousin Bathilda. Have you met my cousin Bathilda yet?"

"I haven't had the honor."

She nodded. "Don't let Mignon bother you. She growls at everyone."

And with those cryptic words, she led him up the stairs and into a light, feminine room, all yellows and whites with dauntingly fragile furniture. Thomas was standing at the far end with a rather stout matron. He looked up at their entrance, seeming less than pleased to see his brother.

"Look who Hero brought home," Lady Phoebe said as they neared.

"Griffin," Thomas murmured in greeting.

"Thomas." Griffin turned to the older lady and eyed the small black, white, and brown spaniel she held in her arms. It was growling at him, low and continually, rather like a bumblebee.

"This is Lord Griffin Reading, Cousin Bathilda," Lady Phoebe murmured. "My lord, this is my cousin, Miss Bathilda Picklewood."

Miss Picklewood dipped into a creaking curtsy as he bowed. "We shall have to tell Panders that there is one more for luncheon."

"I'll try not to eat too much," Griffin said lightly. "What a pretty little spaniel."

"She is, isn't she?" Miss Picklewood had actually pinkened. She stroked the spaniel's head, and it interrupted its rumbling to lick her fingers. "Would you like to pet her?"

"Ah." Griffin examined the dog warily. It hadn't started growling again, but then its protuberant brown eyes didn't look particularly friendly either.

Beside him, Lady Phoebe's eyes were positively

dancing behind her spectacles. "Don't be frightened. If she bites, we'll send for a doctor, I assure you."

"Bloodthirsty baggage," Griffin muttered under his breath before extending a hand toward the dog's nose. If he were going to be bitten, he might as well get it over with. "Mademoiselle Mignon."

The spaniel sniffed daintily and then opened her mouth in a doggy grin as he gingerly fondled her ears.

"I don't understand it," Miss Picklewood said. "She usually hates gentlemen."

Griffin's outraged gaze flew to Lady Phoebe's own, and she covered her mouth to stifle a giggle.

The girl shrugged. "She's never actually *bitten* a gentleman before. Just threatened to."

"She came close with me," Thomas remarked drily. "You must've rubbed your fingers in bacon, Griffin."

"Perhaps she just has very good taste," Griffin said as he scratched Mignon's chin.

"In any case, she certainly seems fond of you," Miss Picklewood muttered. She nodded as the butler made some sort of signal. "I think we're ready to go in. Perhaps you can see what's taking your sister so long, Phoebe?"

Lady Phoebe slipped from the room, and Thomas made a social remark, but Griffin wasn't paying attention. He absently stroked the little spaniel and wondered if he was the reason Hero was reluctant to come to luncheon.

Damn, damn, damn. He'd made the worst mistake of his life.

"Here she is."

He looked up at the sound of Lady Phoebe's voice. Hero was standing beside her, composed, though color still flew high in her cheeks.

She walked straight to Thomas and held out her hand. "My lord, it is good to see you."

Thomas bent over her hand in a polite, everyday gesture that in no way could be construed as passionate, and pain arched through Griffin's body in a searing flame. In that moment, he wanted to shove aside his brother, lift up Lady Hero, and bear her away. Take her someplace where he could wipe that look of bored serenity from her face and replace it with lust. Lust for *him*.

Instead he took a breath and offered his arm to Lady Phoebe. "Will you accompany me into luncheon, my lady?"

She smiled up at him, her round, rosy cheeks merry. "I'd be delighted, my lord."

The luncheon, like the room, proved to be a feminine affair. A clear soup hardly more than a broth, delicate little pastries more pretty than filling, and a variety of breads and cheeses. The wine was good, though, and in ordinary circumstances, Griffin might've enjoyed himself.

"I understand you manage the family estates," Miss Picklewood said with a queer look fixed on her face. She sat at the head of the table. One of her hands drifted beneath the table.

"*Manage* is surely too strong a word," Thomas drawled from the foot of the table. "My brother is preoccupied with his amusements, and we do have several land stewards."

Griffin picked up his knife. "What my brother is trying to say is that, yes, I do oversee the Mandeville estates as well as my private ones."

Thomas gave him a blank, unfriendly stare as he sipped his wine.

To Thomas's right, Lady Hero straightened as her hand

disappeared beneath the table. "Are your lands in Lancashire as well, Lord Griffin?"

"Yes." Griffin toyed with his knife. "A result of prudent marriages by my ancestors."

"But that's so far from London," Lady Phoebe exclaimed. "Surely you must get lonely in the country."

She bit her lip and stared straight ahead as her hand, too, suddenly darted underneath the table.

Thomas, seemingly oblivious to all this, snorted. "My brother can find excitement no matter where he is. And he has his trips to London should he find a need to debauch himself."

Griffin narrowed his eyes, staring at Thomas, feeling the blackness boil at the back of his eyeballs. He smiled and dropped the knife. It clattered onto his plate.

The ladies started.

Thomas merely raised his eyebrows.

Griffin shifted his gaze to Lady Phoebe, who sat between him and Thomas. "I enjoy riding and hunting, my lady, and overseeing the planting and harvest takes up much of my time, so no, I'm not lonely, though I do thank you for your concern."

She was frowning, her eyes darting between him and his brother, but at his words she smiled tentatively. "Well, we shall have to be sure to see that you are properly entertained when you are in London, won't we, Hero?"

Lady Hero pressed her lips together. "Phoebe..."

"What?" Lady Phoebe looked confused.

Lady Hero's expression was wooden. Even Miss Picklewood's face looked more welcoming.

At that moment, Griffin felt tiny paws on his knee. They tapped quite imperiously.

"I'd be delighted to go anywhere you have a mind, Lady Phoebe." He smiled and broke off a piece of pastry, feeding it to Mignon beneath the table.

"Our time is largely taken up by wedding arrangements," Hero said repressively.

"But you must shop." He picked up the knife again, idly twirling it between his fingers. "And eat and go to fairs and the like."

Lady Phoebe giggled nervously.

Hero's eyes dropped to her plate. Her cheeks had gone pale, her mouth crimped in a straight line.

He shrugged easily, though his heart had shriveled. "Or perhaps not."

Thomas stirred in his seat. "I wouldn't think you'd be inclined to go to any more fairs."

Lady Phoebe perked up. "Why do you say that?"

Griffin arched an eyebrow at his brother, a sudden memory lightening his mood.

"Because Griffin nearly got himself killed by a pack of traveling tinkers at the last fair he attended," Thomas drawled.

"Really?" Phoebe leaned forward.

"Indeed. He was in the act of stealing—"

"Merely examining," Griffin interjected.

"*Stealing*," Thomas rolled over him with his parliamentary voice, "a trinket of some kind."

"A penknife," Griffin murmured to Phoebe. "It had a ruby on the hilt."

Thomas snorted. "Paste, most likely. In any event, one of the tinkers, a man of at least six feet tall, caught him by the scruff of the neck, and had I not intervened, I would be one brother shorter today."

Griffin smiled wryly, putting down the knife and taking a sip of wine. "Even then Thomas was rather renown for his oratory."

Thomas grinned and Griffin remembered that long-ago day. The sudden fear, the complete relief and gratitude when his bigger, older brother had come to his rescue. He looked down at his plate, nudging the knife with his fingertip. That time seemed centuries ago now.

"How old were you?" Hero asked softly.

He inhaled and looked up, meeting her far-too perceptive eyes. "Nearly twelve."

She nodded and the conversation moved on to a piece of gossip Miss Picklewood had heard.

But Griffin was silent, contemplating that past when he and Thomas had been so close.

And the present when they were so very far apart.

Chapter Nine

*Queen Ravenhair looked at the offerings of her three
suitors and nodded regally. "Thank you," she said,
and led them into the dining room where she
turned the conversation to other matters.
But that night as Queen Ravenhair stood upon her
balcony, the little brown bird flew to the railing.
She took the bird into her cupped palms and saw that he
had a string about his neck, and at the end of the
string was a small iron nail.
And then she smiled. For her people used nails to build
their houses, and that—her people and their homes—was
the foundation of her kingdom....*
—from *Queen Ravenhair*

Hero stared at herself in her dressing room mirror the
next afternoon and wondered what sort of woman let
her fiancé's brother make love to her. The woman in the
mirror looked the same as she remembered—widely set
gray eyes, neatly coiffed red hair, steady, serene gaze—
everything in place, in fact. But somehow she was different than the person she'd thought herself just a week
before. *That* woman—that Hero—would never have
sinned, would've scoffed at the mere suggestion that she
might.

And yet she had.

Hero lightly touched a curl at her temple.

"It's quite lovely, my dear." Lady Mandeville's voice broke into her thoughts.

Hero glanced down at herself. Yards of shimmering pale silk apricot swathed her form, pulled back in front to reveal a cream underskirt embroidered with green, blue, and pink posies. The embroidery continued along the seams of the dress and framed the deep, round neckline. It was indeed a lovely dress.

Why, then, did she feel like weeping?

"You do like it, don't you?" Lady Mandeville inquired. "We can have it remade or have an entirely new one made if you don't. There's still time before the wedding."

"No, no," Hero said quickly. "It's a lovely dress. The seamstresses have done a wonderful job."

The little woman kneeling at her feet flashed her a grateful smile before bending again to the hem.

She'd always known who she was, Hero reflected. A lady of principles. A woman with compassion and a few ideals, but one who had a level head on her shoulders. She'd always prided herself on her common sense. Yesterday had been a very sad blow to both common sense and the image she'd had of herself. She was four and twenty—a mature number of years. One would think by now that she'd have a firm grasp of who she was.

Apparently not.

"There," the head seamstress said, sitting up. She eyed the hem critically. "We'll take that up and then add some lace to the sleeves and bodice. It'll be very fine when we finish, my lady, never you fear."

Hero dutifully pivoted to eye the dress from the side.

Such a perfect dress. If only the woman inside was as perfect. "I'm sure it will be very nice."

"We'll require three more fittings, I think. May we call upon you next Tuesday morning, my lady?" The seamstress and her helpers were already extracting her from the dress.

"That will be fine," Hero murmured.

"I shall come to that fitting as well," Lady Mandeville announced. "We can discuss the family jewelry and what pieces you might want to wear."

"Of course."

Hero met her own eyes in the mirror as the seamstresses worked around her. Calm and gray. She'd committed a sin. She wasn't sure she could ever resurrect her perfect facade again. She should be wracked with guilt and despair and yet... and yet, doing what she had done with Lord Reading yesterday had felt fundamentally right.

Soul-deep right.

That feeling was perhaps the most disturbing thing of all.

It took another half hour to dress again. Lady Mandeville chatted lightly as Hero made her toilet, and if the older lady saw anything odd about her future daughter-in-law, she made no sign. The seamstresses left after carefully packing away Hero's wedding dress, and then Lady Mandeville rose as well. She drew on her gloves, watching as Wesley crossed the room to fetch a jacket for Hero from the wardrobe.

"Are you sure you like the dress, my dear?" Lady Mandeville said softly.

Hero looked at her kind face and had to blink suddenly.

She didn't deserve this wonderful woman as a mother-in-law. "Oh, yes."

"It's just"—Lady Mandeville touched Hero's shoulder lightly with one finger—"you seem rather melancholy this afternoon."

Hero smiled, pulling the crumbling shards of her facade about her. "Bridal nerves, I expect."

Lady Mandeville looked uncertain, but in the end she nodded. "Of course. But if you would like to talk to me about anything—anything at all—well, I do hope we'll have that sort of a relationship."

"I hope so too," Hero said in a rush. How she longed to confess all her doubts and worries! But Lady Mandeville would no longer look at her quite so kindly if she knew how Hero had deceived her son. "Thank you."

Lady Mandeville gave one last tug to her gloves. "Good, my dear. I'm glad. Now, don't keep Thomas waiting too long. I know he expects to take you driving this afternoon." So saying, the lady bid her farewell and left.

Hero donned a pretty green jacket with Wesley's help.

Wesley stood back to admire her work and nodded, satisfied. "My Lord Mandeville will be quite taken with you today, my lady."

Hero smiled slightly. "Thank you, Wesley."

She descended the stairs and found Mandeville already waiting for her in the sitting room.

"My dear," he said as she entered. "Your beauty puts the sun to shame."

She curtsied. "Thank you, my lord."

"And how are the wedding plans progressing?" he asked as he guided her from the sitting room and down the front steps. "I hear the dress is nearly finished."

"Yes, only a few more fittings." Hero glanced at Mandeville curiously. This might be the most personal interest he'd ever shown in her. "Your mother told you before she left?"

He nodded and he helped her into his open carriage. "My mother loves a wedding. You should've seen the flurry she was in when Caroline was married. I think her only disappointment now is that a son does not require a trousseau."

Hero glanced at her hands folded in her lap and hid a smile at the thought of Mandeville being outfitted in new stockings and chemises. "I quite like your mother. She's been a great help with the wedding plans."

"I am happy to hear it." He concentrated on the ribbons for a moment, guiding his lovely matched bays into the crowded London street.

Hero tilted her face up surreptitiously. The sun was out today, a welcome last stand of autumn. The London traffic ebbed and flowed around the carriage in a giant stream. A heavy miller's cart trudged along ahead of them, and sedan chairmen deftly wove in and out of slower pedestrians, their passengers jogging along in upright boxes. A few soldiers on horses clattered by, ignoring the shouted insults of a pair of butcher's boys who'd been splattered by the horses' hooves. A single tattered woman bawled a song by the side of the road, her two children at her feet with hands outstretched.

"She likes you, you know," Mandeville said.

"Your mother?"

"Yes." He slapped the reins as the carriage cleared the miller's cart, and the horses stepped into a trot. "She has a dowager house, naturally, but I find it's easier if the two of you get along."

"Of course," Hero murmured. She straightened the edge of her glove. "Did she like your first wife?"

Mandeville glanced at her warily. "You mean Anne?"

Was it such an odd question? "Yes."

He shrugged, returning his gaze to the horses. "Mother manages to get along with nearly everyone, it seems. She never showed any outward dislike or disapproval."

"Did she show any approval, though?"

"No."

She watched him for a moment as he handled the reins with expert ease. He was a private man, she knew, but in only weeks they would be man and wife. "Did you love her?"

He flinched as if she'd said something obscene. "My dear..."

"I know it's none of my business," she said softly. "But you never speak of her to me. I just would like to know."

"I see." He was silent a moment, a slight frown between his eyebrows. "Then I shall endeavor to assuage your curiosity. I was...fond of Anne and quite sad when she died, but I hold no disappointed love for her. You need have no worries there."

She nodded. "And Reading?"

"What about him?"

"I'm afraid I've heard the rumors," Hero said carefully. She remembered Reading's own reply on the matter when she pressed him about whether he'd seduced his brother's wife. *No, God, no.* "Do you truly believe your brother could've betrayed you so?"

"I don't have to believe," he said very drily. "Anne herself told me."

*   *   *

THOMAS WATCHED HIS fiancée's delicately curved eyebrows arch in surprise and felt irritation crawl under his skin. What had she thought? That he'd harbored some insane suspicion without any evidence?

And why the hell was she quizzing him anyway?

He faced forward again, guiding the bays around a shepherd with a herd of sheep milling in the middle of the road. They were nearing Hyde Park, and he longed for the open air. Wished he could give the bays their heads and let them run wildly down the lane.

Hardly a fitting activity for a marquess.

"I'm sorry," Lady Hero murmured beside him, quietly contrite.

Well, even the most perfect of women became emotional once in a while. They could hardly help it, made the way they were. Anne had been a mercurial creature. Lavinia was passionate, but more controlled. In comparison to them, Hero was a model of restraint, really.

He sighed. "It was a long time ago in any case. I cannot ever forgive Griffin, but I can certainly try and lay the matter aside and go on. As I've said, you needn't worry about what happened in my marriage to Anne. It's in the past."

For a moment he tried to remember what Anne had looked like that terrible night. She'd been hysterical, weeping as she tried to push her poor, dead babe from her body. At one time he'd thought the sights and sounds of that night would be engraved in his nightmares for the rest of his life. But now all he could remember was the still, gray body of the baby, its features curiously flattened, and the thought that all of the blood and hysteria hadn't mattered anyway. The child had been a girl.

A tiny, dead girl.

"I see," Lady Hero said beside him.

Thank God the gates of the park were within sight. He hated thoughts like these, useless and dispiriting. Ones that challenged his authority and his place in the universe: A marquess should not have to hear the dying confession of infidelity from his wife. Should not have to see the dead body of his baby girl.

"We won't discuss this again," he said. "Now that you've had your questions answered."

She didn't say anything, but then she didn't have to. Naturally she would acquiesce to his wishes. It occurred to him that Lavinia would've kept arguing the point. Odd thought—and hardly helpful. He endeavored to put it from his mind.

The park was crowded today, the fine weather drawing out all walks of society. He guided the bays into the slowly moving line of carriages and horses revolving about one end of Hyde Park.

"I saw Wakefield yesterday," he commented.

"Did you?" Her voice seemed a little cool, but then she was probably distracted by the passing parade.

"Indeed. He tells me that there is a possibility that he soon will have a titled gin distiller in his grasp."

She stiffened beside him. Many women found political talk dreary, but he'd thought her more tolerant than most. After all, she was sister to one of the foremost parliamentarians of the day. And of course she knew of his own political ambitions.

"Do you know who?" she asked, calming his sudden worry.

"He hasn't said. Most likely keeping the matter under

his hat until he's certain. Your brother is a dark horse. Ah, there's Fergus." Thomas nodded to Lord Fergus sitting with his rather plain-faced wife. Behind them sat their two daughters, also, alas, plain-faced. "He's in the naval department," he murmured sotto voce as he pulled the bays alongside the Fergus carriage.

And then he was proud, for Lady Hero graciously nodded at the introduction of the ladies and then complimented Lady Fergus on her bonnet, prompting the lady's sallow complexion to turn pink. The two girls leaned slightly forward, and all four were soon in animated discussion.

"A good match, Mandeville," Fergus rumbled after they'd discussed the latest Lords scandal. "You're a lucky man."

"Indeed, indeed," Thomas murmured.

His recent ridiculous doubts fled. Lady Hero was above all a calm and demure creature, not given to the type of awful drama Anne often acted out.

Fergus nattered on for another ten minutes—the man was prone to be didactic—and then they made their farewells.

Thomas took up the reins again. "I hope you didn't find talking to Lady Fergus and her daughters too boring."

"Not at all," Lady Hero replied. "They were quite nice. Besides, I know how important these kinds of little meetings are for you and your career, Mandeville. I want to do everything I can to aid you."

He smiled. "I keep forgetting that your perception rivals your beauty, my lady. I am indeed a lucky man."

"You flatter me."

"Don't all ladies wish to be flattered?"

She didn't answer and he glanced her way. Lady Hero's face was in profile as she looked fixedly to the side. He followed her gaze and felt as if he'd been struck in the belly.

Lavinia Tate was two carriages over, laughing up into the face of that Samuel fellow who'd escorted her to Harte's Folly. She wore a quilted jacket the color of spring poppies, and the sunlight glinted off her damnably bright red hair. If any man in Hyde Park hadn't noticed her yet, it was because he was dead.

Or a fool.

"Who is she to you?" Lady Hero asked quietly.

"No one," Thomas said through stiff lips.

"Yet you stare at her as if she's someone very important indeed."

"What?" He tore his eyes from the sight of Lavinia and looked at his fiancée, her face too pale, her hair merely a tasteful, *natural* shade of light copper. She was a watercolor next to Lavinia's vivid oil. "She's ... someone I once knew."

"You no longer know her?" Lady Hero tilted her head in gentle inquiry.

Lavinia's laugh floated on the autumn breeze.

Thomas wanted suddenly to shout at Lady Hero, to make that gentle expression fall from her face, to shake her until she quit her questions and her perceptive looks, and then he wanted to jump from the carriage and plant a facer in that stupid young buck with Lavinia.

But he did none of that, of course. Gentlemen of his rank never acted in such a way. Instead, he merely urged the horses on, waiting interminably to pass Lavinia's carriage.

"She's in my past," he said through cold lips. "I met her when I was rather down, I'm afraid."

He remembered when he was the man who she laughed up at, the way it had made his chest swell. And he remembered the sight of her in the morning light, so carnal, so wise. He'd been able to see every single line in her face, the slight sag to her breasts, and strangely it hadn't made a whit of difference. She'd been the most beautiful woman he'd ever seen.

Would ever see.

He cleared his throat. "That's in the past now. We'll not talk of it."

She sighed beside him, the sound sad and somehow lonely. "Perhaps you're right. It's best to put aside what might have come before. Our future together should be what we focus on."

She laid a gloved hand on his elbow, slim and comfortable. "We'll make an admirable pair, you and I, Thomas."

He was able to summon a smile to give her. "Yes. Yes, we will."

And then they were finally past Lavinia Tate.

WESLEY WAS PUTTING the finishing touches on Hero's toilet the next morning when Phoebe burst in the room.

"You'll never guess!"

Hero started to open her mouth to ask what she'd never guess, but Phoebe continued in a rush. "Lord Griffin and Lady Margaret have called and asked to take us shopping!"

For a split second, Hero's heart leaped at the thought of him. But then her practical side asserted itself.

"Oh, my dear." Hero winced at the excited look on Phoebe's face. Her entire countenance seemed to glow. "You know that Bathilda doesn't want me to be seen with Reading. And after bringing him back to luncheon the other day . . ."

The light went out in Phoebe's face. "But I cannot go alone with them."

No, she certainly couldn't, and Reading was well aware of the fact, Hero thought grimly.

"Please, Hero?"

Hero closed her eyes.

But that didn't shut out Phoebe's voice. "Pleeease?"

Hero's eyes snapped open. "Fine. But only for an hour or so, no more."

She needn't have bothered with caveats—Phoebe was already hopping up and down with excitement.

Hero sighed, knowing already that this was a very bad idea. Still, she had to struggle to contain a smile as she descended the stairs after Phoebe.

Reading waited below, looking quite respectable in a dark blue coat and breeches. He smiled as Phoebe bounced up to him, but his eyes were on Hero.

She fought not to blush.

"I'm glad you could join us, Lady Hero," he said as he escorted them out the door.

She shot him a sharp glance, watching for irony, but he seemed perfectly serious. "Where is your sister?"

His eyes widened mockingly at her. "In the carriage."

And indeed when they entered the carriage, there was Lady Margaret already waiting.

"Oh, I'm so glad you could come on such short notice!" she exclaimed as they settled on the cushions. "I feel we ought to get to know one another since you're marrying my brother."

"Of course," Hero murmured. "We'll soon be sisters, won't we?"

Reading's face went blank as he turned to the window.

"I hope so," Lady Margaret said. "I almost feel as if I know your brother, the duke, better. Thomas talks about him so much, and then they spent all that time last summer drawing up their gin bill. Wakefield's quite passionate on the subject, isn't he?"

"He believes that St. Giles is crime-riddled because of gin," Phoebe said soberly. "So by extension he blames our parents' death on gin."

Hero glanced at her sister, a little surprised that she'd gleaned this information from the censored things that Maximus said in front of her.

Lady Margaret nodded. "Then I suppose you both are also passionate on the subject."

Reading turned to look at Hero, and she tilted her chin up as she answered. "Yes."

"We ladies can't make bills in parliament," Phoebe said, "but Hero has recently become the patroness of a home for foundling children in St. Giles."

"Really?" Lady Margaret asked. "How I admire you, Lady Hero. I've never done anything so selfless."

"But you could." Phoebe leaned forward in her eagerness. "Hero has decided to let other ladies help with the home by donating their money."

"Indeed?" Reading drawled. "And are gentlemen allowed to help, too? Perhaps I shall make a donation."

Hero couldn't quite meet his gaze. He was jesting, of course, but he'd already offered to help her once....

But before she could say anything, Phoebe leaped in. "It's for ladies only, I'm afraid."

"Such discrimination," Reading murmured.

"Gentlemen always want to run things," Hero shot back.

Reading's mouth quirked in amusement.

"That's very true," Lady Margaret said. "I think it's quite smart of you to limit your, er..."

"Syndicate," Phoebe supplied. "It's to be called the Ladies' Syndicate for the Benefit of the Home for Unfortunate Infants and Foundling Children."

"Splendid!" Lady Margaret enthused. "I think that a ladies-only syndicate is quite a wonderful idea. May I join?"

"Naturally," Hero replied as Reading rolled his eyes.

"Except..." Lady Margaret looked suddenly abashed. "I've only a bit of pin money to donate. Perhaps it won't be enough to join?"

"We have no lower limit," Hero said firmly, even as she realized that her syndicate might have to be larger than she'd first envisioned. "Any lady of means who is sincere in her wish to help the orphan children of St. Giles is welcome to join."

"Oh, lovely."

Reading smiled and shook his head. "We're at Bond Street, ladies. Will you come and shop now?"

Phoebe and Lady Margaret eagerly descended the carriage, and somehow Hero found herself with Reading.

He bent over her as their sisters walked ahead. "So you have found a solution to your dilemma over the funds for the home all by yourself."

"Phoebe came up with the idea, but yes, I think it a good solution," she replied.

"As do I," he said unexpectedly. *"Brava."*

His approval sent a warm feeling through her, as if she'd just drunk hot tea on a cold day. Why she should care one way or the other about his feelings on the matter, she did not know, but there it was—she did care.

"Have you told Thomas yet about your involvement with the home?" he asked.

"No." She glanced down guiltily. "I will soon, of course."

"Of course," he murmured. "I just hope Thomas is as liberal as your brother."

"That's an awful thing to say."

He shrugged. "But true nonetheless. Your activities will reflect upon Thomas, and he has a damnably narrow view of what it means to be the Marquess of Mandeville."

She felt a twinge of irritation, though she knew that Reading was but speaking the truth. Mandeville did need to worry about his name—he was a prominent member of parliament. And as his wife, she would be under scrutiny. Still..."I can't think being the patroness of a home for foundling children can be considered so very risqué."

"No, but gallivanting about St. Giles is." He escorted her around a group of ladies gathered about a window display. "He'll want you to stop once you're married."

"You don't know that," she insisted stubbornly. "Besides, I can't think what business it is of yours."

"Can't you?" He turned and suddenly his green eyes met hers. The street, the crowds, seemed to fall away, and she could hear the echo of her heartbeat in her ears.

Hero inhaled, tearing her gaze from his. "No, I can't. Besides, it's natural for Mandeville to want to protect his wife. You must understand that."

"Must I?" He shook his head, his mouth twisting. "I only understand that I prefer birdsong from the meadow instead of a cage."

"Do you? Have you ever thought of the bird?" she asked too quietly, too intensely. Suddenly they were no longer speaking of birds. "Perhaps she feels safer knowing that someone is looking after her in her cage. Perhaps she fears the wide-open space with no one to guard her."

For a moment he was silent; then Reading said low, "How does the bird know she hates the freedom of the meadow if she's never felt it?"

His green eyes were locked with hers, and she couldn't look away. Her breath was caught in her chest, and she longed to simply do as he suggested, to fly free, but she couldn't ... she simply couldn't.

"Here we are!" Lady Margaret called ahead of them, gesturing to a pretty little shop.

The shop turned out to be a milliner's where Phoebe found a lovely length of Belgian lace. Afterward, Reading bought them all buns and tea and then insisted they visit a bookstore. Phoebe and Lady Margaret made for a display of beautifully illustrated books on botany while Reading drew Hero aside toward a small shelf of books in Greek and Latin.

"They have some interesting books here," he said, taking down a tome of plays. "Have you read Aristophanes?"

"I shouldn't," she murmured, even as she took the book from his hands. She fingered the leather spine.

"Why not?" he asked softly. "It's merely a book of plays, a bit scandalous in parts, granted, but nothing to tempt you into sin."

"But it's a book of *plays*," she said, still holding the book. "Not history like Thucydides and Herodotus."

"So?" His eyebrows rose up his forehead.

"So it isn't serious." She placed the book carefully back on the shelf. "It's my duty to occupy my mind with more important matters than comedic plays."

"Duty to whom?" he began rather heatedly, but suddenly there was a cry and a thump from behind him.

Hero looked and saw Phoebe crumpled in a heap at the bottom of a short series of steps. "Oh, dear God!"

She hurried over with Reading.

Phoebe's face was chalk-white, and Lady Margaret, though standing by her, did not look much better.

"What happened?" Reading barked.

"I don't know," Lady Margaret said. "She must've tripped on the stairs."

"I didn't see them," Phoebe said through pale lips. "I was walking to another bookshelf, and the stairs just came up in front of me."

Reading glanced at her sharply before bending and asking, "Can you stand?"

"I . . . I think so."

"Reading, her forehead," Hero said. There was a line of blood dripping down the side of Phoebe's face.

"She must've bumped it." Reading touched Phoebe's hair gently.

"Ow." Phoebe began to raise her right arm and then inhaled sharply, her face turning a ghastly green. "Oh!"

"What is it?" Hero asked.

"I think she's broken her arm," Reading said. "No, don't touch it. Let me." With one athletic movement, he gathered Phoebe into his arms and rose. "I'll carry her back to the carriage, and once we've got her home, we'll send for a doctor."

"Very well," Hero began, but Reading was already striding out the shop door.

She and Lady Margaret trotted to keep up, and they were soon at the carriage. The ride home was an awful journey, each bump causing Phoebe pain. Reading sat beside her, trying to brace her against the worst jostling, his mouth white-rimmed. As soon as they were at the house, Bathilda came out and began efficiently ordering maids and footmen about. Phoebe was carried into the house, and Hero was about to follow her when a restraining hand was laid upon her arm.

She turned and looked up into Reading's angry face. "Why doesn't she have better spectacles? It's obvious she can't see with the ones she has—she didn't see the steps! You need to consult an expert."

Hero closed her eyes, waiting for self-righteous anger to meet his, but all she felt was a deep, despairing sorrow.

"Hero?" he asked, squeezing her arm.

"We have consulted the experts," Hero said wearily. "Some from as far away as Prussia. Ever since a year ago when we realized her eyesight was poor, she's been prodded and poked and any number of 'cures' tried upon her."

He frowned. "And?"

She blinked back tears, trying to smile and failing miserably. "And none of them has worked. Phoebe is going blind."

*   *   *

IT WAS PAST midnight by the time Griffin entered St. Giles that night, and those who were easy prey were already scurrying to ground. He'd not seen hide nor hair of the Vicar's men in the nights since Reese's body had been thrown over the wall. Maybe the man had lost interest in this part of London. Maybe the talk that the Vicar was going to attack again was simply rumors. Maybe the man was dead.

Maybe, but Griffin wasn't counting on it. He rode with his eyes alert, one hand on the loaded gun in his saddle. The Vicar had been known to demonstrate patience when he was after something he wanted. And it appeared he wanted Griffin's still very much.

A shadow moved to his right, slipping from a doorway, and Griffin pulled one of the pistols from the saddle. He turned, raising the pistol, and then he blinked at what he saw. A man in some sort of close-fitting costume, wearing a short cape and an extravagantly plumed hat. The apparition bowed slightly, flourishing his hat, and then leaped and swarmed straight up a house wall, disappearing onto the roof.

Good God. Griffin looked up but caught no sight of the Ghost of St. Giles—for it must be he. The apparition had been wearing black and red motley. Was the ghost a footpad? But if so, the man had made no move to try and rob him. What exactly was the purpose of the ghost's wanderings? Griffin shook his head and kneed Rambler into motion again. Too bad he couldn't tell Megs of his sighting—she'd be all agog.

It was full dark by the time Griffin arrived at the distillery. He pounded on the gate and waited for what seemed like an overlong time for an answer, his back crawling all the time at the knowledge of how exposed he was. When Nick Barnes finally opened the door, Griffin felt his nerves tighten. Nick's face was grim.

"What is it?" Griffin asked as he dismounted inside the courtyard wall. He took the two loaded pistols from the saddle and shoved them in a wide leather belt he had strapped over his coat.

"Another man gone just this morn," Nick growled. "Don't know if 'e was taken by th' Vicar or if 'e plain ran away."

"Damn." Griffin pulled off his coat and picked up a shovel to stoke the fires beneath one of the big copper caldrons. This day just kept getting worse and worse. He still saw little Phoebe in his mind's eye, her face drawn tight by pain, the knowledge that she was losing her sight making him feel helpless. Damn it, a young girl like her shouldn't have to go blind. God shouldn't let it happen.

When Griffin looked up again, he saw Nick was staring at him thoughtfully. "Bad business."

Griffin grunted and pushed a shovelful of coal into the fire.

"We'll not last long like this," Nick said quietly.

Griffin looked around, but none of the men were close enough to overhear. "I'm aware of that fact. All the Vicar needs to do is pick us off a bit at a time and sit back and wait until I can no longer pay enough to keep the men here."

Nick scratched his chin. "Is it worth it, is what I'm a-wondering? You's got a bit put by, I knows. Per'aps it's time to quit. Give up the stills and find some other way to make a shillin'.'"

Griffin turned and glared at him.

Nick shrugged imperturbably. "Then maybe we should do something a bit more activelike."

"Jesus." Griffin bent and shoveled more coal.

He knew what Nick was getting at: an attack of their own. This had started as a simple business—never respectable, of course, but a business nevertheless. When had it descended into warfare? Maybe it was time to give up this illicit means of making money, but what else did he have? Land that his farmers labored to get a stingy crop from. How else could he turn his grain to money?

Nick watched him shovel coal silently for a moment.

"I seen that lady what came with you th' other day," Nick said chattily after a bit.

Griffin straightened and propped an elbow on his shovel, raising an eyebrow. Nick didn't chat.

Nick pursed his lips—not a pleasant sight. "Seemed a mite put out, she did. Something you said, maybe, m'lord?"

"She doesn't approve of gin distilling," Griffin said flatly.

"Ah." Nick rocked back on his heels. "Not a proper occupation for toffs, I'm thinking?"

"That's right." Griffin winced and rubbed the nape of his neck. "No, that's not entirely correct. She champions a foundling home in St. Giles. She thinks gin is the reason there's so many orphans. It's the root of every evil in London as far as she's concerned."

"The 'Ome for Unfortunate Infants and Foundlin' Childr'n."

Griffin glanced at him, surprised. "You know of it?"

"'Ard not to, livin' in these parts." Nick tipped back his

head to stare at the shadowed ceiling of the warehouse. "A good place, is what I 'ear. Not like those what sell the mites into bad apprenticeships. Pity the 'ouse burned last winter."

Griffin grunted. "She's having it rebuilt. Bigger and grander."

"Sounds like a right angel of good will, she does."

Griffin stared at him, suspicious of mockery.

Nick looked innocent. "Makes one wonder what she was doin' wi' you, don't it, m'lord?"

"She's affianced to my brother." Griffin shoveled in more coal, though the fire was well enough stoked now.

"Oh, then she 'as but a sisterly interest in you."

"Nick," Griffin growled in warning.

But Nick was never the type to be cowed.

"It's the saintly ones, I find, that needs watchin'," he mused. "Now, whores, they be simple—fuck 'em an' pay 'em. No problems, everything nice an' tidy an' never a thought afterward. But with a respectable woman, why there's talk an' feelings an' suchlike. Trouble, the lot of them. Not, mind you, that it's not worth it in the end, just that there's a bit of worry up front. A man best be warned."

"Nick," Griffin said slowly, "are you giving me romantic advice?"

Nick pushed his hat to the back of his head so he could scratch his scalp. "Wouldn't dream of it, m'lord."

Griffin grunted. "She's soon to be my sister-in-law anyway."

"O' course, o' course," Nick murmured.

He didn't look at all convinced by the reminder.

Griffin wasn't sure he was convinced himself. He

sighed and threw aside the shovel. "Do you remember when we first started this all those years ago?"

Nick chuckled. "That little still on Tipping Lane? You were a right green 'un then, m'lord. Suspicious, too."

"I wasn't sure I could trust you."

Nick grinned. "Nor I you. You was this toff down from that fancy school, all lace and fripperies. Weren't sure as you'd last a week."

Griffin snorted. He'd met Nick in a seedy Seven Dials tavern—not the place one usually found business partners. But something about the glaring former boxer had struck him as essentially honest. Nick had been the one to introduce him to the man he'd bought his first still from. The thing had been rickety in the extreme.

"Remember when we thought the still would blow?" he asked.

Nick spat into the straw. "Which time? I'm thinkin' of more 'n one."

Griffin grinned and looked around the warehouse. It was a far cry from that small single still on Tipping Lane. It had taken years to build his business to this point, to be where he didn't have to lie awake at night worrying over money flow and harvests. To where he could tell his mother to plan for Megs's next season and be fairly sure they'd actually be able to afford it. He only needed a little more time to get entirely financially stable.

"We worked hard to get here, didn't we?" he said.

"That we did."

"Damned if I'll let the Vicar take it from me now."

"Amen to that." Nick dug a short clay pipe from his waistcoat. He took a moment to light it with a straw stuck in the still fire. Then he said, "'Ave you ever thought of doin' somethin' else?"

Griffin looked at him in surprise. "No. I suppose I've never had time to think of finding other business. Have you?"

"No." Nick scratched the back of his head. "Well, not rightly. Me father was a weaver, but I never learned the craft. Seemed a tedious task when I were young, an' now I'm too old a dog for learnin' new tricks."

"Weaving." Griffin thought of the Mandeville lands in Lancashire. They'd always been too rocky for growing grain. Many of their neighbors had put in sheep for wool and meat.

"Mam and me sisters spun the thread for Pa," Nick said. "I did, too, when I were a lad."

Griffin smiled at the thought of Nick spinning thread with his great hamlike hands.

A shout came from behind them. Griffin whirled, snatching a pistol from his belt. Smoke was pouring out from one of the big chimneys that climbed the outer walls. The men were milling, coughing from the rolling black smoke.

Nick swore foully. "They've stopped th' chimney from without!"

"Put out the fire!" Griffin shouted. "I'll guard the walls."

He gestured to the men, slapping his hands on the backs of those turned away, and ran to the warehouse entrance. Griffin slammed himself against the wall next to the door and shoved it open a crack with one foot. The guards outside were wrestling with attackers next to the walls. Already three men were past them and into the courtyard.

"They're coming in," he told his men. "Make damn sure they don't get to the warehouse."

And with that he kicked the door wide and drew his other pistol, firing both straight-armed. One attacker went down, crashing to the cobblestones. More shots exploded from his men's guns, and the second man went down. But one man still rushed the door while others were overwhelming the courtyard guards. In a corner of the courtyard, Rambler squealed and reared in terror.

"Get them!" Griffin shouted, his words sounding muffled to his own ears.

His men flew past him toward the walls. He threw down one pistol and drew his sword to meet an attacker. The man was short but burly, and he held a huge cutlass in his hand. The attacker swung and Griffin dodged. He was afraid his thinner sword would break under the cutlass. He slid closer while the man was still turned aside from the force of his own blow and stabbed him under the arm through the armpit. The man didn't even flinch. He struck at Griffin with his other hand, a blow Griffin was just able to duck, taking it on his shoulder instead of his face, his hand still on the sword stuck in the man's body. The man raised his cutlass again, but then staggered. He crumpled all at once, like a marionette whose strings had been cut.

Griffin stuck his foot on the man's chest and pulled his sword from the attacker's body. He turned toward the wall, sword ready, but there was no need. Four bodies lay on the cobblestones and a man—one of his own—was sitting with his back against the wall, moaning. All the other attackers had retreated.

The skirmish was over—at least for now.

"Get him inside." Griffin gestured at the moaning man. "You others stay and guard the courtyard from further attack."

He left eight men guarding the walls and turned back to the warehouse. Rambler still snorted and shook where he was tethered in a corner.

Griffin went to him and placed a hand on the gelding's sweaty neck. "It's all right, lad. All right now."

The horse rolled his eyes at him.

Griffin spoke quietly to him for a few more minutes and then filled a nosebag from the saddle with a handful of oats. He left Rambler contentedly munching and strode to the warehouse. Smoke still slipped from the doorway, drifting into the night, but it was thinner now. He picked up the pistol he'd thrown down and ducked inside.

It was dim, the smoke swirling about the ceiling. Griffin squinted against stinging ash.

Nick loomed out of the dark like Satan himself, his face blackened. "We got it out, sure enough, but we can't work the still on that 'earth now."

Griffin nodded. "We need guards on the roof."

Nick cocked an eyebrow, looking positively evil. "And 'ow will we get men for that duty?"

"Pay them triple," Griffin said grimly.

"At some point you'll be paying more than you're makin'," Nick warned.

"I'm well aware of that fact."

Nick nodded and turned to look back at the wreckage of the blocked chimney. "Could've been worse."

"How so?"

"They tried to block another of the chimneys, but the wad fell through. Merely made a smokin' mess on the fire." He looked back at Griffin. "We got it out well enough."

Griffin sat on a barrel wearily and began reloading his pistols from a sack of powder and balls. "This time."

"Aye," Nick grunted, and turned to the chimneys, his words drifting back over his shoulder. "Just pray our luck 'olds out."

Chapter Ten

*The next day, the queen called for her horse and
assembled the princes so they might go hunting with
falcons. And as they sat mounted in the stable yard,
she turned to her suitors and asked, "What is the
strongest thing in my kingdom?" Then she rode out
of the stable yard without a backward glance.
Well, the princes wore looks of consternation as they
followed the queen to the hunt, but the stable master
only nodded his head thoughtfully....*
—from *Queen Ravenhair*

It was midmorning by the time Griffin arrived home from
St. Giles. He wearily dismounted Rambler outside his
town house and gave the reins to a stable lad.

"See he's rubbed down well and given some oats," he
instructed the boy.

With a last pat for Rambler, he climbed the front steps
of his town house and let himself in. He kept only a small
staff at his London residence since he did no entertaining
here. A cook, a few maids, a bootblack boy, and Deedle
were quite sufficient for his needs. The price for such lax-
ity, however, was that there was often no one to meet him
at his own door.

Griffin threw his hat at a hall table and didn't bother

to pick it up when it fell to the floor. He began climbing the stairs. God, he ached like an old man. Another night awake was added to the fight and the ride to and from St. Giles. Now all he wanted was a hot bath and bed. Not necessarily in that order.

But Deedle knew well his master's ways.

The manservant poked his head out of Griffin's room as soon as he heard his steps in the upper hall. "I've got the water boiling, m'lord. We'll 'ave a bath ready in two ticks."

"Bless you, man," Griffin said. He sat upon his bed and began drawing off his boots as the maids hurried in with steaming kettles.

Twenty minutes later, Griffin winced and then sighed as he lowered himself into a tub of hot water.

Deedle fussed about for a moment, putting clothes away. Then he picked up Griffin's muddy boots. "I'll take these down to the boy, shall I?"

Griffin, eyes closed, waved a hand.

The door shut behind the valet.

He'd already soaped the smoke from his head and body, but the rising steam was wonderful. Griffin lay there, soaking, and let his mind drift. He'd left orders for Nick to find more men—if there were some to be had at any price. The Vicar wasn't just targeting Griffin's stills. Overnight there'd been news of two different fires destroying other gin makers. At least one man was dead in the flames. Could he keep his business going?

Griffin snorted softly. Lady Hero would certainly be happy if he went under. One less gin maker among hundreds—if not thousands—in St. Giles. But then maybe she was right to disapprove of his business.

The thought of her disapproval brought other thoughts of her as well. He remembered the little line that knit itself between her delicately arced brows when she lectured him. The way her pale rose lips softened when she listened to his response. And how her lashes had drifted closed when he'd kissed her neck.

Griffin groaned and his hand drifted along his thigh to his cock, already half erect. He brought up images of those sweet little breasts, the red nipples large in contrast and somehow unbearably erotic. They'd been drawn hard and tight for him, and he imagined biting gently down on them. He could almost hear the moan she'd make at his touch.

He grasped his cock in his hand, pulling up, feeling his own hardness, the exquisite sensitivity at the tip.

He'd draw the laces from her stays, bare her fully for his own enjoyment. And under her skirts, there lay that sweet, warm, wet—

Downstairs, someone began pounding on his front door.

Griffin groaned. Surely there was someone to answer it. He didn't have many servants, but he did have enough to answer a bloody door. Or perhaps the caller would give up.

But the knocking continued.

"Hell," he spat, letting go of his now-rigid cock. The visitor might be Nick Barnes with more news.

Griffin climbed from the tub, splashing water on the rug, then swiped a towel across his body and pulled on breeches and a shirt. He ran down the stairs barefoot and stomped across the hall floor to fling open the door.

"What?"

He found himself glaring into Lady Hero's startled gray eyes. She glanced down the length of him, making him very aware of the damp shirt clinging to his chest and the breeches covering his half-aroused state.

Her gaze snapped back up to his. "Oh!"

"What are you doing here?"

"Oh, thank God!" she said low. "I'd heard reports this morning of a gin still burning in St. Giles. They said a man was dead."

"Well, it wasn't me," he said, not very graciously.

"I can see that." She cleared her throat. "Might I come in?"

He looked up and down the street. No one appeared to be paying attention to them. He reached out, wrapped his fingers around her upper arm, and yanked her inside his house.

Lady Hero stumbled in with a squeak. "What do you think you're doing?"

"Trying to salvage your reputation," Griffin muttered. He turned and stomped into the library without bothering to see if she'd follow. "What do *you* think you're doing visiting a bachelor's residence—unaccompanied—in the middle of the day?"

"I wanted to make sure you were all right," she said from behind him. "And I need to talk to you."

Griffin grunted. The damned woman no doubt wanted to continue her harangue about the still. He picked up a decanter of brandy and splashed some into a glass. He turned with the glass in his hand and found her frowning at the scatter of papers on his desk. Probably disapproved of the mess.

He tossed back some of the brandy. "About what?"

She turned, still frowning. "I'm sorry?"

He gestured with the glass, spilling some of the brandy onto the floor. "What do you want to talk about?"

She pursed her lips in a fussy little moue that only served to draw attention to her mouth. He had a sudden image of her mouth pursed and filled. His cock, ever at the ready, came to full, raging arousal.

Griffin slammed back the rest of the brandy.

She opened that luscious mouth. "I—"

"Perhaps you wanted to chat about the weather?" Griffin said silkily. He refilled his glass. "That would be an appropriate topic of discussion for an early morning call."

She blinked. "I—"

He held up a finger to stop her and took another gulp of brandy. It burned going down, but his shoulder, which had been aching from this morning's fight, began to loosen.

"Should you be drinking so much before noon?" she asked disapprovingly.

"Yes." He glared and took another sip to prove his point. "I always drink when I'm half dressed and entertaining ladies."

She flushed a becoming pink. "Perhaps I should come back another time."

"Oh, no." He set down the glass with a crack and stalked toward her. "You've interrupted my bath, interrupted my quite *pleasurable* pursuits there, in fact. You might as well tell me what you want to say."

She stared at him, mute.

"Perhaps you wanted to take me to task for my gin-making ways yet again, hmm?" He leaned over her, not caring if he intimidated or even frightened her. "Or chide me for fucking too much."

She flinched at the word but stood her ground bravely.

He narrowed his eyes viciously. How dare she stand there like a martyr when he ached—literally *ached*—for her? He snapped his fingers as if remembering something. "But you can't chide me for seduction when you've fallen victim to my lewd advances yourself, can you? Not so saintly now, are you?"

Her eyes widened, and he thought he saw a shimmer that might've been tears. He wouldn't give ground now. Not when he might finally drive her out of his house, out of his life, and out from under his skin.

Griffin bent and murmured in her ear, "But perhaps that's what you really came here to discuss—seduction. Perhaps all that stuff about gin making was merely an excuse you seized upon to come see me. Perhaps you want me to kiss more than your sweet breasts this time."

HE'D TAUNTED HER, baited her, argued with her, and made her feel far more than she should. And now he loomed over her, clearly trying to scare her away.

But she wasn't frightened.

Lord Reading's warm breath washed over her bare neck, scented with brandy, and his wicked words sparked something deep within her. It might be—definitely *should* be—shame, but she very much feared it was something else entirely.

"Is that what you want?" he purred. "My hand on your belly? Stroking down until my fingers tangle in your maidenhair? I'd wager it's as soft as a kitten's fur, your hair down there."

She drew in a shuddering breath, pressing one hand to her stomach. He shouldn't say these things. She should make him stop. She should leave. Except...except she wanted with all her heart to stay. To meet him on equal ground—just this once.

To be a woman to his man.

He didn't touch her, simply stood over her too close and whispering those shameful, shocking, seductive words. "But what's below is even softer, isn't it? Your sweet petals, all wet and silky, blooming open for me. I'd find your secret bud hidden in among them, and I'd circle it just so. Never hard enough to hurt you—oh, no, I'd not hurt you—but not so soft that you couldn't feel it. For I want you to feel it, Hero. I want you to feel *me*."

She moaned, and she couldn't help it—didn't want to help it anymore. She turned her head toward him. His face was inches from hers. His eyes were a pale, implacable green, arrogant and sinful. If that was all she saw in his gaze, she would've walked from the room.

It was the hint of vulnerability that made her stay.

Her gaze dropped to his lips. They were curled in a sneer, but the lower one was still wet from the brandy. The sight sent a rush of warmth low in her belly. "Griffin."

He groaned and muttered something vile under his breath. Then she was caught in his arms, not gently at all, and his mouth was on hers, wild and needy.

"Hero," he muttered as his lips feasted on hers. "Hero."

He'd seemed to have let slip some essential control. His movements were jerky and ungraceful, starkly primitive in their intent. He knocked her hat to the floor. His mouth bit along her jaw and down her neck as he grappled with her wrap, tearing it from her arms. He swore and lifted his head, staring down as he got her bodice off and began rapidly unlacing her stays.

She should be horrified. Frightened and appalled, but instead his savagery seemed to feed some need within herself. Her hands were helping his; she was stripping the clothing from her limbs as fast as he. The room was hot, her breath was coming in gasps, and the scent of brandy and need filled her nostrils, making her feel faint.

Her skirts suddenly dropped, and then she stood in only her chemise, stockings, and shoes.

He blinked, his eyelids dropping to half-mast as his movements suddenly stilled. For an awful moment, she feared he might come to his senses and stop.

Instead he slowly moved his hand to the chemise's edge at her shoulder. He fingered the fine material gently, his gaze locking with hers. Then, his green eyes holding hers, he twisted his fingers in the fabric and pulled sharply downward. A seam ripped, something gave way, and he tore the fragile fabric from her body.

She gasped, shocked, standing there nude before him. She'd never revealed herself to a man. She was aware of her nipples, pointed and red in the chill air of the room, and the knobbiness of her knees. Except—dear Lord!—he wasn't looking at her knees. Her chest heaved and his eyes rose to her breasts. His mouth twisted in a smile. Before she'd even completed the thought, his hands flashed out to shackle her wrists.

"No." He shook his head slowly, his gaze never leaving her body. "Let me look. Let me *feast*."

She shuddered. Her whole body was hot, prickling with sensation, as if his eyes physically touched her. This was almost torture, standing nude before him, letting him look at her without even her hands to cover herself with.

He chuckled, low and dark, and then, still holding her

wrists, he swooped down and covered her right breast with his mouth.

She jumped and her head fell back helplessly. His mouth was hot, sucking hard on her flesh. She wanted to feel more, she *needed* more, and her hips of their own accord jerked toward him.

"Oh, not yet," he whispered over her wet, sensitive nipple. "Not nearly yet. I've been thinking of this for a long time."

What? she wondered wildly. *What could he possibly have been thinking about?*

He sank to his knees before her, and she lifted her heavy head, blinking down curiously at him. What was he...?

He let go of her wrists to place his hands on her thighs and force her legs farther apart. Her dazed mind stuttered to life. He was too close to her center. He could see and, more importantly, *smell* everything.

He lifted one of her legs—her foot still shod in an elegant heeled slipper—and draped it over his shoulder, which placed him squarely underneath her.

"No," she said frantically. "I don't—"

He looked up at her, and his pale green eyes seemed to glow. "*Yes.* Hold on to the back of the settee, and whatever you do, *don't* let go."

And then, before she could move or think, he dipped his head forward and licked across her folds.

She gasped and grabbed wildly for the settee behind her. She'd heard whispers of this, but in no way was she prepared for it. He was kissing—no, worse, *licking*—her intimate flesh. It was the most extraordinary thing she'd ever experienced in all her life. His tongue was hot and faintly raspy, stroking firmly over and over, burrowing deeper until he did indeed find what he'd called her bud.

She puffed out air and bit her lip. Her eyes squeezed tight. She mustn't scream, mustn't make a sound, but, dear Lord, it was hard not to. He was licking delicately, exquisitely, over and over again. She felt him pull apart her folds with his thumbs, and then he set his mouth directly over her center.

And sucked.

She gasped, the sound loud in the room. It was almost painful it was so sweet. She felt tremors rock her legs, and for the life of her she couldn't help it.

She peeked.

His dark, shorn head was between her thighs, his thick lashes shuttered over his eyes as he ministered to her. One brown hand was splayed on her pale hip, the difference in their skin tones in shocking contrast. He was so big, so masculine, and he was servicing her. This must be wrong, must surely be a sin, for it felt too, too good.

His eyes suddenly flashed open, and he was looking up at her, green eyes intent as he kissed her between her thighs, in that place *no one* but she had ever touched.

The sight was too much. An implosion started at her center, sending out sparkling waves. She bit her lip and shut her eyes, unable to hold his gaze while suffering this final, intimate pleasure. It was shameful. It was wonderful. She shuddered and quaked beneath the shattering release, and she did it all in front of *him*. She thought he would draw away, but he continued with tiny, intimate kisses, making the aftershocks go on and on until her legs trembled and she feared she would fall.

Then he was surging up her, catching her about her waist and setting her on the settee. He threw her clothes on top of her, and before she could wonder what he was about, he lifted her high against his chest.

She clutched at his shoulders as he strode to the library door, and she realized what he meant to do. "You can't!"

"Watch me," he replied.

She feared servants, but no one was about as he ran across the short hallway and up the stairs. He strode down an upper hall and shouldered open a door at the far end. She just had time to see a full bath, a few crumpled towels, and a huge bed with atrocious flaming orange drapes, and then she was bouncing on the bed.

Griffin flung her clothes rather cavalierly to the floor, stripped off her slippers, and then stood looking down at her.

She held her breath, wondering what he expected of her. She'd never done this, hadn't planned it, and was in no way prepared. She started to prop herself on one elbow, but he slowly shook his head.

"Stay there." He raised his hands over his shoulders, grasping the back of his shirt. "Stay still."

He drew his shirt off over his head and doffed his breeches.

She'd seen naked males before. Statues, pale and entirely denuded of hair. A few living boys or even young men, their shirts removed for labor.

She'd never seen *this* man nude, though. He was brown all over. What she'd taken for skin tanned by the sun was instead naturally olive toned. His shoulders were wide and square, and in contrast to those unliving statues, there was hair upon his body. Sprinkles of it, dark and curling, from one brown nipple to the other, a bare patch between chest and belly and then a gradually widening line of dark hair from his navel to the bush about his genitals. The hair there was thick and black, and his penis rose ruddy and dark from it, a strange, foreign, *male* thing.

She looked and looked and felt herself clench internally at the sight, the wonder, of being free to inspect his nude body. She'd held that part of him in her hands, but she'd never seen it. It rose almost vertical to his belly but stood away from his body. Thick veins twined about its length, leading to a fleshy cap, swollen past his foreskin. It gleamed faintly in the candlelight, reddish purple and ready. It was the most magnificent thing she'd ever seen in her life—and the most frightening.

"Do you like it?" he asked, grasping himself.

She watched, mesmerized, as he pulled the skin down the shaft and then up again, cupping the head in his palm. Her eyes rose to his, and she could only speak the truth. "Yes."

A corner of his mouth kicked up, though he looked far from amused. "Good. I've heard of virgins running screaming from the sight."

She bit her lip at the word *virgin*.

"You are, aren't you?" he said in a voice that in any other man she might think gentle. "A virgin?"

She nodded. A virgin. She was about to lose her virginity. This was wrong. This was a sin. This was—

"Don't think," he ordered. He stepped forward to place a knee on the bed, making it dip beneath his weight. "Don't think, don't wonder, don't worry. Only feel." He lowered himself, his hands on either side of her head, his body suddenly heating hers. "Feel *me*."

And she did. He pressed his legs between hers, widening her thighs until there was a place for his hips, and settled himself on her. She could feel the rough hair of his legs sliding along hers, the hard slab of his belly, and above all, the hot iron rod lying across her mound.

She looked up at him as he lowered his head toward hers, murmuring, *"Feel me."*

His lips were gentle but not soft. He inserted his tongue into her mouth, and she knew now how to suckle upon it, how to tilt her head so that their mouths fitted together perfectly. His hands were in her hair, pulling pins out, burrowing beneath the tresses to palm her scalp, and she realized suddenly that she could explore as well.

She lifted her hands along his sides, stroking, touching his warm skin. His back was smooth, a little damp now from his bath or perhaps the heat they made between them. She skated up and felt the muscles of his shoulders move beneath her palms. This was so intimate, so quietly special: to touch a man's naked back, to feel him as he made love to her.

He muttered something and lifted away from her, breaking their kiss. He rocked to the side a bit and reached between them. She felt his fingers sliding through her maidenhair. Then he was pushing his penis against her folds, swirling the head in her wetness, pressing against her apex. She watched his face, seeing the grim set of his mouth, the slight furrow between his brows. Sweat shined on his forehead, and it occurred to her that though he'd no doubt done this innumerable times before, he was taking *this* time very seriously.

That gave her comfort.

Then he shifted and looked up, and at the same time she felt the tip of his cock at her entrance.

She gripped his shoulders in sudden doubt.

He ducked his head, catching her eyes. "Don't think. Just feel."

And he flexed his hips.

She expected pain, but there was only a strange sort of pinch. She panted, waiting for more—pain or pleasure, she wasn't sure.

He slid a little way out and then farther in.

Her lips parted as she realized that he was not fully sheathed in her.

"Relax," he whispered against the corner of her mouth.

He withdrew and shoved again, this time only a little more inside. The pinch had lessened, but the stretching, the pressure was still there, not a painful sensation, but not entirely pleasant either. He shifted then and brought her legs up, wrapping them about his waist. Suddenly there seemed to be more room. He slid partly out, his penis rubbing against her, and then shoved forcefully, his hip bones meeting hers.

She looked up at him, so full of his flesh. Was this all there was?

He seemed to understand the question in her eyes. He lay against her, his upper half braced away from her on straight arms. He smiled again, this time rather grimly, and grunted, "Feel."

Then he slid against her, his penis slowly pistoning out and into her. She gasped. He did it again, his eyes watching hers, and swiveled his hips, grinding down on her.

"Oh!" With her hips tilted up, his body was hitting that spot exactly, each pull of his cock adding somehow to the exquisite sensation.

"Feel, my heart," he whispered, and she saw that his

eyes were glistening. Before she could speak he dipped his head to tongue her nipple.

She arched helplessly underneath him. His strong body guided and pleasured hers, his hips moving relentlessly, grinding down on that one special spot. It began again, a glistening heat between her legs, growing and spreading outward until she quaked and clutched at his shoulders. There was something else here as well. It was a terrible sorrow, a welling joy, as if all the emotion she'd ever held in check or pushed away was suddenly rising to the surface. She couldn't control her face, couldn't control her body. She was coming apart, and she'd never be able to pin herself back together again.

Griffin was making love to her, and she knew in that moment that this was a once-in-a-lifetime experience. Here and only here would she ever be truly free. She held him close, terrified he would somehow stop and leave her behind.

But he didn't. He gently bit down on her nipple and rocked against her faster and faster, sweat gleaming on his neck and on his chest, until she shattered under him. She opened her mouth in a silent scream, and he filled it with his tongue and lips, shuddering into her, continuing his ride, until he suddenly left her.

She felt the splash of warm liquid on her belly and opened her eyes. He was above her, his cock in his hand, his face relaxing from the sexual tension of before.

It was over. She was no longer a virgin.

CHARLIE WATCHED AS the dice fell from his fingers. A deuce and a trey. Five could be lucky or not; it just depended on the play.

"The attack failed, then." He knew without looking up that Freddy shifted his weight from one foot to the other.

"Aye. Three men killed outright and another two injured and lyin' in bed."

Charlie grunted, scooping up the dice. He rolled them between his fingers, the familiar clink of the bones soothing to his ears. "And we're still dealing with the duke's damned informers."

Freddy didn't answer that, probably because there was no need.

"But you say Reading was seen with the duke's sister?" Charlie asked thoughtfully.

"Twice in St. Giles," Freddy replied.

Charlie nodded, feeling the skin on his cheeks pull as he smiled. "The duke, the duke. It always comes back to the duke, doesn't it? The duke and Reading, our dear friend."

Freddy licked his lips nervously.

A thump and a feverish murmur came from overhead.

Charlie glanced up as if he could see the woman lying above. "How is she today?"

Freddy shrugged. "The nurse says she took some broth this morn."

Charlie looked down without comment and threw the dice. They tumbled to the edge of the table, a trey again and a *cater*—four. Lucky seven. "Perhaps it's time we use the duke's informers to our own end. Perhaps it's time His Grace learns what Reading really does in St. Giles."

Chapter Eleven

*That night, Queen Ravenhair again called her suitors to
her throne room and asked them what their answers were.
Prince Westmoon snapped his fingers. Instantly a groom
led a prancing black stallion into the throne room.
Westmoon bowed low. "This horse is the strongest thing in
your kingdom, Your Majesty."*
*Prince Eastsun waved a hand, and a huge warrior
marched into the throne room, his chest armored in silver,
his sword sheathed in a golden scabbard. "This man is the
strongest thing in your kingdom, Your Majesty."*
*Finally, Prince Northwind presented a snowy bullock
with gilded horns. "This bullock is the strongest thing
in your kingdom, Your Majesty."*
—from Queen Ravenhair

Griffin slumped to the bedsheets, his body slaked. He lay
there on his back, an arm over his eyes, his mind entirely
blank, and all his muscles in a state of total relaxation. He
might as well have been poleaxed.

Which apparently could not be said of Hero.

When the bed shook, he realized that his lover might
not be in a similar state of enervated shock.

Griffin cracked one eyelid and watched, bemused, as
Lady Hero jumped from the bed and ducked below the

side. She straightened a minute later, trying to struggle into the remains of her chemise.

He yawned. "I know you're new to this, sweeting, but the usual thing is to lie about for a bit, perhaps do the thing over again, God and my cock willing. No need to go haring off."

As soon as the words left his lips, his brain finally—belatedly—roused itself, and he knew, absolutely and fatally, that it was the exact wrong thing to say.

She gave up on the chemise and bent to pick up her stays. Her face was half averted, but he could see even in profile when her lips thinned. "I must go."

He couldn't think very well—something more than the ordinary had happened here—but he knew he didn't want her to go. Griffin scrubbed his hand over his head, trying to find some measure of wakefulness. "Hero—"

She ducked down again.

He propped himself up and peered over the side of the bed. She knelt, rummaging through her pile of clothes. Her head, even down-bent, did not look welcoming.

He sighed. "Stay a little while and I'll call for some tea."

She stood again, pulling on her petticoats. "I can't be seen here."

He was tempted to ask why she'd bothered to come in the first place, then, but prudence—not usually a virtue of his—stilled his lips. He knew he should talk to her, but he couldn't think of the words that would persuade her to stay. His head felt thick, filled with dirty lint and smoke left over from the night awake in the warehouse.

He wasn't prepared for this, damn it.

She had on her stays now and was clumsily lacing

them. No doubt she usually had the aid of a maid. He felt a strange kind of tender pang at the sight.

He rolled to sit on the edge of the bed, his legs spread, and pulled a corner of the sheets over his lap. "Let me help you."

She stumbled back—and half turned away. "I...I can manage."

"Are you weeping?" he asked in horror.

"No!"

But she was. *Dear God.* She was *crying.*

He didn't know what to do, how to make this *right.* "Marry me."

She stilled and turned, her eyelashes spiked with tears. *"What?"*

Had he just said that? But he looked her in the eye and repeated the words. "Marry me."

It was as if something clicked into place—a missing piece he hadn't even known he lacked—and he knew, suddenly and completely, that marrying Hero was the right thing to do. He didn't want anyone to ever hurt her. He wanted to be a shield for her. For the first time since he'd come back to London, he felt as if he knew what his purpose was. He felt *right.*

Unfortunately, she didn't seem to feel the same way.

She shook her head, stifling a sob, and bent to pick up her dress.

His pride was pricked. He stood, the sheet falling away. "What say you?"

"Don't be silly," she muttered as she fought her way into the dress.

His head reared back as if she'd struck him. "You find an offer of marriage from me *silly*?"

"Yes." She had the dress over her head and started lacing up the front. "You only ask because you've bedded me."

He set his hands on his hips as anger rose in his chest. His head throbbed—he hadn't enough sleep in days—and he tried to keep his voice even. "I've taken your virginity, my lady. Pardon me if I think that a good reason to take you to wife as well."

"Oh, dear Lord." She turned to face him. Her eyes skipped over his nude body, and then she held her gaze firmly above his waist. "Have you not listened to a word I've said these last days? Marriage is a contract, a bargain between families. A pact for the future, solemnly thought out and sincerely entered into. It isn't something one just jumps into on a whim."

He shook his head. "This isn't a whim."

"Then why didn't you ask me before you bedded me?"

He stared at her, tempted to answer that he'd been thinking with the smaller of his two heads before he'd bedded her, thank you very much.

But she was already continuing, her voice horribly gentle. "You and I have no similar goals or intentions. You told me less than a fortnight ago that you never intended to marry. You're offering out of guilt or misplaced gallantry, neither of which is a solid foundation for a marriage. I've made a terrible mistake"—her voice wobbled, making his heart constrict—"but calling off my marriage to Mandeville would simply compound it."

He gaped at her. When had she thought all of this out?

He could refute all of her points, given a night's sound sleep, but one stuck out in particular. "You're not going to marry Thomas."

She arched her eyebrows. "Is that why you bedded me?"

"No!" he roared.

"Good," she said, perfectly reasonable, perfectly perfect. "My arrangement with Thomas is between him and me. It has nothing to do with you."

"I beg to differ," he said, the words sounding stupidly pompous even to his own ears, standing there naked, arguing with the woman he'd ignobly deflowered. "I'm Thomas's brother and the man you just fucked."

She flinched. "I hate that word. Please don't use it around me anymore."

"Damn it, Hero!"

"I need to leave now," she said politely, and did just that.

For a moment he stared, incredulous and stunned, at the closed door. What had happened? What had he done?

His eyes dropped to the white sheets on the bed, and he saw a small smear of blood there. The sight tore at his heart. Griffin swore and slammed his fist into the bedpost, splitting his knuckles.

Deedle came in the room, looking around brightly. "I passed a lady in the hallway, m'lord, in quite the hurry. Right pretty, though. Didn't think you was up for it, if'n you know what I mean, after last night."

Griffin groaned and dropped back to the bed, his aching head in his hands. "Shut up, Deedle."

THE DAY WAS bright and sunny, even in St. Giles, and Silence Hollingbrook smiled as she made her way through the morning market.

"Mamoo!" Mary Darling cried from her perch on

Silence's hip, and stretched out plump baby hands toward a pile of shiny red apples.

Silence laughed and stopped. "How much?" she asked the bonneted apple seller. William had once praised her apple pie—long ago when they'd first been married.

The woman winked, the wrinkles in her tanned face deepening. "For you and such a bonny lass, only three-pence a half dozen."

Normally, Silence would bargain the seller down, but the apples did look good and the price was fair. "I'll take a dozen."

She handed over the coins and called Mary Evening over with the marketing basket she held. She watched as the seller carefully picked out and filled the basket for her. The apples would make a nice pie or two for the children.

She continued on her way through the stalls. Besides Mary Evening, she had Mary Compassion and Mary Redribbon to carry her purchases, and the girls trailed her like obedient ducklings. They'd already purchased onions, turnips, and a nice lump of fresh butter, and Silence was making for a stall with a pretty display of beetroots when a shout made her glance to the right.

A small gang of boys was there—a common sight in St. Giles and indeed all of London. These boys were intent on some type of dicing game on the ground, and one boy had obviously won or lost. He jumped up and down and was immediately cuffed by another lad. In a moment, both boys were rolling in the dust, no one paying much attention to them other than to walk around the scuffle. Then as she was idly watching, she saw something—someone—beyond the boys. A graceful male figure, inky black curls brushing broad shoulders, the hint of wide, cynical lips.

It couldn't be.

She dodged to the side, trying to get a better look. He'd turned away, and there were other people, other stalls, between them. She couldn't be sure, but if she could just get a good glimpse...

"Where are we going, ma'am?" Mary Evening panted.

Silence looked around and realized that the girls were running to keep up with her swift steps. She turned back, searching the place where she'd last seen that too-familiar face.

But he was gone.

Perhaps she'd imagined him; perhaps she'd mistaken another man with long hair worn undressed about his shoulders. Mary Darling fretted and reached for an apple in Mary Evening's basket. Silence picked one out with fingers that trembled and gave it to the baby. She'd not seen him since that one awful night; surely she must be mistaken.

But she knew she wasn't. She'd caught a glimpse of Charming Mickey O'Connor, the most notorious river pirate in London.

"It's time we were home," she told the children.

She turned, hurrying away from the market. Perhaps it was merely a coincidence that Charming Mickey should be in the market at the same time as she. He did live in St. Giles, as she had good reason to know. Except she really couldn't see Mr. O'Connor doing his own marketing. Her steps quickened until she was nearly trotting. Her heart was beating in triple time, so fast and light she thought she might faint.

Mustn't show fear before the wolf.

She half laughed, but the sound was more a sob. Mickey wasn't anything like a wild, savage wolf—at least on the surface. The one time she'd seen him, he'd been dressed in velvet and lace, every finger of his hands adorned with jeweled rings. He'd been elegant and suave. But underneath, dear God, *underneath* he'd been exactly like a ravenous wolf.

Silence was panting by the time they made the home. Her fingers were clumsy with the key, and she nearly dropped it twice before getting it in the door. With a last nervous look over her shoulder, she pushed the girls inside the home and slammed the door shut behind her. Quickly she flung down the bar.

"Are you all right, ma'am?" Mary Evening asked anxiously.

"Yes." Silence placed a hand over her breast, trying to calm her breathing. Mary Darling munched messily on her apple, unconcerned. At least she hadn't alarmed the baby. She smiled. "Yes, quite, but I'm dying for a cup of tea, aren't you?"

"Yes, ma'am!" was the general consensus.

So she marched back to the kitchen with her charges, feeling marginally better.

That feeling stopped, though, when she saw Winter standing in the kitchen, his face grave. Winter never came home before his luncheon at one of the clock.

She frowned. "What are you doing home at this hour?"

Winter looked at the eldest girl. "Mary Evening, please set the marketing on the table and take the other girls with you upstairs. I believe Nell has just made some tea for the children there."

The girls obediently trailed from the kitchen.

Silence looked at Winter, her chest squeezing, "Winter?"

He glanced distractedly at Mary Darling, still in her arms. "Perhaps we should send the baby upstairs as well."

"No." Silence swallowed, laying a cheek against Mary Darling's soft, black curls. "Let her stay with me."

Winter nodded. "Will you sit?"

She lowered herself to one of the kitchen benches. "What is it? Tell me."

"We've received word from the owners of William's ship," he said gently.

Her head started to spin, Winter's words becoming indistinct.

Still, when he continued, she heard him. "William's ship has been lost at sea. There were no survivors. I'm afraid William is dead."

"YOU SEEM TIRED, my dear," Cousin Bathilda observed that night as she and Hero rocked in the carriage. "Perhaps you shouldn't have sat with Phoebe all afternoon."

They were on their way to a ball. Hero frowned for a moment, thinking. Oh, yes, the Widdecombe's ball. She might find a lady tonight interested in helping the home if only she put her mind to it. Funny how she'd had trouble concentrating all day.

"My dear?" Cousin Bathilda prompted.

"Phoebe didn't tire me." Hero smoothed her brow. "I have a slight headache."

"Shall I tell the driver to turn around?"

"No," Hero said too sharply, then inhaled. "No, it's quite all right, cousin."

"Well, I can't think it's all right when you use that tone," Cousin Bathilda said, her feathers all ruffled.

Hero stifled a sigh and made herself smile calmly. "Truly, I'm sorry to have snapped at you."

"Very well, then," the other lady replied. "It's rather late to turn about now anyway; we're nearly there. Although I do feel bad about leaving poor Phoebe abed at home. Has Maximus talked to you about her yet?"

"No, not yet."

"He must make a decision soon, I think." Cousin Bathilda had lines of worry about her eyes. "Thank the Lord the physician said her arm will heal. It would be terrible if she were crippled as well as…" Bathilda's voice died away as if she couldn't quite make herself say the word.

Hero sighed and turned to gaze out the window, though there was nothing to see in the dark. How strange she felt! As if she'd become disconnected from her body and the events around her. She should be thinking deeply at this moment, coming to decisions and making things right somehow. Instead, she found it hard to concentrate on anything at all. Anything but thoughts of Griffin and how it had felt to accept him into her body this morning. She could almost smell his skin, hot and salty, feel the hair on his chest rasping against her bare nipples, see his eyes watching her always.…

"I do hope Lord Griffin isn't at the ball tonight," Cousin Bathilda said, making her start.

Fortunately, her cousin didn't seem to notice Hero's wild glance.

"Bad enough that Phoebe seems entirely charmed by him," Cousin Bathilda huffed. "I cannot believe you invited that man to luncheon!"

"Phoebe doesn't know the particulars of his reputation," Hero replied, attempting to move the conversation away from herself.

"Naturally not!" Bathilda was shocked at the mere notion. "A precious, innocent girl like her having knowledge of the extent of Lord Griffin's scandalous ways— the very thought."

"He has his good points as well," Hero said before she could stop herself. "He's funny, and an interesting conversationalist, and he can be very kind."

"Funny and kind do not excuse a man's rakishness."

"He will soon be part of the family," Hero replied, and felt like weeping.

"Humph!" was all Cousin Bathilda had to say to that.

Her obvious indignation made Hero smile faintly. "Mignon likes him, remember."

The little dog raised her head at her name. She was curled up beside Bathilda on the carriage seat.

Cousin Bathilda stared severely at her pet. "She usually has better taste, I must say."

Mignon decided their conversation was uninteresting, since the topic didn't involve doggy tidbits. She yawned and laid her head back down again.

"Ah, here we are," Cousin Bathilda said as the carriage rolled to a stop. She gathered Mignon in her arms and preceded Hero down the steps.

Outside, the Widdecombe town house was ablaze with torches. Liveried footmen bowed and ushered them up the steps and inside.

"I see Helena has made an extra effort this year," Cousin Bathilda whispered loudly in Hero's ear. "And well she should after *last* season's debacle."

Hero was still trying to remember the debacle in question when they came upon the receiving line.

"Bathilda." A very thin lady with silvery gray hair leaned forward and almost touched her cheek to Cousin Bathilda's. "How wonderful to see you again. And you brought your darling dog," she observed with pursed lips as Mignon rumbled at her.

"Helena." Cousin Bathilda put a soothing hand on Mignon's head. "You remember my dear relative, Lady Hero Batten."

"My lady." Hero dipped into a curtsy.

"Engaged to the Marquess of Mandeville, yes?" Lady Widdecombe peered at her with faint approval. "A very good match, my dear. Congratulations."

"Thank you, my lady," Hero murmured. She felt a suffocating weight, as if a large boulder sat upon her chest. How scandalized everyone here would be if they knew what she truly was beneath her facade. She'd lost her perfection. She'd lost her place. For a wild moment she had the urge to simply turn and flee from the ballroom.

"There's Mandeville now," Cousin Bathilda exclaimed.

Hero glanced up and saw her fiancé, looking the same as ever. He was quite elegant tonight in deep brown velvet overembroidered in gold and red.

He made a leg at the sight of her. "Miss Picklewood, Lady Hero. You are the fairest damsel here tonight, I vow."

"My lord." She wondered what he would say if she asked him what feature he found so especially beautiful about her? Was it her eyes? Her neck? Her breasts? But then he'd never seen her bare breasts. Only one man had and it wasn't her fiancé.

She looked away, biting her lip as guilt battered against her.

"I hope your dear sister is better?" Mandeville asked gravely.

"As well as can be expected, my lord," Cousin Bathilda answered. "The doctor has prescribed bed rest, but he thinks the arm will knit."

"I am so glad."

"I see my good friend Mrs. Hughes over there," Cousin Bathilda said. "If you young people will excuse me?"

"Of course," Mandeville murmured. He held out his arm to Hero without really looking at her. "Shall we stroll?"

"Please," she answered sedately, calming the hysterical voices in her head.

She laid her hand on his sleeve as he led her into the crowd. The room was too hot, it seemed. Lady Helena had chosen to decorate the ballroom with hundreds of roses, and the scent of the wilting flowers was almost overwhelming. She nodded her head and murmured inanities to passing people until she thought she might scream. Her world had tumbled off balance, and she didn't know how to right it again.

And then, suddenly, Griffin stood in front of them, dressed elegantly in blue and gold, his wig snowy white. His arm was crooked, as he idly fondled something in his hand. His green eyes flicked from her face to her hand, laid on Mandeville's sleeve, then rose slowly to his brother's face.

Hero tried to swallow, but her throat was dry. Surely he wouldn't say anything, do anything, *here*?

Griffin bowed stiffly. "Good evening, Thomas, Lady Hero."

She nodded, unable to speak.

"Griffin," she heard Mandeville say beside her. "I didn't know you were invited tonight."

"It's amazing the places where I'm welcome."

She lifted her eyes at his cynical tone. His green eyes clashed with hers, his expression grim.

She caught her breath.

"What have you got there?" Mandeville asked.

Griffin raised his eyebrows and opened his hand. Hero inhaled silently. Her diamond earbob lay on his palm—the one she'd thrown at him in the sitting room at her engagement ball.

He smiled thinly. "A trinket I found upon the floor. Do you think it becomes me?"

He held the earring to his ear as Hero widened her eyes in warning. Surely Mandeville would recognize it as hers!

"Or perhaps it's better suited to a lady," Griffin drawled. He reached out, and Hero felt the heat of his fingers as he dangled the earring near her ear.

Mandeville frowned, looking confused. "Don't be an ass."

"No?" Griffin's smile had disappeared as he looked at her. "Well, maybe I'll make it a keepsake."

He pushed the earring into his waistcoat pocket.

Hero stared at him, her chest aching as if she'd been weeping. She'd lost him, she suddenly realized. They could never again be friends now.

Griffin looked at Mandeville. "With your permission, I'd like to offer your fiancée a dance."

"Certainly," Mandeville replied.

And just like that, she was handed from one man to the other, rather like a prize pony at a country fair.

Hero waited until they'd strolled some distance from Mandeville. "I don't want to talk to you."

"I know," Griffin replied low. "You seem to only want to do, er, *other* things with me."

"Hush!" she hissed desperately.

In any other man, the look he gave her might be mistaken for hurt. "I'm not going to disgrace you here in front of everyone, never fear."

She didn't know how to reply to that, and while she was contemplating it, he led her swiftly through a pair of French doors and outside.

She looked around the lovely paved balcony with wide steps that led into a shadowed garden and turned to him accusingly. "You told Mandeville we were to dance."

He shrugged, unconcerned. "We'll tell him you felt overwarm. You certainly appear overwarm."

She lifted a hand to her flushed cheek. "That's not a very gentlemanly thing to say."

He laughed shortly and without humor. "Nothing I say ever pleases you, my Lady Perfect. Have you noticed? Only the things I do please you."

She looked away, but he placed a thumb under her jaw and turned her head back so that she had no choice but to look him in the face. "You were pleased this morning, were you not?"

Hero wanted to lie, but in the end she could not, so she simply stayed mute.

He grimaced and let his hand drop with a gesture of disgust. "You won't admit it, but I know you were. I felt you as you came apart in my arms, as your sweet cunny clenched about my cock."

She shivered, remembering the feel of him, too. "Please."

He stared at her hard and then drew her down the steps and into the shadows of the garden. Pulling her along until they were out of earshot of the ballroom doors.

He turned and placed his hands on her upper arms. "We must discuss it, even if you want to forget it forever."

"That's just it," she whispered, emboldened by the dark. "I don't want to forget."

"Hero," he said low, and her name sounded like a prayer on his lips.

He bent over her, there in the dark garden, and she felt the brush of his lips over hers. They were whisper-soft, like the kiss of a knight for a maiden he held in high esteem. Did he think of her that way, even now that she'd proven herself unvirtuous? She drew back and tried to search his face, but it was in shadow. He might as well have been a stranger.

She made to step back, but he caught her hand, holding her against himself. "Will you marry me?"

She shook her head, tilting her face to look at the stars, still and empty and so very far away. "How can I?"

"How can you not?" he retorted, his voice deep. "I've pierced your maidenhead."

She closed her eyes.

"Hero." His hands rose to grip her shoulders hard. "You *must* marry me."

"Do you love me?" she asked.

His head jerked back. "What?"

"Do you love me, Lord Griffin?"

"I . . . have feelings for you."

She felt her heart tear a little. "*Feelings* are not the same as love."

"You don't love Thomas."

She shook her head. "No, that wasn't our pact together."

"Then for God's sake, why demand it of me?" he growled low and urgent. "If I'm good enough to bed, surely I'm good enough to wed."

She merely shook her head again. Panic was rising in her chest, a suffocating sense that she could never undo her wrong, that she'd never recover the place that she'd always had in society and her family.

"Do you love me?" he demanded.

"No!" The denial burst from her lips without thought or preparation. The mere notion of falling in love with this man made fear surge in her breast.

"Then why come to me? Why let me make love to you?"

"I don't know." She inhaled to steady her voice. "I... I came this morning to see if you were all right, to talk to you about the home, about your gin making. I had no notion of doing what we did."

But was that the truth? a small voice asked deep inside her. Her heart had been beating hard when she'd knocked on his door. She'd been excited, her hands trembling in anticipation. Maybe without knowing it herself, she had gone there to submit to him. To find out, once and for all, if she was more than the facade of a duke's daughter.

He shook his head, clearly confused. "At least answer my question: Why not marry me?"

She shook her head frantically. "I... I can't think. You don't understand the magnitude of this decision. If I marry you, my life will never be the same again. Maximus will hate me. He may repudiate me, keep me from the family."

"For God's sake." For a moment she could tell he was struggling to keep his voice low. Then he said urgently, "I may be a rake, but my reputation isn't *that* sordid. I doubt your brother will be happy with our match, but to cast you out—"

"He hates gin making," she whispered back fiercely. "You are a gin distiller. How long before he finds that out? You have no idea of the depths of his hatred for gin and gin makers. What he will do to you—and me—when he does find out."

He shoved her away suddenly, as if he didn't trust his hands on her. "Have you even thought of the alternative? If you go through with this marriage with Thomas, we'll be knotted together for the rest of our lives with *this* between us."

"I know," she cried. "Dear God, don't you think I've known that from the moment I rose from your bed this morning?"

He backed from her vehemence as if stunned, and in that moment she did what she'd never done in her entire life.

She turned and ran.

Chapter Twelve

*Queen Ravenhair eyed the stallion, the warrior, and the
bullock for some time, but in the end she merely nodded
and thanked her suitors for their answers. She dined in
state with the princes, but though they had much to
talk—and argue—about, the queen was nearly silent
throughout the meal. She was relieved when at last
she retired to her rooms. Once there, Queen Ravenhair
hurried to the balcony.*
*There, already waiting, was the little brown bird.
And about his neck was an acorn on a string. . . .*
—from *Queen Ravenhair*

Griffin stalked back into the ballroom, trying to look civilized, as if he wasn't actually hunting Hero down. Which was a lie, of course, because he *was* most definitely hunting her.

He paused just inside the French doors, glancing casually about, and caught a glimpse of red curls to his right. He smiled at a passing matron, who looked alarmed, and began strolling in that direction.

He'd always loved women. Ever since that first sweet tavern owner's daughter—Belle or Betty or perhaps Bessie. She'd had wide blue eyes and tits with freckles on them, and she'd shown him infinite pleasure at the age of nearly sixteen. He'd never had any particular problem attracting women, both low and quite high. They seemed to be drawn by his smile and his ease. One of his lovers had called him charming, and maybe he was. All he knew was that he took care of them for the short period they were with him, and when they inevitably left, either with a laugh or a quiet tear, he smiled and kissed them and sent them on their way. He didn't moon over them, he didn't lie awake thinking about them, and he never, ever, *ever* went chasing after them like some pie-faced simpleton.

And yet here he was stalking through a crowded ballroom, his brother and her cousin in attendance. Well. That only made the hunt more interesting, didn't it?

She was skittering around the edge of the crowd. She looked over her shoulder, and he stopped, half turned away from her, to greet an elderly gentleman he'd never met. The old man arched his eyebrows, confused but pleased, and Griffin leaned a little closer to hear his reply.

She fell for the ruse, silly, silly chit, and darted down a hallway. He straightened and turned from the old man, moving with purpose now. One glance showed that Thomas was clear across the room with a gentleman Griffin vaguely recognized as a member of the House of Lords. Griffin made sure no one was paying him any particular attention and ducked into the hallway.

The hall was lit, but the candelabra were few and far between. This wasn't one of the main thoroughfares where the ladies went to mend their appearance. He tutted. She couldn't have chosen a better place for his purposes had she acted under his own instructions.

Statuary lined the hall, eerily lifelike in the candlelight. The first room was on his left, the door ajar. He glanced inside and saw two shapes moving in the darkened room. His mouth curved in a cynical smile. She hadn't gone to ground there. The next sitting room was empty. He carefully searched it while keeping an eye on the door so she wouldn't double back past him.

The moment he entered the third room, however, he knew. It might have been the faint scent of a woman, or perhaps he heard a low gasp. Or perhaps he simply knew on a level below his senses and skin, a level as deep as his soul: She was here. He closed the door behind him, enclosing them both in near darkness. A single candle flickered, abandoned, on a side table.

Griffin glanced about the room. It seemed to be a small library or retiring room. A trio of chairs was by the fireplace on the far side, facing away from the door. Two settees were nearer to him, at right angles around a low table in the center of the room. One of the settees had its back to him, but the trio of chairs was the more obvious choice.

He smiled slightly, feeling his pulse spike, and walked slowly toward the fireplace.

She waited until he was bent over the nearest chair. There was a scuffling and a sudden flurry, but he was watching.

Griffin whirled and made it to the door before she did.

Hero halted, panting, inches from his chest.

He cocked his head, smiling not at all nicely. "Going somewhere, my Lady Perfect?"

"Let me out," she demanded. Any other woman would've pleaded.

He took a step toward her, forcing her to step back or let him run into her. "No."

She flung back her head, regal and palely beautiful.

The diamonds in her red hair glittered. "I've told you I won't marry you."

"So you have," he agreed pleasantly. "But I'm not looking for marriage at the moment."

Her lips parted, and he saw the delicate skin on her throat flutter under her heartbeat. He'd bedded her only this morning. She'd been an innocent; she'd still be sore. They were in a public gathering, for Christ's sake.

None of it mattered.

He was ragingly hard for her.

"Come here," he whispered.

"Griffin."

He half closed his eyes at her murmur. "You say my name like a lover, so soft, so sweet. I want to lick the word from your lips, sip the exhaled breath from your mouth. I want to possess you utterly. Right now. Right here."

She darted then, a hart flushed from cover, and tried to leap around him. He caught her by her waist and flung her up against the closed door.

Then he bent his head and looked her in her brilliant diamond-gray eyes. "What will it be, madam?"

HERO LOOKED INTO those demonic green eyes and knew stark despair mixed with freedom: She couldn't resist him. Why, she wasn't sure. Any other man she would've walked away from. But not Griffin.

Never Griffin.

She let her own worst impulses fly free. She raised her hands, framed his lean cheeks, and pulled his head down to hers.

Oh, yes, she needed this. She needed *him*.

His mouth was warm and luscious, and she feasted on

it like a starved child. She hadn't even known that she'd missed the taste of his lips. The taste of liberty.

He groaned and fumbled with her skirts, pulling, yanking them up. She felt a draft of cool air on her bare thighs, and then his big, hot palms were on her bottom. He squeezed and fondled her, all the while kissing her passionately, his tongue in her mouth. His fingers dipped into the crevice of her buttocks and stroked down until they met her wetness from behind.

He tore his mouth from hers, panting. "Put your arms around my shoulders."

She complied, with no idea what he might have in mind. Then he was lifting her bodily, supporting her whole weight in just his arms. She hung gracelessly for a moment until she instinctively wrapped her legs about his waist.

"Good girl," he breathed.

His hand was between them, fumbling awkwardly, and she bit her lip against a wholly inappropriate fit of the giggles. They were both completely dressed. He even still wore his white wig. How could he possibly think—

And then she felt the naked heat of his cock.

She gasped, staring into his eyes, only inches from her own.

"Shhh," he hissed quietly. "You must make no noise."

He made a movement and that broad head slid through her slick folds.

She bit her lip.

He braced one hand on the door and lowered his head to whisper against her lips. "Now."

And his cock breached her.

There was a tiny pinch, a stretching. She watched him swallow, his strong throat working. His mouth pulled in a slight grimace; there were white lines at the corners of his lips. He pushed again. She opened her mouth in a silent gasp as he invaded her another couple of inches.

The door thumped against her back.

Hero squeaked in alarm. Griffin slipped his palm over her mouth and leaned hard into the door. She looked at him, her eyes wide. He shook his head.

"I say, the door won't open," came a slurred male voice from outside.

A feminine giggle was the reply.

The door thumped again, which had the effect of driving Hero's hips hard against Griffin. His cock slid exquisitely against her, seating him fully, his pelvis brushing hers.

"Shall I try again?" the male voice asked.

Griffin leaned his full weight on her and the door, his legs braced, his head beside hers, his forehead against the wood of the door. She was spread wide, helplessly open and impaled upon his strong flesh, waiting to see if they'd be discovered.

The door gave another shudder, actually opening a crack. Griffin lunged into her hard and slammed the door back shut. Hero closed her eyes, close, so close, to ecstasy.

"Damn me, we'll find another room, shall we?" the man without said.

Footsteps tromped away.

He didn't move, holding her up, still impaled, still arched against him. They breathed together, their chests moving as one. Slowly, so very slowly, his hand drifted down from the door. He brushed over the tops of her breasts, lightly, almost casually.

She waited, her hand on his neck, feeling the animal heat of him. He burrowed beneath her skirts and traced leisurely up her thigh, toward her center, toward that point where he was joined with her. She turned her head and took his earlobe between her teeth. He circled, delicately, almost too lightly, his fingers trailing through her folds stretched wide. He reached the apex of her sex and spread his hand, pressing down quite explicitly on her clitoris.

And she jerked, hard and hot, falling from a great height, the wind whistling past her ears, glorious in her descent.

He arched away from her and pulled his cock partway out, then slammed it back into her, rough and fast and relentless. He thrust in and out in short, jerky, controlled movements, never so hard as to rattle the door, never so soft as to let her down from her fall from on high.

She wanted to scream, wanted to shout aloud with joy. This rapid energy was too much, was not enough. She wanted him to continue forever. She bit, gently, precisely, on his earlobe and his mechanical rhythm stuttered. He jerked, arched, jerked again and then thrust one last time, holding himself deep within her.

She felt heat flood her insides.

His breath was loud and harsh in her ear, and she amused herself by licking his earlobe. Then, moving slowly, he unwrapped her legs from his waist and set them on the floor.

She leaned against the door, catching her breath, watching with half-closed eyes as he took out a handkerchief and cleaned himself. How had she become so wanton in the span of less than a day?

He glanced up and saw her watching him. Deliberately, he held out the handkerchief. "My lady?"

She should have felt shame or even degradation, but instead it seemed a curiously intimate gesture. She took his handkerchief and, reaching under her skirts, wiped his semen from her thighs. She let her skirts fall and stood holding the soiled cloth, unsure of what to do with it.

He finished buttoning his breeches and took the cloth from her fingers, folding it and slipping it into his coat pocket. He twitched at her skirts, straightening them carefully as she stood there, as complacent as a child. Griffin caught her eye, reaching gravely to push a lock of hair behind her ear.

"There," he whispered almost sadly. "Your toilet is done, my Lady Perfect. No one will ever know how I've despoiled you. You are as lovely as ever."

She swallowed and leaned her head back against the door. "You've never called me lovely before."

"Haven't I?" he asked lightly. He turned away, glancing about the room, presumably to make sure there was no evidence left behind. He looked back at her, his wide mouth curled at the corner. "Perhaps I never found the need with Thomas constantly praising your beauty."

"He does it by rote," she said. "Do you?"

"No," he murmured, and touched her hair lightly. "Nothing I do with you is ever rote."

Her heart gave a pang then. What was he telling her? She inhaled to say something—what she wasn't sure—but his hand fell, and he stepped back, executing a graceful bow.

His face wore a polite mask when he said, "The usual thing in these instances is for the lady to leave first. I'll wait an appropriate amount of time before following you so that we are not seen together."

"Oh," she said, feeling suddenly naive, "of course."

Hero smoothed her skirts one last time and peeked out the door. The dim hallway was deserted. She looked over her shoulder at Griffin, feeling as if she should say something, *wanting* to say something.

He cocked an amused eyebrow at her.

Well, she could play the sophisticate, too. She inhaled and sailed forth, moving without hurry. She was new to this type of subterfuge, but it seemed sensible to appear unruffled. She walked to the end of the hall, took another breath, and slipped into the ballroom.

She was just congratulating herself on having succeeded in avoiding detection when her brother's voice spoke beside her. "There you are, Hero."

She didn't quite jump, but she may have squeaked before she turned to face Maximus.

His dark, heavy brows drew together. "Something the matter?"

"No." She made herself unclench her fingers as she inhaled and smiled brightly. "No, of course not. I didn't realize you were attending tonight."

His lips pressed together in an expression that wasn't quite a grimace as he scanned the room. "I need to discuss an urgent matter with Mandeville. Have you seen him?"

She nodded. "I talked to him earlier."

"How is Phoebe?"

She blinked and glanced at her brother. His razor-sharp eyes were suddenly focused on her. "Better. Will you come to see her again? She asks after you."

"Yes. Tomorrow afternoon, I think. I will have to tell her when I see her."

Hero inhaled, closing her eyes. "Then you've come to a decision."

"I have. She cannot have a season."

"She's been dreaming of one—you know that." Her heart was aching.

"Would you have her make a fall at a dance?" he asked gently. "Can you imagine her humiliation? I will not let her endanger either her pride or her person. We'll keep her safe with us, with her family."

"How will she make a match?" Hero bit her lip. "Surely you don't mean for her to remain a spinster all her life?"

Maximus shrugged one shoulder impatiently. "She is only seventeen. When the time is right, I can introduce a select number of gentlemen to her. Never fear. I will take care of her."

Hero nodded. Of course he would. Maximus always took care of those around him. And perhaps he was right—a season might prove too stressful for Phoebe with her failing eyesight.

Still, it would be a terrible blow to Phoebe. She had been so excited at the prospect of her season.

"You've made the correct decision," Hero murmured, glancing down at her hands.

Maximus brought his eagle-eyed gaze back to her. "Are you sure you're all right?"

"Naturally." She smiled at him rather wistfully.

It would be so nice if she could talk to him about her troubles. About Griffin and the strange, tangled relationship they had, her doubts about the coming marriage to Mandeville, and whether it would even take place. There was so much she'd like to share with him, her elder brother. She'd lost Papa and Mama too young to really miss them overmuch, but at times like these, she longed for them. To have someone who truly cared about her.

But she'd never had that kind of rapport with Maximus. Perhaps it was because of her own reserved personality or because he was so much older than she and shouldered so many duties as the Duke of Wakefield. Or maybe it was simply never meant to be. Whatever the case, she realized now that she didn't really know her brother. Not, at least, in the deeper sense. She didn't know what he feared—if indeed he feared anything. If he'd ever loved or ever cried or if, late at night, he ever suffered any self-doubt.

Of course, he didn't really know her either, did he?

Maximus surprised her by taking her hand. "I care for you and your welfare—you know that, don't you?"

She nodded silently, feeling guilt mixed with pain at his words.

"If you ever need me, Hero, you have merely to ask," he said.

He squeezed her fingers and then tucked them into the crook of his elbow. "Come. I see Mandeville in the far corner. I'm sure he'd be much pleased to see his fiancée."

She agreed because she could hardly do otherwise, but she searched the ballroom as they crossed to Mandeville. She couldn't see Griffin. Perhaps he'd already gone in to dinner.

"What is the urgent matter you wish to discuss with Mandeville?" she asked idly.

"It's his brother."

Hero stopped, causing Maximus to halt as well. "What about Reading?"

Maximus frowned down at her. "He's distilling gin in St. Giles. I will have to arrest him."

The blow was so sudden, so sharp, that for a moment she didn't feel the pain. "No!"

"I'm sorry, my dear," Maximus began. "I know he's Mandeville's brother—"

She clutched his arm with shaking fingers. "You cannot arrest Griffin. You simply cannot."

Maximus's eyes narrowed sharply. "*Griffin*?"

This was it. She'd betrayed herself. She was going to lose Maximus, lose her family and friends.

Carefully, Hero took her hands from her brother's sleeve and clasped them primly in front of herself. She must remember that they stood in a crowded ballroom.

"For me, Maximus," she whispered, her lips barely moving. "Promise me you won't touch him."

Around them the crowd talked and laughed and even shouted, but Maximus was as still as a graven image and just as silent.

Hero closed her eyes and prayed.

Finally he spoke. "Whatever Reading is to you, it must stop immediately."

Her eyes flew open. His face was pale and set, his lips bloodless. She opened her mouth to speak.

His hand rose, sharp and commanding, between them. "Wait. I will not move against him for your sake, but in return you will promise me that you will quit him. Hero, he distills *gin*." The word was spat from his lips.

She bowed her head, her heart beating fast in relief.

"Your word, sister."

She nodded mutely.

Maximus took a deep breath, and she realized suddenly that his entire body was tense and trembling, like a racehorse held back from the starting gate.

"We will not speak of this again," he murmured, and then he took her arm.

They walked sedately to Mandeville's side as Hero fought to catch her breath.

Mandeville's first words didn't help.

"Wakefield, my dear." The marquess bowed to them both, then frowned. "I shall have to take my brother to task, my lady. He seems to have abandoned you to your own devices."

"It's of no matter," she replied. "I'm sure there was someone he wanted to talk to."

The gentlemen made noises of vague assent, and then Maximus drew Mandeville into a discussion of a bill he wanted passed in parliament.

Hero listened long enough to make sure the bill had nothing to do with gin, and then she fixed a pleasant, interested expression on her face and let her mind wander. She opened her fan and behind its painted scene scanned the ballroom. Griffin wore blue and gold tonight, and for a moment she thought she saw his broad shoulders leading a lady in the minuet. Then the man turned and she saw it wasn't him. She had to warn him somehow, but she must not be seen in his company. Perhaps she could send word to his house tomorrow.

Maximus bowed and made some parting comment, but Hero was hardly aware, so caught up was she in searching for Griffin.

"I must beg your pardon for both my brother and I," Mandeville said.

"Hmm?" She glanced up to find him regarding her seriously.

"I am just as much at fault for neglecting you as my brother," Mandeville said. "I fear I have not played the attentive fiancé very well these last several days."

"Oh, my lord," she said with a pang. "I am perfectly happy with your attention."

He frowned. "You're kind as you always are, my lady, but I've been remiss." He hesitated a moment, then said, "I admire the duke very much. He is, I think, one of the great leaders of our nation. It may seem that I forget at times that it is you I have pledged to wed, not he."

She felt her lips tremble on a smile at the thought of Mandeville and her brother at an altar wedding each other, but she suppressed it. She knew it would hurt Mandeville's feelings if she found his words amusing. He meant them from his heart.

She laid her palm on his sleeve. "He admires you as well, my lord, and I assure you, I am not jealous of the time you spend with my brother. I know you both have grave matters of the nation to decide. Indeed, I am glad that our government is in such capable hands."

Mandeville gave her one of his rare, unpracticed smiles, his face becoming boyishly handsome, and she was reminded why she'd consented to become this man's wife in the first place.

He bowed. "Come, my dear. Let us discover what awaits us in the dining room."

And she accompanied him, her heart more confused than ever.

GRIFFIN HAD HAD perhaps more than his fair share of intimate encounters at balls and other social events. Ladies who were excited by the hazards and the possibility of being discovered. For others it was simply easier to meet at a ball than to risk the danger of him climbing in her window at night.

Such sophisticated seductions were urgent at the time but easily forgotten afterward. The various fumblings in anonymous dark rooms became, after a parade of similar encounters, merely ordinary. Once Griffin stepped out of whatever dark room he'd chosen for the evening, he rarely thought about the lady involved.

But as she'd proven already on numerous occasions, Hero was different.

The moment he stepped back in the ballroom, his entire attention was on her. Was she having second thoughts? Perhaps realizing this moment how very sordid a rendez-vous in the midst of a crowded social event was? Damn it, he should never have followed her down that hall. Hero wasn't like the cynical matrons he usually seduced. She was idealistic, proud, sure of her own infallibility. And he had been the one to prove how very human she was.

The thought did not shine a flattering light on him. Worse, this maidenish nervousness was enough to make a rake think hard about reform. He snorted, startling a plump matron nearby. Perhaps it was time to settle down and spend his evenings with a warm cup of milk by the fire.

His musings were still dark when he caught sight of Megs, lovely in a yellow frock with black and red embroidery, but looking a bit like a wilted buttercup.

"Oh, Griffin," she sighed when she saw him.

He raised his eyebrows. "Oh, Megs."

She plucked limply at her skirts. "Do you think I'm the sort of lady a gentleman would like to kiss?"

"Not if I'm about, I hope," Griffin growled.

She rolled her eyes. "I cannot remain a virgin forever, Griffin. I'd hope to someday have children without it being a divine miracle. That is"—her brief show of spirit suddenly flew away again—"if any man ever shows enough passion to take me to wife."

Griffin straightened, his eyes narrowing. "What has that ass Bollinger done?"

"It's rather more what he *hasn't* done," Megs moaned. "He's refused to take me into the garden."

"And a good thing, too," Griffin said with vast disapproval. Good God, anything could happen in a garden at a ball—and he should know.

"No, really, Griffin," Megs said soberly. "I know you have all those big-brother feelings to overcome, but try for a moment. How can I contemplate marriage to a man who looks appalled at the mere notion of kissing me?"

"How do you know he was even thinking of kissing you?" Griffin pointed out. "Perhaps he was worried about the cold, or good God, Megs, your *reputation*. He may—"

"Because I asked him," she interrupted.

"To...?"

"Kiss me," she confirmed. "And he looked like I'd asked him to lick an octopus. A *live* octopus."

Griffin wondered if he could punch a man for *not* kissing his sister.

"Oh," he said, which was an entirely inadequate response.

But oddly Megs seemed content with it. "Yes. You see the problem? If he's not even tempted, if he's even *disgusted* by the thought, well, what hope can there be for a satisfactory union?"

"I don't know." Griffin shook his head, trying for something better. "You know people of our rank don't marry for love, Meggie. That's just the way it is."

The thought depressed him unaccountably.

"Don't you think I know that?" she said. "I'm well aware that I'm expected to make a good marriage in which, if I'm lucky, my husband won't have half a dozen mistresses and give me the pox."

"Megs," Griffin protested, truly shocked. When had his little sister become so jaded?

She waved away his male outrage. "But I can at least find some kind of...of *friendship*, don't you think? A common understanding, a desire to do more in the bedchamber than produce an heir?"

"Of course," he soothed. He knew he should be remonstrating her over her shocking language, but he just hadn't the stamina for such hypocrisy at the moment. "We'll find you a good husband, Megs."

She sighed. "It is possible, isn't it? Caro jogs along comfortably enough with Huff. And Thomas seems content with Lady Hero."

Griffin stiffened at Hero's name, but Megs didn't seem to notice.

She wrinkled their nose. "He isn't exactly demonstrative with her, but she's a pleasant sort. I quite like her, really, and she understands that he must be pompous sometimes."

Griffin unwillingly snorted a laugh.

"It's just that..." Megs tilted her head back, staring at the shimmering chandeliers overhead for a moment. "Well, if Lady Hero suddenly died—tragically, you know, like in a terrible horse-riding accident or from a lightning strike—I think Thomas would be sad, but he wouldn't be *prostrate*." She looked at him a little wistfully. "He wouldn't want to die himself. I just think it would be nice to be married to a man who would truly mourn my loss if I died. Does that make sense?"

"Yes," he said as he caught sight of Hero across the room, ethereal and lovely and entirely out of his reach. If she died, he suddenly knew that he wouldn't much care if he lived or died. "Yes, it makes all the sense in the world."

Chapter Thirteen

The queen smiled in delight when she saw the acorn about the little brown bird's neck. An acorn grows into an oak, the strongest tree in the forest, and the forests of her kingdom were filled with mighty oaks. Truly, then, the acorn was the strongest thing in her kingdom.

Queen Ravenhair carefully plucked the acorn from the little bird's neck. She cupped the bird in her palms and whispered her secrets to him before letting him fly. Then she leaned over her balcony, searching the castle grounds, but all was silent and dark. Only a single light flickered in the stables....

—from *Queen Ravenhair*

"We lost another 'un," Nick said as Griffin entered the warehouse early that morning.

Griffin sighed and unpacked the pistols he'd brought with him onto a wooden barrel. The men were working, but there wasn't the usual laughter and loud talk. The still was eerily quiet.

"Run away or caught by the Vicar's men?" he asked.

Nick shrugged. "Don't know. 'E just disappeared."

Griffin nodded and sat to begin loading the pistols. He'd bought them used, but he'd made sure they all worked well enough.

"An' word is, the informers picked up three more gin sellers today," Nick said.

Griffin looked up. "You're just a font of good news."

Nick grinned nastily. "Between th' Vicar and the informers, I'm feelin' a bit like a doxy wi' two sailors—one takin' 'er from in front and the other goin' at it from behind."

Griffin winced at the graphic image. "Thank you for that thought."

"It's just the way I sees it, m'lord," Nick said cheerfully. "Now if we could just get the informers and th' Vicar to pay us for the favor, why, we'd be rollin' in gold."

Griffin laughed reluctantly. "That's not likely to happen any time soon."

"Naw, it isn't." Nick scratched his chin contemplatively for a moment. "'Ow's that lady what you brought 'ere the other day?"

"I asked her to marry me."

"Why, felicitations, m'lord!"

"And she turned me down."

Nick shrugged. "The ladies need time to think some matters over like."

Griffin grimaced and set down the pistol he'd just loaded. "It's more than giving her time to think. She doesn't see me as fit husband material. And then there's the small matter of her still being engaged to my brother."

"Any woman 'oo'd pick your brother over you is soft in th' 'ead, if you don't mind me sayin' so, m'lord."

Griffin smiled wryly.

"'Ave you given any more thought as to what you might do if we lose the still?" Nick asked.

Griffin shrugged, staring at the pistols.

"Me granddad was a shepherd," Nick said, gazing into the blackened rafters of the warehouse. "Grew up around sheep. Dumbest creatures in the world, mind you, so me da said, but easy and the livin's not bad."

Griffin contemplated that odd information for a moment and why it might've been offered. "You want to tend sheep?"

"Naw." Nick sounded offended. "But wool, there's money to be made in that."

"How so?"

"Yer get some sheep up north, see? You've said before that the land's bad for crops. What's no good for grain is often fine enough for animals to graze."

"That's true enough," Griffin said slowly. He was surprised that Nick seemed to have put some thought into the matter.

Nick's raspy voice was eager. "You send the wool t' London, an' it's spun and woven. I still know some weavers, used to be friends of me da. Might start a shop. I could oversee th' operation here."

"You want to become a *weaver*?"

"It's an 'onest trade," Nick said with dignity and a hint of hurt. "One that'd make us both money, too."

Griffin frowned. "Who would spin the wool?"

Nick's big shoulders moved in a shrug. "Children or women can spin."

"Huh." There was a growing demand for woolen cloth in London, both for export and to clothe its population. And as for children to spin the wool, there might be a ready source nearby.

Nick slapped his knee. "Forgot to tell you—the chandler shop on the corner makes a fine dish of jellied eels.

'Ad some just yesterday. Right tasty they are. Half a tick and I'll have you a bowl."

"Uh—"

Nick whirled and was off out of the warehouse before Griffin could finish demurring to the offer. Griffin sighed. Nick had a particular fondness for jellied eels, which he didn't share.

But then between the Vicar and Hero, the prospect of having to consume a full bowl of jellied eels was the least of his worries.

Griffin strolled out of the warehouse to wait for his disgusting breakfast. The sky above the courtyard wall was turning a pearly gray as the sun began to rise. Nick was already thinking ahead to what they might do instead of distill gin, and if there was one thing that Griffin had always trusted, it was Nick's head for business. If Nick thought they could make money off of sheep, well then—

The shot was loud in the still morning air.

Griffin ran to the gate, and only as he flung it open did he realize that he was unarmed. If this was a trap to draw him out…But, no, the narrow alley outside the warehouse was deserted.

Griffin frowned. "Nick! Where are you, Nick?"

He nearly turned back, but then he heard the groan.

He found Nick slumped inside a doorway only feet from the warehouse entrance.

Griffin swore and bent over his friend. Blood and jellied eels were splashed upon the cobblestones. Nick was trying to stand, but something was wrong with the big man's legs.

"Spilled me eels," Nick wheezed. "Buggers spilled me jellied eels."

"Forget about your damned eels," Griffin growled. "Where are you hit?"

Nick looked up and the sun suddenly rose, lighting every ugly cranny in his face. His eyes were sliding to the side, his mouth lax. Griffin inhaled and then found he couldn't breathe properly.

"Best eels in St. Giles," Nick whispered.

"Goddamn you, Nick Barnes," Griffin hissed. "Don't you die."

He grabbed Nick's arm and bent, hauling the other man's weight over his shoulder, staggering as he stood. Nick was solid muscle and heavy as a horse. Griffin made it back through the gate to the warehouse and locked it before setting Nick down on the cold, damp cobblestones of the courtyard.

"Get some cloths!" he roared to the guards. The blood was everywhere, soaking into Nick's breeches, splattering Griffin's jacket. Griffin turned back to Nick, holding his head in his hands. "Nick!"

Nick opened his eyes and smiled sweetly up at him. "They were awaitin' for me. Vicar's men. Fuckin' jellied eels."

Nick's eyes closed and no matter how Griffin swore at him, they did not open again.

HERO KNOCKED FOR the second time at the Home for Unfortunate Infants and Foundling Children that afternoon. She stood back and glanced at the upper-story windows, puzzled. Every one was shuttered.

"Perhaps no one's here, my lady," George, the footman, offered.

Hero frowned. "Someone is always about—it's a home for children, after all."

She sighed and glanced up the street nervously. She still half expected Griffin to discover that she'd journeyed into St. Giles without his escort. He'd seemed to have an uncanny ability to know when she was planning to go into St. Giles. Yet today there'd been no sign of him.

The door opened and Hero turned in relief, but her smile soon faltered when she saw the grave little figure in the doorway. "Why, Mary Evening, whatever is the matter?"

The child ducked her head, opening the door wider to let her in. Hero instructed George to wait by the door. She crossed the threshold and was immediately struck by how silent the house was. Instead of letting her into the sitting room, Mary Evening led her back to the kitchen. The child darted out of the room, leaving her alone.

Hero looked around. A kettle was simmering on the fireplace, and clean dishes were stacked to dry on a sideboard, the obvious debris from luncheon. She wandered to a cabinet and opened a door curiously, finding tea, flour, sugar, and salt.

Footsteps sounded in the hall. Silence Hollingbrook entered. For a moment Hero couldn't figure out the difference in the woman's appearance. Then she realized that instead of her usual brown or gray costume, Mrs. Hollingbrook was clad entirely in flat black.

There could be only one reason.

"I'm so sorry to keep you waiting," Mrs. Hollingbrook said distractedly. "I don't know why Mary Evening put you in the kitchen."

"You're in mourning," Hero said.

"Yes." Mrs. Hollingbrook smoothed a hand down her black skirts. "Mr. Hollingbrook...my husband, I mean."

She inhaled on a broken gasp.

"Sit down." Hero hurried over, pulling out one of the kitchen benches.

"No, I'm sorry, I just...I..."

"Sit," Hero repeated, pushing gently on Mrs. Hollingbrook's shoulder. "Please."

Mrs. Hollingbrook sank onto the bench, her expression dazed.

"When did you find out?" Hero went back to the cabinet and took down the tin of tea leaves. A brown pottery teapot was drying with the other dishes. She righted it and began spooning in tea leaves.

"Yesterday. I...Yes, it was only yesterday," Mrs. Hollingbrook murmured wonderingly. "It seems so long ago."

Hero went to the hearth and, catching up a cloth, picked up the kettle and poured boiling water into the teapot. Fragrant steam rolled up from the teapot before she replaced the lid. She'd come to inform Mrs. Hollingbrook about the new architect and the further delays in building the new home, but that information would obviously have to wait. This was more important.

She brought the full teapot to the table. "He was lost at sea?"

"Yes." Mrs. Hollingbrook fingered her skirt. "His ship went down. One and fifty men aboard, and all lost at sea."

"I'm so sorry." Hero fetched two cups from the sideboard.

"It is sad, isn't it?" the other woman said. "At sea. I keep remembering those lines from *The Tempest:* 'Full fathom five your father lies/ Of his bones are coral made/ Those were pearls that were his eyes...'" Her voice trailed away as she stared fixedly at the table.

Hero poured some tea and put a heaping spoonful of sugar into the cup before placing it in front of Mrs. Hollingbrook.

"How long does it take, do you think?" Mrs. Hollingbrook murmured.

"What?" Hero asked.

The other woman glanced up, her eyes looking bruised. "For a corpse to turn into something else in the sea? I've always found it somewhat comforting that we all turn to dirt in the end—when we're buried in the ground at least. Dirt can be a very good thing, after all. It nourishes the flowers, makes the grass grow that sheep and cattle feed upon. A cemetery can be a very peaceful place, I think. But the sea . . . It's so very cold and lonely. So lonely."

Hero swallowed, looking at her tea. "Did Captain Hollingbrook like sailing?"

"Oh, yes." Mrs. Hollingbrook seemed surprised. "He talked about it even when he was home on land. He'd always wanted to be a sailor ever since he was a little boy."

"Then perhaps he never saw the sea quite like you and I would," Hero said tentatively. "I mean, I don't presume to know what his mind was like, but wouldn't it make sense that he might have a different opinion of the sea? That he might even like it?"

Mrs. Hollingbrook blinked. "Maybe. Maybe so."

She reached forward and took the hot tea in both hands, raising it to take a tentative sip.

Hero drank from her own cup. Although the tea wasn't as fine as the type she was used to, it was strong and hot and at the moment seemed just the thing.

"I'm sorry," Mrs. Hollingbrook said vaguely. "I should . . . What did you come for today?"

Hero thought of the news she'd wanted to share about the new architect for the home. "Nothing important."

"Oh." Mrs. Hollingbrook knit her brows, seemingly deep in thought. "It's just..."

"What?" Hero asked gently.

"I shouldn't tell you these things," Mrs. Hollingbrook murmured distractedly. "It's not your concern."

"I think," Hero said, "that I would like it to be my concern. If that would be all right with you."

"Yes," Mrs. Hollingbrook said. "That would be all right with me." She took a breath and said in a rush, "It's just that when he left—when William sailed last—we were not in the concord of mind that we usually were."

Hero looked down at her tea, remembering the rumors that had swirled last winter about this woman. There were those who had been quite eager to tell her then that it was well known that Mrs. Hollingbrook had sold her virtue to a man called Mickey O'Connor. At the time, she'd decided to disregard the rumors. She trusted both Temperance and Winter Makepeace, and if they had confidence that their sister was fit to run a foundling home, then she was content with their opinion.

Hero had dealt directly with Mrs. Hollingbrook all summer and fall, and in that time she had found no reason to doubt her. She didn't know the truth of the rumors, whether they were groundless or if Mrs. Hollingbrook had somehow compromised herself. But she no longer had quite the moral authority to judge other women on their failings, did she? And even if she had, Hero would still feel at a soul-deep level that Mrs. Hollingbrook was a good woman. A woman deserving of the epithet "virtuous."

But whether the rumors were true didn't really matter at this moment. Trust could be broken over falsehoods as easily as lies.

"I'm sorry," she said, because she didn't know what else to say.

Mrs. Hollingbrook didn't seem to need an eloquent speech. "I wish I could have but one more chance to speak to him. To tell him…" Her voice faded away, and she shook her head before drawing in a shaky breath. "I just wish we had not parted on such unfriendly terms."

Hero hesitantly reached out a hand toward the other woman. She didn't know her well—they were of different classes—but grief was universal.

Mrs. Hollingbrook clutched her hand convulsively. "It's selfish, I know, but I keep thinking 'it's over now.' "

"What is?" Hero asked gently.

Mrs. Hollingbrook shook her head again, and tears suddenly ran down her cheeks. "My life, everything I… I thought I'd have. This was my love; this was my marriage. William and I were happy once. I'm explaining it badly." She closed her eyes. "Love—*happiness*—isn't so very common, really. Some people never find it in all their lives. I *had* it. And now it's gone." She opened her eyes, staring without hope. "I don't think love like that comes twice in a lifetime. It's over. I have to go on without it now."

Hero looked down, tears misting her own eyes. *Love isn't so very common.* She'd known that in an intellectual sort of way, but here was someone who'd had it and then lost it. She had a sudden, near-panicked urge to see Griffin. She had to warn him that Maximus knew of his distillery. She had to touch his hand, to assure herself that he was whole and alive. She had to hear him breathe. Was this love, this longing? Or was it a sly facsimile?

"Pardon me," Mrs. Hollingbrook said, wiping at her tears. "I'm not usually so maudlin."

"Don't apologize," Hero said firmly. "You have suffered a great shock. It would be strange if you were not melancholy."

Mrs. Hollingbrook nodded wearily.

Hero stayed a few minutes longer, drinking the tea in companionable silence. But her urge to see Griffin—to feel for herself that he was alive and well—was still strong. She soon excused herself and walked rapidly to the door.

On the tedious carriage ride back to the better parts of the West End, she couldn't stop herself from dwelling on the most grotesque thoughts: Griffin dragged before a magistrate, condemned and humiliated, and the most horrifying of all—his limp body swinging from a hangman's knot.

By the time she mounted the step to his town house, she was near hysterical with her own morbid imaginings.

The door was pulled open by Griffin himself. He didn't seem to employ very many servants. He scowled down at her, the stubble thick on his jaw, his shirt open at the throat, and his bare head tousled. Deep shadows circled his eyes.

"What are you doing here?" he growled.

Her relief at seeing him well, albeit surly, brought contrary irritation to her chest. "Will you let me in?"

He shrugged and stepped back, his grudging movement ungracious.

She entered anyway, following when he turned his back

and led the way into his library. She took a moment to look about. Last time she'd come here, their argument had flared so fast and intense she hadn't had time to notice his house.

Now she saw that his library was expensively if carelessly appointed. An exquisite painted globe of the world was draped with a waistcoat. Several small paintings of saints, delicate and fine and looking very old, hung on the wall, but two were crooked and all were dusty. The bookshelves were filled to overflowing, the books crammed against each other in whatever way they'd fit. In just a glance, she saw a large book of maps, a history of Rome, a naturalist's study, Greek poetry, and a recent edition of *Gulliver's Travels*.

"Have you come to critique my reading taste, my lady?" Griffin poured himself a brandy.

"You know I have not." She turned and looked at him. "I've begun the Thucydides, though I'm afraid I'm very slow. My Greek is rusty."

"Do you like it?"

"Yes," she said simply, because it was true. The work necessary to understand the Greek script made her feel all the more accomplished when she did finish a paragraph.

She waited for a reply from him.

But he shrugged and tossed back the brandy. "Why have you come?"

"To warn you about my brother." She removed a stack of books from one end of a settee and sat since he made no move to offer. "He knows that you're distilling gin in St. Giles."

He stared at her. "That's it?"

She frowned, her irritation increasing. Didn't he care about his own safety?

"Isn't that enough? You must give up your still at once, before Maximus sends soldiers to arrest you."

He studied the amber liquid in his glass. "No."

She felt wild frustration rising within her breast. Maximus may have given his word that he wouldn't act against Griffin, but as long as Griffin had his still, he was in danger. "Whyever not? You're more than a man who is good at making money, Griffin. So much more. You're caring and funny and noble. Can't you see that—"

He looked up at her, and she caught her breath, cutting off her words. His green eyes shone as if with tears.

"What is it?" she whispered.

"Nick is dead," he said. "Nick Barnes. He started the still with me. You may not remember him—he was with me when you saw the still. The big man with the scarred face."

"I remember." She remembered that they had seemed to be friends despite the difference in their station. She looked at him. "What happened?"

"Nick went out this morning to get jellied eels." Griffin made an odd face, half grimace, half smile. "He loved jellied eels. The Vicar's men shot him and I found him...."

His voice trailed away as he shook his head.

She rose and crossed to him, unable to stay so far away when he was in pain. "I'm sorry." She took his face between her palms. "I'm so sorry."

"I can't leave it now," he rasped, his pale green eyes intense. "Don't you see? They murdered Nick. I can't let them get away with it."

She bit her lip. "But your life is in danger."

"And what is it to you?"

Her mouth dropped open. "What?"

He let his glass fall to the carpet, where it rolled under the settee. His hands grasped her shoulders. "What do you care if my life is endangered? Am I a friend you share a bed with? A brother-in-law you'll invite to your wedding? What, Hero? What am I to you?"

She stared at him, trying to find the words. She cared for him, that much was true, but beyond that she couldn't tell him. She hadn't the words to describe her feelings.

She simply didn't know.

He seemed to understand her dilemma. Frustration warred with despair in his eyes.

"Damn you," he hissed, and kissed her.

HER LIPS WERE soft and yielding, but that didn't assuage Griffin's anger. He wanted to imprint himself upon her. To make her acknowledge that he was more than simply a *friend* or a potential brother-in-law. To ensure she never forgot him.

He wanted to engrave himself upon her very bones.

His grief and anger over Nick's death seemed to twist and transform until all he felt was a raw ache for Hero. Right here. Right now.

He arched her over his arm, cruelly putting her off balance as he ravished her mouth. He could feel the clutch of her fingers in his back, but she wasn't struggling. She made no effort to escape him or his savage plundering of her mouth.

That placated the beast within him a little. He pulled back and looked into her diamond eyes. They were dazed, blurred with sensuous need. He picked her up, ignoring her squeak, and bore her from the library like a rapacious Viking marauder.

Deedle had just entered the hallway. The valet's mouth dropped open as his master passed.

Griffin shot him a glare, ensuring there would be no unasked-for comments. Then he was mounting the stairs with Hero in his arms.

She buried her face against his chest. "Oh, Lord! He saw us."

"And he won't say a damned thing if he wants to keep his position," Griffin growled.

He strode down the upper corridor and carried her into his bedroom, kicking the door closed behind him. He flung her down on the bed and immediately began prowling up her supine form.

She looked at him with sleepily erotic eyes and whispered, "But he'll know what we're doing in here."

"Good." He straddled her, caging her with his body. "Were it up to me, all of London would know what we do here."

Her eyes widened at his words and he expected protestations. Instead she reached up and ran her palms over his head.

"Griffin," she said, low and a little sadly. "Oh, Griffin."

The sadness made his chest hurt, but he wouldn't have been deterred even if she had argued. Not now. Not this time. A great urgency was building inside of him, a need to complete this with her before it was too late. He tore at the laces to her bodice like a ravening beast.

She didn't try to stop him but simply lay beneath him and smoothed her hands over his short hair as if to soothe him. He got her bodice open and threw it aside, impatient. Her stays seemed to resist him willfully. He who had never had trouble removing the clothing of any woman.

"Let me," she murmured, and gently set aside his shaking hands.

She unlaced her stays, and he filled his hands with her warm flesh. He made himself calm, touching her as delicately as he was able to in this state.

"All of it," he ordered. "Take off all of it."

She raised her eyebrows but complied, slowly working herself out of the miles of expensive fabric while he went quietly insane. When at last she'd kicked off her shoes and reached for her ribbon garters, he reared up.

"Leave them."

He examined her, like a connoisseur with a particularly fine piece of artwork. Her body was slight, her breasts high and delicate, her hips slim, and her moonlight skin seemed to glow in his dim bedroom. The tuft of hair at the apex of her thighs was a gleaming red beacon.

His cock was hard and throbbing, but it wasn't lust he felt looking at her, naked and vulnerable beneath him. It was a strange kind of possessiveness, a need to keep her close, to defend and honor her. She could be hurt in so many ways, this proud woman, and the thought of each was like the cut of a knife, so that in the end his very soul seemed to be awash in blood.

Couldn't she see his blood? Couldn't she keep him from hurt in return?

He looked at her, wanting, hating, needing. She had a trio of faint freckles on her left shoulder, and he bent to lick them.

Her hands clutched at his head. "Griffin."

"Hero," he murmured mockingly. He bit gently at the juncture of her shoulder and her neck. "Do you like that?"

"I...yes," she whispered, and he was filled suddenly with a kind of melancholy yearning.

"What else do you like?" he asked.

"I want to touch you."

He drew back and looked at her. She lay quietly, watching him with those serious diamond eyes. He was used to being the one who led the seduction. He did things to his lovers; they rarely reciprocated. Possibly it was a need to be in control or simply the dominant male animal asserting itself. In any case, he was unused to handing over the reins of lovemaking.

"Please," she said.

Reluctantly he moved aside, ready to catch her should she jump up and try to escape. But she rose and knelt beside him, looking at him curiously. He still wore his breeches and shirt.

She touched his throat with a single finger, trailing it down to where his shirt parted on his chest. "Take this off, please."

He shifted enough to tear the shirt off over his head.

"Now your breeches."

He kicked them and his smallclothes off and lay back down, naked.

She sat on her knees for a moment, her head tilted curiously as she simply looked at his body. He itched to move. To grab her and roll her under him. But he took a breath and let her have her moment of silent examination.

Then she placed both hands on his chest, her fingers tightening a little, kneading the muscle above his nipples. Her eyes half closed.

"I didn't know men had such hair upon their bodies," she said quietly. "It's never there on statues—unless in neat small whorls over the groin. But you have more than that, don't you?"

Her hands stroked up, his chest hair curling over her fingers before springing back. It tickled a little, pulled a bit more. He moved his legs restlessly. He'd never thought much about his own body, save as it could please either him or a lover.

"Does it disgust you?" he asked.

"No," she said consideringly. "It's just so very… foreign."

Her fingers were tracing over his belly now, circling his navel. She glanced at him. "Does it itch?"

His eyebrows rose in sudden humor. "No. Sometimes it catches in my clothing, which is quite painful, but that doesn't often happen."

She nodded, seemingly content with that answer. Her fingers were stroking through his pubic hair now, close to but not quite touching his cock.

"You have it, too," he whispered. He lifted a hand to thread his fingers through her pretty red curls. Her legs were closed tightly, so he could do no more than pet.

She looked down, watching his hand in her maidenhair as if fascinated by the sight. "It's strange, isn't it? We wear so many clothes, laced, buckled, and tied up tight, and yet underneath we are like"—she spread her fingers, catching the base of his cock in the crook of her thumb and forefinger—"*this*."

She looked up, meeting his gaze, her own solemn. "Do all lovers think like this? That they have a secret just between the two of them? Is this what it was like with your other women?"

Something about the way she classed herself in with

the faceless other women he'd bedded disturbed him deeply. They were transitory. Mere phantoms that came and went in his life.

She was more to him than that.

He wrapped his hands about her slim waist and lifted her up and over him so that her legs straddled his thighs. "What other women? I can't remember any woman before you."

He pulled at her, intending to bring her closer so he could kiss her, but she forestalled him with a hand against his chest. "Your words are pretty, my lord, but the fact remains. There were other women in the past, and there will be other women in the future."

"No." His denial was hard, immediate, and given without any prior thought. By talking of a future in which he had other lovers—a future in which they were apart—she implied that someday she would have another lover. Neither possibility was admissible.

He jerked her close and rolled her beneath him, lying on her heavy and hard. He might be crushing her, but he didn't care.

She had to understand.

"There are no others, either for you or for me," he said, his nose nearly pressed against hers. "No other people live outside this room. There is only you and I and *this*."

He shoved into her. She was tight and not quite ready, but he pressed relentlessly. He would not be forestalled; he would not retreat.

"Griffin," she gasped. She arched beneath him, her legs widening.

That gave him a little more room. He took advantage of that fact, pressing forward into her lush heat.

"You and I," he panted, "are special. This isn't like what everyone else does. It isn't like anything I've ever had before. We are unique together."

"That can't be," she said stubbornly, even as her slim fingers gripped his buttocks.

"It is," he said against her mouth. Why wouldn't she believe him? Why this denial of something nearly mystical? "Listen to me. I will never have another lover like you. You will never have another lover like me. What we have should be cared for and cherished."

And he pushed one last time and seated himself finally. She was wet now, grasping at his penis in erotic little twists that made his balls draw up tight, made his brain go fuzzy.

"But I don't think—" she began, maddening, maddening creature.

And since he could no longer form a coherent argument, he did the next best thing. He covered her mouth with his, thrusting his tongue into her honeyed warmth, his hips moving of their own accord. God! This was heaven, though he'd surely be damned by that blasphemous thought. She was soft and giving beneath him, making small animal sounds against his mouth, her hips cradling his, and all that time her sweet cunny gave and gave and gave.

He'd lost the ability to move with any finesse. Years of sophisticated practice in lovemaking fell by the wayside because he'd not been lying: This was unlike anything he'd ever experienced before. Where before he'd been performing a physical act, now he did something that involved both body and soul.

With Hero, this ancient movement was making love.

He threw back his head, glorying in the sensations, physical and mental. She made him believe he could fly. He looked down and watched her face, glowing with exertion. Her eyes were closed, a slight frown between her brows, her mouth a little parted. She bit her bottom lip as he watched, and he knew she was close.

Close and he could make her fall over the edge.

He hitched himself up, pressing against the apex of her thighs with each thrust, rubbing against her little bud. She swallowed, her delicate throat working.

He grit his teeth and held out. He was close as well, but he'd not go until she'd found her bliss. He lowered his head and whispered in her ear, "Come for me, sweeting."

She shook her head stubbornly.

"Yes," he murmured against her neck. He could taste salt and woman, and his cock jumped within her.

She moaned.

"Let me feel your honey." He licked down over her breast. "Come for me."

She arched, her legs moving restlessly.

"Come, my love," he murmured against her nipple, and then sucked that tender bit of flesh into his mouth. He drew it between his teeth and bit carefully, gently.

And she came apart in his arms, her cunny squeezing so exquisitely about his cock he let go of her nipple and arched back. He shouted his agony, holding himself deep within her as he jerked and jerked again in almost painful bliss.

She was his, he was hers, and at this moment in time their world was complete.

HERO STARED AT the canopy over Griffin's bed and traced circles on his broad back. He'd collapsed on top of her

after their lovemaking and showed no signs of moving.
Her legs were splayed wide beneath him, his penis still
lodged within her. It was not a graceful pose, but at the
moment she didn't care.

She held him tenderly in her arms, this big, strong man.
This man who shouted at her and carried her off—twice
now!—to his bedroom to have his wicked way with her.
He was stubborn and rude and made his living making
gin. He was everything she disapproved of, in fact, and
yet, if he stirred right now and indicated he wanted to
make love again, she'd do it.

And what's more, she had no doubt that she'd enjoy it.

Was this love? Silly question. She was too mature to
mistake physical lust for love, but still…the question
whispered in her brain. If she felt nothing for him, surely
she wouldn't have this near-constant longing to be with
him? Surely she wouldn't be already mourning their coming separation?

He sighed and lifted off of her, his penis sliding from
inside her. She felt bereft.

"I'm sorry," he said, his words slurring a bit. "I didn't
mean to crush you."

"You didn't," she replied, as polite as if he'd apologized
for stepping on her foot while dancing.

He grunted and threw an arm around her shoulders,
scooping her close to his side. She lay against him, watching the rise and fall of his chest, the flutter of his eyelashes
as he drifted into sleep.

She inhaled and smelled his scent—male and sexual.
She thought about how she felt when she was with him,
about the way he looked at her sometimes, as if she were
a strange and very precious bird whose song he couldn't

quite figure out. She thought about Mandeville and his perfection and about Maximus and his pride and his hate. She thought about herself and what she'd learned since that fateful carriage ride when she'd placed her hand on a bare male cock. *Griffin's* bare cock.

And as the shadows began to lengthen along the wall, she came to a decision.

She knew what she must do.

Chapter Fourteen

The next morning, the three princes—looking somewhat
grim—assembled in the stable yard, for the queen
wished to go riding. When everyone was mounted,
Queen Ravenhair faced her suitors and asked, "What is
the heart of my kingdom?"
She glanced once at the stable master, so swiftly that no
one might have noticed. But the stable master touched
his finger to his cap, and his lips curved just a tiny
bit at the corners.
Then the queen rode out of the stable yard with
the princes....
—from *Queen Ravenhair*

"I do not see why Mrs. Vaughan must hold a musicale every season," Cousin Bathilda said the next morning at breakfast. She waved an invitation furiously in the air, causing Mignon, sitting on her lap, to snap at it.

Hero surreptitiously moved Cousin Bathilda's imperiled teacup away from the edge of the table.

"She never spends the money necessary to employ musicians of any talent," Cousin Bathilda continued, "and thus we are all forced to listen to off-key violinists and tipsy sopranos while partaking of squashy cakes and watered wine."

"If her events are so awful, why go?" Phoebe asked reasonably. It was the first morning she'd felt well enough to come down to breakfast. Her right arm was bound tight to her chest, and she used her left a little awkwardly to eat.

"My dear gel," Cousin Bathilda said severely, "Mrs. Vaughan is sister to the Duchess of Chadsworth, who is mother to the future Duke of Chadsworth, a very fine catch indeed. It would not do to insult her."

Phoebe wrinkled her nose. "Well, Hero is already engaged and *I* think the future Duke of Chadsworth is mentally deficient. *And* he has no chin." She popped a bite of roll into her mouth.

"Hero, explain to your sister the importance of remaining in the good graces of duchesses, irrespective of whether their sons have chins or not," Cousin Bathilda commanded.

Hero opened her mouth to say something vague. Her mind wasn't really on the conversation. All she could think about was the appointment she intended to make immediately following breakfast.

Fortunately, Cousin Bathilda hadn't really wanted someone else speaking for her. "No matter one's own rank, one should never irritate the sister of a duchess. It's simply bad form."

"*I* think it's bad form for her to hold boring musicales," Phoebe said pertly.

"You are but a child," Cousin Bathilda pronounced. "You'll understand better when you come of age, won't she, Hero?"

"Um..." Hero looked at the older woman blankly for a moment as her mind caught up with the breakfast-table conversation. "I suppose so."

Cousin Bathilda was feeding Mignon a bit of bacon and wasn't paying much attention to her, but Phoebe looked at her curiously, squinting a bit through her spectacles. "Are you feeling quite the thing?"

"Oh, yes." Hero took a sip of her tea and found it had gone cold. "Why?"

Phoebe shrugged. "You seem distracted."

"Wedding nerves," Cousin Bathilda said. "I've seen it before. A gel gets all fuzzy-minded the closer the date comes. Soon she'll not make a lick of sense at all."

"You make getting married sound like a debilitating disease," Phoebe laughed.

"For some it is," Cousin Bathilda said darkly. "Now finish up your breakfast. Maximus said he'll be calling on you this morning."

Bathilda gave Hero a significant glance, and Hero realized that Maximus must be coming to tell Phoebe the bad news about her season—or lack thereof.

On that ominous note, Hero excused herself and called for a carriage to be brought round. She couldn't bear to sit at the table any longer, listening to Cousin Bathilda talk about her marriage, and she was worried about Phoebe. Poor Cousin Bathilda was going to be so upset when she heard what Hero was about to do.

The thought wasn't pleasant, and it brought with it the realization of all the other people she was about to disappoint. Dear Lord, her family might never forgive her. But her plan was the right thing to do, even if it was not the easiest, so she held her head high as she stepped down from the carriage outside Mandeville House.

The hour was unfashionably—indeed scandalously—early, and she hadn't brought a chaperone. The butler lifted his eyebrow faintly when she requested to see Mandeville, but he showed her into the sitting room readily enough. Hero paced to the mantel and stared sightlessly at some Mandeville ancestor's portrait. What she planned to do would infuriate Maximus, nullify their bargain, and put Griffin in danger. After talking to Thomas, she would have to go to Maximus and throw herself on his mercy. Perhaps if she promised to—

Thomas opened the door.

He crossed to her immediately, his handsome features worried. "What is it, my dear? Has something happened?"

Now that he was before her, tall and imposing, Hero found she had trouble putting together the words. "I..." She cleared her throat and looked about the room. A group of chairs sat together in one corner. "I need to talk to you. Will you be seated?"

He blinked and she fought down nervous laughter. No doubt he was rarely if ever told to take a seat in his own home—or anywhere else for that matter. He was a marquess. What she was about to do suddenly made her quail. Before she could change her mind, she hurried to the chairs and sat down. Mandeville followed more slowly, frowning now.

Hero waited until he sat across from her and then just said it. "I cannot marry you."

He shook his head, his expression clearing. "My dear, such bridal nerves are common, even for a woman as level-headed as you. Don't worry that—"

"No," she said, causing him to abruptly close his mouth. "I'm not suffering from nerves or...or any kind of womanly hysteria. I simply cannot marry you."

She bit her lip as he stared at her.

"I am sorry," she offered belatedly, conscious that she was making a hash of this.

He stiffened at her apology, possibly realizing for the first time that she was serious. "Perhaps if you explain to me the problem, I can help."

Oh, Lord, if only he weren't so reasonable!

She looked down at her hands. "I've simply come to the understanding that... that we won't do together."

"Is it something I've done?"

"No!" She looked up quickly, leaning forward earnestly. "You're everything a lady could hope for in a husband. This has nothing to do with you. It's me, I'm afraid. I just can't marry you."

He shook his head. "The marriage contracts have been drawn up and our engagement announced. It's too late to change your mind, my dear. You protest otherwise, but I believe this is simply a case of bridal anxiety. Perhaps if you go home and rest, spend the day abed with some tea. I do feel—"

"I'm not a virgin any longer, Thomas."

His head reared back as if she'd struck him. "My dear..."

"I can't with good conscience marry you," she said softly. "It would not be fair to you."

For a moment he simply stared at her, and she thought he'd realized that this was final.

Then he spoke.

"I cannot pretend joy at this news," he began ponderously. "But it isn't as earth-shattering as all that. I will, of course, want to wait long enough to make sure any offspring is mine, but—"

Dear God, but she wanted to scream! "I lay with your brother, Thomas."

He stared at her, his face slowly going red.

She stood. "I've compromised myself and sacrificed both my virtue and perhaps more importantly my self-worth. I'm sorry, Thomas. You do not deserve this. If I'd—"

One moment she was babbling and he was staring at her stony-faced. In the next he was towering over her, his expression red and awful and completely terrifying. She had only a second of fear.

And then he struck her full in the face.

GRIFFIN MOUNTED THE steps of Mandeville House, his mind in a weary fog. Was this what grief was—a mind-numbing fatigue? It seemed so to him. He'd spent the night burying Nick. He'd paid for a coffin and burial clothes, a plot and headstone, and he watched all alone as Nick had been lowered into that cold grave. Then Griffin had returned to his still and begun making arrangements to destroy the Vicar. Just a few days more and everything would be in place to bring down the Vicar and avenge Nick. Just a few more days and then he could rest.

But in the meantime, he had other duties to attend to. This morning he was to escort Mater to the shops to pick out a settee or sideboard or some other frippery. Why she had to do her shopping so blasted early in the morning he wasn't sure, but she'd been quite adamant about the time.

He nodded to the butler as he entered. "Where's my brother?"

"The marquess is in the crimson sitting room," the butler intoned.

Griffin began striding in that direction. "I'll just show myself in."

"He has a guest, my lord."

Griffin turned, still backing toward the sitting room. "Who?"

"My Lady Hero."

Griffin paused. Hero had been very quiet yesterday as she'd left him. He'd hoped that her silence meant she was rethinking marriage to him, but surely she wouldn't say anything to Thomas without—

A shout came from the sitting room.

Griffin pivoted and ran toward the sound. A crash came and then another shout.

He flung open the door as the shout coalesced into a single screamed word. "Whore!"

Thomas was standing, shoulders hunched, face blood-red, over something on the floor. The place where he glared was concealed by the settee. Griffin felt his blood turn to sharp, stabbing ice in the second it took him to cross the room and look over the settee.

She was alive. That much he saw and comprehended. She lay in a pool of emerald green skirts but she was alive.

Then his attention was drawn to the red mark on the side of her beautiful face.

It was in the shape of a man's hand.

Roaring filled his head, white and complete, drowning out sound, sight, and reason. He took Thomas low, his shoulder slamming into his brother's belly. Thomas staggered back, hitting a chair, and they both went over, chair and all. Thomas swung a fist, and Griffin took it on the shoulder, not even feeling the blow.

Not feeling anything but murderous rage.

He lowered his head and beat, fists balled, teeth clenched, the roaring in his ears loud and total. He saw only Thomas's bloody face, his brother's mouth moving, saying something, perhaps pleading, and Griffin's heart swelled with gleeful rage.

He'd touched her. He'd *hurt* her. And for that he deserved to walk upon crippled legs.

Someone pounded on his back, but he didn't pay attention. Not until Hero shouted in his ear. "Griffin, stop!"

He became aware, slowly it seemed, of people in the room. Of an ache in his shoulder and, strangely, his jaw. He glanced up and saw Mater's face.

She was crying.

His arms fell to his side, and he stared at her, his chest heaving.

"Oh, Griffin," she said, and he wanted to weep as well. To howl his shame and sorrow.

He looked down and saw Thomas lying between his knees, trying to staunch the blood flowing from his nose with one hand. Over his hand, his brother's blue eyes glittered with rage and an answering shame.

"Griffin," Hero said, her hand on his shoulder as light as a bird's, and finally he turned to look at her.

Tears sparkled in her eyes, and one side of her face was reddened and beginning to swell. The sight enraged him all over again, but this time he didn't glance at his brother. Instead he reached for her face, his hands bloody and trembling.

He cradled her with his bruised hands. "Are you all right?"

"No," she said. "No."

"I'm sorry," he said. "I am so sorry."

He rose and tried to take her into his arms, to somehow try and make right this bloody, awful mess.

But she shook her head, backing away. "Don't."

"Hero," he pleaded, and his vision blurred. "Please."

"No." Her hand rose, delicate and pale, to halt him. "No, I can't...just don't."

And she turned and fled the room.

Griffin looked around. The butler, a footman, and several maids were standing about gawking while his mother's frail shoulders shook.

"Get out, the lot of you," he barked to the servants.

They fled silently.

He took Mater into his arms, feeling the fragile bones of her shoulder blades. "I'm so sorry. I'm a beast."

"I don't understand," she said. "What has happened?"

"Griffin seduced my fiancée," Thomas said indistinctly through swelling lips. He still lay on the floor. "He couldn't keep his hands off her any more than he could keep his hands off poor Anne."

"Griffin?" Mater looked at him, her eyes bewildered, and it nearly broke his heart.

"Shut up, Thomas," he growled.

"How dare you—"

Griffin turned his head slowly and glared at his brother silently, his upper lip lifting in a threat so primal, even Thomas understood. "You'll not talk of this. You'll not insinuate. You'll not even speak her name—do you understand?"

"I—" Thomas shut his mouth.

"Not a word, or I'll finish what I began."

Mater laid a protesting hand on his shoulder, but this was too important, even if it distressed her further. Griffin held Thomas's gaze until his elder brother nodded and looked away.

"Good," Griffin said. "Come, Mater. Let's have some tea and I'll try to explain."

And he led her from the room, leaving Thomas on his arse on the floor.

"I CANNOT PRETEND joy over your actions," Cousin Bathilda said to Hero an hour later. "But I think you have been quite punished enough for whatever transgressions you may have committed."

She gently replaced the wet cloth on Hero's swollen cheek. Hero closed her eyes, not wanting to see the anxious worry in Cousin Bathilda's eyes. She lay in her own bed now, hiding from the turmoil outside her room. The entire side of her face throbbed where Thomas had struck her. Mignon was beside her, the little dog's nose against her good cheek as if to give comfort.

Sudden tears flooded Hero's eyes. "I don't deserve your care."

"Nonsense," Cousin Bathilda said with some of her former vigor. "The marquess had no right to strike you. The very idea of hitting a lady! It's very lucky he didn't break your cheekbone. Really, it's for the best that you shan't marry the man after all if he has such violent impulses."

"He was provoked," Hero said drily.

The memory of Thomas's enraged face as he stood over her made her shiver. And then when Griffin had entered with such force. The sight of the brothers locked in mortal combat seemed like a terrible dream. She'd actually worried that Griffin would not be stopped until he killed his brother. How had things come to this?

"We'll have to make it a small wedding, of course," Cousin Bathilda said now.

Hero blinked. "But I'm not marrying Mandeville."

Cousin Bathilda patted her shoulder. "No, dear, Reading. And as soon as possible, before any gossip gets out."

Hero closed her eyes in weariness. Did she want to marry Griffin? Would Maximus even let her? But thoughts of her brother brought a realization.

"Oh, dear Lord, I forgot Maximus!" Hero sat upright, the wet cloth sliding from her face. She looked at Cousin Bathilda in panic. "Does he know yet?"

Cousin Bathilda blinked, looking taken aback. "I certainly haven't told him, but you know how he is."

"Yes, I do," Hero said, climbing from the bed.

"What are you doing?"

"He'll have found out by now—you know he will," Hero muttered as she searched for her slippers. "I don't know if it's by informants or gossip or plain alchemy, but he finds out *everything* sooner or later, and considering the scandalous nature of this news..." She trailed off as she bent to look under the bed. There her slippers were!

"My dear, far be it for me to stop you seeking solace from your brother, but wouldn't it be better to wait a while until he has had time to properly, er, digest the news?"

"And what do you think he'll do then?" Hero demanded as she shoved her feet into the slippers. Her hair must be a mess! She rushed to the mirror to look.

"Do? You mean...?" Cousin Bathilda gasped.

Hero turned and saw from the blanched expression on the other woman's face that at last she'd realized the peril. Without her marriage to Thomas to stop him, Maximus would attack Griffin—or worse.

She nodded and gave her hair a distracted pat. It would simply have to do—she didn't have the time to wait for it to be dressed again. "He'll want to do something, perhaps even something violent. And frankly I've had enough male violence for today."

She dashed out of the room and down the stairs, then had to pause in the front hall while a carriage was called.

"Wait for me, dear," Cousin Bathilda panted behind her. She held Mignon in her arms like a shield.

"He's bound to be in a terrible mood," Hero said. "You needn't accompany me."

Cousin Bathilda lifted her chin. "I've taken care of all of you since your parents' death. I'll not let you face him without me. Besides," she added a bit more prosaically, "it may take two females to calm him."

The thought did not make Hero more cheerful, but she entered the carriage with determination.

Half an hour later, they were knocking on the door of Wakefield House, the imposing residence her father had built. He'd expected to raise his family here, but only Maximus inhabited the grand town house now.

A flustered butler opened the door, his back straightening at the sight of her. "My lady, I don't think..."

Hero pushed past him and turned. "Where is my brother?"

"His Grace is in his private rooms, but—"

Hero nodded briskly and mounted the stairs. Normally she would never invade Maximus's bedroom, but the circumstances were extraordinary.

As it turned out, his door was open, a secretary scurrying out like a chastised dog.

Hero took a deep breath and entered the room.

Maximus was in his shirtsleeves, bent over a desk, writing something. Three other men stood in the room, including Craven, Maximus's long-time valet. Craven was tall and thin and looked more like a coffin-maker than a valet, dressed as he was all in black.

He saw her and Cousin Bathilda and turned to Maximus. "Your Grace."

Maximus looked up and met Hero's gaze.

"Leave us," he said to the servants.

Craven ushered the other men from the room, closing the door behind him.

Maximus stood and crossed to her. He stared down into her face, his own curiously blank.

Then he touched a finger to her aching cheek. "He'll die for this."

She wasn't sure which "he" Maximus referred to, but it hardly mattered. "No, he won't."

He frowned and half turned toward his desk again. "I've already sent my seconds to Reading. The matter is settled."

Cousin Bathilda drew in her breath and moaned softly.

Hero caught his arm. "Then call them back."

He raised his eyebrows. Maximus was a duke, after all. No one talked to him thusly, not even she.

But this was life or death.

"I don't want a duel," she told him, holding his eyes firmly. "I don't want any more violence, and I certainly don't want a death."

"It does not concern you."

"It most certainly does!" she said. "I am the one responsible for Mandeville's rage. I am the one who chose to give away my virtue and cause this problem."

He shook his head. "Hero—"

"No, listen," she said low. "I am ashamed of what I've done, but I will not let shame make me hide from the consequences. Call back your seconds, Maximus. Don't fight a duel that will ruin you on my behalf. I don't think I could bear to live with that."

He gazed at her silently for a moment, then crossed to the door and cracked it open. Craven must still have been waiting outside, because Maximus held a murmured conversation before closing the door again and coming back to her.

"I do this for you," he said. "Only for you, and I do not promise that I will not pursue a duel at a later date if I feel this matter is not adequately settled."

Hero swallowed. It was a great concession, even if it was only a partial one. "Thank you."

"Thank *God*!" Cousin Bathilda pronounced, and plopped into a chair.

Maximus nodded and crossed to the desk. "Now, we must settle how soon you can marry Mandeville. I've no doubt the servants will have started gossiping over this morning's affair already."

Alarm climbed Hero's spine. "Maximus—"

He frowned down at the papers on his desk. "No doubt he's upset about your liaison with his brother, but I think he will come around when he has a chance to think. The marriage settlement was very much to his liking, after all."

"Maximus!" she repeated a little desperately.

Her brother looked up, frowning.

Hero lifted her chin. "I'm not marrying Mandeville."

"Do you want me to arrest Lord Reading?"

She swallowed. "No."

He looked at her a moment and then glanced down again at his papers as if her feelings hardly mattered. "Then you'll marry the Marquess of Mandeville."

His flat tone sent a chill down her spine. She knew that voice: It was the voice of the Duke of Wakefield.

And the Duke of Wakefield did not change his course once set.

Chapter Fifteen

*That night the queen summoned her suitors to her throne
room to hear what their answers might be.*
*Prince Westmoon came forward and unfurled a
magnificent flag at her feet. On it was the emblem of her
kingdom along with an embroidered castle. "This castle,"
he said, "is the heart of your kingdom, Your Majesty."*
*Next, Prince Northwind unveiled a silver compass,
cleverly inlaid with mother-of-pearl and coral. "The
harbor, Your Majesty. That is the heart of your kingdom."*
*Finally, Prince Eastsun laid before her a sparkling crystal
globe that held a miniature town at its center. "The city is
the heart of your kingdom, Your Majesty...."*
—from *Queen Ravenhair*

The Duke of Wakefield was not an easy man with whom
to procure an audience.

Griffin had spent half the afternoon cooling his heels
in first one sitting room and then another at Wakefield
House. Presumably he was moving closer to the great
man, but at the rate he was going, it would be well past
Christmas before he got there.

Which was why he was striding down a long and formi-
dably elegant hallway in search of His Grace's study. He
had no doubt that the man didn't want to see the seducer

of his sister—and a gin distiller to boot—but that was just too bad. His and Hero's future depended on this meeting.

He passed a small library and yet another sitting room—how many did one man need?—before coming to a closed door on the right.

Griffin opened it without knocking.

Considering that he had a huge mansion with an over-abundance of rooms, the Duke of Wakefield had chosen a relatively small space for his study. The room must be nearly at the back of the house, an odd situation for the master. The study's walls and ceiling were covered in dark wood, intricately carved as if from some medieval monastery. Beneath his feet was a carpet richly embroidered in amber, ruby, and emerald. At one end, taking up nearly the entire width of the room, was a huge, rather ugly desk, also carved from dark wood. Behind the desk was the duke, scowling at him.

Griffin made a leg. "Your Grace, I hope I am not disturbing you."

One ducal eyebrow slowly rose at this bit of blatant lying. "What do you want, Reading?"

"Your sister."

Wakefield's eyes narrowed dangerously. "According to her, you've already had her."

"I have." No use trying to pretend innocence. "And that is why I desire her hand in marriage now."

Wakefield leaned back in his chair. "If you think I'm letting my sister be seduced into a trumped-up marriage with a fortune hunter—"

"I'm not a fortune hunter." Griffin flexed his fist, still sore from his brother's jaw. Losing his temper now would not serve his cause well. "I have enough money of my own."

The duke's upper lip curled ever so slightly. "Think you that I haven't made inquires about you and your business?"

Griffin stiffened.

"You're a profligate rake," Wakefield said. "You enjoy the affections of numerous ladies—the majority married. You have only a small inheritance yourself, but your brother for some reason sees fit to let you manage both it and the Mandeville lands. Add to that the fact that you are distilling gin illegally in St. Giles, and it's not a very nice picture, is it?"

Griffin looked the other man in the eye. "I don't gamble or drink to excess. I have increased what you term a *small* inheritance fourfold since I got it and confidently intend to continue to build it. I may be known for my affairs of the heart, but I fully plan to be faithful to your sister when she marries me."

Wakefield smiled cynically. "Few men of our class refrain from keeping a mistress once married, and yet you expect me to take you on your word alone that you will not?"

"Yes."

"And what of your still? Will you give it up for my sister?"

Griffin thought of Nick covered in jellied eels and his own life's blood. "No, not yet anyway."

The duke watched him silently for what seemed like a full minute. Griffin could feel a bead of sweat trickle down the small of his back. The urge to say something was nearly overwhelming, but he knew he'd laid his case before the man as strongly as possible. Speaking now in the face of the intimidating stare would only show weakness.

Finally, Wakefield spoke. "It doesn't matter anyway. This entire discussion is moot. I've already informed Hero that she will be marrying your brother on Sunday. And if you haven't given up your still by then, no doubt I will be visiting you with my soldiers very soon thereafter."

He picked up a piece of paper from his desk. The interview was obviously over.

Today was Wednesday. Sunday was only four days away. Griffin took one step toward the big desk and swiped his arm across the entire top. Pens, papers, books, a small marble bust, and a gold inkwell all crashed to the floor.

Griffin leaned across the desk, his arms braced on the now-clear top, and stared into Wakefield's outraged eyes. "We seem to be under a confusion of communication. I did not come here to *ask* for your sister's hand. I came to *tell* you I will marry Hero, with or without your permission, Your Grace. She has lain with me more than once. She may well be carrying my child. And if you think that I'll give up either her or our babe, you have not done nearly enough research into my character or history."

Griffin pushed himself off the desk before the other man could utter a word and strode out the door.

IT WAS VERY, very late at night, and Thomas squinted as he propped himself up with one hand on the doorjamb while he used the other to pound on the door. It was the second time he'd knocked, and he stepped back to squint up at the town house. This was the correct house all right, he wasn't likely to ever forget it. Which meant the jade was either not answering him or, worse, was visiting one of her many young paramours. If she was, he'd—

The door opened abruptly to reveal a large, menacing manservant he'd not met before.

Thomas scowled. "Where is she?"

The manservant began to close the door.

Thomas set his shoulder against the door, shoving hard. But his footing wasn't as firm as he thought it. Suddenly he found himself on his arse—the second time today—and red washed over his vision. He was the Marquess of Mandeville, damn it! His life wasn't supposed to be like this.

There was a flurry of movement at the door, and then Lavinia was bending over him in a purple wrap, her outrageously red hair about her shoulders. In dishabille, without the artful application of her paint pots, she looked every year of her age. And yet when he stared up at her, he thought her the most beautiful woman in the world.

"What has happened to you?" she cried.

"I love you," he said thickly.

She rolled her eyes. "You're drunk. Hutchinson, help me get him inside."

Thomas began to protest the help of the manservant, but as his legs did appear to be a bit wobbly, it really seemed a moot point. A few minutes more and he was ensconced in her sitting room on the yellow settee.

"I've always liked this settee," he said, patting the cushion beside him. He gave her a seductive look. "Some of my best memories took place here."

She sighed, which was *not* how he remembered her responding to his seductive looks in the past. "Why aren't you at your fiancée's house, Thomas?"

"Not my fiancée anymore," he said, sounding petulant even to his own ears.

Her delicate eyebrows rose. "I thought you'd signed the marriage papers?"

"She fucked Griffin."

Lavinia merely looked at him, her arms folded beneath her magnificent bosom.

He shook his head irritably, glancing about the room. "Fucked him under my own nose. Jus' like Anne. Whores, all of 'em."

She moved slightly at the second use of the crude verb. "You know I dislike such language, Thomas."

"Sorry." He laid his head in his hands, for it had begun to spin slowly.

"What happened to your face?" she asked softly.

"Griffin." He laughed, feeling his nose. It was large and lumpy and no doubt broken, but at the moment he hardly felt it. "He attacked me, if you'll credit it. After seducing my fiancée, *he* hit *me*. Should call him out."

"Did you deserve it?"

He shrugged guiltily. "I hit her. Lady Hero. I've never before struck a woman in my life."

"Then it does sound like you deserved it," Lavinia said briskly. She bent to examine him. "Even so, your nose looks quite painful."

He looked at her slyly. "You always cared for me, Lavinia."

"Not anymore."

He frowned. She could at least pretend a sentimental affection. "Lavinia..."

She sighed. "You need cold water for that nose."

She moved to the sitting room door, and he watched her longingly as she called for the hulking butler and asked for cold water and a cloth. Her wrap was a deep amethyst that hugged her luscious bottom. He noticed that her slippers were worn, though, the embroidery tattered. She should have new slippers, ones with jeweled heels. He'd give her jeweled slippers and much, much more if only she came back to him. He closed his eyes a moment.

When next he opened them, Lavinia was beside him with a basin of water. She draped a cold cloth over his nose.

"Ouch." Thomas winced.

"Hold still," she said.

He watched her as she leaned over him, her brows knit.

"Why did you leave me?" he asked.

"You know why."

"No, but really," he said somewhat indistinctly. He needed the question answered right this moment. "Why?"

"Because," she said as she lifted away the cloth and rewetted it. "You decided it was time to marry. You asked Lady Hero to be your wife."

"But why leave me?" he asked stubbornly. "You know I could've kept you in luxury for the rest of your life."

"The rest of my life?" Her brown eyes met his, and he couldn't read the emotion that lay within them.

"Yes," he said, suddenly sober. "For forever. I would not take any other mistress. I would've been true to only you."

"And to your wife, you mean." The strange spell that had been between them broke. She shook her head. "I'd not take well to being a kept woman, I'm afraid, Thomas."

"I can't marry you, damn you," he snarled.

He knew he wasn't charming anymore. Wasn't anything

but ugly, but he couldn't prevaricate. The emotion welled up in him too strongly.

"I know you can't marry me," she said, sounding almost bored. "But that doesn't mean I can't marry some other gentleman."

His head jerked back, the blow more painful than his brother's fist. "You will not!"

She raised her eyebrows. "Whyever not? You have no claim on me."

"Damn you," he hissed. He threw aside the silly cloth and grabbed her close. "Damn you!"

And he kissed her with all the desperation of a man with a torn and bloodied heart.

She tore her mouth away even as he delved beneath the amethyst silk wrapper. "This won't solve anything, Thomas."

"Might not," he grunted as he licked her neck. "But it sure as hell will make me feel better."

"Oh, Thomas," she sighed, and since that didn't sound like a rejection of any sort, he went ahead and did what he'd been wanting to do for months now.

Make love to Lavinia.

GRIFFIN WAS DOZING in one of his brother's chairs when the front door of Mandeville House opened and closed. He jerked awake, rubbing at his face groggily.

He'd tried Thomas's house the night before—after seeing the Duke of Wakefield—but Thomas had been out. When it was clear that his brother wasn't returning home any time soon, Griffin had decamped to St. Giles.

This morning he'd come directly to Thomas's house to catch his brother before he left for the day. Except

Thomas, that most staid of bachelors, appeared to have spent the night out.

Curious.

Griffin peered into the hall.

There was Thomas, looking damnably grumpy, and with a nose the size of a turnip, speaking sharply to his butler. "I don't care who has come to call. I'm not at home."

"Not even for blood relations?" Griffin drawled.

Thomas swung violently in his direction and then winced and lifted a hand to his head as if it ached. "Especially not to bloody blood relations!"

He turned toward the stairs in dismissal.

Griffin was beside him in a couple of strides. "That's just too damn bad, brother mine. You and I are overdue for a heart-to-heart."

"Damn you," Thomas started.

"No." Griffin leaned into his brother's face. "Not unless you want me hanging out your dirty laundry here and now and within earshot of the servants."

Thomas eyed him sourly for a moment, then jerked his head toward the stairs and began climbing without a word.

Since this was a better reception than Griffin had hoped for, he followed.

They ended up in a study on one of the upper floors. Griffin prowled around the room while Thomas crossed to a crystal decanter and splashed amber liquid into a glass.

Griffin raised his eyebrows. "Bit early in the day, isn't it?"

"Not for me," Thomas replied moodily.

Griffin grunted as he studied a medieval etching on the wall. "This was father's study, wasn't it?"

Thomas looked up as if surprised. "Yes. Don't you recognize it?"

Griffin shrugged. "I didn't come in here much."

"Father used to call me in every Sunday evening," Thomas mused. "Before I went away to school. Then when I was home, we'd retire here after dinner."

"What did you do?" Griffin asked.

"Talk." Thomas shrugged. "He'd ask me about my studies. Have me recite my Latin lesson when I was younger. Discuss politics when I was older."

Griffin nodded. "He was preparing you to be the marquess."

"I suppose he was." Thomas looked at him. "Didn't he do the same with you?"

"No. I wasn't invited," Griffin said without heat.

Thomas stared at him a moment as if baffled, then looked down at his glass. "What do you want with me, Griffin?"

"I want you to decline to marry Hero."

"She's already declined me."

Griffin looked at him. Apparently he hadn't heard yet from Wakefield. "Her brother wants her to marry you this Sunday."

Thomas narrowed his eyes. "Does he indeed?"

"Yes." Griffin grit his teeth. "I want you to refuse to marry her."

Thomas snorted angrily. "Of course you do. I suppose you want her for yourself, just as you wanted my first wife for yourself."

"This has nothing to do with Anne," Griffin said as calmly as he could.

"Oh, no?" Thomas sneered. "Poor, poor Anne! What would she do if she knew her lover had forgotten her so easily? But then you do go through women fast enough. I suppose there's little point in learning their names, much less remembering them when dead. Have you told Hero about Anne?"

"Yes."

The reply pulled Thomas up short. He blinked before recovering. "What? That you make a habit of seducing your brother's women?"

"No. I told her that I'd never touched Anne." Griffin met his brother's somewhat bloodshot eyes grimly.

Thomas barked a laugh. "You lie."

"No, I do not." Griffin couldn't stop the heat entering his tone. God! He'd lived with this slander for *years.* "I never made love to Anne, never seduced her, never had any intention of seducing her. If she told you otherwise, she lied."

"Anne told me on her *deathbed* you were her lover." Thomas banged his glass down on the side table. "She told me the baby was yours. She said you'd been lovers for months, that you'd started seducing her before we'd even wed."

"And I told you at her funeral that she lied!"

"Do you really expect me to believe a known rake over my *wife*?"

"I expect you to believe your *brother*!" Griffin's shout echoed about the room. He bent forward, grasping the back of a chair, trying to regain his composure. "Jesus, Thomas. How could you? How could you believe I would seduce your wife? I'm your brother. You never even thought to give my words credence. You just believed a hysterical woman dying in childbirth over me. It was as if you'd been expecting it all along, and her words merely confirmed your suspicions."

"I had been expecting it." Thomas picked up his glass and drained it. "You flirted with Anne, admit it."

"Yes! Fine! I flirted with her. I flirted with her like every other gentleman does with every other lady in a ballroom." Griffin threw up his hands. "But that was all it ever was. It never went beyond silly words in public. I never *meant* it to go beyond that."

"She loved you."

Griffin inhaled. "If she loved me, it wasn't because I encouraged her. You know that, Thomas. Once you were married, once I realized that she might be taking our social flirtation at all seriously, I went north."

But Thomas was shaking his head. "You knew she had a tendre for you and you exploited it."

"Why the hell would I do such a thing?" Griffin asked in exasperation.

"Jealousy." Thomas gestured with his glass. "You said it yourself: Father never invited you to his study. You weren't the heir."

Griffin laughed incredulously. "Do you think me such a pathetic man that I'd seduce my brother's wife out of *jealousy*?"

"Yes." Thomas downed the rest of his glass with one gulp.

Griffin closed his eyes. If Thomas had been any other man, Griffin would have called him out. The insult to his honor, to his integrity, to his very character was unbearable. But this was Thomas.

His brother.

And he still needed something from him.

Griffin inhaled slowly. "I think you know, somewhere under that stuffy, stubborn hide, that I'm innocent of this heinous charge."

Thomas started to talk, but Griffin held out his hand. "Let me continue."

After a moment, Thomas nodded stiffly.

"Thank you." Griffin looked at him. "You don't love Hero. She has admitted being my lover. I don't think you want to marry her. Let me have her, Thomas."

"No."

Despair clawed at his chest, but Griffin didn't let the weakness show. "You don't want her. I do. Don't be a dog in the manger."

Thomas laughed. "The tables have turned, haven't they? Not so cocky now, are we?"

"Don't. *Don't*, Thomas." Griffin closed his eyes.

"If Wakefield has decided we'll marry this Sunday, I fully intend to comply."

"I love her."

Griffin opened his eyes on the stark words. They were true, he realized. The understanding should've been a shock. Instead, it felt strangely right.

He stared at his brother without hope, but without fear either.

Thomas looked startled a second; then he glanced away uneasily. "More fool you." And he left the room.

HERO WAS LYING in bed that night, sleepless, her mind running in tight, erratic circles, when she heard the sound at her window. It was a tiny thing, something like a scratch, and if she hadn't been wide awake and worrying, she wouldn't have heard it at all. Could a cat have climbed up to her balcony? She propped herself up and stared toward the long windows. Her room was black, but muted moonlight lit the window dimly. She squinted. Surely—

A large shape suddenly loomed, silhouetted black against the window.

Hero gasped and choked, struggling to scream.

The shadow moved, the window opened, and Griffin calmly stepped into her bedroom.

Hero found her voice, even as her heart leaped in gladness at the sight of him. "What do you think you're doing?"

"Hush!" he said, sounding like a disapproving schoolmaster instead of a midnight marauder. "Do you want to wake the entire house?"

"I'm most definitely contemplating it," she replied, though he no doubt knew as well as she that she lied. Hero sat up in her bed and tucked the sheets primly under her arms. She wore a chemise, but she didn't want him to get any ideas that she was wanton.

Well, even more wanton than she'd already shown herself to be.

He didn't make a reply but prowled closer. The room was dark, and as he moved, she lost his shape behind the bed curtains. She felt an awful moment of panic as he disappeared from her sight, as if she'd never see him again. She reached out to brush aside the curtains and saw him by her dresser. He seemed to be studying the things on the top. Could he see in the dark?

"I've talked to your brother."

She tensed. "Oh?"

"He tells me you're going to marry Thomas on

Sunday," he said. "Our…conversation did not end well, I'm afraid."

She was silent.

"Well? Are you going to marry Thomas?"

She squinted but still couldn't make out his expression. "That's what Maximus wants me to do."

His head swiveled toward her. "What do *you* want?"

She wanted Griffin, but it wasn't that simple. If she refused to marry Thomas, there would be nothing to stop Maximus from going after Griffin. Nothing to stop him from arresting Griffin and hanging him by his neck until dead. And even if that were not the case, could she marry Griffin knowing that she would have to give up her family? Perhaps never see Phoebe or Cousin Bathilda or Maximus again? A stifling panic rose in her throat at the mere notion.

"Have you decided to give up the still?" she asked softly, desperately.

"I can't." His voice was hard. "Nick died defending it. I can't just walk away from him."

"Then I'll have to marry Thomas," she said, feeling helpless. She let the curtain fall, deliberately cutting herself off from him. "Perhaps it's for the best."

"You don't mean that." His voice was low and gritty and sounded nearer.

"Why can't I?" she asked wearily. Her heart had ached for days now, for so long that she didn't notice it anymore. It was simply there: a constant pulse of sorrow. "I can't marry you. We're nothing alike."

"True," he whispered, and it sounded like he was close beside her, the breath of his words separated from her only by the gauze of her bed curtains. "We are nothing alike, you and I. You're more similar to Thomas—staid, cautious in your decisions, careful of your actions."

"You make me sound a terrible bore."

He laughed, an intimate brush of sound in the dark. "I said you are similar to Thomas—not alike. I'd never find you boring."

"How kind." She touched the curtain with a fingertip, pressing gently until she felt the plane of his cheek through the gauzy fabric.

"I think that it's our very differences that make us a perfect match," he said, and his jaw moved under her fingertips. "You'd die of boredom with Thomas within a year. If I found a lady with a temper similar to mine, we'd tear each other apart within months. You and I, though, we're like bread and butter."

She snorted. "That's romantic."

"Hush," he said, his voice quivering with laughter but also with an undertone of gravity. She cradled his jaw as he said, "Bread and butter. The bread provides stability for the butter; the butter gives taste to the bread. Together they're perfect."

Her eyebrows drew together. "I'm the bread, aren't I?"

"Sometimes." His voice was a thread of rumbled sound, low and ominous. She could feel his words as they drifted over her palm. "And sometimes I'm the bread and you're the butter. But we go together—you understand that, don't you?"

"I..." She wanted to say yes. She wanted to agree to marry him and turn a deaf ear to all the dissenting voices in her head. "I don't know."

"Hero," he whispered, and she traced the movement of his lips through the curtain as he spoke. "I've never felt this way about any other woman. I don't think I ever will again. Don't you see? This is a once-in-a-lifetime event. If you let it slip through your fingers, we'll both be lost. Forever."

His words made her shudder. *Lost forever.* She couldn't bear the thought of him lost. Impulsively she leaned forward and set her lips against his through the curtain, feeling his heat, feeling his presence.

But he drew his head back. "Do you understand how much you mean to me? What we are together?"

She shook her head. "Don't you see how much you're asking of me? To leap into an abyss on just your words. I can't see how—"

"Then let me show you."

The bed curtains were shoved aside, and he was in bed with her. He pulled the curtains closed, and suddenly her bed was small, intimate, and dark. They were enclosed in their own tiny world, just the two of them, outside of time and space.

He drew the covers from her grasp, and she let him without even token protest. The fabric made a shushing sound as it slid down her legs, and she swallowed, her body beginning to throb with want for him. She knew him now—knew what he could do to her. What he could make her feel.

His hands touched her ankles, encircling them, warm and firm. "Hero." His voice was gritty, deep and threaded with intense emotion.

She felt his hands smooth up her calves, his touch almost too tender here in the dark. He was only a shadow, so she closed her eyes and concentrated on his fingertips, trailing over her thighs, trying to forget that this would surely be their last time together. He traced swirls on her skin, and when her breath hitched, it sounded loud in her ears. He reached the tops of her thighs, and she moved her legs restlessly, but his touch left her as he drew her chemise off over her head. She lay nude, her skin prickling with the chill of the night air.

Then his fingertips descended again, lightly skimming circles on her sides, almost tickling. Her skin seemed to tune itself to him, coming alive with tingling sensation.

She reached for him impatiently. "Griffin..."

"Hush," he whispered. "Just let me show you."

His fingers trailed from her sides to her belly, meeting over her navel. She sucked in a breath, unable to keep completely still under his touch. He breathed a laugh and scraped his nails lightly up to just under her breasts. Her nipples were tightly drawn already, pricking with anticipated pleasure. He traced the tender curve of the underside of her breast, tickling, faintly scratching, and she had to squeeze her thighs together to contain her own excitement.

When his mouth descended on one trembling nipple, hot and wide open, she jumped. She clutched at his hair as he traced around her nipple with his wet tongue, then sucked strongly. He was pinching at her other nipple, nearly painfully, his entire mouth over her breast, devouring her flesh in erotic hunger.

"Griffin," she sobbed.

He nipped at her in punishment. She gasped and raised her legs, shocked to feel his breeches against her inner thighs. He was still dressed, but at this moment she no longer cared. She raised her hips and ground desperately against him. She found him, hard and big inside the fabric of his breeches, and she widened her thighs still farther to press her aching flesh against him.

But he dropped his weight on her, pinning her open and vulnerable beneath him.

"Not yet," he murmured, and moved his mouth to her other nipple.

She tried to shift her hips, to rub against him somehow, but he lay, large and male and implacable, upon her. He held his upper body off her with his arms as he leisurely ravished her breasts, but his hips pinned her completely.

She grasped at his hair, trying to tug his head up. But his locks were shorn too short, and he merely chuckled against her nipple.

He was pulling strongly on her oversensitive nipples, and she was close—so close! If he'd just let her—

"Griffin!" she hissed in frustrated exasperation.

She felt herself heating from within, the entire surface of her body alert and ready for him. She could feel him, hard and long, against her clitoris, but he would not *move*.

"Shhh." He raised his head and licked lazily at a nipple, his breath caressing her wet skin as he whispered merely another torment. "Easy, sweetheart."

He spoke as if she were a mare in need of gentling, and at any other time, she would've made him aware of his insult. But at this moment she was entirely at his mercy.

"Griffin, please," she whispered.

"Do you want me?" he asked.

"Yes!" She tossed her head restlessly. She'd explode if he didn't give her release soon.

"Do you need me?" He kissed her nipple too gently.

"Please, please, please."

"Do you love me?"

And somehow, despite her extremis, she saw the gaping hole of the trap. She peered up at him blindly in the dark. She couldn't see his face, his expression.

"Griffin," she sighed hopelessly.

"You can't say it, can you?" he whispered. "Can't admit it either."

He rubbed his face against her breasts, and she thought his cheek might be wet.

"Griffin, I—"

He raised his head and tilted his body to the side. "Never mind."

For a moment, she thought he meant to leave her, and her heart dropped in panic. She grabbed his arms desperately.

But she could feel his muscles moving beneath her fingers as he worked his hands between them.

"Shhh, it's all right," he murmured as he settled between her thighs again. His penis was naked and big. "I've got what you want and need, if not love."

She shook her head, no longer sure, no longer able to decide what was real and what was sexual excitement. "I don't—"

"Hush." The head of his cock nudged her entrance, and she felt the delicious stretch. "That's good, isn't it?"

A rough edge lined his voice now. He entered her, one slow inch at a time, and it was torture. She made to arch up, to embed him all at once, but he shifted one hand, holding her hips firmly down.

"Take it," he growled. "Let me give you this at least."

He withdrew a bit, and she mewled in protest; then he was crowding into her again, his length endless and rock hard. He shoved and shoved again, and she felt his pubis meet her mound.

He paused, and she could hear his breath coming in quick pants, but when he spoke, his voice was even and smooth. "There. That's better, isn't it? That's what you want—good, hard *cock*."

On the last word, he reared and withdrew his length to the very tip before slamming his hot flesh back into hers. And he was right: It *was* what she wanted. It was perfect, in fact. Him moving on her like a stallion, all muscle and sweat, intent on their mutual pleasure.

He grabbed her knees and raised them higher, spreading her wide for his pleasure as he hitched himself up her. He pounded into her in a strong, insistent rhythm. With every thrust, he shoved her up the bed until her head was buried into her pillow, the pillow hard against the spindles of her bed. She gasped helplessly, glorying in his savagery. She loved this, wanted it to continue forever, wanted him to thrust into her until she forgot who he was. Who she was.

Until time itself stopped.

But neither of them could continue indefinitely. His thrusts were becoming jerky and hard, and she felt herself at the edge of her own release. She arched beneath him, her hands scrabbling at his shoulders. He slammed his mouth over hers just as she opened it to scream. Hot flashes of lights were going off behind her eyes. His cock was rubbing, rubbing, rubbing over that one delicious spot, and she was going to die from the endless pleasure.

He thrust his tongue into her mouth, and she sucked it helplessly. He ground his hips into her and shuddered. She felt the tremors wrack his big shoulders. He tore his mouth from hers and groaned, long and low, his body shaking as it poured life into hers.

He dropped like a stone onto her and lay unmoving for a moment while she tried to catch her breath.

Finally he turned his head toward her face and brushed a kiss over her cheek. "I love you and I believe with all my heart that you love me as well. Why can't you say it, Hero?"

Chapter Sixteen

*Queen Ravenhair looked at the answers to her question
and nodded in acknowledgment. "I shall see you
on the morrow, gentlemen."
But as she rose to leave the throne room, Prince Eastsun
spoke. "What is your decision, Your Majesty?"
She looked and saw that all three princes were
staring at her rather sternly.
"Yes, which of us have you chosen?" Prince Northwind
demanded. "We have answered each of your questions,
yet you have said nothing."
"You must decide," Prince Westmoon said. "You must
decide and tell us on the morrow which of us
you will marry...."*
—from *Queen Ravenhair*

Griffin got up and lit a candle from the banked embers in
her fireplace. He walked back to the bed, arrogantly nude,
the candlelight shining on his smooth stomach. He set the
single candle on her bedside and climbed in beside her
again, large and male and demanding.

"Well? Why can't you say it?"

Hero looked at Griffin and felt her heart begin to crumble. "Does it matter so much, three little words?"

"You know it does."

But she shook her head. "I can't. You want me to give up my family, all that I know, and you won't even give up your awful still. Can't you see that what you're asking is impossible?"

She expected anger and harsh words. Instead, he merely closed his eyes as if too weary to keep them open. "I need but a little time with the still. After I take down the Vicar. After—"

"How long, Griffin?" Her voice rasped in her throat. "Days? Weeks? Years? I cannot wait that long. Maximus and your brother will not let me."

He opened his eyes, and his gaze was hard now. "So it comes down to this: You will choose marriage to my brother over marriage to me?"

"Yes."

"How can you do this to me? To us?"

She bit her lip, trying to find the words. "I've spent my life obeying the rules set before me by society and my brother. Maximus has decided that Thomas is the better man for me."

"You accuse me of not giving up my still for you," he said quietly. "But I think you are the greater coward. You will not give up your brother's approval for me."

"Perhaps you're right," she answered. "I cannot go against Maximus now. I cannot. He has the power to ban me from my family. Besides, he's made the right choice. Thomas is reliable. He's *safe*."

"And I'm not?"

"No." The word dropped between them like a leaden weight. Hero felt tears fill her eyes, though she wasn't sure for what she mourned.

The bed shook and suddenly Griffin was atop her, his

weight pressing her into the mattress, his breath hot and angry against her cheek. "He might be safe, but do you love him, Hero?"

"No," she sobbed.

"Does he make you blush with anger and then with want?" He kicked apart her legs, settling hot and heavy between them. "Does he know how sensitive your nipples are? That you can come just by me sucking them?"

"God, no."

"Does he watch you like I do? Does he know that your eyes turn to diamonds when you're aroused?" He nipped along her neck, his kisses insistent and hard. "Does he know that you like to read in Greek but loathe drawing? Does he wait with bated breath for you to arch your left eyebrow so prissily—and then grow hard when you do?" He thumbed both her nipples at once, bringing a surge of heat between her thighs. "Tell me, Hero, goddamn it to bloody hell, *tell* me: Does he make you feel like I do?"

"No!" Her answer was a despairing wail.

His thumbs were between them, spreading her folds as if he had every right, as if she was *his*, now and forever, until the end of time, amen. And then he was in her. Hard and hot, moving so exquisitely she began to cry.

She wrapped her legs tightly around his narrow hips, her arms about his shoulders, holding on to him with her entire body as he rode her.

His big penis slid in and out of her slick folds. She was already sensitive from their previous lovemaking. She was gasping, hardly able to keep up, his pace rough and fast. It was too much; she couldn't hold herself together anymore. She wanted to push him away. To flee this room and him and his too-strong lovemaking. He wasn't giving her time to yield to him, to hide or assimilate his angry urgency. He was simply pushing her to experience what they shared—what they made—here and now.

He bent and caught her mouth, kissing her possessively even as his cock worked in and out of her. She moaned, opening her mouth, accepting the invasion of his tongue, tasting her own tears on his lips.

"Hero," he murmured. "Hero. Hero. Hero."

He punctuated each utterance of her name with a hard thrust of his hips as if to brand her as his. Sweat was dripping from his body, his breath was coming in hard gasps, and the bed was quaking.

She shook her head against the pillow—in denial of him or their lovemaking or of her own urges, she was no longer sure. But he pursued her, catching her head between his hands, holding her and making her look at him as he thrust himself into her body.

"Do you love me, Hero?" His pale green eyes were full of torment. "Do you love me like I love you?"

And she cracked apart on his words, a stream of liquid heat pouring forth from her center. She trembled beneath him, trying to tear her gaze from his as her passion exploded within her. As rivers of sweet pleasure spread through her thighs and belly. As her heart fractured and re-formed.

But he wouldn't let her look away. He held her gaze as his own eyes half closed and the muscles of his face, neck, and chest tightened. She watched helplessly as he convulsed above her, his big, strong shoulders gleaming with sweat.

He thrust into her once, twice, three times more and held himself there, tight against her, their bodies locked, as he orgasmed. His eyes pled silently with hers, defiant and proud.

Her vision blurred.

He slumped onto her, his chest heaving.

Hero closed her eyes, running her hands over his slick shoulders. She wanted to imprint this memory on her mind: the musk of their lovemaking, the weight of him on her, the sound of his harsh breaths in her ear. Someday, perhaps soon, she would want to draw upon this memory, to cherish and hold it in her heart.

He suddenly rolled off her, and her hands clutched after him, but he wasn't leaving her bed. Not yet at least.

He gathered her close, nestling her bottom into his groin, surrounding her back with his wide shoulders. He brushed the hair from her nape and kissed her there.

"Sleep," he said.

And so she did.

THE DAY WAS gray, but then every day seemed gray now, Silence thought as she gazed out the grubby kitchen window.

"Mamoo!" Mary Darling cried, clutching fretfully at the front of Silence's dress with grubby hands. "Mamoo!"

"Oh, Mary Darling," Silence sighed.

She'd forgotten to don an apron before sitting down to a late breakfast with the toddler. Now there were two smears of grease across her black bodice. She stared down at herself, feeling helpless and blank. She ought to rise and wash herself off—or at least find an apron—but she didn't seem to have the energy.

"Give the child to me, sister." Winter hung his round

black hat by the door as he entered the kitchen, then placed a plain wooden box on the table. He plucked Mary Darling from her arms and flung the child in the air, catching her easily as she squealed and giggled.

Why must men fling babies about? Even Winter, the most staid of her brothers, was prone to the disease. "I'm always afraid you'll drop her when you do that."

"But I never do," he replied.

"What are you doing home in the middle of the morning?"

"Half the boys were absent, sick from some type of fever, and the other half could not concentrate." Winter shrugged. "I sent the remaining boys home. Where is everyone?"

"The children have already eaten. Nell has taken them for a morning walk."

Winter glanced over the baby's shoulder, eyebrows raised. "*All* of the children?"

"The ones big enough to walk anyway," Silence said, feeling guilty. "I should have gone with her."

"No, no," Winter said hastily. He tucked the baby against his side and took down a plate from the cupboard. "We all must take a respite from work now and again."

"You don't."

"I haven't lost a dear one recently," he replied softly.

She pressed her lips together for a moment, then rose and took the plate from her brother. Silence crossed to the hearth and filled the plate with porridge from a pot hanging there. She brought the plate back to the table and set it in front of him.

"Let me take Mary. She'll have the porridge all over your coat in no time."

"Thank you," Winter said. He spooned up a mouthful of the thick porridge and murmured in contentment as he ate it. "That's very good."

"Nell made it," Silence said drily. Her own cooking left much to be desired.

"Ah." Winter swallowed and gestured to the wooden box. "I found that on the front step."

"Did you?" Silence felt a spark of curiosity and looked at the box with more animation than she'd had in days. "Do you think it's Mary Darling's admirer?"

Winter smiled gently. "I could venture a guess, but it seems more logical to simply open it and find out."

Silence stuck out her tongue at her brother. She turned the box over in her fingers. It was no bigger than the size of her palm. As she examined the box, she realized that although it was very plain, without marking or paint, the box was finely worked. It shone with beeswax. She frowned uneasily. The box was much dearer than Mary's other gifts.

Mary Darling grabbed for the box, held so temptingly in front of her.

"Not yet, sweetie," Silence said. "We need to see what's inside first."

She laid the box on the table, opened the lid, and gasped.

"What is it?" Winter half rose to look.

Silence turned the box so that he could see the strand of pearls coiled inside.

He was quiet a moment; then he lifted the necklace with his long, elegant fingers. He held the pearls up, watching as they gleamed in the light. "This is a very expensive present for a child."

"It's not for Mary Darling," Silence whispered. She held up the scrap of paper that had lain under the pearls. Two words were written upon it.

Silence Hollingbrook.

WHEN HERO WOKE, she knew even before she opened her eyes that Griffin was no longer with her. She lay, unmoving, eyes shut, as if to put off the inevitable realization that he was gone. The bed was cold. He'd been gone a long time.

She curled her fingers into fists and was startled to feel something in her right hand. She opened her eyes to see and brought her hand closer to her face. It was late morning, the light shining from her window bright and strong.

The thing in her hand was her diamond earring. Hero traced the bobble with one fingertip. The diamond earring Griffin had picked up after she'd thrown it at him so long ago now. She looked at it, and tears filled her eyes as she understood the message.

He wasn't coming back.

IT WAS LATE morning by the time Griffin climbed the steps to his town house. His legs felt leaden, his chest heavy and clogged.

"Where have you been?"

He raised his head at the familiar voice. Mater stood on his step, wrapped in a velvet cape.

He stopped and said stupidly, "What are doing here? Has something happened?"

"Has something happened?" she repeated incredulously. "Yes, something *happened*—you beat Thomas, say you've seduced his fiancée, and then you both virtually disappear! I want to know what is going on and how you'll resolve this horrible difference between you two. It's worse now than before you came back to London. What has happened to our family?"

He stared at her, this strong little woman, and saw her shoulders sag. She'd withstood Pater's death, withstood debt and scandal, and now she was near defeat because of him. His mouth tasted of ashes.

Add his mother's disillusionment to his sins.

He glanced around and realized they were in a public place. One of his neighbors was peering at them avidly from behind her curtains.

Griffin took Mater's arm. "Come inside, dearest."

She looked up at him uncertainly, and in the morning sunshine, the lines about her eyes were clear. "Griffin?"

"Come inside," he repeated.

He led her into his library and realized his mistake immediately when he glanced to the spot beside the settee where he'd made love to Hero. He swore under his breath, but where else was he to put her? Half the rooms were in sheets because he didn't bother using them.

"What is it?" she asked, touching his arm worriedly.

"It's nothing," he said, and strode to the door to bellow for a servant. A full minute elapsed before a blowsy maid scurried into view. "Bring some hot tea and cakes."

She curtsied. "'Aven't any cakes, m'lord."

Griffin grimaced. "Bread, then, or whatever else Cook can find."

He closed the door and turned back to the room, running his hands over his head. He wasn't wearing a wig, hadn't shaved in days, and his house and staff were wretched. Well, the last hardly mattered anymore. Once he'd dealt with the Vicar, he'd let the lease lapse and remove himself and Deedle to the north. Deedle hated it there, but Griffin would be damned if he'd stay in the same city as Thomas and Hero.

"Griffin?" Mater said softly.

Damn it. Mater had never cared to rusticate. He'd be leaving her behind as well. Unless she decided to take up residence in a city nearer the Mandeville estate. But that still wasn't London.

Nothing was the same as London.

"Griffin!" His mother crossed the room and took his hands. "You must tell me what you're thinking."

He smiled wearily. "It's not so very dramatic as all that, Mater. I'm making plans to leave London."

"But why?"

He closed his eyes. "I can't live here with Thomas and *her*."

"Lady Hero, you mean." She half laughed, and he opened his eyes to see her staring at him in exasperation. "Are we not to speak her name now?"

"That would be rather hard for Thomas," he said wryly.

She blinked. "He's not…"

He nodded. "They will be married Sunday."

He dropped her hands and crossed to pour himself a healthy glassful of brandy.

"But I thought…"

"That I'd marry her?" he asked, his back still turned to her. "Apparently not."

"Why not?"

He shrugged. "Does it matter? Anyway, Thomas will have his revenge for my seduction of Anne."

"Don't be silly." She made a dismissive sound. "I never believed you'd seduced Anne."

He turned, vaguely surprised—and rather grateful. "No? Everyone else did."

"I'm your mother, Griffin." She placed her hands on her hips and looked at him with exasperation. "Do give me some credit."

"Oh, Mater, I love you so." He smiled wryly and drank some brandy, wincing slightly as it burned his gullet.

"No one believes that old gossip anymore."

"Thomas does."

She stared. "What?"

He nodded and drank some more brandy. The second sip was smoother. Perhaps he'd become a sot.

"But that can't be!"

"Said so himself," he assured her. "Got it from Anne's own lips as she lay dying."

"That girl always was a ninny, God rest her soul," Mater muttered. "Did you tell him point-blank that you didn't do it?"

"Yes, and he point-blank did not believe me, perhaps because of my recent actions with Lady Hero."

"That's an entirely different matter," Mater said.

"Is it?" he asked. "To Thomas I doubt it is."

"Anne was his wife. Lady Hero is only affianced to him. Besides…" She trailed off, biting her lip.

Griffin narrowed his eyes at her suspiciously. "Besides what?"

She waved an irritable hand. "It's not my secret to divulge."

"Mater."

"Don't growl at me." She locked gazes with him for a moment, then looked away. "He can be so foolish sometimes."

"Tell me."

"It's none of your business, Griffin."

"If it involves Hero, it is. I love her."

Her face softened immediately. "Oh, do you?"

"Yes, unfortunately," he said. "Now tell me."

"It's just that Thomas took up with a rather risqué lady last season, a Mrs. Tate. He tried to hide it from me, of course, but I saw nonetheless. He couldn't keep his eyes off her when he'd see her at a ball or some other such place."

"Thomas has a mistress? Damn it, I knew it! He was following her at Harte's Folly."

"Rather more than a mistress I think, although perhaps he doesn't know it himself," she said somewhat obscurely.

Griffin's anger was building. How dare Thomas marry Hero already encumbered by a mistress? "Has he broken it off?"

"That's just it," Mater replied. "I thought he had when he proposed to Lady Hero, but now I think he's seeing Mrs. Tate again."

"To punish Hero," Griffin growled.

"No, I don't think so. I think he's formed a tendre for the woman." Mater shook her head sadly. "I love Thomas dearly—he is my firstborn son—but he can be so *very* boneheaded. He should let Lady Hero go."

"Ah." Griffin tossed back the rest of the brandy. "But I'm afraid that doesn't matter to me in any case."

"What do you mean?"

"She doesn't love me." He tried to smile and failed. "She won't marry me."

"Humph." Mater frowned ferociously. "She might say she doesn't want to marry you, but I don't for a moment believe she doesn't love you. A woman like Lady Hero does not let a man into her bed out of the bonds of wedlock unless she's fallen head over heels for him."

He looked down at his glass, unable to meet her gaze. He suddenly found it hard to speak. "She's hiding it well if she does love me."

"If only we had more time," his mother burst out. "I'm sure she'd come to her senses if Thomas would just *wait* to marry her."

"It's Wakefield who is pushing the marriage." Griffin shook his head. "And in any case, I truly don't think she'll be changing her mind. I have business to finish here, and then I'll be leaving for Lancashire."

"But you can't leave!" Mater cried. "Don't you see? If you just give her time—"

"I can't stay and watch her marry Thomas!" he hissed, the pain surfacing despite his efforts to keep it submerged. He glanced at her and then away again at the pity in her eyes. "I simply can't."

"Griffin—"

"No." He cut the air with the blade of his hand. "Just listen. I'll finish my business, and then I'm moving north permanently. I'll either transfer my business north somehow or have my agents act for me in London. I'm not coming back."

She watched him silently, but tears swam in her eyes. He could see them clearly.

It was more than he could bear.

"She doesn't love me. I have to accept that fact and go on." He picked up the decanter and a glass and strode to the door. He paused there, his back to her.

"I'm sorry," he said.

And then he fled to his rooms. If he was lucky, he'd be insensibly drunk in an hour.

Chapter Seventeen

The queen returned to her rooms that night with a heavy heart. Her suitors were right: She must make a decision and choose the perfect man to wed, but the thought filled her with sorrow. She went to her balcony and saw that the little brown bird was already perched there.
Queen Ravenhair picked up the bird and found about his neck a string with a tiny mirror tied to the end. She untangled the mirror and held it up—and of course saw herself reflected in its surface. And then she knew the message: She was the heart of her kingdom....
—from Queen Ravenhair

Hero absently turned the diamond earring over in her fingers late that afternoon. She had retired to the sitting room with a pot of tea, now cooling on the low table in front of her. The room smelled of roses, because a giant vase of the flowers sat on the corner table. They were pale pink—her favorite—but she glanced away from the sight of them.

Cousin Bathilda had had hysterics over Maximus's demand that Hero marry on Sunday. She'd gone off to try and reason with Maximus, but Hero had very little hope that even Cousin Bathilda would persuade Maximus to put off the wedding. Once Maximus set his mind to something, he was like a granite boulder: hard and immovable.

Not that it mattered, really.

If she were to marry Thomas, this Sunday or a Sunday months from now it made no difference. She didn't even care about the inevitable scandal. She knew she should. A small part of her mind was wailing that she should be panicked, should be pacing or throwing hysterics herself. And yet she couldn't bring herself to care.

She was making a mistake.

Hero sighed and dropped the earring next to her teacup. She couldn't shake the feeling that she was making a terrible, irredeemable mistake.

"There you are," Phoebe called from the doorway as she entered. "Wherever has Cousin Bathilda gone? I can't seem to find her."

"I'm sorry, love," Hero said, feeling guilty. "She's gone off in a frenzy to speak to Maximus."

"Oh," Phoebe said, sitting down on a chair at right angles to Hero's settee.

Phoebe's little shoulders drooped. Hero bit her lip. "Did Maximus talk to you?"

Phoebe nodded, looking down.

"I'm so sorry."

"It's all right." Phoebe straightened a bit. "All those balls and such. It would have been wearying, I expect, don't you?"

"Yes, it is rather tiring," Hero said gently.

"It's just…" Phoebe wrinkled her nose. "I would've liked to have danced with a gentleman not related to me once. Just once."

Hero felt tears prick her eyes.

"It's for the best. I do understand that." Phoebe inhaled and looked up. "Did Cousin Bathilda go to talk to Maximus about your marriage?"

Her voice was diffident and Hero felt worse. They'd not told Phoebe anything, but she must've been aware of the household turmoil the last couple of days.

"You know Maximus said I had to marry this Sunday?" Hero asked.

"One of the servants overheard something and told me." Phoebe's eyes dropped. "I thought you didn't like him anymore?"

"It's rather complicated."

"But he hit you, didn't he?" Phoebe looked at her worriedly. "That's where you got that bruise on your cheek, isn't it?"

"Yes." Hero winced as she touched her cheek. It was turning a rather vivid purple. "But he has sent his apologies." She gestured to the vase of roses.

Phoebe examined them. "So that's who they're from?"

"Yes."

"They're quite extravagant. He must be feeling guilty. But then he *should* feel guilty. I don't think you ought to marry him," Phoebe said earnestly. "Not if he's hurt you. What is Maximus thinking?"

"It's not quite that simple." Hero sighed and picked up the diamond earring, twisting it between her fingers. "Maximus is doing what he thinks is best for me."

"I don't see how."

"Mandeville acted out of anger—I did something to anger him terribly. He's a very trustworthy man usually.

Maximus knows this and knows he will make a responsible, solid husband for me."

Phoebe wrinkled her nose. "Responsible. Solid."

When repeated flatly like that, Thomas's attributes sounded less sterling. Nevertheless, Hero nodded. "Yes."

"It seems rather boring reasons for marrying someone."

Hero bit her lip. "Marriage is supposed to be boring."

"Why?" Phoebe asked. "Why can't it be exciting and... and an adventure? I'm sure if you looked a bit more, you could find a man who made your heart thrill when you saw him."

Made her heart thrill. That was what she felt like when she saw Griffin. But he was wholly inappropriate, wasn't he? Phoebe was simply too young to understand.

Hero shook her head, staring at the earring in her hand.

Phoebe leaned forward to peer at her hand. "Isn't that the earbob you lost at your engagement ball?"

"Yes." Hero folded her fingers protectively around the little piece.

"But how wonderful that you've found it again," Phoebe said. "It's almost like having an entirely new set when one finds a lost earring, I always think."

Hero raised her eyebrows in faint amusement. "How often do you lose earrings?"

"Quite often, I'm afraid," Phoebe said. "They just seem to—"

"Your brother is as stubborn as a mule!" Cousin Bathilda cried as she entered the sitting room. Mignon barked as if to emphasize the pronouncement.

"He wouldn't move the date?" Hero asked.

"Not only would he not move the date, but he also

wouldn't even discuss the matter." Cousin Bathilda plopped onto the settee beside Hero, earning a growly grumble from Mignon. "Then he had the temerity to tell me that he had business to conduct and that our interview was over! Can you imagine? Where that man became so rude, I haven't the faintest. Your mother was the height of civility, my dears, a true lady, even without the title, and *I* certainly never led him to believe that such conduct to his elders was a matter of course."

Cousin Bathilda was busy twitching her skirts in her agitation, and the constant movement was apparently too much for Mignon. The little spaniel got up from her lap and delicately stepped onto Hero's lap, where she settled with a long-suffering sigh.

Hero stroked Mignon's silky ears. "Would you like some tea, Cousin?"

"Tea would be quite the thing," Cousin Bathilda said. "But this pot has gone cold no doubt. Phoebe, will you be a dear and call for another?"

"Yes, Cousin Bathilda." Phoebe obediently rose.

Bathilda cast a glance at the girl as she crossed to the door. "How much does she know of the matter, do you think?"

"Probably everything," Hero said wearily. "The servants can't help but overhear and they gossip, you know."

"Wretched gossip!" Cousin Bathilda humphed. Phoebe returned and Bathilda smoothed her face. "Thank you, my dear. I'm glad to know that I instilled some manners in you girls at least."

"I don't think anyone could make Maximus do something he didn't want to do, manners or not," Phoebe said cheerfully. "He's the duke, after all. Sometimes it's hard to imagine him as anything else, but he must've been a baby with pap on his face once upon a time." She frowned uncertainly. "He was, wasn't he?"

"Of course!" Bathilda said. "He was an adorable baby, although very grave even when in leading strings. Your mother used to laugh at his solemn face."

"Did she?" Phoebe leaned forward. She was always interested in discussions of their parents. Since she'd only been an infant when they died, she had no memories of them.

"Oh, yes," Cousin Bathilda said, "though your father chided her for it. He said such solemnity in a boy would make a good duke in a man. And he was right—Maximus is a magnificent duke, even if he is stubborn as a mule."

The maids entered with new tea things, and there was silence a moment as they cleared the old tea away and set out the new. Hero thanked them and they curtsied and quietly left the room.

"This looks nice and hot," Cousin Bathilda said as she sat forward to pour. "Phoebe, would you like a dish? Hero?"

Hero shook her head, and Cousin Bathilda assembled a dish of tea for Phoebe and one for herself.

Cousin Bathilda sat back with her dish, inhaling the steam. "Ah, this is restorative. I can't think why your brother must torment me so, my dears."

"Perhaps his business was very important," Phoebe offered as she sipped her own tea.

Cousin Bathilda snorted delicately. "He *said* so and perhaps *thought* so, but I don't see how arresting some illicit gin maker in the worst part of St. Giles can be all that important no matter what he says or thinks."

Mignon squeaked as Hero clutched involuntarily at her ear. Maximus was after a gin maker in St. Giles—today! Griffin had said just last night that he'd argued with Maximus. If Maximus saw Griffin as a threat to her marriage to Thomas, he might consider it a deed well done to get Griffin out of the way.

Hero shivered as fear raced up her spine. Her brother could be very ruthless, but surely—*surely!*—he wouldn't move against Griffin when she was about to marry Thomas. Hadn't he promised her? But, no, he hadn't actually put the promise into words—he'd simply asked if she wanted Griffin arrested. The implication had been that he *would* have Griffin arrested if she didn't marry Thomas. But after that, Griffin had argued with Maximus. Had Maximus decided to eliminate the threat that Griffin posed to her marriage to Thomas?

Cousin Bathilda glanced at her. "Something the matter, my dear?"

"I...I was just wondering when Maximus plans to arrest this gin distiller." Hero dug her fingers into Mignon's soft fur, and Mignon licked her hand.

"At this very moment," Cousin Bathilda replied, causing Hero's heart to nearly stop. "Well, soon in any case. He was muttering something about taking soldiers and finding his informant as he escorted me to his door."

Hero leaned forward urgently. "Then he hasn't done it yet? There's still time?"

Cousin Bathilda looked startled and slowly lowered her teacup. "Why, yes, I suppose so, dear. Whyever do you ask?"

"I-I've remembered an appointment," Hero said, standing and unceremoniously dumping Mignon to the floor.

The little dog squawked and retreated under the settee. "Is the carriage still in front?"

"I don't know," Cousin Bathilda called behind Hero as she rushed to the door. "Hero, what is this about?"

But Hero was already in the outer hallway making for the stairs. She hadn't time to explain to either Bathilda or Phoebe. She hadn't time to find help. She had to go to St. Giles and warn Griffin before her brother threw him in gaol...

On a hanging charge.

THOMAS WAS SURPRISED to see a coach outside Lavinia's house when he climbed down from his carriage late that afternoon. He frowned, a vague worry beginning to niggle at the back of his mind as he knocked at her door.

The imposing butler answered and scowled down at him. Thomas didn't bother with any niceties. He brushed past the man, noticing crates and baskets piled against the walls of the hall.

"Where is she?"

"Mrs. Tate is in her rooms," the man said sourly—and he dropped the "my lord," Thomas noted.

Thomas ran up the stairs without another word. Damn the man anyway; he was but a mere servant. Thomas was determined to have a word with Lavinia about her staff, but when he reached her rooms, he stopped dead instead. Every drawer was opened in her bureau, and her wardrobe was flung wide. Dresses, petticoats, stockings, shoes, chemises, and other female odds and ends were strewn on every available surface. And in the midst of all this chaos, Lavinia was directing two maids as they packed the clothes into boxes.

"What are you about?" he asked sharply.

She looked up at his voice, and her face went completely blank.

Something in the vicinity of his heart constricted. "Lavinia?"

"Martha, Maisie, please help the footmen in the downstairs sitting rooms," Lavinia said.

The maids bobbed curtsies and left the room, shooting him curious looks.

He didn't care what was going through their pea brains. "What are you doing?"

She lifted her chin. "I'm packing to leave of course."

She wore a simple gray dress today—not at all her usual style—and against her bright wine-red hair, it gave her a severe look.

He had a savage urge to tear it from her body.

"I thought…" He had to stop and swallow past a sudden swelling in his throat. He had a wrenching, horrifying notion that he might weep. "I thought you would stay with me."

"Because I let you bed me?"

"*Yes*, damn you!"

She sighed. "But I told you already that I will not be your mistress while you are married to another woman, Thomas. I never changed my mind."

She turned back to the bed, but he grabbed her arm roughly. "You love me."

"Yes, I do." She raised her eyebrows and looked at him, sadly it seemed. "But you know love has very little to do with it."

"Damn you," he whispered, and because he was in despair, he took her mouth.

She let him. She stood silent and complacent, made no move to struggle, as he ground her lips beneath his. She tasted of mint and tea, and he groaned, growing erect. She'd always done this to him, since the very first time he'd seen her, laughing at some other man in a ballroom. She brought out the animal side of him, made him forget he was a peer, a respected member of parliament, and a gentleman who owned vast amounts of land.

She made him into a man, only a man, and in the past he'd hated her for it: reminding him that beneath the ermine robes he was merely blood and bone like any other wretch who scrabbled for a living in London. But here, now, he no longer cared. He was going to lose her, once and for all. She would simply walk away, wine-red hair, maddening laugh, and those plain brown eyes that saw all of his most shameful secrets and loved him anyway.

And in the end, when he finally took his mouth from hers, she simply looked at him and turned away. She picked up a stocking and began carefully rolling it. "Good-bye, Thomas."

He sank to his knees, there in her room on the carpet that was worn in spots, and said the first thing that popped into his mind. "Please marry me, Lavinia."

"YOU LOOK LIKE you've died, been buried for three days, and then been dug up," Deedle greeted Griffin cordially that evening in St. Giles. Deedle tilted his head and took a closer look. "And been to 'ell in the meantime, too."

"Thank you, I have," Griffin growled as he filled a nosebag for Rambler.

He'd not sufficiently trusted any of the men at the still to put them in charge, so he'd been forced to press Deedle into service. His valet stood, armed like a buccaneer, two pistols in his belt and a sword as well. Griffin looked up at the sky. The day was fleeing fast as night cast long shadows in St. Giles.

Deedle pushed his tongue through the hole in the front of his teeth. "What's 'appened to you, m'lord?"

Griffin shook his head, then stopped as it throbbed in warning. "Nothing to worry yourself over."

Deedle snorted. "If you say so."

"Take it or leave it, I don't give a damn." Griffin strode into the dim interior of the still warehouse. He hadn't the patience to argue semantics with Deedle this evening.

"Then I'll leave it," Deedle said, skipping to keep up with him.

"What's happened since I was here last?" Griffin asked.

Deedle sighed. "We've lost two more men overnight. That brings us to five, not including we two."

"You doubled their pay again?"

Deedle nodded. "Just like you said to. Didn't keep those two fellows from doin' a runner."

"I don't suppose it matters much anymore anyway," Griffin said. He watched dispassionately as his remaining men filled oaken barrels with gin. "The whole thing'll be over after tonight."

Deedle came around to face him. "Then it's tonight?"

"Yes." Griffin gazed at the big copper kettles, the barrels of waiting gin, the fires, and the huge warehouse itself. Everything he and Nick had worked so hard to build. "Yes, tonight."

"Jesus," Deedle breathed. "Are you sure? We've less than a dozen men and not all the supplies you wanted. M'lord, it'll be near suicide."

Griffin stared back at Deedle, his gaze level, his head

pounding, his mouth tasting of blood and bile. He'd lost Hero, would lose his mother to London, never had a chance of reconciling with Thomas in the first place, and Nick, his dear friend, was dead and buried. The bloody still was the last thing he had left in London.

"Tonight or never. I'm not waiting any longer. I want this over with." He turned and picked up one of the wicked-looking swords his men used and then glared back at Deedle. "Are you with me or not?"

Deedle swallowed and gripped his pistol. "Aye, m'lord, I am."

Chapter Eighteen

Tears filled Queen Ravenhair's eyes at the simplicity
and beauty of the tiny mirror's message.
She held the bird in the hollow of her palms. "What
shall I do?" she whispered into the downy feathers.
"Who shall I take as husband?"
She let the bird go and he flew away. But instead of
disappearing for the night as usual, it was back again
within minutes. It alighted and opened its beak to sing.
Let the heart of the heart decide....
—from *Queen Ravenhair*

"'E's cornered," Freddy said with satisfaction that evening. "Reading won't be getting out of this one alive, I'm thinking. 'E's lost Nick Barnes and most of 'is men have deserted 'im."

Charlie nodded, listening with one ear to the click of the dice in his fingers and with the other for any sound overhead. "Our informant has told Wakefield where Reading's still is?"

"Told 'im and is leading 'im to Reading's still as we speak," Freddy said. So great was his glee that he almost looked Charlie full in the face.

Almost, but not quite.

Charlie spilled the dice to the table. Two aces. Deuce.

For a moment he stared, mesmerized by the ill omen. Deuce could foretell death, but whose—his enemy's or his own... or perhaps the woman who lay above?

"We'll draw him out," Charlie whispered, still mesmerized by the unlucky dice throw. "Draw him out, kill him, and fire the still."

THE SKY WAS turning gray as Hero climbed from her carriage at the edge of St. Giles.

"I don't like this, my lady," George the footman said. He hoisted a lantern and fingered one of the pistols she'd given him.

A shout rose from the group of men arguing over an overturned cart in the road. Her carriage was stuck behind the accident in a street too narrow to turn around.

"I understand your objections," Hero murmured. "But I cannot wait for them to clear the road. It could take hours."

"Beggin' your pardon, my lady, but couldn't we send word back home for another footman or two to join us?"

"I've told you. I haven't the time." Hero picked up her skirts and began to walk briskly away from her carriage and the accident.

"But after dark," George fretted. "What if we're attacked, my lady?"

"You've got the pistols," Hero said soothingly.

George looked unconvinced by this assurance, but he made no more protestations. Instead he fixed a suspicious eye on their surroundings.

Hero bit her lip as she wrapped her cloak about herself. She couldn't blame George. This expedition was dangerous—*very* dangerous. Normally she'd never even contemplate going into St. Giles after dark, let alone on foot and with but a single bodyguard. She was quite aware of the dangers St. Giles posed.

But what other choice did she have? She needed to get to Griffin's still as soon as possible. She hadn't wanted to risk arousing Cousin Bathilda's suspicions by taking more than one footman.

Hero glanced about them. The street they were in was darkening and becoming deserted as she watched. Everyone seemed to want to get inside before full dark. She shivered. Dear Lord, what if she was too late and Maximus had already made his raid on the still? The thought of Griffin in chains, of him being thrown into some wretched prison, was almost more than she could bear. He was so proud! Worse, what if he resisted being taken? What if he were shot?

She nearly sobbed at the thought. This was insane. Just last night she'd rejected him as thoroughly as if she'd written it all down on paper. Now she was racing through the St. Giles alleys in fear for his life.

Had she gone insane? Or had she simply made a terrible mistake?

Why had she sent him away in the first place? All the considered arguments she'd given him, all the well-reasoned points, none of them made sense anymore. All she knew was what her innermost heart felt: she wanted Griffin. Despite his wild ways, despite his shady past, despite the fact that her brother was about to arrest him for distilling gin.

She wanted Griffin. She'd die if anything happened to him, and she very much feared that her life would be a long, gray, boring test of endurance without him in it. She wanted him, she needed him, and *yes*, she loved him—she'd admit it now that it might be too late. She loved him.

And that was all that mattered.

"THIS'S BARMY," DEEDLE hissed under his breath.

Griffin glanced back at him over his shoulder. Night had fallen, and the alley behind the warehouse still was swallowed by shadows. The blackness was a boon for the predators of the night, hiding any lurking assassin or creeping attacker.

Of course, the shadows also hid those who *preyed* upon the predators. Tonight that included Griffin and Deedle.

Griffin checked with his fingers that his gun was cocked. "It might be barmy, but it's our only chance."

Deedle grunted. "The Vicar and 'is gang won't be expecting us—that's for certain. Not sitting out 'ere in the dark."

Something scraped and Griffin turned his head toward the sound, alert and silent. A low shape darted across the alley.

"Cat," Deedle whispered. "Think the Vicar will attack tonight?"

"He's been waiting since they killed Nick," Griffin murmured. "He's hoping most of my men have fled—which they have, damn him—and he wants me desperate and afraid. I'd say there's a good chance that tonight's the night."

Deedle gripped Griffin's shoulder just as Griffin saw the shadow move. Three men were creeping up the alley. One leaped and clawed at the wall of the warehouse. They were going to stop the chimneys again in preparation for the rest of the attack, if Griffin wasn't mistaken.

Griffin charged low and fast and without sound. He caught the first man by the hair and clubbed him with the butt of his gun. The man went down like a felled tree. The second man shouted, but Deedle shot him. Griffin turned and aimed at the man scaling the wall. He squeezed the trigger and felt his chest expand in savage triumph when the man fell.

Then someone hit him from the side. His pistol flew from his hand as he was thrown violently against the wall. His attacker was a giant with a giant's fists, pounding at his face, his belly. Griffin gasped, winded, the world spinning. He drew his pistol and shot point-blank into the other man's face.

He felt the sting of gunpowder against the side of his face, the spray of something wet and sticky. He pushed aside the body and glanced up, his ears strangely muffled. Men were pouring in at the far end of the alley, running toward him and Deedle, at least twenty of them, maybe more.

It was a trap, he thought, oddly composed. The Vicar had been waiting for them to emerge from the walls of the still warehouse. And they had. They had.

Griffin walked to the middle of the alley and turned, drawing his sword to face the oncoming slaughter.

"M'lord," Deedle wheezed beside him. "Who the 'ell is that?"

And Griffin looked over his shoulder and realized that a *second* group of men blocked the *other* end of the alley, marching in line, coming toward them. Behind them were men on horseback.

"Soldiers." He spat blood into the dust at his feet. "The Duke of Wakefield is coming to arrest me if I'm not mistaken."

"Dear God in heaven," Deedle muttered. "We're dead, m'lord. Dead!"

And Griffin threw back his head and laughed. The sound echoed off the filthy brick walls that enclosed the alley he was about to die in.

SILENCE HURRIED HOME, through the darkened streets of St. Giles.

She'd meant to take only a quick trip to visit one of the home's wet nurses and her tiny charge. But the moment she'd entered the woman's apartment, she'd immediately caught the astringent scent of gin. That had led to recriminations, protests, and a rather awful scene before she'd finally walked out with the orphaned infant. No matter how sorry she might feel for the wet nurse—a widow with a child of her own—Silence couldn't risk the well-being of such a tiny baby. The nursling was only a month or so old—a fragile age for a baby.

She'd known of another possible wet nurse for the baby, but the second woman lived nearly a mile away from the first, and in the opposite direction of the home. She'd hurried there as fast as she could walk with the babe in her arms. And in the end, Silence had been very satisfied with the placement. The new wet nurse, Polly, had been employed in the past by the home and had always given satisfactory service. Although her own children were now weaned, Polly assured Silence that she had enough milk for the orphaned infant.

A good day's work, but an exhausting one, and the reason she was now caught out after dark.

Silence pulled her light woolen cloak more securely about her shoulders and eyed a dark doorway as she passed it. She was trying very hard not to think of some of the awful tales she heard from Nell—an inveterate teller of horror stories. The woman who'd been strangled by a lover. The woman who'd been dragged into an alley and savagely attacked by three drunken men. The woman who had gone out to buy a meat pie for her four children and simply disappeared, her shoe found the next day in an alley.

Silence shivered. All of Nell's stories had two common elements: They were all about women out alone.

And they all took place after dark.

A cry came from up ahead, and Silence's steps faltered. She was in a wide street, but there were no cross streets nearby. Only a single flickering lantern hung over a tiny cobbler's shop. Voices could be heard and lights, growing stronger, coming nearer.

Silence looked about desperately. A man shouted an angry curse. Then a crowd came tearing around the corner of the street up ahead. There were men holding torches, but also women. They milled and shouted, and in the middle was some kind of wretched *thing* that they were dragging by a collar.

Someone smashed a window and Silence flinched. She was already backing away, turning to hurry up the street she'd just walked down. But that direction was *away* from the home. She looked over her shoulder as two men dragged the wretch they'd caught to the middle of the street and began beating him with cudgels.

"'Ave mercy!" she heard their victim cry.

There were more curses and amid them a single hoarse shout she could make out: *"Informer!"*

Dear Lord, they were lynching a gin informer.

Doors opened up ahead, but when she looked there hopefully, more people came out and ran toward the horrible scene behind her. The street was suddenly filled with shouting madmen. Someone jostled her and Silence tripped. She fell against a house wall, pressing herself back.

A drunken man loomed in front of her, hands twitching, ugly mouth leering. Without a word, he snatched the hood from her head, pulling her hair painfully as he did so. Behind him, flames shot up to the sky, framing his black face with orange. What in God's name were they doing to the poor informer?

But she had worse to think about right in front of her. The ugly man leaned over her menacingly.

Silence darted to the right and for a split second felt a rush of welcome relief because she thought she was free.

Then a heavy hand caught her by the hair, and she knew the night was about to become a nightmare.

Chapter Nineteen

*The queen tossed and turned that night on her royal
bed, but in the morning she had come to a decision. She
dressed with care, wearing her best cloth of gold gown
and a diamond and ruby crown. Then she strode into the
throne room to meet her suitors. The princes had dressed
in their best as well. Prince Eastsun shone in robes of gold
and silver, Prince Westmoon wore a doublet sewn with
emeralds, and Prince Northwind was fairly encrusted with
pearls. All three men stood tall and handsome, perfectly
perfect in their splendor.*

"Have you made your decision?" Prince Eastsun asked.

Queen Ravenhair tilted her chin. "Yes...."

—from *Queen Ravenhair*

The first wave of attackers hit like a battering ram. They
didn't seem to have pistols, but they were armed with
cudgels, and a few bore swords. Griffin fired his last shot
from his remaining pistol, taking down the man leading
the charge.

Griffin drew his sword. "For Nick Barnes!"

A shot came from behind him, and then the Vicar's
men from one end and the soldiers from the other con-
verged, and he and Deedle were in the middle of a melee.
Griffin swung his sword with one hand, nearly severing

a man's arm. The man howled and fell and was trampled by a horse.

For a moment, through the mass of heaving men, Griffin saw a face—or what might be a face in a nightmare. The man's flesh looked as if it had turned to wax and melted down the side of his skull before hardening in a grotesque parody of facial features. Griffin blinked and the vision was gone.

Griffin punched another man and was shoved hard in return. Someone swung a cudgel at him, and he took the blow on his left shoulder, his entire arm going numb. He shook his head, trying to clear a trickle of blood from his eyes. He didn't even remember the wound from which it came. He expected at any moment to be shot or impaled from behind but didn't bother looking.

Death would find him soon enough.

Beside him Deedle cursed. Griffin turned to see Deedle stagger back from three men. His arm was painted red.

Griffin shouted and charged Deedle's attackers. He felt his face stretch into a grin as he threw the first man aside. The other two turned tail and ran. Then, suddenly, there was a break and he was face-to-face with a gleaming black boot ornamented with a gold spur. He looked up and saw Wakefield glowering down at him from atop a huge black horse.

"Reading!" Wakefield shouted. "Is this your still?"

"Fuck you," Griffin replied, and elbowed a short, bandy-legged tough in the face.

Wakefield drew a pistol, aimed it over Griffin's head, pulled the trigger, and nearly deafened Griffin with the *boom!* He looked at Griffin again, frowning, and his lips moved, but Griffin couldn't hear him.

He was jostled from behind and Griffin turned. Deedle was using one of his pistols to beat a man about the head.

Griffin felt a touch on his shoulder and swung his sword.

Wakefield jerked up, then cupped his hand about his mouth, shouting. "Are these your men?"

"Would I be fighting my own men?" Griffin asked in exasperation.

He dodged aside as a man staggered toward him, then kicked the fellow's feet out from under him before stomping him once viciously in the head. He glanced around. Most of the Vicar's men were fleeing in disorder, routed by the more experienced fighting of the soldiers.

"It appears you have a business rival, then," Wakefield observed.

He drew his sword and leaned down to slap the blade against the face of a charging rough. The man spun with the force of the blow and his own momentum, and Griffin finished him off by hitting him across the back of the head with the hilt of his sword. Griffin watched the man slump to the ground and then turned to Wakefield with a sarcastic reply on his lips.

But he saw a movement beyond Wakefield's giant horse, and Griffin's shoulders tensed in horror instead.

There at the mouth of the alley, Hero was picking her way delicately toward the fight, the footman beside her armed only with a lantern and a wavering drawn pistol.

"*Christ,*" Griffin breathed.

Wakefield glanced over his shoulder. "What the hell is my sister doing here, Reading?"

*   *   *

THOMAS HAD NEVER knelt to anyone. He was aware as he looked up at Lavinia how humble the position was, but that was appropriate: He was a petitioner for her hand. Indeed, he was desperate for her hand. If Lavinia left him, he'd have *nothing*. If she asked him, he'd crawl to her on hands and knees.

Had she any idea the straits she'd left him in?

But her brown eyes had filled with tears that made them glitter. "You know you cannot marry me, Thomas. You've told me so many times before."

She started to turn from him, but he was up and off the rug in a thrice, taking her hand, holding it between his own. "I've told you so, but I lied, Lavinia. Both to me and to you. I can marry you."

"But what about Anne? What about your fears of betrayal?"

He felt ignoble panic rise in his chest. "They don't matter."

"Yes." She took a deep breath. "Yes, they do. Anne horribly betrayed you, and you haven't trusted a woman since. I can't live with the constant fear that I'll do something that you'll misinterpret."

"No!" He closed his eyes, trying to control himself so he could make this important plea. "I was a cad, I admit it, to ever doubt you. You never strayed from me when we were together. You weren't the one who found someone else. *I* was."

"But—"

"No, hear me out." He squeezed her hand. "I know I am the problem. Griffin told me that he'd never seduced Anne, yet I refused to give him the satisfaction of believing him. Please, please, Lavinia, trust me. Let me prove I can change."

She was shaking her head, trying ineffectually to wipe at the tears. "What of parliament? Or the succession of the marquessate?"

"Don't you see?" He shook his head, searching for the words, he who was known for his eloquence on the floor of the House of Lords. "None of that matters. Without you, I am a shadow of a man, a mere wisp. Parliament, even the marquessate, can survive without me, but *I* cannot survive without *you*."

She made a sort of gasping sound.

"I love you, Lavinia," he said, desperate now. "I don't think that's ever going to change, because I've tried to stop and I can't. I love you and I want to marry you. Will you marry me?"

"Oh, Thomas!" She was half laughing, half crying. Her eyes were red, her cheeks blotchy, and strangely she was the most beautiful woman he'd ever seen. "Yes, I'll marry you."

HERO STARTED RUNNING the moment she saw Griffin beside Maximus on his horse. They were lit by flickering torches and in the midst of a desperate battle, but all she could see were the two men. Dear God, was her brother about to kill her lover?

"My lady!" George shouted, and blocked a blow from a man with a large stick. "My lady, please!"

Griffin ducked around Maximus's horse. He shoved aside a man in his way, stabbed another with his sword, and punched and then kicked a third. In all of this, he never took his eyes from Hero. Even in the dimly lit alley, his pale green eyes seemed to glow with a savage light. He reached her just as George gave a shout and fired his pistol.

Hero flinched and turned to see a man falling, bloody, at George's feet.

Then her shoulders were grabbed, and she was swung around. Griffin glared down at her. He'd lost his wig and was bleeding from a cut on his forehead. Blackened blood was drying on the right side of his face, his right eye gleaming in the midst of the gore like a demon.

She almost fainted from the relief of seeing him alive and whole. Thank God she'd arrived in time. Thank God she'd not have to spend the rest of her life mourning him. Thank God—

Griffin opened his mouth. "What the hell are you doing here, you bloody stupid woman?"

She blinked and stiffened. "I just spent the last hour traveling across London to get to you!"

"I told you never to go into St. Giles alone!" He shook her.

"I had George—"

He snorted. "George! One man! And after dark. Have you completely lost your senses?"

She thrust up her chin. "I was coming to rescue *you*, you...you *cad*!"

Tears of humiliation and hurt were flooding her eyes. She shoved away from him and turned to flee.

He muttered a completely inappropriate curse and grabbed her from behind. He swung her around, and then his mouth was on hers, hot and angry and oh so alive.

She was glad—so very glad—that he was well, even if he'd just been awful to her, that she opened her lips beneath his and wrapped her arms as tightly as she could around his neck. Sight and sound and place disappeared until it was just the two of them, alone in their own world. Her heart was beating loud in her ears. She could smell gunpowder and sweat on him, and the sharp, acrid scents made him more real. More alive. She could taste her own tears on his lips—tears of joy.

"Hero," he groaned.

"Griffin," she sighed.

"Jesus," someone muttered in disgust nearby.

Griffin raised his head but didn't take his emerald eyes from hers. "Go away, Wakefield."

Hero's eyes widened, and she glanced wildly around until she saw her brother, still seated on his black horse, staring disapprovingly down at them.

"You can't take him!" she cried, and clutched at Griffin's broad shoulders. Maximus could hardly arrest Griffin if she clung to him bodily.

"He's not going to arrest me," Griffin said, arrogant as always. "Not if you marry me."

"Are you blackmailing my sister?" Maximus growled.

"If I have to." Griffin's gaze had returned to hers, and what she saw there suddenly made her heart fly free. "I'll do whatever it takes to marry you, Hero."

She caressed his jaw—the only part of him not covered in blood—with unsteady fingers. "You don't have to blackmail me to marry you. I love you."

His eyes flared and he pulled her close again. "Do you mean that? You'll marry me?"

"Gladly," she breathed.

He bent his head and kissed her, but just as she opened her mouth beneath his, he jerked his head up.

"My lord!" A soldier had come running up to Maximus. "There's rioting just to the west of here. Shall we send for reinforcements?"

Hero looked at Griffin in horror. "That's where the home is!"

He nodded. "Right." He glanced about and bellowed, "Deedle!"

Griffin's valet appeared, his hair on end, one arm bloodied, but he was standing upright. "Aye, m'lord?"

"Have the Vicar's men taken the bait?" Griffin asked cryptically.

Maximus frowned. "What's this?"

Deedle grinned from ear to ear. "'Is men are in and ours are out, m'lord."

"Then do it."

Deedle nodded. He placed two fingers between his lips and blew a shrill, piercing whistle.

Griffin turned to Maximus. "I suggest you call your men to you."

Maximus raised his eyebrows suspiciously but shouted, "To me!"

At once the remaining soldiers started for him.

"Taking a while, isn't it?" Deedle said worriedly.

BOOM!

A huge concussion made the very ground shake. Bricks tumbled from the nearest buildings while at the same time an intense light lit the night. The smell of smoke filled the air.

Hero grabbed for Griffin. "What was that?"

"That'll cut the Vicar down to size." Griffin grinned ferociously. "Nick would've liked the pretty trap we set for the Vicar and his men."

Maximus, who had been eyeing the explosion, turned to look down at them. "You blew the still, didn't you?"

Griffin grinned. "I haven't the faintest idea what you're talking about. But if a still did blow, it might be because a very insistent lady recently showed me the evils of gin and gin distilling."

Hero's heart swelled as tears pricked her eyes. "Oh, Griffin!"

Maximus grunted. "You're an annoying prick, but I suppose I must accept you into the family."

He glanced at Hero.

She tilted her chin up. "Unless you prefer I elope?"

Maximus shuddered. "I'd never hear the end of it from Cousin Bathilda if you did." He leaned down and offered his hand to Griffin. "Pax?"

Griffin took the proffered hand. "Pax."

"Now." Maximus straightened in the saddle. "Where is this orphanage?"

SILENCE LOOKED UP at the drunken tough advancing on her and wondered if she would want to live after he finished with her.

A shout came from behind the man. Since it was merely one of many raucous voices raised in the night, her attacker ignored it. But he couldn't ignore the gloved hand that slapped down on his shoulder. The drunken lout began to turn, but he suddenly spun in an oddly graceful movement that ended with him face-first on the ground.

Silence blinked and glanced up at her savior.

And then she could only stare. The man before her looked like something out of a pantomime. He wore breeches and a tunic patterned all over in a harlequin's red and black diamonds. On his feet were tall black jackboots, and cuffed black gloves covered his hands. A grotesque half-mask with an enormous hooked nose concealed his features, leaving only his mouth and chin bare. As she looked at him, he doffed a huge wide-brimmed black hat and swept her a courtly bow.

"You're the Ghost of St. Giles!" she blurted.

His mouth curled at the corner, but he made no sound, simply gesturing with his hat before him as if to direct her path.

"I live over there," she said, feeling a bit foolish for talking with a mute comic actor.

His mouth tightened, and again he bowed and most definitely directed her in the *opposite* way from the home.

"I suppose I can trust you?" she said.

He grinned, which did not at all set her mind at rest. On the other hand, he *had* saved her, and with such a notorious escort, she had no fear of being accosted again.

"Very well." She lifted her skirts and then stopped as she saw someone beyond him.

There on the other side of the street was Mickey O'Connor. He stood facing her, hands on hips, a slight frown between his beautiful brows, making no attempt to conceal himself from her.

But then why would he have any reason to hide from her?

He nodded, acknowledging he knew she'd seen him, and she looked away, her breath trembling in her throat. That was when she realized that the Ghost had tightened his fist on the hilt of his sword.

"No, don't," she said, laying a hand on his arm.

He looked at her, his head cocked to the side in inquiry.

Silence didn't know if she was worried for him or for Mr. O'Connor. She only knew she'd seen enough bloodshed for the night. "Please."

He nodded once and removed his hand from the hilt of his sword.

Silence couldn't help it. She looked again across the street.

Mr. O'Connor's black gaze bored into her. He didn't look at all happy.

She deliberately turned away. "This way, did you say?"

The Ghost nodded and they set off. For the first couple of minutes, as Silence picked her way over the cobblestones, she felt Mr. O'Connor's gaze on her back. She refused to turn around, to acknowledge him in any way, and after a bit she no longer felt the sensation.

She let out a breath and concentrated on her surroundings. The Ghost walked with an almost soundless tread, light and athletic. His head was up, and he seemed almost to *scent* the wind. Twice he stopped and turned down a different street as if to avoid the mob. Once he took her arm and urged her into a run, just before she heard shouts from behind them. Oddly, though he never spoke and she couldn't see most of his face, she never felt afraid of him.

When at last they came within sight of the temporary home, Silence stopped short. There was a crowd of people outside the home's doors, but she could see in the light of the lanterns they held that they were soldiers.

"Whatever are soldiers doing here?" she asked.

Obviously she didn't expect an answer, but when she turned, she was surprised to find herself alone. She glanced quickly up the street, but there was no sign of the Ghost.

The Ghost had disappeared as abruptly as he'd appeared.

"Men are so maddening," Silence muttered to herself, and started for the home.

"Mrs. Hollingbrook!" Nell appeared at the home's door and ran toward her. "Oh, ma'am! We were that worried for you. Three informers have been murdered tonight— or so they say. There was rioting in the streets, and Mr. Makepeace has been beside himself. I've never seen him in such a state before."

"Where is Winter?" Silence asked distractedly. "Is that Lady Hero?"

"Yes, ma'am," Nell said. "And the Duke of Wakefield himself! You can't credit the excitement there's been."

Silence squinted. It looked very much as if . . . "Is Lady Hero kissing Lord Griffin?"

Nell nodded. "She's engaged to him."

"But I thought she was engaged to his *brother*, the Marquess of Mandeville," Silence said, feeling very confused.

Nell shrugged. "Not by the looks of it."

And indeed Lady Hero seemed quite affectionate with Lord Griffin. Silence was still trying to puzzle the matter out when Winter suddenly appeared, hatless and panting.

"Thank God!" He wrapped her in a bear hug, an extraordinary demonstration of affection for Winter. "We feared the worst."

"I'm sorry," Silence gasped. "I had to move the baby to a new wet nurse, and by the time I was done, it was already dark."

Winter stepped back and closed his eyes. "Well, no more. I don't think I could survive another night like this one. From now on, we only go out in pairs."

Silence nodded. "You're right. If it hadn't been for the Ghost of St. Giles—"

He turned suddenly and pierced her with a stare. "What?"

She blinked, taken aback. "The Ghost of St. Giles. I saw him. He was the one who escorted me home safely."

No need to go into *how* he'd found her. Winter was already anxious about her well-being without telling him how close she'd come to rape—and worse.

Winter lifted his head, glancing about the dark street. "He was here?"

"Yes," Silence said slowly. "He brought me here and then disappeared. Why do you ask?"

Winter shrugged. "The Ghost always seems to be about when I'm not. I'd like to catch a glimpse of this phantom apparition someday."

"He isn't a phantom, that I can assure you," Silence said. "He was as real as you and I."

Winter grunted. "Well, in any case, we don't have the time to speculate about the Ghost at the moment. Our illustrious visitors require our attention."

"Lady Hero said she had something to speak to you about," Nell said. "I just remembered."

"What is it?" Silence asked.

Nell knit her brows. "Something about spinning. I can't think what, but she did seem most insistent."

"Spinning?" Silence couldn't think how spinning might concern Lady Hero, but then the aristocracy was a breed apart at times. "We'd best go see."

Chapter Twenty

❦

"I have one last question for you," the queen announced
to her frowning suitors. "What is in my heart?"
Well! Her question was not met with joy by the three
princes. Prince Eastsun frowned and for a moment
simply opened and closed his handsome mouth before
admitting defeat and bowing from the room. Prince
Westmoon scowled and stomped out, muttering about the
frivolousness of queens and women in general. Prince
Northwind shook his head and said, "Who can understand
the heart of a woman?" And then he, too, left.
The advisers, ministers, and men of letters fell to arguing,
but Queen Ravenhair quietly left the throne room and
made for the stables....
—from *Queen Ravenhair*

Six weeks later...

"He's a priggish ass, and I don't see why I should bother
to even reply." Griffin threw the letter from Thomas on
the breakfast room table.

Across from him, his wife of only one week continued
to serenely pour her tea. "You need to not only answer
him, but also agree to see him for dinner because he is
your brother."

"Humph." Griffin crossed his arms on his chest and attempted to glare at Hero but was somewhat diverted by the magnificence of her décolletage. "Is that a new frock?"

"Yes, and don't change the subject," she replied with adorable severity. It always rather aroused him when she attempted to be severe with him.

Of course, his wife could arouse him by reciting the alphabet, too.

"What are you going to do today?" he asked, ignoring her order.

"I'm going to inspect the progress Mr. Templeton's made on the new home. He thinks they may actually be done before spring. After that, I'll stop by the home and see how the spinning lessons are going."

"Splendid!" Griffin had already bought a prize ram and breeding ewes. By spring the children would have new wool to spin.

She smiled. "And then I'm off to a tea at Lady Beckinhall's, where I hope to persuade her to join my Ladies' Syndicate for the Benefit of the Home for Unfortunate Infants and Foundling Children."

He made a show of shuddering. "The name alone strikes fear into my heart."

"Why?"

"A syndication of ladies involving both one's wife and one's sister," he replied darkly, "would strike fear into any man's heart."

"Silly," she said blithely. "Margaret will laugh when I tell her you said so."

"And prove my point."

She gave him a look and set down her cup of tea. "Now, as to your brother—"

"Name me one good reason why I should see him"—Griffin held up a finger as she opened her lips—"*besides* the fact that I'm unfortunately related to him."

She smiled sweetly, which he had begun to realize in the last week was a warning sign. "It would please your mother."

"Huh," was his devastating reply. The fact was that he'd do almost anything to make Mater happy, and Hero well knew it.

"And," she said, picking up a piece of toast, "it would please me as well."

Griffin straightened in outrage at that. "He *hit* you!"

"And I've forgiven him," she said. "He did give me that incredibly expensive emerald necklace in apology."

"Lavinia made him do that," he pointed out.

"It was still a lovely gesture nonetheless." She eyed him as she crunched her toast. "And that was after he sent me roses daily for three weeks straight. I don't know why you stopped him."

"Whole damned house smelled of wilting roses," Griffin muttered. "Irritating as hell."

His wife looked at him with those diamond eyes. "Don't you think that if I can forgive him, you should, too?"

"Huh." He was huhing a lot since marrying Hero. Rather lowering for one's self-esteem, that. A devious thought suddenly presented itself. Griffin widened his eyes. "If I endure what will no doubt be a horrible dinner with Thomas, will you kiss me?"

She narrowed her eyes. Lovely, but no fool, was his wife. "I always kiss you."

"Not," he said silkily, "*that* kind of kiss."

He watched as pink rose in her cheeks. Married a week

and he could still make his wife blush, by God! One had to take one's victories where one could.

"Are you trying to blackmail me?" she hissed incredulously. "That's rather low, even for you."

He straightened the cuffs on his coat. "I prefer to think of it as an incentive."

She snorted delicately.

"Just one kiss." His eyelids drooped lazily at the thought of her kissing him *there*. "One tiny, little kiss."

It was a delight to see her cheeks flame pinker. "Rogue."

He smiled lazily. "Tease."

"Will you go?"

"Will you kiss me?"

She bit her lip, and his cock stood at attention. "Perhaps."

Which was why, several hours later, Griffin found himself mounting the steps of Mandeville House. Not even the remembrance of Hero's eyes as she'd murmured that "perhaps" improved his mood. He knocked, half hoping that his brother wouldn't answer and he could just go home to his wife.

But the door opened, and he was admitted and escorted into a dining room. Griffin looked around. At one end of a long mahogany table, his brother was seated. One other place setting lay at Thomas's right hand. Otherwise the table was empty.

He hadn't seen Thomas since the day they'd argued. In the intervening weeks, they'd both married, and Thomas—in an interesting role reversal—had endured something of a miniature scandal for marrying the notorious Mrs. Tate.

Griffin strolled toward Thomas. "Where is Lavinia?"

Thomas, who had stood on his entrance, picked up his glass of wine and took a deep drink, eyeing Griffin sourly over the rim. "She said it would be best if we dined alone."

Griffin dropped into his chair. "Hero wouldn't come either."

Thomas's gaze lowered. "I'm truly sorry for hurting her."

"As well you should be," Griffin growled. He looked away. "She says she's forgiven you."

Thomas sighed. "I'm glad."

Griffin stared at his glass for a bit. If he drank it down, he might keep drinking and on the whole, he'd rather be sober when he returned home to Hero and her kiss.

Thomas cleared his throat. "Lavinia says I must tell you that I believe you."

It took a moment for Griffin to work out that complicated comment; then he straightened in his chair. "You do?"

Thomas nodded, sipping his wine.

Griffin slammed his palm down on the table. All the dishes jumped, and a fork fell off the edge. "Then why the hell didn't you say so earlier?"

Thomas scowled. "She always liked you."

"Anne?" Griffin asked incredulously.

Thomas nodded.

"So? *You* were the one she married."

"But if I hadn't had the title—"

"But you *did* have the title," Griffin near roared. Of all the stupid, soft-brained—

Thomas slammed his own hand down. A glass crashed to the floor. "You don't understand! You've never understood. *I* might have the title and Father's affections, but *you* have Mother's and everyone else's!"

Griffin blinked. "You were...*jealous*? Of me?"

Thomas looked away, a muscle ticking in his jaw.

And it was suddenly too much for Griffin. He shouted with laughter, holding his belly, doubled over the table.

"It's not that funny," Thomas said when Griffin paused to take a breath.

"It bloody well is," Griffin assured him. "You've barely talked to me for over three years and all because you were jealous. Jesus, Thomas! You're richer, older, and scads more handsome than me. What more do you want?"

Thomas shrugged. "She always liked you better."

Griffin sobered. "Who? Anne or Mater?"

"Both." Thomas stared moodily into his glass. "When Father died, I thought I'd be the one in charge. I was the marquess, after all. But then we realized Father's debts, and she called you home from Cambridge."

"I do have the better head for business."

Thomas nodded stiffly. "You do. You did. Even though you were only twenty—and two years younger than I— you immediately set to improving our finances."

"Would you prefer I'd let us all go to debtor's prison?" Griffin asked drily.

"No." Thomas raised his face and looked him frankly in the eye. "I'd prefer that I were the one who could save Mother from financial ruin."

Griffin stared at him for a moment and thought about what it must have cost Thomas to admit that he wasn't good at something.

He leaned forward and poured his brother some more wine. "Every time you've ever made a speech in parliament,

Mater has written all about it to me—pages and pages of details, the points you made and the reaction of the Lords."

Thomas's mouth dropped open. "Truly?"

Griffin nodded. "Truly. Haven't you ever noticed her in the ladies' gallery?"

"No." Thomas shook his head, looking a little dazed. "I had no idea."

"Well, now you do." Griffin set the bottle down and leaned back in the chair. "Besides, what good would *two* financial geniuses in the family do?"

THE OPENING OF the bedroom door woke Hero that night. She yawned and stretched indolently as Griffin set down the candle he carried and took off his wig.

It was sadly unsophisticated but they'd decided they preferred to share a room—and a bed—at night. So upon their marriage, she'd moved into his bedroom and was in the process of redecorating the sitting room on one side into a dressing room for her.

"You were out late," she murmured, her voice husky from sleep.

Griffin, who'd splashed water on his face from the basin on his dresser, turned to her with a cloth in his hand. "Thomas wanted to discuss his estates."

His voice was relaxed—a far cry from the tension in his body when he'd left this evening for his brother's house. "It went well, then?"

"Well enough. He's very interested in the new weaving venture." He threw the cloth to the dresser top and prowled toward her, his gaze roaming over the silk coverlet she held to her chest. "Are you wearing anything under there?"

She lowered her eyes demurely. "No . . . Well, yes."

He cocked an eyebrow as he shrugged out of his coat. "What?"

She tilted her head.

His gaze went to her left ear. "Ah. Your diamond earbob." He tugged at his neckcloth. "Where's the other one?"

She lifted one bare arm out from underneath the covers and pointed mutely at the table beside the bed.

He dropped his neckcloth and waistcoat onto a chair, then came over to look. Griffin picked up the other earbob. "Is this the one you threw at me?"

"Yes." She lay back against the fluffy down pillows.

"I see." He toed off his shoes and crawled over the bed at her, the mattress sinking beneath his weight. "May I?"

She licked her lips, feeling the acceleration of her pulse. "Please."

He straddled her, kneeling on the coverlet, trapping her beneath, and leaned over her. Gently he took her earlobe in his warm fingers, and she felt him insert the fine gold wire into her ear.

She shivered.

He cocked his head, examining his handiwork. "Beautiful."

"They are my favorite," she said.

His eyes moved to hers, amused, aroused, and dangerously possessive. "I wasn't referring to the earring."

She arched her brows innocently. "Weren't you?"

"No." He bent and licked her throat.

Goose bumps rose over her skin, making her nipples come almost painfully erect.

"I think I first fell in love with you when you threw that earbob at me," he whispered against her skin.

"How could you?" she gasped. She wanted to take her arms out from underneath the covers, but his weight on the sheets prevented her. "You were making love to another woman."

"Not making love," he contradicted her choice of words. "I never made love until I met you. And besides, it doesn't matter. I forgot her the moment I saw you."

She laughed, though her lips trembled. "Do you expect me to believe such balderdash?"

"Oh, yes," he murmured, tugging the sheet lower on her bosom. "Believe me and love me in return."

He raised his head, and she met his gaze, suddenly serious. "I do. I do love you."

A corner of his mouth quirked up. "When did you know?"

She bit her lip, wishing he'd go back to kissing her, wanting at the same time to draw this out endlessly. "You're fishing for compliments."

"And if I am?" He took the coverlet between his teeth and tugged it down beneath one breast. He hovered over the nipple, close enough that she felt his hot breath, but he didn't touch her.

"I think it was when you kissed me at Harte's Folly," she whispered.

He snorted. "You thought I was Thomas."

She laughed. "I didn't! I was only teasing you by pretending I thought you were he—you'd made me so irritated. I'd never mistake you for—Oh!"

He'd leaned down and delicately taken her nipple between his teeth. She felt the flick of his tongue against the sensitive tip, and then he was sucking strongly on her.

She moaned, low and shockingly animal.

He let go of the nipple. "You were saying?"

"I'd never mistake you for another," she whispered, watching him from beneath half-closed lids. "We talked about true love on that first night. Do you remember?"

"How could I forget?" He pulled the coverlet down another inch and exposed her other breast. Idly he played with her nipples. "I had an uneasy feeling, even then, that you were the one for me."

She swallowed, having trouble forming words with his hands working so exquisitely on her. "You are my true love, Griffin, now and forever. Sometimes when I think how close I came to turning away from you out of pure cowardliness, I want to weep."

"Hush," he murmured, brushing kisses over her lips, still pinching and fondling her nipples. "You didn't. We are together—and we'll remain together. Forever."

"Promise?" she whispered beneath his lips.

"Promise," he said just before kissing her deeply.

When he raised his head again, she was wet and wanting, but he still had her pinned beneath the coverlet.

"Are you ever going to let me go?" she asked.

"No," he said, looking very satisfied. "I think I rather like you in this position, unable to move or object to whatever I want to do to you."

She squirmed a little, feeling the slide of the silken covers against her bare skin. "I do like this, but it does have one drawback."

"What is that?" he asked absently as he traced circles on her breasts.

"I might find it hard to kiss you."

"What do you mean? It's easy enough for..." He trailed away as he obviously rethought her words.

"Not *there*," she purred. Really, she'd had no idea she could make such a sound.

His gaze flew to hers, suddenly very green and hopeful. He was off the bed in a thrice, doffing his clothes eagerly.

Hero took the opportunity to remove the covers. She lay like a wanton, head propped on one hand, watching as her husband, nude and gloriously erect, turned to her.

His gaze swept over her naked form and came to rest on what she knew was the blush on her face. "I love you."

"I love you as well." She inhaled, feeling very scandalous as she crooked one finger. "Come here and I'll give you a kiss you'll never forget."

And she did.

Epilogue

Queen Ravenhair walked into her stables and found there,
away in the back, her stable master currying her
favorite mare. "My suitors have all fled, Ian,"
she said to the man.
The stable master looked faintly surprised.
"You know my name, Your Majesty?"
"Oh, yes," she said, drawing nearer. "I wonder
if you might answer me a question?"
"I'll do my best," said he.
"What is in my heart?"
The stable master threw down the curry brush and turned to
face the queen. He looked at her gravely with warm brown
eyes. "Love, Your Majesty. Your heart is filled with love."
She raised a haughty eyebrow. "Indeed? And will
you tell me what is in your heart, Ian?"
He stepped closer and took her dainty,
white hands in his own big, calloused ones.
"Love, Your Majesty. Love for you."
"Then I think you ought to call me Ravenhair, hadn't
you?" she murmured as she kissed him.
He threw back his head and laughed. "I am far from
perfect, my darling Ravenhair, but I would be the happiest
man in the world if you would take me as your husband."
"And I will be the happiest woman in the world to be your
wife." She smiled back, her heart overflowing with joy,
and rose on her tiptoes to whisper in his ear, "I don't
think I truly want perfection anyway."
—from *Queen Ravenhair*

"Mamoo!" Mary Darling giggled as she knocked over the tin cups Silence had carefully helped her stack on the kitchen floor.

The cups fell with a great clatter, and the little girl clapped her hands in glee.

"Goodness! That was very loud," Silence said fondly.

The baby bounced on her bottom. "Mo'! Mo'!"

"Very well, we'll stack them once more, and then, young lady, I think it'll be time for a nap." Silence had found that though Mary Darling might protest mightily at the thought of a nap, she was much happier with one.

"You look cheerful this afternoon, sister." Winter came in the kitchen and set down his bundle of books.

"Do I?" Silence was aware that Winter had been keeping a close eye on her since William's death.

"Yes." Winter made a sudden horrible face at Mary, which sent the baby into gales of laughter. "I think that cap becomes you."

Silence smiled a little sadly. It wasn't the cap, she knew. It was little Mary Darling. One couldn't let oneself wallow in grief with an active baby to care for. And perhaps that was for the best. She stroked a finger over Mary's downy cheek. Life had to go on, after all.

"Is it stew again?" Winter peered into the pot on the hearth.

"Beef and cabbage," Silence replied.

"Good." Winter never seemed to notice what was set before him, but like all men, he had a deep appreciation for tasty food. "I'll just go and wash before luncheon."

"Hurry," she called after his retreating back. "I've still got to put Mary down for a nap."

He waved over his shoulder to indicate he'd heard her.

"Let's just hope Uncle Winter doesn't start reading a book up there," she confided to Mary.

The baby chortled and knocked over a tin cup.

"Mrs. Hollingbrook!" Joseph Tinbox, one of the home's older boys, ran into the kitchen. "Look what I've found on the step."

He held out a small wooden box.

Silence stared at the offering like it was an adder. Their step had been mercifully free from any gifts since the morning of the riots, and she'd been hoping that perhaps the giver had forgotten them.

"Shall I open it?" Joseph asked eagerly.

"*No*," Silence said a little too sharply. She inhaled. "Shouldn't you be at your afternoon lessons?"

"Aw!"

She lifted a brow. "Now, Joseph."

Joseph wrinkled his nose but slumped off obediently to his lessons.

Silence picked up the box with trembling fingers. She prized open the lid and stared inside. A lock of hair lay there, tied with a scarlet ribbon. She picked it up between thumb and forefinger, but no note was hidden underneath.

"Whose do you suppose it is?" she whispered to the baby.

It was a black lock, the hair so dark it shone blue-black. In fact, it was very like Mary Darling's own hair. Now that her curls had grown in thickly, they'd revealed themselves as inky black. Silence held the lock to the baby's head experimentally as Mary bent over her tin cups.

The hair was a perfect match.

But the lock didn't come from Mary Darling's head.

Silence would know if someone had cut it, and besides, Mary's hair was still too short. No, the lock of hair was long and curling, and really rather beautiful. A woman with hair like this—

Silence suddenly dropped the lock in shock.

Or a *man*. She knew of one man who had long, curling, inky-black hair. She gazed in horror at the baby playing before her. The baby she'd nursed and played with and sung to like she was her very own for the last seven months. The baby she'd given her heart to.

Mary's hair matched Charming Mickey's hair exactly.

Don't miss the stunning
conclusion to the
Maiden Lane series!

Turn the page for an excerpt from

Duke of Desire

Chapter One

Once upon a time there lived a poor stonecutter...
—from *The Rock King*

APRIL 1742

Considering how extremely dull her life had been up until this point, Iris Daniels, Lady Jordan had discovered a quite colorful way to die.

Torches flamed on tall stakes driven into the ground. Their flickering light in the moonless night made shadows jump and waver over the masked men grouped in a circle around her.

The *naked* masked men.

Their masks weren't staid black half masks, either. No. They wore bizarre animal or bird shapes. She saw a crow, a badger, a mouse, and a bear with a hairy belly and a crooked red manhood.

She knelt next to a great stone slab, a primitive fallen monolith brought here centuries ago by people long forgotten. Her trembling hands were bound in front of her, her hair was coming down about her face, her dress was in a shocking state, and she very much suspected that she might *smell*—a result of having been kidnapped over four days before.

In front of her stood three men, the masters of this horrific farce.

The first wore a fox mask. He was slim, pale, and, judging by his body hair, a redhead. His inner forearm was tattooed with a small dolphin.

The second wore a mask in the likeness of a young man's face with grapes in its hair—the god Dionysus if she wasn't mistaken—which, oddly, was far more terrifying than any of the animal masks. He bore a dolphin tattoo on his upper right arm.

The last wore a wolf mask and was taller by a head then the other two. His body hair was black, he stood with a calm air of power, and he, too, bore a dolphin tattoo—directly on the jut of his left hipbone. The placement rather drew the eye to the man's...erm...*masculine attributes*.

The man in the wolf mask had nothing to be ashamed of.

Iris shuddered in disgust and glanced away, accidentally meeting the Wolf's mocking gaze.

She lifted her chin in defiance. She knew what this group of men was. This was the Lords of Chaos, an odious secret society composed of aristocrats who enjoyed two things: power and the rape and destruction of women and children.

Iris swallowed hard and reminded herself that she was a *lady*—her family could trace its line nearly to the time of the Conqueror—and as such she had her name and honor to uphold.

These...*creatures* might kill her—and worse—but they would not take her dignity.

"My Lords!" the Dionysus called, raising his arms above his head in a theatrical gesture that showed very little taste—but then he *was* addressing an audience of nude, masked men. "My Lords, I welcome you to our spring revels. Tonight we make a special sacrifice—the new Duchess of Kyle!"

The crowd roared like slavering beasts.

Iris blinked. The Duchess of...

She glanced quickly around.

As far as she could see in the macabre flickering torchlight, *she* was the only sacrifice in evidence, and she was most certainly *not* the Duchess of Kyle.

The commotion began to die down.

Iris cleared her throat. "No, I'm not."

"Silence," the Fox hissed.

She narrowed her eyes at him. In the last four days she'd been kidnapped on her way home from the wedding of the *true* Duchess of Kyle, she'd been bound, hooded, and thrown on the floor of a carriage, where she'd *remained* as the carriage bumped over road after rutted road, and then, on arrival at this place, she'd been shoved into a tiny stone hut without any sort of fire. She had been starved and had only a few cups of water to drink. Last, but most definitely *not* least, she'd been forced to relieve herself in a *bucket*.

All of which had given her far too much time to contemplate her own death and what torture would precede it.

She might be terrified and alone, but she wasn't about to surrender to the Lords' plans without a fight. As far as she could see she had nothing to lose and quite possibly her life to gain.

So she raised her voice and said clearly and loudly, "You have made a mistake. I am *not* the Duchess of Kyle."

The Wolf turned to the Dionysus and spoke for the first time. His voice was deep and smoky. "Your men kidnapped the wrong woman."

"Don't be a fool," the Dionysus snapped at him. "We captured her three days after her wedding to Kyle."

"Yes, returning *home* to London from the wedding," Iris said. "The Duke of Kyle married a young woman named Alf, not me. Why would I leave the duke if I'd just married him?"

The Dionysus rounded on the Fox, making the other man cringe. "You told me that you *saw* her marry Kyle."

The Wolf chuckled darkly.

"She lies!" cried the Fox, and he leaped toward her, his arm raised.

The Wolf lunged, seized the Fox's right arm, twisted it up behind his back, and slammed the other man to his knees.

Iris stared and felt a tremble shake her body. She'd never seen a man move so swiftly.

Nor so brutally.

The Wolf bent over his prey, both men panting, their naked bodies sweating. The snout of the Wolf mask pressed against the Fox's vulnerable bent neck. "Don't. Touch. What. Is. *Mine.*"

"Let him go," the Dionysus barked.

The Wolf didn't move.

The Dionysus's hands curled into fists. "*Obey* me."

The Wolf finally turned his mask from the Fox's neck to look at the Dionysus. "You have the wrong woman—a corrupt sacrifice, one not worthy of the revel. I want her."

"Take care," murmured the Dionysus. "You are new to our society."

The Wolf tilted his head. "Not so new as all that."

"Perhaps newly *rejoined*, then," the Dionysus replied. "You still do not know our ways."

"I know that as the host, I have the right to claim her," growled the Wolf. "She is forfeit to me."

The Dionysus tilted his head as if considering. "Only by my leave."

The Wolf abruptly threw wide his arms, releasing the Fox and gracefully standing again. "Then by your *leave*," he said, his words holding an edge of mockery.

The firelight gleamed off his muscled chest and strong arms. He stood with an easy air of command.

What would make a man with such natural power join this gruesome society?

The other members of the Lords of Chaos didn't seem happy at the thought of having their principal entertainment for the evening snatched out from under their noses. The masked men around her muttered and shifted, a restless miasma of danger hovering in the night air.

Any spark could set them off, Iris suddenly realized.

"Well?" the Wolf asked the Dionysus.

"You can't let her go," the Fox said to his leader, getting to his feet. There were red marks beginning to bruise on his pale skin. "Why the bloody hell are you listening to him? She's *ours*. Let us take our fill of her and—"

The Wolf struck him on the side of the head—a terrible blow that made the Fox fly backward.

"*Mine*," growled the Wolf. He looked at the Dionysus again. "Do you lead the Lords or not?"

"I think it more than evident that I lead the Lords,"

the Dionysus drawled, even as the muttering of the crowd grew louder. "And I think I need not prove my mettle by giving you this woman."

Iris swallowed. They were fighting over her like feral dogs over a scrap of meat. Was it better if the Wolf claimed her? She didn't know.

The Wolf stood between Iris and the Dionysus, and she saw the muscles in his legs and buttocks tense. She wondered if the Dionysus noticed that the other man was readying for battle.

"However," the Dionysus continued, "I can grant her to you as an act of . . . *charity*. Enjoy her in whatever way you see fit, but take care that her heart no longer beats when next the sun rises."

Iris sucked in a breath at the sudden death sentence. The Dionysus had ordered her murder as casually as he would step on a beetle.

"My word," the Wolf bit out, and Iris's fearful glance flew to him.

Dear God, these men were monsters.

The Dionysus tilted his head. "Your word—heard by all."

A low growl came from behind the wolf mask. He bent and gripped Iris's bound wrists and hauled her to her feet. She stumbled after him as he strode through the mass of angry masked men. The crowd jostled against her, shoving her from all sides with bare arms and elbows until the Wolf finally pulled her free.

She had been brought to this place hooded, and for the first time she saw that it was a ruined church or cathedral. Stones and broken arches loomed in the dark, and she tripped more than once over weed-covered rubble. The spring night was chilly away from the fires, but the man in the wolf mask, striding naked in the gloom, seemed unaffected by the elements. He continued his pace until they reached a dirt road and several waiting carriages.

He walked up to one and without preamble opened the door and shoved her inside. "Wait here. Don't scream or try to escape. You won't like my response."

And with that ominous statement the door closed. Iris was left panting in terror in the dark, empty carriage.

Immediately she tried the carriage door, but he'd locked or jammed it somehow. It wouldn't open.

She could hear men's voices in the distance. Shouts and cries. *Dear God*. They sounded like a pack of rabid dogs. What would the Wolf do to her?

She needed a weapon. Something—*anything*—with which to defend herself.

Hurriedly she felt the door—a handle, but she couldn't wrench it off—a small window, no curtains—the walls of the carriage—*nothing*. The seats were plush velvet. Expensive. Sometimes in better-made carriages the seats...

She yanked at one.

It lifted up.

Inside was a small space.

She reached in and felt a fur blanket. Nothing else.

Damn.

She could hear the Wolf's growling voice just outside the carriage.

Desperately she flung herself at the opposite seat and tugged it up. Thrust her hand in.

A pistol.

She cocked it, desperately praying that it was loaded.

She turned and aimed it at the door to the carriage just as the door swung open.

The Wolf loomed in the doorway—still nude—a lantern in one hand. She saw the eyes behind the mask flick to the pistol she held between her bound hands. He turned his head and said something in an incomprehensible language to someone outside.

Iris felt her breath sawing in and out of her chest.

He climbed into the carriage and closed the door, completely ignoring her and the pistol pointed at him. The Wolf hung the lantern on a hook and sat on the seat across from her.

Finally he glanced at her. "Put that down."

His voice was calm. Quiet.

With just a hint of menace.

She backed into the opposite corner, as far away from him as possible, holding the pistol up. Level with his chest. Her heart was pounding so hard it nearly deafened her. "No."

The carriage jolted into motion, making her stumble before she caught herself.

"T-tell them to stop the carriage," she said, stuttering with terror despite her resolve. "Let me go now."

"So that they can rape you to death out there?" He tilted his head to indicate the Lords. "No."

"At the next village, then."

"I think not."

He reached for her and she knew she had no choice.

She shot him.

The blast blew him into the seat and threw her hands up and back, the pistol narrowly missing her nose.

Iris scrambled to her feet. The bullet was gone, but she could still use the pistol as a bludgeon.

The Wolf was sprawled across the seat, blood streaming from a gaping hole in his right shoulder. His mask had been knocked askew on his face.

She reached forward and snatched it off.

And then gasped.

The face that was revealed had once been as beautiful as an angel's but was now horribly mutilated. A livid red scar ran from just below his hairline on the right side of his face, bisecting the eyebrow, somehow missing the eye itself but gouging a furrow into the lean cheek and catching the edge of his upper lip, making it twist. The scar ended in a missing divot of flesh in the line of the man's severe jaw. He had inky black hair and, though they were closed now, Iris knew he had emotionless crystal-gray eyes.

She knew because she recognized him.

He was Raphael de Chartres, the Duke of Dyemore, and when she'd danced with him—once—three months ago at a ball, she'd thought he'd looked like Hades.

God of the underworld.

God of the dead.

She had no reason to change her opinion now.

Then he gasped, those frozen crystal eyes opened, and he glared at her. "You idiot woman. I'm trying to *save* you."

RAPHAEL GRIMACED IN pain, feeling the scar tissue on the right side of his face pull his upper lip. No doubt the movement turned his mouth into a grotesque sneer.

The woman who'd shot him had eyes the color of the sky above the moors just after a storm: blue-gray sky after black clouds. That particular shade of blue had been one of the few things his mother had found beautiful in England.

Raphael agreed.

Despite the fear that shone in them, Lady Jordan's blue-gray eyes were beautiful.

"What do you mean you're trying to save me?" She still held the pistol as if ready to club him over the head should he move, the bloodthirsty little thing.

"I mean that I don't intend to ravish and kill you." *Years* of anguish and dreams of revenge followed by months of planning to infiltrate the Lords of Chaos, only to have the whole thing collapse because of *blue-gray eyes*. He was a bloody fool. "I merely wished to spirit you away from the Lords of Chaos's debauchery. Oddly enough, I believed you would be grateful."

Her lovely brows drew together suspiciously over those eyes. "You promised the Dionysus that you'd *kill* me."

"I *lied*," he drawled. "If I'd meant you harm, I assure you, I'd have trussed you up like a Christmas goose. You'll note I didn't."

"Oh, dear Lord." She looked stricken as she flung down the pistol, staring at his gory shoulder. "This is a mess."

"Quite," he said through gritted teeth.

Raphael glanced down at his shoulder. The wound was a mass of mangled flesh, the blood pumping from within at a steady pace. This was not good. He'd meant to have her securely on the road back to London tonight, guarded by his men. If the Dionysus heard that she'd shot him, that he was *weakened*—

He grunted and tried to sit up against the swaying of the carriage, eyeing her, this woman he'd only truly met once before.

He'd first seen her in a ballroom where he'd gone to meet members of the Lords of Chaos. In that den of corruption, swarming with his enemies, she'd stood out, pure and innocent. He'd warned her to leave that dangerous place. Then, when she'd walked alone back to her carriage, he'd shadowed her to make sure she made it safely there.

And that would've been that—had he not discovered that she was all but engaged to the Duke of Kyle—a man tasked, on orders of the King, with the risky job of bringing down the Lords of Chaos. Raphael knew that as long as Kyle pursued the Lords, Lady Jordan would be in danger. Because of this, Raphael had spent no little time worried about her. Had even gone so far as to trail her into the country to Kyle's estate.

There he'd seen her marry Kyle—or so he'd thought.

At that point Raphael had been forced to consider the matter at an end. Lady Jordan's protection was no longer his concern, but her husband's. Raphael might be loath to admit it, but Kyle was more than equal to the task of protecting his wife. If Raphael had felt some small twinge of longing...well, he'd made sure to bury it deep inside, where it would die a natural death from lack of light.

Yet now...

It was as if his previously stopped heart jolted and started beating again. "Are you truly not the Duchess of Kyle?"

"No." She reached for him, and he was astonished at how gentle her hands were. She had no cause to be gentle with him—not after what she'd been through tonight. Yet she placed both small palms about his left arm—the unharmed side—and helped him stand. He lurched across the moving carriage and half fell into the opposite seat.

"I, too, saw you married to Kyle," Raphael said evenly.

She glared. "*How?* Alf and Hugh were married inside their country manor. The King was there, and I assure you there were guards everywhere."

"I saw Kyle kiss you in the garden at the celebration afterwards," he said. "There might have been guards, but I assure *you* they neglected to search the woods overlooking the garden."

"It rather serves you right that you confused the matter since you were *spying*," she said tartly. "I don't remember Hugh kissing me, but if he did it was in a brotherly manner. We're *friends*. It doesn't matter anyway. Whatever you *imagined* you saw, I'm not married to Hugh."

He closed his eyes for a moment, wondering *why* she'd bothered moving him, when he felt the bulk of a fur rug bunched over his nude body. He hadn't even realized that he was shivering.

Ah, of course. The rug that had been stored in the bench he'd been sitting on. "Yet it was well known in London that you were to marry the Duke of Kyle."

"We let the gossips think I was the bride at the wedding because his real wife is without family or name." She shook her head. "'Twill be a scandal when the news comes out. Is that why you saved me? Because you thought I was the duchess?"

"No." Raphael opened his eyes and watched as she unwrapped the fichu from about her neck, exposing a deep décolletage. Her breasts were sweetly vulnerable. He glanced aside. Such things were not for one as tainted as he. "I would have rescued you in any case—duchess or not."

"But why?" She flipped the fur away from his shoulder and pressed the flimsy fichu hard against the wound.

He inhaled, not bothering to answer her nonsensical question. Did she think him a demon?

But then she *had* just seen him attending what was at base a demonic rite.

"You have to stop the carriage," she was saying. "I can't halt the bleeding. You need a doctor. I should—"

"We're near my home," he said, cutting her off. "We'll be there soon enough. Just keep pressing. You're doing fine, Lady Jordan."

Her blue-gray gaze flicked up to his, wide with surprise. "I wasn't sure if you recognized me."

This was intimate, her face so close to his. He naked and she with the upper slopes of her breasts uncovered. He felt hazy with desperate temptation. He could *smell* her, above the scent of his own blood—a faint flower scent.

Not cedarwood, thank God.

"You're hard to forget," he murmured.

She frowned as if uncertain whether he complimented or insulted her. "Is that why you rescued me? Because you recognized me from that one dance?"

"No." *Not at all.* He hadn't known whom the Dionysus meant to sacrifice tonight. Hadn't known there was to *be* a sacrifice—though of course that was a possibility. Would he have rescued any woman?

Perhaps.

But the moment he'd seen *her*, he'd known he had to act. "You seem oddly competent at handling a gunshot wound."

"My late husband James was an officer in His Majesty's army," she said. "I followed him on campaign on the Continent. There were times when tending a wound became very helpful."

He swallowed, watching her from beneath half-lowered lids, trying to *think*. He couldn't afford to show weakness in these parts—it was why he'd brought his own servants from Corsica. The Lords of Chaos were powerful in this area. If the Dionysus discovered that he was wounded, he—and she—would be in peril. The Dionysus already wanted her dead and expected Raphael to kill her.

A wicked idea crept into his mind.

She was a temptation—a temptation aimed at his one weakness. He'd walked alone for so long. For his entire life, really. He'd never thought to seek another. To permit any light into his darkness.

But she was right here, within his grasp. To let her go again was beyond his control right now. He was weakened, dizzy, lost. Dear God, he wanted to keep her for himself.

And the means to convince her to stay with him had just dropped into his lap.

"The blood has soaked my fichu." She sounded upset, but not hysterical. She was a strong woman—stronger than he'd first realized when he'd pulled her from the revelry.

He made his decision. "You need to marry me."

Her beautiful eyes widened in what looked like alarm. "What? No! I'm not going to—"

He reached up and grasped her wrist with his left hand. Both her hands were pressed firmly on his wound. Her skin was warm and soft. "The Dionysus ordered me to kill you. If—"

She tried to recoil. "You're not going to—"

He squeezed her fragile wrist, feeling the beating of her heart. Feeling this moment in time.

Seizing it.

"*Listen*. I meant to have you safely on the road to London tonight. That isn't possible now that I'm wounded. The only way I can protect you is to marry you. If you're my duchess, you'll have my name and my money to shield you when they come, and believe me, Lady Jordan, the Dionysus's men *will* come for you. They need to silence you, for you know far too much about the Lords of Chaos now."

She snorted. "They thought I was the Duchess of Kyle before. *That* certainly didn't protect me."

"*I* am an entirely different duke than Kyle," he replied with flat certainty. He brought his other hand up and untied the rope around her wrists. "And I also have my servants."

She frowned down at her freed wrists and then at him. "How will they keep me from being murdered?"

"They are Corsicans—brave and loyal to a fault—and I have over two dozen." He'd spent his life filled with rage, grief, and a drive for revenge. He'd never even thought of marriage. This was a flight of fancy. An aberration. A diversion from the strict path he'd set for his life. Yet he could not find it within himself to resist. "My men answer only to me. If you're my wife—my family and my duchess—they will protect you with their lives. If I die due to your gunshot wound and you do *not* marry me, they may look upon you far less favorably."

Her plump mouth dropped open in outrage. "You'd *blackmail* me into marriage? Are you deranged?"

Oh, indeed. Probably on both counts. "I'm *wounded*."

He arched an eyebrow. "And attempting to save your life. You might try thanking me."

"*Thank* you? I—"

Fortunately the carriage halted before she could articulate what she thought of that idea.

Raphael kept a firm hold of the lady's wrist as the door was opened, revealing Ubertino, one of his most trusted men. Ubertino was nearly forty, a short man with a barrel chest and graying hair clubbed back in a tight braid. The Corsican's bright-blue eyes widened in his tanned face at the sight of his master's blood.

"I've been shot," Raphael told him. "Get Valente and Bardo and tell Nicoletta to come."

Ubertino turned to shout the orders in Corsican to the other men behind him and then stepped into the carriage.

Lady Jordan backed away warily.

"Tell Ivo to take the lady into the abbey," Raphael ordered. He wouldn't put it past her to run once she was out of the carriage.

"Did she do this, Your Excellency?" Ubertino muttered in Corsican as he put his shoulder against Raphael's bad side.

Raphael grunted and stood, clenching his jaw. He would not pass out. "A misunderstanding merely. You will forget this."

"I think it will be hard to forget," Ubertino said.

Carefully they negotiated the two steps down from the carriage.

He was cold. So cold.

"Nevertheless, I order it so." Raphael stopped and stared at the servant. In another life he might've counted this man his oldest friend. "You will protect her no matter what happens."

The Corsican inclined his head. "As you wish, Your Excellency."

Valente and Bardo came running into the driveway.

Valente, the younger of the two, began asking questions in Corsican, but Ubertino cut him off. "Listen to *lu duca*."

Raphael's hands were in fists. He would not fall down here before his men. "Go to the vicar in town. You know his house, by the English church?"

Both men nodded.

"Wake him up and bring him here." He could feel the blood trickling down his side, oddly hot against the chill of his body. "Do not let anything he says or does keep you from your task. Hurry."

Valente and Bardo ran to the stables.

They knew only a few words of English. The vicar might very well think he was being robbed or worse. Raphael ought to write a letter explaining the matter.

But there was no time.

Behind them Lady Jordan exclaimed, "Take your hands from me, sir!"

Raphael raised his voice. "Ivo is merely helping you into my home, my lady."

"I don't wish to be helped!"

He turned to see her glaring at him, her blond hair a halo about her head in the carriage's lantern light, and felt his lips quirk. She really was rather extraordinary.

A pity he could not make her his wife in reality.

Her gaze swept past him and to the facade of the building behind him, then widened in what looked very much like horror. "*This* is your home?"

He turned to look as well. The abbey was ancient. The original structure had been a fortified keep, which had been added to and modified over centuries, first by monks and then, after the dissolution of the monasteries, by generations of his ancestors. This was where he'd spent most of his childhood. Where his mother had breathed her last breath. The place he'd hoped never to see again.

His mouth twisted. "*Home* might be a bit of an exaggeration."

Elizabeth Hoyt is the *New York Times* bestselling author of more than twenty lush historical romances, including the Maiden Lane series. *Publishers Weekly* has called her writing "mesmerizing." She also pens deliciously fun contemporary romances under the name Julia Harper. Elizabeth lives in Minneapolis, Minnesota, with three untrained dogs, a garden in constant need of weeding, and the long-suffering Mr. Hoyt.

The winters in Minnesota have been known to be long and cold and Elizabeth is always thrilled to receive reader mail. You can write to her at PO Box 19495, Minneapolis, MN 55419 or e-mail her at Elizabeth@ElizabethHoyt.com.

You can learn more at:

ElizabethHoyt.com
Twitter @elizabethhoyt
Facebook.com/ElizabethHoytBooks
Goodreads.com/ElizabethHoyt
Instagram.com/elizabethhoytauthor
Pinterest.com/elizabethhoyt